128(12/14)2/15

The Best of
CONNIE
WILLIS

The Best of
CONNIE
WILLIS

AWARD-WINNING STORIES

BALLANTINE BOOKS * NEW YORK

Introduction and new text copyright © 2013 by Connie Willis

Published in the United States by Del Rey, an imprint of The Random House Publishing Group, a division of Random House, Inc., New York.

DEL REY is a registered trademark and the Del Rey colophon is a trademark of Random House, Inc.

Most of the stories in this work have been previously published in *Asimov's Science Fiction*. "At the Rialto" was originally published in *Omni*. "The Soul Selects Her Own Society: Invation and Repulsion: A Chronological Reinterpretation of Two of Emily Dickinson's Poems: A Wellsian Perspective": was originally published in *War of the Worlds" Global Dispatches* edited by Kevin J. Anderson (New York: Spectra, 1996).

Previous publication information can be found on page 475.

Library of Congress Cataloging-in-Publication Data
Willis, Connie.
The best of Connie Willis : award-winning stories / Connie Willis.
pages cm
All ten of her Hugo and Nebula award-winning short stories.
ISBN: 978-0-345-54064-5 (hardcover : alk. paper)
ISBN: 978-0-345-54065-2 (eBook)
1. Science fiction, American. I. Title. II. Title: Award-winning stories.
PS3573.I45652B47 2013
813'.54—dc23
2013000495

Printed in the United States of America on acid-free paper

www.delreybooks.com

10 9 8 7 6 5 4 3 2 1

First Edition

To the public library

CONTENTS

INTRODUCTION

Writing an author's introduction to a "Best of" collection is kind of problematic. If you talk too much about the stories, you give away the plot, and if you focus on the "best of" part, it looks uncomfortably like bragging—and usually is.

Telling where you got the idea for each story is usually a terrible letdown and doesn't really explain anything. I mean, I got the idea for "The Last of the Winnebagos" from being stuck behind an RV going fifteen miles an hour up the pass to Woodland Park, and the idea for "All Seated on the Ground" from sitting in the church choir singing some Christmas carol with truly awful lyrics, but that doesn't explain how I got from there to the story, and if I explain all the steps in between (giving away half the surprises in the story in the process), you'll feel as duped and annoyed as you do after a magician explains how he sawed the woman in half.

Besides, I don't know all the steps. Writers don't really understand where their ideas come from, or how they morph into the story on the page. And often what I thought I was doing turned out not to be what was really going on at all. While you're writing one story, your subconscious is busily writing another. Which means that to *really* explain the stories, I'd have to go all autobiographical and get into my childhood and the traumas thereof, which I have *no* intention of doing here.

It's too bad this isn't a theme anthology. It's easy to write an introduction for a theme anthology. If it's about time travel or H. G. Wells–like invasions from outer space or dragons, then you natter on about dragons—or invasions, or time travel—for a few pages, and you're good. But only one of the stories in this collection is about a Wells-like invasion. (There's another invasion from outer space, but the aliens don't try to kill anybody. They don't do *anything*. In fact, that's the problem. They just stand there and look disapproving.)

There are also a couple of time-travel stories here (though only one's about time travel in the traditional sense), there aren't *any* dragon stories, and the other stories are about psychics, RVs, the Pyramids, the post office, Annette Funicello, mystery novels, Kool-Aid, tomato plants, and the footprints out in front of Grauman's Chinese Theatre.

It's kind of hard to detect a common theme in all that, and the settings don't provide one, either. The stories take place in Phoenix; Egypt; the London Tube; Amherst, Massachusetts; and a mall at Christmastime—and in the past, future, afterlife, and end of the world.

About the only thing the stories have in common is that *I* wrote them, and even that's apparently a bit uncertain. There was a conspiracy theory making the rounds of the Internet a while back that there were actually *two* Connie Willises, one who wrote the "funny stuff" and one who wrote the "sad stuff," which I don't understand at all.

I mean, Shakespeare wrote both comedies and tragedies (to say nothing of historical fiction, fantasy, and some pretty darn good poems) and nobody ever said *his* stuff was written by two different people. Although, come to think of it, they *did* accuse him of being someone else altogether, including Francis Bacon, Edward de Vere, and Queen Elizabeth. (And a committee, which I guess counts as two different people.) No one has claimed a committee wrote my stories yet, so that's good.

And it *is* true that there's more than one kind of story in this collection. But in writing them, I wasn't so much following in Shakespeare's footsteps (though the world would definitely be a better place if *everybody* tried to write like Shakespeare—or at least read him) as in the footsteps of some of my favorite science-fiction writers.

They didn't stick to just one kind of story, either. Shirley Jackson wrote both chilling studies in human behavior ("The Lottery") and hilarious ones ("One Ordinary Day, with Peanuts"). So did William Tenn, penning the savage "The Liberation of Earth," the bleak "Down Among the Dead Men," and the uproarious "Bernie the Faust."

And Kit Reed wrote—and is still writing—all across the spectrum, from the terrifying ("The Wait") to the creepy ("The Fat Farm") to the sweet and funny ("Songs of War").

I was first exposed to all these writers and to many more—Fredric Brown, Mildred Clingerman, Theodore Sturgeon, Zenna Henderson, James Blish, Ray Bradbury—in the Year's Best collections edited by Judith Merril, Robert P. Mills, and Anthony Boucher, and they had an even more profound effect on me than Robert A. Heinlein, whose work I found at the same time.

To quote Mr. Heinlein, "How it happened was this way." In one of those serendipitous moments that make you ponder how much of the course of your life depends on the vagaries of chance, I happened to see a copy of Heinlein's *Have Space Suit, Will Travel*, thought it had a funny title (for you young'uns, there was a TV show in those days called *Have Gun, Will Travel*—and yes, we had TV back then!), and checked it out. And fell in love with the very first line: "You see, I had this space suit."

I also fell in love with its seventeen-year-old hero (I was thirteen), his ten-year-old-girl sidekick Peewee, and the Mother Thing. And in love with the humor and the adventure and the science and the literary references. Kip's dad is reading Jerome K. Jerome's *Three Men in a Boat* in the first chapter, and Shakespeare's *The Tempest* figures heavily in saving the planet. (I *told* you the world would be a better place if everybody read Shakespeare.)

I immediately devoured the rest of the Heinleins my library had— *Time for the Stars, Tunnel in the Sky, The Star Beast, The Door into Summer, Double Star, Space Cadet*—and then set out to find other stuff like them.

There was no science-fiction section in the library back in those days (they were days of dark oppression), so this was harder than it might seem. But I'd noticed that the Heinleins all had this symbol of a spaceship and an atom on the back, so I scoured the library for other books with the symbol. I found, I remember, *Pebble in the Sky* and *The Space Merchants* and *Revolt on Alpha C.* And the Year's Best collections—a whole row of them.

They were a revelation to me. Here, cheek by jowl, were stories by John Collier and C. M. Kornbluth and Ray Bradbury and C. L. Moore, a kaleidoscope of stories and styles and themes, from the funny (Fredric Brown's "Puppet Show") to the frighteningly dystopic (E. M. Forster's "The Machine Stops") to the achingly sad ("Flowers for Algernon").

A realistic story about a man walking across the moon on foot stood between a lyrical remembrance of things past and a nightmarish take on the *"good* life," and there were tales of tidal flats and amusement parks and department stores and spots in the Arizona desert where it was possible to see "a miracle of rare device."

Stories about robots and time-travelers and aliens, and stories about the cold equations of the physical universe and the hidden costs of technological advance, about the endless difficulty of determining what a human is—and how to be one. Science fiction in all her infinite variety, spread out like a feast in front of me.

And the stories were *good*. These were, after all, short stories and novelettes and novellas being written by authors at the height of their powers. Nowadays, science-fiction writers tend to think of the short story only as a way to get their foot in the publishing door or as a practice run for the three-volume trilogy they *really* want to write, and after they sell that first novel, they tend not to write any more short stories.

But back then very few science-fiction novels were being published (they were *really* days of dark oppression), and *everybody*, from the talented beginner to old hands like Jack Williamson and Frederik Pohl, was writing for the magazines. Including Heinlein, who I was thrilled to find was also in the collections, with gems like "They" and "All You Zombies"—and my favorite, "The Menace from Earth."

These were people who really knew how to write, and I reaped the benefit, reading classics like "Evening Primrose" and "Nightfall" and "Vintage Season" and "Ararat."

Even in this exalted company, some stories stood out as exceptional. One of them was "Lot," by Ward Moore, which starts out seeming to be a simple tale about a dad packing the family car for a trip and turns into a horrific (and all-too-possible) nuclear nightmare, a story that managed to embody not only the loss of civilization but the loss of our humanity, and one that has reverberated in my mind ever since I read it.

A second standout was Philip K. Dick's "I Hope I Shall Arrive Soon," a story about a man in cold sleep traveling to a far distant planet who keeps dreaming his arrival. It deals with an entirely different kind of nightmare, one in which we can no longer tell what's reality and what's a dream.

But my favorite had to be Bob Shaw's "The Light of Other Days," a simple little tale about a couple driving out to the country on a summer afternoon to buy a piece of window glass for their apartment. It somehow managed to dissect marriage, loss, grief, and the bitter knowledge that technology can be a two-edged sword, all in the space of a few thousand words.

I had had no idea stories could *do* stuff like this.

I've always considered myself incredibly lucky (the "chance" thing again) that I discovered those collections when I did. Heinlein was great, but novels devoted to blasting through space and discovering planets infested with multieyed monsters didn't have all that much to say to me, and that was what most of the science-fiction novels in my library were about. And the movies were even worse. (We were still *years* away from *Star Wars*.)

With only *Daring Rangers of the Sky* to read and *Attack from Venus* to watch, my infatuation with science fiction might have proved short-lived. But through the brilliance of Bob Shaw and Philip K. Dick and all those other writers, I'd glimpsed what science fiction could be. So I kept reading, discovering Samuel R. Delany and J. G. Ballard and

James Tiptree, Jr., and Howard Waldrop and a host of other brilliant writers, and falling more and more in love with the field. And I started writing stories of my own.

Well, maybe not entirely my own. When I look back at "A Letter from the Clearys," I can see how much it owes to Ward Moore's "Lot." When I reread "Fire Watch," I see the impact of Heinlein and his hapless heroes on me, and in "Even the Queen" and "At the Rialto" the influence of his breezy style and bantering characters.

But it's not just those two authors. They *all* influenced me. They taught me all sorts of techniques I could use in my stories—the onion-like layered revelations of Daniel Keyes, the understated ironies of Kit Reed, the multiple meanings Shirley Jackson could cram into a single line of dialogue. More important, they showed me that a story didn't have to be all flash and pyrotechnics (though they taught me how to do that, too). They showed me that stories could be told simply and straightforwardly—and have hidden depths.

But mostly they made me fall so madly in love with their stories that I wanted to be just like them, so madly in love that I've written science-fiction short stories for more than forty years—and am still writing them.

This year I was honored to be awarded the Grand Master Nebula for my work and my life in science fiction. It is fitting that the award is named after Damon Knight, who wrote several of my favorite short stories in those Year's Best collections, including "The Country of the Kind" and "The Big Pat Boom," and I'd like to think I got the award as much for the stories you'll find in this volume as for my novels.

In my acceptance speech I thanked all of the writers and editors and agents who've helped me along the way, and I concluded with this:

But mostly I have to thank the people to whom I owe the most:
—Robert A. Heinlein, for introducing me to Kip and Peewee,
and to Three Men in a Boat *and to the whole wonderful world*
of science fiction.

—And Kit Reed and Charles Williams and Ward Moore, who showed me its amazing possibilities.
—Philip K. Dick and Shirley Jackson and Howard Waldrop and William Tenn, who taught me how science fiction should be written.
—And Bob Shaw and Daniel Keyes and Theodore Sturgeon, whose stories—"The Light of Other Days" and "Flowers for Algernon" and "The Man Who Lost the Sea"—taught me to love it.
I wouldn't be here without them.

I couldn't have done any of the things I've done without them, and in a sense, when you read this collection, you're reading their stories as well as mine. At least, I *hope* a little of them has rubbed off on me. Because they were truly the year's—and any year's—best. And when my stories are comic and tragic and about everything from Thomas More to Christmas carols, from murder to exasperated mothers, I'm following firmly in their footsteps. And they were following firmly in Shakespeare's.

So, enjoy! And then, when you've read all these stories, go read Philip K. Dick's "We Can Remember It for You Wholesale" and C. L. Moore and Henry Kuttner's "Mimsy Were the Borogoves" and Kit Reed's "Time Tours, Inc." and Theodore Sturgeon's "A Saucer of Loneliness." And all the other wonderful, wonderful stories of science fiction!

Connie Willis

The Best of
CONNIE
WILLIS

A LETTER FROM THE CLEARYS

There was a letter from the Clearys at the post office. I put it in my backpack along with Mrs. Talbot's magazine and went outside to untie Stitch.

He had pulled his leash out as far as it would go and was sitting around the corner, half-strangled, watching a robin. Stitch never barks, not even at birds. He didn't even yip when Dad stitched up his paw. He just sat there the way we found him on the front porch, shivering a little and holding his paw up for Dad to look at. Mrs. Talbot says he's a terrible watchdog, but I'm glad he doesn't bark. Rusty barked all the time and look where it got him.

I had to pull Stitch back around the corner to where I could get enough slack to untie him. That took some doing because he really liked that robin. "It's a sign of spring, isn't it, fella?" I said, trying to get at the knot with my fingernails. I didn't loosen the knot, but I managed to break one of my fingernails off to the quick. Great. Mom will demand to know if I've noticed any other fingernails breaking.

My hands are a real mess. This winter I've gotten about a hundred burns on the back of my hands from that stupid woodstove of ours. One spot, just above my wrist, I keep burning over and over so it never has a chance to heal. The stove isn't big enough and when I try to jam a log in that's too long that same spot hits the inside of the stove every time. My stupid brother David won't saw them off to the right length. I've asked him and asked him to please cut them shorter, but he doesn't pay any attention to me.

I asked Mom if she would please tell him not to saw the logs so long, but she didn't. She never criticizes David. As far as she's concerned he can't do anything wrong just because he's twenty-three and was married.

"He does it on purpose," I told her. "He's hoping I'll burn to death."

"Paranoia is the number-one killer of fourteen-year-old girls," Mom said. She always says that. It makes me so mad I feel like killing her. "He doesn't do it on purpose. You need to be more careful with the stove, that's all." But all the time she was holding my hand and looking at the big burn that won't heal like it was a time bomb set to go off.

"We need a bigger stove," I said, and yanked my hand away. We do need a bigger one. Dad closed up the fireplace and put the woodstove in when the gas bill was getting out of sight, but it's just a little one because Mom didn't want one that would stick way out in the living room. Anyway, we were only going to use it in the evenings.

We won't get a new one. They are all too busy working on the stupid greenhouse. Maybe spring will come early, and my hand will have half a chance to heal. I know better. Last winter the snow kept up till the middle of June and this is only March. Stitch's robin is going to freeze his little tail if he doesn't head back south. Dad says that last year was unusual, that the weather will be back to normal this year, but he doesn't believe it, either, or he wouldn't be building the greenhouse.

As soon as I let go of Stitch's leash, he backed around the corner like a good boy and sat there waiting for me to stop sucking my finger and untie him. "We'd better get a move on," I told him. "Mom'll have a fit." I was supposed to go by the general store to try and get some tomato seeds, but the sun was already pretty far west, and I had at least a half hour's walk home. If I got home after dark I'd get sent to bed without supper and then I wouldn't get to read the letter. Besides, if I didn't go to the general store today they would have to let me go tomorrow and I wouldn't have to work on the stupid greenhouse.

Sometimes I feel like blowing it up. There's sawdust and mud on everything, and David dropped one of the pieces of plastic on the stove while they were cutting it and it melted onto the stove and stinks to high heaven. But nobody else even notices the mess, they're so busy talking about how wonderful it's going to be to have homegrown watermelon and corn and tomatoes next summer.

I don't see how it's going to be any different from last summer. The only things that came up at all were the lettuce and the potatoes. The lettuce was about as tall as my broken fingernail and the potatoes were as hard as rocks. Mrs. Talbot said it was the altitude, but Dad said it wasn't, either, it was the funny weather and this crummy Pikes Peak granite that passes for soil around here. He went up to the little library in the back of the general store and got a do-it-yourself book on greenhouses and started tearing everything up and now even Mrs. Talbot is crazy about the idea.

The other day I told them, "Paranoia is the number-one killer of people at this altitude," but they were too busy cutting slats and stapling plastic to even pay any attention to me.

Stitch walked along ahead of me, straining at his leash, and as soon as we were across the highway, I took it off. He never runs away like Rusty used to. Anyway, it's impossible to keep him out of the road, and the times I've tried keeping him on his leash, he dragged me out into the middle and I got in trouble with Dad over leaving footprints. So I keep to the frozen edges of the road, and he moseys along, stopping to sniff at potholes, and when he gets behind, I whistle at him and he comes running right up.

I walked pretty fast. It was getting chilly out, and I'd only worn my sweater. I stopped at the top of the hill and whistled at Stitch. We still had a mile to go. I could see the Peak from where I was standing. Maybe Dad is right about spring coming. There was hardly any snow on the Peak, and the burned part didn't look quite as dark as it did last fall, like maybe the trees are coming back.

Last year at this time the whole peak was solid white. I remember because that was when Dad and David and Mr. Talbot went hunting and it snowed every day and they didn't get back for almost a month. Mom just about went crazy before they got back. She kept going up to the road to watch for them even though the snow was five feet deep and she was leaving footprints as big as the Abominable Snowman's. She took Rusty with her even though he hated the snow about as much as Stitch hates the dark. And she took a gun. One time she tripped over a branch and fell down in the snow. She sprained her ankle and was frozen stiff by the time she made it back to the house. I felt like saying, "Paranoia is the number-one killer of mothers," but Mrs. Talbot butted in and said the next time I had to go with her and how this was what happened when people were allowed to go places by themselves, which meant me going to the post office. And I said I could take care of myself and Mom told me not to be rude to Mrs. Talbot and Mrs. Talbot was right, I should go with her the next time.

Mom wouldn't wait till her ankle was better. She bandaged it up and we went the very next day. She wouldn't say a word the whole trip, just limped through the snow. She never even looked up till we got to the road. The snow had stopped for a little while and the clouds had lifted enough so you could see the Peak. It was really neat, like a black and white photograph, the gray sky and the black trees and the white mountain. The Peak was completely covered with snow. You couldn't make out the toll road at all.

We were supposed to hike up the Peak with the Clearys.

When we got back to the house, I said, "The summer before last the Clearys never came."

Mom took off her mittens and stood by the stove, pulling off chunks of frozen snow. "Of course they didn't come, Lynn," she said.

Snow from my coat was dripping onto the stove and sizzling. "I didn't mean that," I said. "They were supposed to come the first week in June. Right after Rick graduated. So what happened? Did they just decide not to come or what?"

"I don't know," she said, pulling off her hat and shaking her hair out. Her bangs were all wet.

"Maybe they wrote to tell you they'd changed their plans," Mrs. Talbot said. "Maybe the post office lost the letter."

"It doesn't matter," Mom said.

"You'd think they'd have written or something," I said.

"Maybe the post office put the letter in somebody else's box," Mrs. Talbot said.

"It doesn't matter," Mom said, and went to hang her coat over the line in the kitchen. She wouldn't say another word about them. When Dad got home I asked him about the Clearys, too, but he was too busy telling about the trip to pay any attention to me.

Stitch didn't come. I whistled again and then started back after him. He was all the way at the bottom of the hill, his nose buried in something. "Come *on*," I said, and he turned around and then I could see why he hadn't come. He'd gotten himself tangled up in one of the electric wires that was down. He'd managed to get the cable wound around his legs like he does his leash sometimes and the harder he tried to get out, the more he got tangled up.

He was right in the middle of the road. I stood on the edge of the road, trying to figure out a way to get to him without leaving footprints. The road was pretty much frozen at the top of the hill, but down here snow was still melting and running across the road in big rivers. I put my toe out into the mud, and my sneaker sank in a good half inch, so I backed up, rubbed out the toe print with my hand, and wiped my hand on my jeans. I tried to think what to do. Dad is as paranoiac about footprints as Mom is about my hands, but he is even worse about my being out after dark. If I didn't make it back in time he might even tell me I couldn't go to the post office anymore.

Stitch was coming as close as he ever would to barking. He'd gotten the wire around his neck and was choking himself. "All right," I said, "I'm coming." I jumped out as far as I could into one of the rivers and then waded the rest of the way to Stitch, looking back a couple of times to make sure the water was washing away the footprints.

I unwound Stitch like you would a spool of thread, and threw the loose end of the wire over to the side of the road where it dangled from the pole, all ready to hang Stitch next time he comes along.

"You stupid dog," I said. "Now hurry!" and I sprinted back to the side of the road and up the hill in my sopping wet sneakers. He ran about five steps and stopped to sniff at a tree. "Come on!" I said. "It's getting dark. Dark!"

He was past me like a shot and halfway down the hill. Stitch is afraid of the dark. I know, there's no such thing in dogs. But Stitch really is. Usually I tell him, "Paranoia is the number-one killer of dogs," but right now I wanted him to hurry before my feet started to freeze. I started running, and we got to the bottom of the hill about the same time.

Stitch stopped at the driveway of the Talbots' house. Our house wasn't more than a few hundred feet from where I was standing, on the other side of the hill. Our house is down in kind of a well formed by hills on all sides. It's so deep and hidden you'd never even know it's there. You can't even see the smoke from our woodstove over the top of the Talbots' hill. There's a shortcut through the Talbots' property and down through the woods to our back door, but I don't take it anymore. "Dark, Stitch," I said sharply, and started running again. Stitch kept right at my heels.

The Peak was turning pink by the time I got to our driveway. Stitch peed on the spruce tree about a hundred times before I got it dragged back across the dirt driveway. It's a real big tree. Last summer Dad and David chopped it down and then made it look like it had fallen across the road. It completely covers up where the driveway meets the road, but the trunk is full of splinters, and I scraped my hand right in the same place as always. Great.

I made sure Stitch and I hadn't left any marks on the road (except for the marks he always leaves—another dog could find us in a minute. That's probably how Stitch showed up on our front porch, he smelled Rusty) and then got under cover of the hill as fast as I could. Stitch isn't the only one who gets nervous after dark. And besides, my feet were starting to hurt. Stitch was really paranoiac tonight. He didn't even take off running after we were in sight of the house.

David was outside, bringing in a load of wood. I could tell just by looking at it that they were all the wrong length. "Cutting it kind of close, aren't you?" he said. "Did you get the tomato seeds?"

"No," I said. "I brought you something else, though. I brought everybody something."

I went on in. Dad was rolling out plastic on the living room floor. Mrs. Talbot was holding one end for him. Mom was standing holding the card table, still folded up, waiting for them to finish so she could set it up in front of the stove for supper. Nobody even looked up. I unslung my backpack and took out Mrs. Talbot's magazine and the letter.

"There was a letter at the post office," I said. "From the Clearys."

They all looked up.

"Where did you find it?" Dad said.

"On the floor, mixed in with all the third class stuff. I was looking for Mrs. Talbot's magazine."

Mom leaned the card table against the couch and sat down. Mrs. Talbot just looked blank.

"The Clearys were our best friends," I said. "From Illinois. They were supposed to come see us the summer before last. We were going to hike up Pikes Peak and everything."

David banged in the door. He looked at Mom sitting on the couch and Dad and Mrs. Talbot still standing there holding the plastic like a couple of statues. "What's wrong?" he said.

"Lynn says she found a letter from the Clearys today," Dad said.

David dumped the logs on the hearth. One of them rolled onto the carpet and stopped at Mom's feet. Neither of them bent over to pick it up.

"Shall I read it out loud?" I said, looking at Mrs. Talbot. I was still holding her magazine. I opened up the envelope and took out the letter.

"'Dear Janice and Todd and everybody,'" I read. "'How are things in the glorious West? We're raring to come out and see you, though we may not make it quite as soon as we hoped. How are Carla and David and the baby? I can't wait to see little David. Is he walking yet? I bet Grandma Janice is so proud she's busting her britches. Is that right? Do you Westerners wear britches or have you all gone to designer jeans?'"

David was standing by the fireplace. He put his head down across his arms on the mantelpiece.

"'I'm sorry I haven't written, but we were very busy with Rick's graduation and anyway I thought we would beat the letter out to Colorado, but now it looks like there's going to be a slight change in plans. Rick has definitely decided to join the Army. Richard and I have talked ourselves blue in the face, but I guess we've just made matters worse. We can't even get him to wait to join until after the trip to Colorado. He says we'd spend the whole trip trying to talk him out of it, which is true, I guess. I'm just so worried about him. The Army! Rick says I worry too much, which is true, too, I guess, but what if there was a war?'"

Mom bent over and picked up the log that David had dropped and laid it on the couch beside her.

"'If it's okay with you out there in the Golden West, we'll wait until Rick is done with basic the first week in July and then all come out. Please write and let us know if this is okay. I'm sorry to switch plans on you like this at the last minute, but look at it this way: You have a whole extra month to get into shape for hiking up Pikes Peak. I don't know about you, but I sure can use it.'"

Mrs. Talbot had dropped her end of the plastic. It hadn't landed on the stove this time, but it was so close to it, it was curling from the heat. Dad just stood there watching it. He didn't even try to pick it up.

"'How are the girls? Sonja is growing like a weed. She's out for track this year and bringing home lots of medals and dirty sweat socks. And you should see her knees! They're so banged up I almost took her to the doctor. She says she scrapes them on the hurdles, and her coach says there's nothing to worry about, but it does worry me a little. They just don't seem to heal. Do you ever have problems like that with Lynn and Melissa?

"'I know, I know. I worry too much. Sonja's fine. Rick's fine. Nothing awful's going to happen between now and the first week in July, and we'll see you then. Love, the Clearys. P.S. Has anybody ever fallen off Pikes Peak?'"

Nobody said anything. I folded up the letter and put it back in the envelope.

"I should have written them," Mom said. "I should have told them, 'Come now.' Then they would have been here."

"And we would probably have climbed up Pikes Peak that day and gotten to see it all go blooey and us with it," David said, lifting his head up. He laughed and his voice caught on the laugh and kind of cracked. "I guess we should be glad they didn't come."

"Glad?" Mom said. She was rubbing her hands on the legs of her jeans. "I suppose we should be glad Carla took Melissa and the baby to Colorado Springs that day so we didn't have so many mouths to feed." She was rubbing her jeans so hard she was going to rub a hole right through them. "I suppose we should be glad those looters shot Mr. Talbot."

"No," Dad said. "But we should be glad the looters didn't shoot the rest of us. We should be glad they only took the canned goods and not the seeds. We should be glad the fires didn't get this far. We should be glad . . ."

"That we still have mail delivery?" David said. "Should we be glad about that, too?" He went outside and shut the door behind him.

"When I didn't hear from them I should have called or something," Mom said.

Dad was still looking at the ruined plastic. I took the letter over to him. "Do you want to keep it or what?" I said.

"I think it's served its purpose," he said. He wadded it up, tossed it in the stove, and slammed the door shut. He didn't even get burned. "Come help me on the greenhouse, Lynn," he said.

It was pitch-dark outside and really getting cold. My sneakers were starting to get stiff. Dad held the flashlight and pulled the plastic tight over the wooden slats. I stapled the plastic every two inches all the way around the frame and my finger about every other time. After we finished one frame I asked Dad if I could go back in and put on my boots.

"Did you get the seeds for the tomatoes?" he said, like he hadn't even heard me. "Or were you too busy looking for the letter?"

"I didn't look for it," I said. "I found it. I thought you'd be glad to get the letter and know what happened to the Clearys."

Dad was pulling the plastic across the next frame, so hard it was getting little puckers in it. "We already knew," he said.

He handed me the flashlight and took the staple gun out of my hand. "You want me to say it?" he said. "You want me to tell you exactly what happened to them? All right. I would imagine they were close enough to Chicago to have been vaporized when the bombs hit. If they were, they were lucky. Because there aren't any mountains like ours around Chicago. So if they weren't, they got caught in the firestorm or they died of flash burns or radiation sickness, or else some looter shot them."

"Or their own family," I said.

"Or their own family." He put the staple gun against the wood and pulled the trigger. "I have a theory about what happened the summer before last," he said. He moved the gun down and shot another staple into the wood. "I don't think the Russians started it, or the United States, either. I think it was some little terrorist group somewhere or maybe just one person. I don't think they had any idea what would happen when they dropped their bomb. I think they were just so hurt and angry and frightened by the way things were that they just lashed out. With a bomb." He stapled the frame clear to the bottom and straightened up to start on the other side. "What do you think of that theory, Lynn?"

"I told you," I said. "I found the letter while I was looking for Mrs. Talbot's magazine."

He turned and pointed the staple gun at me. "But whatever reason they did it for, they brought the whole world crashing down on their heads. Whether they meant it or not, they had to live with the consequences."

"If they lived," I said. "If somebody didn't shoot them."

"I can't let you go to the post office anymore," he said. "It's too dangerous."

"What about Mrs. Talbot's magazines?"

"Go check on the fire," he said.

I went back inside. David had come back and was standing by the fireplace again, looking at the wall. Mom had set up the card table and the folding chairs in front of the fireplace. Mrs. Talbot was in the kitchen cutting up potatoes, only it looked like it was onions the way she was crying.

The fire had practically gone out. I stuck a couple of wadded-up magazine pages in to get it going again. The fire flared up with a brilliant blue and green. I tossed a couple of pinecones and some sticks onto the burning paper. One of the pinecones rolled off to the side and lay there in the ashes. I grabbed for it and hit my hand on the door of the stove.

Right in the same place. Great. The blister would pull the old scab off and we could start all over again. And of course Mom was standing right there, holding the pan of potato soup. She put it on the top of the stove and grabbed up my hand like it was evidence in a crime or something. She didn't say anything, she just stood there holding it and blinking.

"I burned it," I said. "I just burned it."

She touched the edges of the old scab, like she was afraid of catching something.

"It's a burn," I shouted, snatching my hand back and cramming David's stupid logs into the stove. "It isn't radiation sickness. It's just a *burn!*"

"Do you know where your father is, Lynn?" she said as if she hadn't even heard me.

"He's out on the back porch," I said, "building his stupid greenhouse."

"He's gone," she said. "He took Stitch with him."

"He can't have taken Stitch," I said. "He's afraid of the dark." She didn't say anything. "Do you *know* how dark it is out there?"

"Yes," she said, and went and looked out the window. "I know how dark it is."

I got my parka off the hook by the fireplace and started out the door.

David grabbed my arm. "Where the hell do you think you're going?"

I wrenched away from him. "To find Stitch. He's afraid of the dark."

"It's too dark," he said. "You'll get lost."

"So what? It's safer than hanging around this place," I said and slammed the door shut on his hand.

I made it halfway to the woodpile before he grabbed me again, this time with his other hand. I should have gotten them both with the door.

"Let me go," I said. "I'm leaving. I'm going to go find some other people to live with."

"There aren't any other people! For Christ's sake, we went all the way to South Park last winter. There wasn't anybody. We didn't even see those looters. And what if you run into them, the looters that shot Mr. Talbot?"

"What if I do? The worst they could do is shoot me. I've been shot at before."

"You're acting crazy, you know that, don't you?" he said. "Coming in here out of the clear blue, taking potshots at everybody with that crazy letter!"

"Potshots!" I said, so mad I was afraid I was going to start crying. "Potshots! What about last summer? Who was taking potshots then?"

"You didn't have any business taking the shortcut," David said. "Dad told you never to come that way."

"Was that any reason to try and shoot me? Was that any reason to *kill* Rusty?"

David was squeezing my arm so hard I thought he was going to snap it right in two. "The looters had a dog with them. We found its tracks all around Mr. Talbot. When you took the shortcut and we heard Rusty barking, we thought you were the looters." He looked at me. "Mom's right. Paranoia's the number-one killer. We were all a little crazy last summer. We're all a little crazy all the time, I guess, and then you pull a stunt like bringing that letter home, reminding everybody of everything that's happened, of everybody we've lost . . ." He let go of my arm and looked down at his hand like he didn't even know he'd practically broken my arm.

"I told you," I said. "I found it while I was looking for a magazine. I thought you'd all be glad I found it."

"Yeah," he said. "I'll bet."

He went inside and I stayed out a long time, waiting for Dad and Stitch. When I came in, nobody even looked up. Mom was still standing at the window. I could see a star over her head. Mrs. Talbot had stopped crying and was setting the table. Mom dished up the soup and we all sat down. While we were eating, Dad came in.

He had Stitch with him. And all the magazines. "I'm sorry, Mrs. Talbot," he said. "If you'd like, I'll put them under the house and you can send Lynn for them one at a time."

"It doesn't matter," she said. "I don't feel like reading them any-more."

Dad put the magazines on the couch and sat down at the card table. Mom dished him up a bowl of soup. "I got the seeds," he said. "The tomato seeds had gotten soaked, but the corn and squash were okay."

He looked at me. "I had to board up the post office, Lynn," he said. "You understand that, don't you, that I can't let you go there anymore? It's just too dangerous."

"I told you," I said. "I found it. While I was looking for a magazine."

"The fire's going out," he said.

After they shot Rusty I wasn't allowed to go anywhere for a month for fear they'd shoot me when I came home, not even when I promised to take the long way around. But then Stitch showed up and nothing happened and they let me start going again. I went every day till the end of summer and after that whenever they'd let me. I must have looked through every pile of mail a hundred times before I found the letter from the Clearys. Mrs. Talbot was right about the post office. The letter was in somebody else's box.

Afterword for "A Letter from the Clearys"

I wrote "A Letter from the Clearys" when we were living in a town in the Rocky Mountains called Woodland Park, up the pass from Colorado Springs. Woodland Park was at that time a little town with dirt roads, lots of pine trees, aspens, and wildflowers, and a gorgeous view of Pikes Peak.

What it didn't have was home mail delivery. I had to walk up to the post office to get the mail. With my dog. So I suppose you can figure out where I got the idea for the story.

But I also remember the post office for what was the worst day of my writing life up till then, and one of the worst two or three of my whole career. In those days you had to mail your manuscript in to the magazine instead of e-mailing it, and you had to enclose a self-addressed stamped envelope (SASE) so the editor could send it back to you with a rejection slip attached.

Since this meant numerous trips to the post office, I used to buy extra stamps and make out two manila envelopes and two SASEs at the same time, one for the magazine I was sending it to and a second set for the magazine I'd send it to after the first one rejected it.

I got *lots* of rejection slips in those days (usually literally a slip of paper only an inch wide with "We are sorry, but your manuscript does not meet the needs of our publication" typed on it), but I was always able to keep my spirits up by telling myself that even though this one had been rejected, there was still a chance I might sell the one I had out to *Galileo*. Or to *Asimov's*.

But on this particular day when I went to get the mail, I found not a rejected manuscript, but a yellow slip telling me to go to the counter. *Oh, goody,* I thought. *My grandmother's sent me a present,* and traipsed up to the counter to collect it.

It wasn't a present, or even a package. It was a stack of manila envelopes with my handwriting on them, all eight of the stories I had had out at the time, *all* rejected. Not a single one left at *Omni* or *F and SF* for me to convince myself I might sell.

Hmm, I thought on the long walk home. *Maybe they're trying to tell me something.* And the something was obviously that I should quit, give up, stop making an idiot of myself, and go back to teaching school.

What saved me from doing just that was those already made-out and stamped envelopes and SASEs. I mean, stamps were expensive, and what would it hurt to send everything out one last time?

Luckily, one of the stories in that batch—"The Child Who Cries for the Moon"—sold to an anthology, *A Spadeful of Spacetime,* which encouraged me enough that I kept writing till I eventually sold to *Galileo,* and to *Asimov's* and *Omni* and *F and SF.* And till I wrote "A Letter from the Clearys" and "Fire Watch," which won the Nebula. And changed the whole course of my life.

But it was close. And even though it sounds like a funny little anecdote now, there was nothing funny about it *at all* when it happened.

So, to any struggling young writers who may be reading this, my message to you is, "Keep slogging on no matter how many rejection slips you get or how discouraged you are." Or, as my hero Winston Churchill would put it, "Never, never, never give up."

AT THE RIALTO

Seriousness of mind was a prerequisite for understanding
Newtonian physics. I am not convinced it is not a handicap in
understanding quantum theory.

—Excerpt from Dr. Gedanken's keynote address to the 1989
International Congress of Quantum Physicists Annual
Meeting, Hollywood, California

I got to Hollywood around one-thirty and started trying to check into the Rialto. "Sorry, we don't have any rooms," the girl behind the desk said. "We're all booked up with some science thing."

"I'm with the science thing," I said. "Dr. Ruth Baringer. I reserved a double."

"There are a bunch of Republicans here, too, and a tour group from Finland. They told me when I started work here that they got all these movie people, but the only one so far was that guy who played the friend of that other guy in that one movie. You're not a movie person, are you?"

"No," I said. "I'm with the science thing. Dr. Ruth Baringer."

"My name's Tiffany," she said. "I'm not actually a hotel clerk at all. I'm just working here to pay for my transcendental posture lessons. I'm really a model/actress."

"I'm a quantum physicist," I said, trying to get things back on track. "The name is Ruth Baringer."

She messed with the computer for a minute. "I don't show a reservation for you."

"Maybe it's in Dr. Mendoza's name. I'm sharing a room with her."

She messed with the computer some more. "I don't show a reservation for her, either. Are you sure you don't want the Disneyland Hotel? A lot of people get the two confused."

"I want the Rialto," I said, rummaging through my bag for my notebook. "I have a confirmation number. W37420."

She typed it in. "Are you Dr. Gedanken?" she asked.

"Excuse me," an elderly man said.

"I'll be right with you," Tiffany told him. "How long do you plan to stay with us, Dr. Gedanken?" she asked me.

"*Excuse* me," the man said, sounding desperate. He had bushy white hair and a dazed expression, as if he had just been through a horrific experience. Or had been trying to check in to the Rialto.

He wasn't wearing any socks. I wondered if *he* was Dr. Gedanken. Dr. Gedanken was the main reason I'd decided to come to the meeting. I had missed his lecture on wave/particle duality last year, but I had read the text of it in the *ICQP Journal*, and it had actually seemed to make sense, which is more than you can say for most of quantum theory. He was giving the keynote address this year, and I was determined to hear it.

It wasn't Dr. Gedanken. "My name is Dr. Whedbee," the elderly man said. "You gave me the wrong room."

"All our rooms are pretty much the same," Tiffany said. "Except for how many beds they have in them and stuff."

"My room has a *person* in it!" he said. "Dr. Sleeth. From the University of Texas at Austin. She was changing her clothes." His hair seemed to get wilder as he spoke. "She thought I was a serial killer."

"And your name is Dr. Whedbee?" Tiffany asked, fooling with the computer again. "I don't show a reservation for you."

Dr. Whedbee began to cry.

Tiffany got out a paper towel, wiped off the counter, and turned back to me. "May I help you?" she asked.

Thursday, 7:30–9 P.M. Opening Ceremonies. Dr. Halvard Onofrio, University of Maryland at College Park, will speak on the topic, "Doubts Surrounding the Heisenberg Uncertainty Principle." Ballroom.

I finally got my room at five-thirty after Tiffany went off duty. Till then I sat around the lobby with Dr. Whedbee, listening to Abey Fields complain about Hollywood.

"What's wrong with Racine?" he said. "Why do we always have to go to these exotic places, like Hollywood? And St. Louis last year wasn't much better. The Institut Henri Poincaré people kept going off to see the arch and Busch Stadium."

"Speaking of St. Louis," Dr. Takumi said, "have you seen David yet?"

"No," I said.

"Oh, really?" she said. "Last year at the annual meeting you two were practically inseparable. Moonlight riverboat rides and all."

"What's on the programming tonight?" I said to Abey.

"David was just here," Dr. Takumi said. "He said to tell you he was going out to look at the stars in the sidewalk."

"That's exactly what I'm talking about," Abey said. "Riverboat rides and movie stars. What do those things have to do with quantum theory? Racine would have been an appropriate setting for a group of physicists. Not like this . . . this . . . Do you realize we're practically across the street from Grauman's Chinese Theatre? And Hollywood Boulevard's where all those gangs hang out. If they catch you wearing red or blue, they'll—" He stopped. "Is that Dr. Gedanken?" he asked, staring at the front desk.

I turned and looked. A short roundish man with a mustache was trying to check in. "No," I said. "That's Dr. Onofrio."

"Oh, yes," Abey said, consulting his program book. "He's speaking tonight at the opening ceremonies. On the Heisenberg uncertainty principle. Are you going?"

"I'm not sure," I said, which was supposed to be a joke, but Abey didn't laugh.

"I must meet Dr. Gedanken. He's just gotten funding for a new project."

I wondered what Dr. Gedanken's new project was—I would have loved to work with him.

"I'm hoping he'll come to my workshop on the wonderful world of quantum physics," Abey said, still watching the desk. Amazingly enough, Dr. Onofrio seemed to have gotten a key and was heading for the elevators. "I think his project has something to do with understanding quantum theory."

Well, that let me out. I didn't understand quantum theory at all. I sometimes had a sneaking suspicion nobody else did, either, including Abey Fields, and that they just weren't willing to admit it.

I mean, an electron is a particle except it acts like a wave. In fact, a neutron acts like two waves and interferes with itself (or each other), and you can't really measure any of this stuff properly because of the Heisenberg uncertainty principle, and that isn't the worst of it. When you set up a Josephson junction to figure out what rules the electrons obey, they sneak past the barrier to the other side, and they don't seem to care much about the limits of the speed of light, either, and

Schrödinger's cat is neither alive nor dead till you open the box, and it all makes about as much sense as Tiffany's calling me Dr. Gedanken.

Which reminded me, I had promised to call Darlene and give her our room number. I didn't have a room number, but if I waited much longer, she'd have left. She was flying to Denver to speak at C.U. and then coming on to Hollywood sometime tomorrow morning. I interrupted Abey in the middle of his telling me how beautiful Racine was in the winter and went to call her.

"I don't have a room yet," I said when she answered. "Should I leave a message on your answering machine, or do you want to give me your number in Denver?"

"Never mind all that," Darlene said. "Have you seen David yet?"

To illustrate the problems of the concept of wave function, Dr. Schrödinger imagines a cat being put into a box with a piece of uranium, a bottle of poison gas, and a Geiger counter. If a uranium nucleus disintegrates while the cat is in the box, it will release radiation, which will set off the Geiger counter and break the bottle of poison gas. Since it is impossible in quantum theory to predict whether a uranium nucleus will disintegrate while the cat is in the box, and only possible to calculate uranium's probable half-life, the cat is neither alive nor dead until we open the box.

—FROM "THE WONDERFUL WORLD OF QUANTUM PHYSICS," A SEMINAR PRESENTED AT THE ICQP ANNUAL MEETING BY A. FIELDS, PH.D., UNIVERSITY OF NEBRASKA AT WAHOO

I completely forgot to warn Darlene about Tiffany, the model-slash-actress.

"What do you mean, you're trying to avoid David?" she had asked me at least three times. "Why would you do a stupid thing like that?"

Because in St. Louis I ended up on a riverboat in the moonlight and didn't make it back until the conference was over.

"Because I want to attend the programming," I said the third time around, "not a wax museum. I am a middle-aged woman."

"And David is a middle-aged man, who, I might add, is absolutely charming. In fact, he may be the last charming man left in the universe."

"Charm is for quarks," I said and hung up, feeling smug until I remembered I hadn't told her about Tiffany. I went back to the front desk, thinking maybe Dr. Onofrio's success signaled a change.

Tiffany asked, "May I help you?" and left me standing there.

After a while I gave up and went back to the red and gold sofas. "David was here again," Dr. Takumi said. "He said to tell you he was going to the wax museum."

"There *are* no wax museums in Racine," Abey said.

"What's the programming for tonight?" I said, taking Abey's program away from him.

"There's a mixer at six-thirty and the opening ceremonies in the ballroom and then some seminars."

I read the descriptions of the seminars. There was one on the Josephson junction. Electrons were able to somehow tunnel through an insulated barrier even though they didn't have the required energy. Maybe I could somehow get a room without checking in.

"If we were in Racine," Abey said, looking at his watch, "we'd already be checked in and on our way to dinner."

Dr. Onofrio emerged from the elevator, still carrying his bags. He came over and sank down on the sofa next to Abey.

"Did they give you a room with a semi-naked woman in it?" Dr. Whedbee asked.

"I don't know," Dr. Onofrio said. "I couldn't find it." He looked sadly at the key. "They gave me 1282, but the room numbers only go up to seventy-five."

"I think I'll attend the seminar on chaos," I said.

The most serious difficulty quantum theory faces today is not the inherent limitation of measurement capability or the EPR paradox. It is the lack of a paradigm. Quantum theory has no working model, no metaphor that properly defines it.

—Excerpt from Dr. Gedanken's keynote address

I got to my room at six, after a brief skirmish with the bellboy-slash-actor who couldn't remember where he'd stored my suitcase, and unpacked.

My clothes, which had been permanent press all the way from MIT, underwent a complete wave function collapse the moment I opened my suitcase, and came out looking like Schrödinger's almost-dead cat.

By the time I had called housekeeping for an iron, taken a bath, given up on the iron, and steamed a dress in the shower, I had missed the "Mixer with Munchies" and was half an hour late for Dr. Onofrio's opening remarks.

I opened the door to the ballroom as quietly as I could and slid inside. I had hoped they would be late getting started, but a man I didn't recognize was already introducing the speaker. "—and an inspiration to all of us in the field."

I dived for the nearest chair and sat down.

"Hi," David said. "I've been looking all over for you. Where were you?"

"Not at the wax museum," I whispered.

"You should have been," he whispered back. "It was great. They had John Wayne, Elvis, and Tiffany the model-slash-actress with the brain of a pea-slash-amoeba."

"Shh," I said.

"—the person we've all been waiting to hear, Dr. Ringgit Dinari."

"What happened to Dr. Onofrio?" I asked.

"Shh," David said.

Dr. Dinari looked a lot like Dr. Onofrio. She was short, roundish, and mustached, and was wearing a rainbow-striped caftan. "I will be your guide this evening into a strange new world," she said, "a world where all that you thought you knew, all common sense, all accepted wisdom, must be discarded. A world where all the rules have changed and it sometimes seems there are no rules at all."

She sounded just like Dr. Onofrio, too. He had given this same speech two years ago in Cincinnati. I wondered if he had undergone some strange transformation during his search for room 1282 and was now a woman.

"Before I go any farther," Dr. Dinari said, "how many of you have already channeled?"

Newtonian physics had as its model the machine. The metaphor of the machine, with its interrelated parts, its gears and wheels, its causes and effects, was what made it possible to think about Newtonian physics.

—Excerpt from Dr. Gedanken's keynote address

"You *knew* we were in the wrong place," I hissed at David when we got out to the lobby.

When we stood up to leave, Dr. Dinari had extended her pudgy hand in its rainbow-striped sleeve and called out in a voice a lot like Charlton Heston's, "O Unbelievers! Leave not, for here only is reality!"

"Actually, channeling would explain a lot," David said, grinning.

"If the opening remarks aren't in the ballroom, where are they?"

"Beats me," he said. "Want to go see the Capitol Records building? It's shaped like a stack of LPs."

"I want to go to the opening remarks."

"The beacon on top blinks out 'Hollywood' in Morse code."

I went over to the front desk.

"Can I help you?" the clerk behind the desk said. "My name is Natalie, and I'm an—"

"Where is the ICQP meeting this evening?" I said.

"They're in the ballroom."

"I'll bet you didn't have any dinner," David said. "I'll buy you an ice cream cone. There's this great place that has the ice cream cone Ryan O'Neal bought for Tatum in *Paper Moon*."

"A channeler's in the ballroom," I told Natalie. "I'm looking for the ICQP."

She fiddled with the computer. "I'm sorry. I don't show a reservation for them."

"How about Grauman's Chinese?" David said. "You want reality? You want Charlton Heston? You want to see quantum theory in action?"

He grabbed my hands. "Come with me," he said seriously.

In St. Louis I had suffered a wave function collapse a lot like what had happened to my clothes when I opened the suitcase. I had ended up on a riverboat halfway to New Orleans that time. It happened again, and the next thing I knew I was walking around the courtyard of Grauman's Chinese Theatre, eating an ice cream cone and trying to fit my feet in Myrna Loy's footprints.

She must have been a midget or had her feet bound as a child. So, apparently, had Debbie Reynolds, Dorothy Lamour, and Wallace Beery. The only footprints I came close to fitting were Donald Duck's.

"I see this as a map of the microcosm," David said, sweeping his hand over the slightly irregular pavement of printed and signed cement squares. "See, there are all these tracks. We know something's been here, and the prints are pretty much the same, only every once in a while you've got this"—he knelt down and pointed at the print of John Wayne's clenched fist—"and over here"—he walked toward the box office and pointed to the print of Betty Grable's leg. "And we can figure out the signatures, but what is this reference to 'Sid' on all these squares? And what does *this* mean?"

He pointed at Red Skelton's square. It said, "Thanks Sid We Dood It."

"You keep thinking you've found a pattern," David said, crossing over to the other side, "but Van Johnson's square is kind of sandwiched in here at an angle between Esther Williams and Cantinflas, and who the hell is May Robson? And why are all these squares over here empty?"

He had managed to maneuver me over behind the display of Academy Award winners. It was an accordionlike wrought-iron screen. I was in the fold between 1944 and 1945.

"And as if that isn't enough, you suddenly realize you're standing in the courtyard. You're not even in the theater."

"And that's what you think is happening in quantum theory?" I said weakly. I was backed up into Bing Crosby, who had won for Best Actor in *Going My Way*. "You think we're not in the theater yet?"

"I think we know as much about quantum theory as we can figure out about May Robson from her footprints," he said, putting his hand up to Ingrid Bergman's cheek (Best Actress, *Gaslight*) and blocking my escape. "I don't think we understand anything *about* quantum theory, not tunneling, not complementarity." He leaned toward me. "Not passion."

The best movie of 1945 was *The Lost Weekend*. "Dr. Gedanken understands it," I said, disentangling myself from the Academy Award winners and David. "Did you know he's putting together a new research team for a big project on understanding quantum theory?"

"Yes," David said. "Want to see a movie?"

"There's a seminar on chaos at nine," I said, stepping over the Marx Brothers. "I have to get back."

"If it's chaos you want, you should stay right here," he said, stopping to look at Irene Dunne's handprints. "We could see the movie and then go have dinner. There's this place near Hollywood and Vine that has the mashed potatoes Richard Dreyfuss made into Devil's Tower in *Close Encounters*."

"I want to meet Dr. Gedanken," I said, making it safely to the sidewalk. I looked back at David.

He had gone back to the other side of the courtyard and was looking at Roy Rogers's signature. "Are you kidding? He doesn't understand it any better than we do."

"Well, at least he's trying."

"So am I. The problem is, how can one neutron interfere with itself, and why are there only two of Trigger's hoofprints here?"

"It's eight fifty-five," I said. "I am going to the chaos seminar."

"If you can find it," he said, getting down on one knee to look at the signature.

"I'll find it," I said grimly.

He stood up and grinned at me, his hands in his pockets. "It's a great movie," he said.

It was happening again. I turned and practically ran across the street.

"*Benji IX* is showing," he shouted after me. "He accidentally exchanges bodies with a Siamese cat."

*Thursday, 9–10 P.M. "The Science of Chaos." I. Durcheinander,
University of Leipzig. A seminar on the structure of chaos.
Principles of chaos will be discussed, including the butterfly
effect, fractals, and insolid billowing. Clara Bow Room.*

I couldn't find the chaos seminar. The Clara Bow Room, where it was supposed to be, was empty. A meeting of vegetarians was next door in the Fatty Arbuckle Room, and all the other conference rooms were locked. The channeler was still in the ballroom. "Come!" she commanded when I opened the door. "Understanding awaits!"

I went upstairs to bed.

I had forgotten to call Darlene. She would have left for Denver already, but I called her answering machine and told it the room number in case she picked up her messages. In the morning I would have to tell the front desk to give her a key. I went to bed.

I didn't sleep well. The air conditioner went off during the night, which meant I didn't have to steam my suit when I got up the next morning. I got dressed and went downstairs.

The programming started at nine o'clock with Abey Fields's Wonderful World workshop in the Mary Pickford Room, a breakfast buffet in the ballroom, and a slide presentation on "Delayed Choice Experiments" in Cecil B. DeMille A on the mezzanine level.

The breakfast buffet sounded wonderful, even though it always turns out to be urn coffee and donuts. I hadn't had anything but an ice cream cone since noon the day before, but if David were around, he would be somewhere close to the food, and I wanted to steer clear of him. Last night it had been Grauman's Chinese. Today I was likely to end up at Knott's Berry Farm. I wasn't going to let that happen, even if he was charming.

It was pitch-dark inside Cecil B. DeMille A. Even the slide on the screen up front appeared to be black. "As you can see," Dr. Lvov said, "the laser pulse is already in motion before the experimenter sets up the wave or particle detector."

He clicked to the next slide, which was dark gray. "We used a Mach-Zender interferometer with two mirrors and a particle detector. For the first series of tries we allowed the experimenter to decide which apparatus he would use by whatever method he wished. For the second series, we used that most primitive of randomizers—"

He clicked again, to a white slide with black polka dots that gave off enough light for me to be able to spot an empty chair on the aisle ten rows up. I hurried to get to it before the slide changed, and sat down.

"—a pair of dice. Alley's experiments had shown us that when the particle detector was in place, the light was detected as a particle, and when the wave detector was in place, the light showed wavelike behavior, no matter when the choice of apparatus was made."

"Hi," David said. "You've missed five black slides, two gray ones, and a white with black polka dots."

"Shh," I said.

"In our two series, we hoped to ascertain whether the consciousness of the decision affected the outcome." Dr. Lvov clicked to another black slide. "As you can see, the graph shows no effective difference between the tries in which the experimenter chose the detection apparatus and those in which the apparatus was randomly chosen."

"You want to go get some breakfast?" David whispered.

"I already ate," I whispered back, and waited for my stomach to growl and give me away. It did.

"There's a great place down near Hollywood and Vine that has the waffles Katharine Hepburn made for Spencer Tracy in *Woman of the Year.*"

"Shh," I said.

"And after breakfast, we could go to Frederick's of Hollywood and see the bra museum."

"Will you please be quiet? I can't hear."

"Or see," he said, but he subsided more or less for the remaining ninety-two black, gray, and polka-dotted slides.

Dr. Lvov turned on the lights and blinked smilingly at the audience. "Consciousness had no discernible effect on the results of the experiment. As one of my lab assistants put it, 'The little devil knows what you're going to do before you know it yourself.'"

This was apparently supposed to be a joke, but I didn't think it was very funny. I opened my program and tried to find something to go to that David wouldn't be caught dead at.

"Are you two going to breakfast?" Dr. Thibodeaux asked.

"Yes," David said.

"No," I said.

"Dr. Hotard and I wished to eat somewhere that is *vraiment* Hollywood."

"David knows just the place," I said. "He's been telling me about this great place where they have the grapefruit James Cagney shoved in Mae Clarke's face in *Public Enemy*."

Dr. Hotard hurried up, carrying a camera and four guidebooks. "And then perhaps you would show us Grauman's Chinese Theatre?" he asked David.

"Of course he will," I said. "I'm sorry I can't go with you, but I promised Dr. Verikovsky I'd be at his lecture on Boolean logic. And after Grauman's Chinese, David can take you to the bra museum at Frederick's of Hollywood."

"And the Brown Derby?" Thibodeaux asked. "I have heard it is shaped like a *chapeau*."

They dragged him off. I watched till they were safely out of the lobby and then ducked upstairs and into Dr. Whedbee's lecture on information theory. Dr. Whedbee wasn't there.

"He went to find an overhead projector," Dr. Takumi said. She had half a donut on a paper plate in one hand and a styrofoam cup in the other.

"Did you get that at the breakfast buffet?" I asked.

"Yes. It was the last one. And they ran out of coffee right after I got there. You weren't in Abey Fields's thing, were you?" She set the coffee cup down and took a bite of the donut.

"No," I said, wondering if I should try to take her by surprise or just wrestle the donut away from her.

"You didn't miss anything. He raved the whole time about how we should have had the meeting in Racine." She popped the last piece of donut into her mouth. "Have you seen David yet?"

Friday, 9–10 P.M. "The Eureka Experiment: A Slide Presentation." J. Lvov, Eureka College. Descriptions, results, and conclusions of Lvov's delayed conscious/randomized choice experiments. Cecil B. DeMille A.

Dr. Whedbee eventually came in carrying an overhead projector, the cord trailing behind him. He plugged it in. The light didn't go on.

"Here," Dr. Takumi said, handing me her plate and cup. "I have one of these at Caltech. It needs its fractal basin boundaries adjusted."

She whacked the side of the projector.

There weren't even any crumbs left of the donut. There was about a millimeter of coffee in the bottom of the cup. I was about to stoop to new depths when she hit the projector again. The light came on.

"I learned that in the chaos seminar last night," she said, grabbing the cup away from me and draining it. "You should have been there. The Clara Bow Room was packed."

"I believe I'm ready to begin," Dr. Whedbee said.

Dr. Takumi and I sat down.

"Information is the transmission of meaning," Dr. Whedbee said. He wrote "meaning" or possibly "information" on the screen with a green Magic Marker. "When information is randomized, meaning cannot be transmitted, and we have a state of entropy." He wrote it under "meaning" with a red Magic Marker. His handwriting appeared to be completely illegible.

"States of entropy vary from low entropy, such as the mild static on your car radio, to high entropy, a state of complete disorder, of randomness and confusion, in which no information at all is being communicated."

Oh, my God, I thought. I forgot to tell the hotel about Darlene.

The next time Dr. Whedbee bent over to inscribe hieroglyphics on the screen, I sneaked out and went down to the desk, hoping Tiffany hadn't come on duty yet.

She had. "May I help you?" she asked.

"I'm in room 663," I said. "I'm sharing a room with Dr. Darlene Mendoza. She's coming in this morning, and she'll be needing a key."

"For what?" Tiffany said.

"To get into the room. I may be in one of the lectures when she gets here."

"Why doesn't she have a key?"

"Because she isn't here yet."

"I thought you said she was sharing a room with you."

"She *will* be sharing a room with me. Room 663. Her name is Dar-lene Mendoza."

"And your name?" she asked, hands poised over the computer.

"Ruth Baringer."

"We don't show a reservation for you."

We have made impressive advances in quantum physics in the ninety years since Planck's constant, but they have by and large been advances in technology, not theory. We can only make advances in theory when we have a model we can visualize.

—EXCERPT FROM DR. GEDANKEN'S KEYNOTE ADDRESS

I high-entropied with Tiffany for a while on the subjects of my not having a reservation and the air-conditioning and then switched back suddenly to the problem of Darlene's key, in the hope of catching her off guard. It worked about as well as Alley's delayed choice experiments.

In the middle of my attempting to explain that Darlene was not the air-conditioning repairman, Abey Fields came up. "Have you seen Dr. Gedanken?"

I shook my head.

"I was sure he'd come to my Wonderful World workshop, but he didn't, and the hotel says they can't find his reservation," he said, scanning the lobby. "I found out what his new project is, incidentally, and I'd be perfect for it. He's going to find a paradigm for quantum theory. Is that him?" he said, pointing at an elderly man getting in the elevator.

"I think that's Dr. Whedbee," I said, but he had already sprinted across the lobby to the elevator.

He nearly made it. The elevator doors slid to a close just as he got there. He pushed the elevator button several times to make the doors open again, and when that didn't work, tried to readjust their fractal basin boundaries. I turned back to the desk.

"May I help you?" Tiffany said.

"You may," I said. "My roommate, Darlene Mendoza, will be arriving sometime this morning. She's a producer. She's here to cast the female lead in a new movie starring Robert Redford and Harrison Ford. When she gets here, give her her key. And fix the air-conditioning."

"Yes, ma'am," she said.

The Josephson junction is designed so that electrons must obtain additional energy to surmount the energy barrier. It has been found, however, that some electrons simply tunnel, as Heinz Pagel put it, "right through the wall."

—FROM "THE WONDERFUL WORLD OF QUANTUM PHYSICS,"
A. FIELDS, UNW

Abey had stopped banging on the elevator button and was trying to pry the elevator doors apart.

I went out the side door and up to Hollywood Boulevard. David's restaurant was near Hollywood and Vine. I turned the other direction, toward Grauman's Chinese Theatre, and ducked into the first restaurant I saw.

"I'm Stephanie," the waitress said. "How many are there in your party?"

There was no one remotely in my vicinity. "Are you an actress-slash-model?" I asked her.

"Yes," she said. "I'm working here part-time to pay for my holistic hairstyling lessons."

"There's one of me," I said, holding up my forefinger to make it perfectly clear. "I want a table away from the window."

She led me to a table in front of the window, handed me a menu the size of the macrocosm, and put another one down across from me. "Our breakfast specials today are papaya stuffed with salmonberries and nasturtium/radicchio salad with a balsamic vinaigrette. I'll take your order when your other party arrives."

I stood the extra menu up so it hid me from the window, opened the other one, and read the breakfast entrees. They all seemed to have "cilantro" or "lemongrass" in their names. I wondered if "radicchio" could possibly be Californian for "donut."

"Hi," David said, grabbing the standing-up menu and sitting down. "The sea urchin pâté looks good."

I was actually glad to see him. "How did you get here?" I asked.

"Tunneling," he said. "What exactly is extra-virgin olive oil?"

"I wanted a donut," I said pitifully.

He took my menu away from me, laid it on the table, and stood up. "There's a great place next door that's got the donut Clark Gable taught Claudette Colbert how to dunk in *It Happened One Night*."

The great place was probably out in Long Beach someplace, but I was too weak with hunger to resist him. I stood up. Stephanie hurried over.

"Will there be anything else?" she asked.

"We're leaving," David said.

"Okay, then," she said, tearing a check off her pad and slapping it down on the table. "I hope you enjoyed your breakfast."

Finding such a paradigm is difficult, if not impossible. Due to Planck's constant the world we see is largely dominated by Newtonian mechanics. Particles are particles, waves are waves, and objects do not suddenly vanish through walls and reappear on the other side. It is only on the subatomic level that quantum effects dominate.

—EXCERPT FROM DR. GEDANKEN'S KEYNOTE ADDRESS

The restaurant was next door to Grauman's Chinese Theatre, which made me a little nervous, but it had eggs and bacon and toast and orange juice and coffee. And donuts.

"I thought you were having breakfast with Dr. Thibodeaux and Dr. Hotard," I said, dunking one in my coffee. "What happened to them?"

"They went to Forest Lawn. Dr. Hotard wanted to see the church where Ronald Reagan got married."

"He got married at *Forest Lawn?*"

He took a bite of my donut. "In the Wee Kirk of the Heather. Did you know Forest Lawn's got the World's Largest Oil Painting Incorporating a Religious Theme?"

"So why didn't you go with them?"

"And miss the movie?" He grabbed both my hands across the table. "There's a matinee at two o'clock. Come with me."

I could feel things starting to collapse. "I have to get back," I said, trying to disentangle my hands. "There's a panel on the EPR paradox at two o'clock."

"There's another showing at five. And one at eight."

"Dr. Gedanken's giving the keynote address at eight."

"You know what the problem is?" he said, still holding on to my hands. "The problem is, it isn't really Grauman's Chinese Theatre, it's Mann's, so Sid isn't even around to ask. Like, why do some pairs like Joanne Woodward and Paul Newman share the same square and other pairs don't? Like Ginger Rogers and Fred Astaire?"

"You know what the problem is?" I said, wrenching my hands free. "The problem is you don't take anything seriously. This is a conference, but you don't care anything about the programming or hearing Dr. Gedanken speak or trying to understand quantum theory!" I fumbled in my purse for some money for the check.

"I thought that was what we were talking about," David said, sounding surprised. "The problem is, where do those lion statues that guard the door fit in? And what about all those empty spaces?"

Friday, 2–3 P.M. Panel Discussion on the EPR Paradox. I.
Takumi, moderator, R. Iverson, L. S. Ping. A discussion of the
latest research in singlet-state correlations including nonlocal
influences, the Calcutta proposal, and passion. Keystone Kops
Room.

I went up to my room as soon as I got back to the Rialto to see if
Darlene was there yet. She wasn't, and when I tried to call the desk, the
phone wouldn't work. I went back down to the registration desk. There
was no one there. I waited fifteen minutes and then went in to the panel
on the EPR paradox.

"The Einstein-Podolsky-Rosen paradox cannot be reconciled with
quantum theory," Dr. Takumi was saying. "I don't care what the experiments seem to indicate. Two electrons at opposite ends of the universe can't affect each other simultaneously without destroying the
entire theory of the space-time continuum."

She was right. Even if it were possible to find a model of quantum
theory, what about the EPR paradox? If an experimenter measured one
of a pair of electrons that had originally collided, it changed the cross-
correlation of the other instantaneously, even if the electrons were light-
years apart.

It was as if they were eternally linked by that one collision, sharing
the same square forever, even if they were on opposite sides of the universe.

"If the electrons *communicated* instantaneously, I'd agree with
you," Dr. Iverson said, "but they don't, they simply influence each other.
Dr. Shimony defined this influence in his paper on passion, and my
experiment clearly—"

I thought of David leaning over me between the best pictures of
1944 and 1945, saying, "I think we know as much about quantum theory as we can figure out about May Robson from her footprints."

"You can't explain it away by inventing new terms," Dr. Takumi
said.

"I completely disagree," Dr. Ping said. "Passion at a distance is not just an invented term. It's a demonstrated phenomenon."

It certainly is, I thought, thinking about David taking the macrocosmic menu out of the window and saying, "The sea urchin pâté looks good."

It didn't matter where the electron went after the collision. Even if it went in the opposite direction from Hollywood and Vine, even if it stood a menu in the window to hide it, the other electron would still come and rescue it from the radicchio and buy it a donut.

"A demonstrated phenomenon!" Dr. Takumi said. "Ha!" She banged her moderator's gavel for emphasis.

"Are you saying passion doesn't exist?" Dr. Ping said, getting very red in the face.

"I'm saying one measly experiment is hardly a demonstrated phenomenon."

"One measly experiment! I spent five years on this project!" Dr. Iverson said, shaking his fist at her. "I'll show you passion at a distance!"

"Try it, and I'll adjust your fractal basin boundaries!" Dr. Takumi said, and hit him over the head with the gavel.

Yet finding a paradigm is not impossible. Newtonian physics is not a machine. It simply shares some of the attributes of a machine. We must find a model somewhere in the visible world that shares the often bizarre attributes of quantum physics. Such a model, unlikely as it sounds, surely exists somewhere, and it is up to us to find it.

—EXCERPT FROM DR. GEDANKEN'S KEYNOTE ADDRESS

I went up to my room before the police came. Darlene still wasn't there, and the phone and air-conditioning still weren't working. I was really beginning to get worried. I walked over to Grauman's Chinese to find David, but he wasn't there. Dr. Whedbee and Dr. Sleeth were behind the Academy Award winners folding screen.

"You haven't seen David, have you?" I asked.

Dr. Whedbee removed his hand from Norma Shearer's cheek.

"He left," Dr. Sleeth said, disentangling herself from the Best Movie of 1929–30.

"He said he was going out to Forest Lawn," Dr. Whedbee said, trying to smooth down his bushy white hair.

"Have you seen Dr. Mendoza? She was supposed to get in this morning."

They hadn't seen her, and neither had Drs. Hotard and Thibodeaux, who stopped me in the lobby and showed me a postcard of Aimee Semple McPherson's tomb. Tiffany had gone off duty. Natalie couldn't find my reservation. I went back up to the room to wait, thinking Darlene might call.

The air-conditioning still wasn't fixed. I fanned myself with a Hollywood brochure and then opened it up and read it. There was a map of the courtyard of Grauman's Chinese Theatre on the back cover. Deborah Kerr and Yul Brynner didn't have a square together, either, and Katharine Hepburn and Spencer Tracy weren't even on the map. She had made him waffles in *Woman of the Year,* and they hadn't even given them a square. I wondered if Tiffany the model-slash-actress had been in charge of assigning the cement. I could see her looking blankly at Spencer Tracy and saying, "I don't show a reservation for you."

What exactly was a model-slash-actress? Did it mean she was a model *or* an actress or a model *and* an actress? She certainly wasn't a hotel clerk. Maybe electrons were the Tiffanys of the microcosm, and that explained their wave-slash-particle duality. Maybe they weren't really electrons at all. Maybe they were just working part time at being electrons to pay for their singlet-state lessons.

Darlene still hadn't called by seven o'clock. I stopped fanning myself and tried to open a window. It wouldn't budge. The problem was, nobody knew anything about quantum theory. All we had to go on were a few colliding electrons that nobody could see and that couldn't be measured properly because of the Heisenberg uncertainty principle. And there was chaos to consider, and entropy, and all those empty spaces. We didn't even know who May Robson was.

At seven-thirty the phone rang. It was Darlene.

"What happened?" I said. "Where are you?"

"At the Beverly Wilshire."

"In Beverly Hills?"

"Yes. It's a long story. When I got to the Rialto, the hotel clerk, I think her name was Tiffany, told me you weren't there. She said they were booked solid with some science thing and had had to send the overflow to other hotels. She said you were at the Beverly Wilshire in room 1027. How's David?"

"Impossible," I said. "He's spent the whole conference looking at Deanna Durbin's footprints at Grauman's Chinese Theatre and trying to talk me into going to the movies."

"And are you going?"

"I can't. Dr. Gedanken's giving the keynote address in half an hour."

"He is?" Darlene said, sounding surprised. "Just a minute."

There was a silence, and then she came back on and said, "I think you should go to the movies. David's one of the last two charming men in the universe."

"But he doesn't take quantum theory seriously. Dr. Gedanken is hiring a research team to design a paradigm, and David keeps talking about the beacon on top of the Capitol Records building."

"You know, he may be on to something there. I mean, seriousness was all right for Newtonian physics, but maybe quantum theory needs a different approach. Sid says—"

"Sid?"

"This guy who's taking me to the movies tonight. It's a long story.

Tiffany gave me the wrong room number, and I walked in on this guy in his underwear. He's a quantum physicist. He was supposed to be staying at the Rialto, but Tiffany couldn't find his reservation."

The major implication of wave/particle duality is that an electron has no precise location. It exists in a superposition of probable locations. Only when the experimenter observes the electron does it "collapse" into a location.

—FROM "THE WONDERFUL WORLD OF QUANTUM PHYSICS,"
A. FIELDS, UNW

Forest Lawn had closed at five o'clock. I looked it up in the Hollywood brochure after Darlene hung up.

There was no telling where David might have gone: the Brown Derby or the La Brea Tar Pits or some great place near Hollywood and Vine that had the alfalfa sprouts John Hurt ate right before his chest exploded in *Alien*.

At least I knew where Dr. Gedanken was. I changed my clothes and got in the elevator, thinking about wave/particle duality and fractals and high entropy states and delayed choice experiments. The problem was, where could you find a paradigm that would make it possible to visualize quantum theory when you had to include Josephson junctions and passion and all those empty spaces? It wasn't possible. You had to have more to work with than a few footprints and the impression of Betty Grable's leg.

The elevator door opened, and Abey Fields pounced on me. "I've been looking all over for you," he said. "You haven't seen Dr. Gedanken, have you?"

"Isn't he in the ballroom?"

"No," he said. "He's already fifteen minutes late, and nobody's seen him. You have to sign this," he said, shoving a clipboard at me.

"What is it?"

"It's a petition." He grabbed it back from me. "'We the undersigned demand that annual meetings of the International Congress of Quantum Physicists henceforth be held in appropriate locations.' Like Racine," he added, shoving the clipboard at me again. "*Unlike* Hollywood."

Hollywood.

"Are you aware it took the average ICQP delegate two hours and thirty-six minutes to check in? They even sent some of the delegates to a hotel in Glendale."

"And Beverly Hills," I said absently. Hollywood. Bra museums and the Marx Brothers and gangs that would kill you if you wore red or blue and Tiffany-slash-Stephanie and the World's Largest Oil Painting Incorporating a Religious Theme.

"Beverly Hills," Abey muttered, pulling an automatic pencil out of his pocket protector and writing a note to himself. "I'm presenting the petition during Dr. Gedanken's speech. Well, go on, sign it," he said, handing me the pencil. "Unless you want the annual meeting to be here at the Rialto next year."

I handed the clipboard back to him. "I think from now on the annual meeting might be here every year," I said, and took off running for Grauman's Chinese.

When we have that paradigm, one that embraces both the
logical and the nonsensical aspects of quantum theory, we will
be able to look past the colliding electrons and the mathematics
and see the microcosm in all its astonishing beauty.

—EXCERPT FROM DR. GEDANKEN'S KEYNOTE ADDRESS

"I want a ticket to *Benji IX*," I told the girl at the box office. Her nametag said, "Welcome to Hollywood. My name is Kimberly."

"Which theater?" she said.

"Grauman's Chinese," I said, thinking, This is no time for a high entropy state.

"Which theater?"

I looked up at the marquee. *Benji IX* was showing in all three theaters, the huge main theater and the two smaller ones on either side. "They're doing audience reaction surveys," Kimberly said. "Each theater has a different ending."

"Which one's in the main theater?"

"I don't know. I just work here part time to pay for my organic breathing lessons."

"Do you have any dice?" I asked, and then realized I was going about this all wrong. This was quantum physics, not Newtonian. It didn't matter which theater I chose or which seat I sat down in. This was a delayed choice experiment, and David was already in flight.

"The one with the happy ending," I said.

"Center theater," she said.

I walked past the stone lions and into the lobby. Rhonda Fleming and some Chinese wax figures were sitting inside a glass case next to the door to the restrooms. There was a huge painted screen behind the concession stand. I bought a box of Raisinets, a tub of popcorn, and a box of Jujubes and went inside the theater.

It was bigger than I had imagined. Rows and rows of empty red chairs curved between the huge pillars and up to the red curtains where the screen must be. The walls were covered with intricate drawings. I stood there, holding my Jujubes and Raisinets and popcorn, staring at the chandelier overhead. It was an elaborate gold sunburst surrounded by silver dragons. I had never imagined it was anything like this.

The lights went down and the red curtains opened, revealing an inner curtain like a veil across the screen. I went down the dark aisle and sat down in one of the seats. "Hi," I said, and handed the Raisinets to David.

"Where have you been?" he said. "The movie's about to start."

"I know," I said. I leaned across him and handed Darlene her popcorn and Dr. Gedanken his Jujubes. "I was working on the paradigm for quantum theory."

"And?" Dr. Gedanken said, opening his jujubes.

"And you're both wrong," I said. "It isn't Grauman's Chinese. It isn't movies, either, Dr. Gedanken."

"Sid," Dr. Gedanken said. "If we're all going to be on the same research team, I think we should use first names."

"If it isn't Grauman's Chinese or the movies, what is it?" Darlene asked, eating popcorn.

"It's Hollywood."

"Hollywood," Dr. Gedanken said thoughtfully.

"Hollywood," I said. "Stars in the sidewalk and buildings that look like stacks of LPs and hats, and radicchio and audience surveys and bra museums. And the movies. And Grauman's Chinese."

"And the Rialto," David said.

"Especially the Rialto."

"And the ICQP," Dr. Gedanken said.

I thought about Dr. Lvov's black and gray slides and the disappearing chaos seminar and Dr. Whedbee writing "meaning" or possibly "information" on the overhead projector. "And the ICQP," I said.

"Did Dr. Takumi really hit Dr. Iverson over the head with a gavel?" Darlene asked.

"Shh," David said. "I think the movie's starting." He took hold of my hand. Darlene settled back with her popcorn, and Dr. Gedanken put his feet up on the chair in front of him. The inner curtain opened, and the screen lit up.

Afterword for "At the Rialto"

I wrote "At the Rialto" after an SFWA Nebula Awards Banquet weekend which actually featured many of the elements depicted in the story. It was held at the Roosevelt Hotel, which was right across the street from Grauman's Chinese Theatre; we *did* go to the Bra Museum at Frederick's of Hollywood, which has Madonna's gold cone-shaped bra and Ethel Merman's girdle; the desk clerk *was* a model/actress; and there were definitely signs of quantum effects occurring at a macrocosmic level. We did not, however, see *Benji IX* at the theater. We saw *Willow*. And we didn't make it out to Forest Lawn.

But we had a great time. And what else can you expect from Hollywood? I adore the place. It's so deliciously nutty. I mean, not only is every hotel clerk and waitress and valet car-parker an actor/something-or-other, but the trademark Hollywood sign up on the hill was actually an advertisement for a housing development called Hollywoodland till the last four letters fell over, and the shopping mall has rearing concrete elephants and a massive replica of the Babylon set for D. W. Griffith's 1916 silent film *Intolerance*.

They named one of their cemeteries Hollywood Forever, and during the summer they project movies on the side of the mausoleum (I am not making this up), and the locals bring picnic baskets and sit on the grass among the graves of Douglas Fairbanks and Cecil B. DeMille and Jayne Mansfield.

And all those stories about crazy directors and clueless producers and pitch meetings are true. When they turned the Broadway play *The Madness of King George III* into a movie, they really did insist on changing the title to *The Madness of King George* because they were convinced the audience would otherwise think it was a sequel. You know, like *Spider-Man 3*.

How can you not love a place like that?

DEATH ON THE NILE

Chapter One: Preparing for Your Trip—What to Take

"'To the ancient Egyptians,'" Zoe reads, "'Death was a separate country to the west'"—the plane lurches—"'the west to which the deceased person journeyed.'"

We are on the plane to Egypt. The flight is so rough the flight attendants have strapped themselves into the nearest empty seats, looking scared, and the rest of us have subsided into a nervous window-watching silence. Except Zoe, across the aisle, who is reading aloud from a travel guide.

This one is Somebody or Other's *Egypt Made Easy.* In the seat pocket in front of her are Fodor's *Cairo* and Cook's *Touring Guide to Egypt's Antiquities,* and there are half a dozen others in her luggage. Not to mention Frommer's *Greece on $35 a Day* and the Savvy Traveler's *Guide to Austria* and the three or four hundred other guidebooks she's already read out loud to us on this trip. I toy briefly with the idea that it's their combined weight that's causing the plane to yaw and careen and will shortly send us plummeting to our deaths.

"'Food, furniture, and weapons were placed in the tomb,'" Zoe reads, "'as provi-'"—the plane pitches sideways—"'-sions for the journey.'"

The plane lurches again, so violently Zoe nearly drops the book, but she doesn't miss a beat. "'When King Tutankhamun's tomb was opened,'" she reads, "'it contained trunks full of clothing, jars of wine, a golden boat, and a pair of sandals for walking in the sands of the afterworld.'"

My husband, Neil, leans over me to look out the window, but there is nothing to see. The sky is clear and cloudless, and below us there aren't even any waves on the water.

"'In the afterworld the deceased was judged by Anubis, a god with the head of a jackal,'" Zoe reads, "'and his soul was weighed on a pair of golden scales.'"

I am the only one listening to her. Lissa, on the aisle, is whispering to Neil, her hand almost touching his on the armrest. Across the aisle, next to Zoe and *Egypt Made Easy,* Zoe's husband is asleep and Lissa's husband is staring out the other window and trying to keep his drink from spilling.

"Are you doing all right?" Neil asks Lissa solicitously.

"It'll be exciting going with two other couples," Neil said when he came up with the idea of our all going to Europe together. "Lissa and her husband are lots of fun, and Zoe knows everything. It'll be like having our own tour guide."

It is. Zoe herds us from country to country, reciting historical facts and exchange rates. In the Louvre, a French tourist asked her where the *Mona Lisa* was. She was thrilled. "He thought we were a tour group!" she said. "Imagine that!"

Imagine that.

"'Before being judged, the deceased recited his confession,'" Zoe reads, "'a list of sins he had not committed, such as, I have not snared the birds of the gods, I have not told lies, I have not committed adultery.'"

Neil pats Lissa's hand and leans over to me. "Can you trade places with Lissa?" Neil whispers to me.

I already have, I think. "We're not supposed to," I say, pointing at the lights above the seats. "The seat belt sign is on."

He looks at her anxiously. "She's feeling nauseated."

So am I, I want to say, but I am afraid that's what this trip is all about, to get me to say something. "Okay," I say, and unbuckle my seat belt and change places with her. While she is crawling over Neil, the plane pitches again, and she half-falls into his arms. He steadies her. Their eyes lock.

"'I have not taken another's belongings,'" Zoe reads. "'I have not murdered another.'"

I can't take any more of this. I reach for my bag, which is still under the window seat, and pull out my paperback of Agatha Christie's *Death on the Nile*. I bought it in Athens.

"About like death anywhere," Zoe's husband said when I got back to our hotel in Athens with it.

"What?" I said.

"Your book," he said, pointing at the paperback and smiling as if he'd made a joke. "The title. I'd imagine death on the Nile is the same as death anywhere."

"Which is what?" I asked.

"The Egyptians believed death was very similar to life," Zoe cut in. She had bought *Egypt Made Easy* at the same bookstore. "To the ancient Egyptians the afterworld was a place much like the world they inhabited. It was presided over by Anubis, who judged the deceased and determined their fates. Our concepts of heaven and hell and of the Day of Judgment are nothing more than modern refinements on Egyptian ideas," she said, and began reading out loud from *Egypt Made Easy*, which pretty much put an end to our conversation, and I still don't know what Zoe's husband thought death would be like, on the Nile or elsewhere.

I open *Death on the Nile* and try to read, thinking maybe Hercule Poirot knows, but the flight is too bumpy. I feel almost immediately queasy, and after half a page and three more lurches I put it in the seat pocket, close my eyes, and toy with the idea of murdering another. It's a perfect Agatha Christie setting. She always has a few people in a country house or on an island. In *Death on the Nile* they were on a Nile steamer, but the plane is even better. The only other people on it are the flight attendants and a Japanese tour group who apparently do not speak English or they would be clustered around Zoe, asking directions to the Sphinx.

The turbulence lessens a little, and I open my eyes and reach for my book again. Lissa has it.

She's holding it open, but she isn't reading it. She is watching me, waiting for me to notice, waiting for me to say something. Neil looks nervous.

"You were done with this, weren't you?" she says, smiling. "You weren't reading it."

Everyone has a motive for murder in an Agatha Christie. And Lissa's husband has been drinking steadily since Paris, and Zoe's husband never gets to finish a sentence. The police might think he had snapped suddenly. Or that it was Zoe he had tried to kill and shot Lissa by mistake. And there is no Hercule Poirot on board to tell them who really committed the murder, to solve the mystery and explain all the strange happenings.

The plane pitches suddenly, so hard Zoe drops her guidebook, and we plunge a good five thousand feet before it recovers. The guidebook has slid forward several rows, and Zoe tries to reach for it with her foot, fails, and looks up at the seat belt sign as if she expects it to go off so she can get out of her seat to retrieve it.

Not after that drop, I think, but the seat belt sign pings almost immediately and goes off.

Lissa's husband instantly calls for the flight attendant and demands another drink, but they have already gone scurrying back to the rear of the plane, still looking pale and scared, as if they expected the turbulence to start up again before they made it. Zoe's husband wakes up at the noise and then goes back to sleep. Zoe retrieves *Egypt Made Easy* from the floor, reads a few more riveting facts from it, then puts it facedown on the seat and goes back to the rear of the plane.

I lean across Neil and look out the window, wondering what's happened, but I can't see anything. We are flying through a flat whiteness.

Lissa is rubbing her head. "I cracked my head on the window," she says to Neil. "Is it bleeding?"

He leans over her solicitously to see.

I unsnap my seat belt and start to the back of the plane, but both bathrooms are occupied, and Zoe is perched on the arm of an aisle seat, enlightening the Japanese tour group. "The currency is in Egyptian pounds," she says. "There are one hundred piasters in a pound."

I sit back down.

Neil is gently massaging Lissa's temple. "Is that better?" he asks.

I reach across the aisle for Zoe's guidebook. "Must-See Attractions," the chapter is headed, and the first one on the list is the Pyramids.

"Giza, Pyramids of. West bank of Nile, 9 mi. (15 km.) SW of Cairo. Accessible by taxi, bus, rental car. Admission L.E. 3. Comments: You can't skip the Pyramids, but be prepared to be disappointed. They don't look at all like you expect, the traffic's terrible, and the view's completely ruined by the hordes of tourists, refreshment stands, and souvenir vendors. Open daily."

I wonder how Zoe stands this stuff. I turn the page to Attraction Number Two. It's King Tut's tomb, and whoever wrote the guidebook wasn't thrilled with it, either. "Tutankhamun, Tomb of. Valley of the Kings, Luxor, 400 mi. (668 km.) south of Cairo. Three unimpressive rooms. Inferior wall paintings."

There is a map, showing a long, straight corridor (labeled Corridor) and the three unimpressive rooms opening one onto the other in a row—Anteroom, Burial Chamber, Hall of Judgment.

I close the book and put it back on Zoe's seat. Zoe's husband is still asleep. Lissa's is peering back over his seat. "Where'd the flight attendants go?" he asks. "I want another drink."

"Are you sure it's not bleeding? I can feel a bump," Lissa says to Neil, rubbing her head. "Do you think I have a concussion?"

"No," Neil says, turning her face toward his. "Your pupils aren't dilated." He gazes deeply into her eyes.

"Stewardess!" Lissa's husband shouts. "What do you have to do to get a drink around here?"

Zoe comes back, elated. "They thought I was a professional guide," she says, sitting down and fastening her seat belt. "They asked if they could join our tour." She opens the guidebook. " 'The afterworld was full of monsters and demigods in the form of crocodiles and baboons and snakes. These monsters could destroy the deceased before he reached the Hall of Judgment.' "

Neil touches my hand. "Do you have any aspirin?" he asks. "Lissa's head hurts."

I fish in my bag for it, and Neil gets up and goes back to get her a glass of water.

"Neil's so thoughtful," Lissa says, watching me, her eyes bright.

" 'To protect against these monsters and demigods, the deceased was given *The Book of the Dead,*' " Zoe reads. " 'More properly translated as *The Book of What Is in the Afterworld, The Book of the Dead* was a collection of directions for the journey and magic spells to protect the deceased.' "

I think about how I am going to get through the rest of the trip without magic spells to protect me. Six days in Egypt and then three in Israel, and there is still the trip home on a plane like this and nothing to do for fifteen hours but watch Lissa and Neil and listen to Zoe.

I consider cheerier possibilities. "What if we're not going to Cairo?" I say. "What if we're dead?"

Zoe looks up from her guidebook, irritated.

"There've been a lot of terrorist bombings lately, and this is the Middle East," I go on. "What if that last air pocket was really a bomb? What if it blew us apart, and right now we're drifting down over the Aegean Sea in little pieces?"

"Mediterranean," Zoe says. "We've already flown over Crete."

"How do you know that?" I ask. "Look out the window." I point out Lissa's window at the white flatness beyond. "You can't see the water. We could be anywhere. Or nowhere."

Neil comes back with the water. He hands it and my aspirin to Lissa.

"They check the planes for bombs, don't they?" Lissa asks him. "Don't they use metal detectors and things?"

"I saw this movie once," I say, "where the people were all dead, only they didn't know it. They were on a ship, and they thought they were going to America. There was so much fog they couldn't see the water."

Lissa looks anxiously out the window.

"It looked just like a real ship, but little by little they began to notice small things that weren't quite right. There were hardly any people on board, and no crew at all."

"Stewardess!" Lissa's husband calls, leaning over Zoe into the aisle. "I need another ouzo."

His shouting wakes Zoe's husband up. He blinks at Zoe, confused that she is not reading from her guidebook. "What's going on?" he asks.

"We're all dead," I say. "We were killed by Arab terrorists. We think we're going to Cairo but we're really going to heaven. Or hell."

Lissa, looking out the window, says, "There's so much fog I can't see the wing." She looks frightenedly at Neil. "What if something's happened to the wing?"

"We're just going through a cloud," Neil says. "We're probably beginning our descent into Cairo."

"The sky was perfectly clear," I say, "and then all of a sudden we were in the fog. The people on the ship noticed the fog, too. They noticed that there weren't any running lights. And they couldn't find the crew." I smile at Lissa. "Have you noticed the turbulence stopped all of a sudden? Right after we hit that air pocket. And why—?"

A flight attendant comes out of the cockpit and down the aisle to us, carrying a drink. Everyone looks relieved, and Zoe opens her guidebook and begins thumbing through it, looking for fascinating facts.

"Did someone here want an ouzo?" the flight attendant asks.

"Here," Lissa's husband says, reaching for it.

"How long before we get to Cairo?" I say.

She starts toward the back of the plane without answering. I unbuckle my seat belt and follow her. "When will we get to Cairo?" I ask her.

She turns, smiling, but she is still pale and scared-looking. "Did you want another drink, ma'am? Ouzo? Coffee?"

"Why did the turbulence stop?" I say. "How long till we get to Cairo?"

"You need to take your seat," she says, pointing to the seat belt sign. "We're beginning our descent. We'll be at our destination in another twenty minutes." She bends over the Japanese tour group and tells them to bring their seat backs to the upright position.

"What destination? Our descent to where? We aren't beginning any descent. The seat belt sign is still off," I say, and it bings on.

I go back to my seat. Zoe's husband is already asleep again. Zoe is reading out loud from *Egypt Made Easy*. "'The visitor should take precautions before traveling in Egypt. A map is essential, and a flashlight is needed for many of the sites.'"

Lissa has gotten her bag out from under the seat. She puts my *Death on the Nile* in it and gets out her sunglasses. I look past her and out the window at the white flatness where the wing should be. We should be able to see the lights on the wing even in the fog. That's what they're there for, so you can see the plane in the fog. The people on the ship didn't realize they were dead at first. It was only when they started noticing little things that weren't quite right that they began to wonder.

"'A guide is recommended,'" Zoe reads.

I have meant to frighten Lissa, but I have only managed to frighten myself. We are beginning our descent, that's all, I tell myself, and flying through a cloud. And that must be right.

Because here we are in Cairo.

Chapter Two: Arriving at the Airport

"So this is Cairo?" Zoe's husband says, looking around. The plane has stopped at the end of the runway and deplaned us onto the asphalt by means of a metal stairway.

The terminal is off to the east, a low building with palm trees around it, and the Japanese tour group sets off toward it immediately, shouldering their carry-on bags and camera cases.

We do not have any carry-ons. Since we always have to wait at the baggage claim for Zoe's guidebooks anyway, we check our carry-ons, too. Every time we do it, I am convinced they will go to Tokyo or disappear altogether, but now I'm glad we don't have to lug them all the way to the terminal. It looks like it is miles away, and the Japanese are already slowing.

Zoe is reading the guidebook. The rest of us stand around her, looking impatient. Lissa has caught the heel of her sandal in one of the metal steps coming down and is leaning against Neil.

"Did you twist it?" Neil asks anxiously.

The flight attendants clatter down the steps with their navy blue overnight cases. They still look nervous. At the bottom of the stairs they unfold wheeled metal carriers and strap the overnight cases to them and set off for the terminal. After a few steps they stop, and one of them takes off her jacket and drapes it over the wheeled carrier, and they start off again, walking rapidly in their high heels.

It is not as hot as I expected, even though the distant terminal shimmers in the heated air rising from the asphalt. There is no sign of the clouds we flew through, just a thin white haze, which disperses the sun's light into an even glare. We are all squinting. Lissa lets go of Neil's arm for a second to get her sunglasses out of her bag.

"What do they drink around here?" Lissa's husband asks, squinting over Zoe's shoulder at the guidebook. "I want a drink."

"The local drink is zibib," Zoe says. "It's like ouzo." She looks up from the guidebook. "I think we should go see the Pyramids." The professional tour guide strikes again.

"Don't you think we'd better take care of first things first?" I say. "Like customs? And picking up our luggage?"

"And finding a drink of . . . what did you call it? Zibab?" Lissa's husband says.

"No," Zoe says. "I think we should do the Pyramids first. It'll take an hour to do the baggage claim and customs, and we can't take our luggage with us to the Pyramids. We'll have to go to the hotel, and by that time everyone will be out there. I think we should go right now." She gestures at the terminal. "We can run out and see them and be back before the Japanese tour group's even through customs."

She turns and starts walking in the opposite direction from the terminal, and the others straggle obediently after her.

I look back at the terminal. The flight attendants have passed the Japanese tour group and are nearly to the palm trees.

"You're going the wrong way," I say to Zoe. "We've got to go to the terminal to get a taxi."

Zoe stops. "A taxi?" she says. "What for? They aren't far. We can walk it in fifteen minutes."

"Fifteen minutes?" I say. "Giza's nine miles west of Cairo. You have to cross the Nile to get there."

"Don't be silly," she says, "they're right there," and points in the direction she was walking, and there, beyond the asphalt in an expanse of sand, so close they do not shimmer at all, are the Pyramids.

Chapter Three: Getting Around

It takes us longer than fifteen minutes. The Pyramids are farther away than they look, and the sand is deep and hard to walk in. We have to stop every few feet so Lissa can empty out her sandals, leaning against Neil.

"We should have taken a taxi," Zoe's husband says, but there are no roads, and no sign of the refreshment stands and souvenir vendors the guidebook complained about, only the unbroken expanse of deep sand and the white, even sky, and in the distance the three yellow pyramids, standing in a row.

"'The tallest of the three is the Pyramid of Cheops, built in 2690 B.C.,'" Zoe says, reading as she walks. "'It took thirty years to complete.'"

"You have to take a taxi to get to the Pyramids," I say. "There's a lot of traffic."

"'It was built on the west bank of the Nile, which the ancient Egyptians believed was the land of the dead.'"

There is a flicker of movement ahead, between the pyramids, and I stop and shade my eyes against the glare to look at it, hoping it is a souvenir vendor, but I can't see anything. We start walking again.

It flickers again, and this time I catch sight of it running, hunched over, its hands nearly touching the ground. It disappears behind the middle pyramid.

"I saw something," I say, catching up to Zoe. "Some kind of animal. It looked like a baboon."

Zoe leafs through the guidebook and then says, "Monkeys. They're found frequently near Giza. They beg for food from the tourists."

"There aren't any tourists," I say.

"I know," Zoe says happily. "I told you we'd avoid the rush."

"You have to go through customs, even in Egypt," I say. "You can't just leave the airport."

"The pyramid on the left is Kheophren," Zoe says, "built in 2650 B.C."

"In the movie, they wouldn't believe they were dead even when somebody told them," I say. "Giza is *nine* miles from Cairo."

"What are you talking about?" Neil says. Lissa has stopped again and is leaning against him, standing on one foot and shaking her sandal out. "That mystery of Lissa's, *Death on the Nile?*"

"This was a *movie*," I say. "They were on this ship, and they were all dead."

"We saw that movie, didn't we, Zoe?" Zoe's husband says. "Mia Farrow was in it, and Bette Davis. And the detective guy, what was his name—?"

"Hercule Poirot," Zoe says. "Played by Peter Ustinov. The Pyramids are open daily from eight A.M. to five P.M. Evenings there is a *Son et Lumière* show with colored floodlights and a narration in English and Japanese."

"There were all sorts of clues," I say, "but they just ignored them."

"I don't like Agatha Christie," Lissa says. "Murder and trying to find out who killed who. I'm never able to figure out what's going on. All those people on the train together."

"You're thinking of *Murder on the Orient Express*," Neil says. "I saw that."

"Is that the one where they got killed off one by one?" Lissa's husband says.

"I saw that one," Zoe's husband says. "They got what they deserved, as far as I'm concerned, going off on their own like that when they knew they should keep together."

"Giza is nine miles west of Cairo," I say. "You have to take a taxi to get there. There is all this traffic."

"Peter Ustinov was in that one, too, wasn't he?" Neil says. "The one with the train?"

"No," Zoe's husband says. "It was the other one, what's his name?"

"Albert Finney," Zoe says.

Chapter Four: Places of Interest

The Pyramids are closed. Fifty yards (45.7 m.) from the base of Cheops there is a chain barring our way. A metal sign hangs from it that says CLOSED in English and Japanese.

"Prepare to be disappointed," I say.

"I thought you said they were open daily," Lissa says, knocking sand out of her sandals.

"It must be a holiday," Zoe says, leafing through her guidebook. "Here it is. 'Egyptian holidays.'" She begins reading. "'Antiquities sites are closed during Ramadan, the Muslim month of fasting in March. On Fridays the sites are closed from eleven to one P.M.'"

It is not March, or Friday, and even if it were, it is after one P.M. The shadow of Cheops stretches well past where we stand. I look up, trying to see the sun where it must be behind the pyramid, and catch a flicker of movement, high up. It is too large to be a monkey.

"Well, what do we do now?" Zoe's husband says.

"We could go see the Sphinx," Zoe muses, looking through the guidebook. "Or we could wait for the *Son et Lumière* show."

"No," I say, thinking of being out here in the dark.

"How do you know that won't be closed, too?" Lissa asks.

Zoe consults the book. "There are two shows daily, seven-thirty and nine P.M."

"That's what you said about the Pyramids," Lissa says. "*I* think we should go back to the airport and get our luggage. I want to get my other shoes."

"*I* think we should go back to the hotel," Lissa's husband says, "and have a long, cool drink."

"We'll go to Tutankhamun's tomb," Zoe says. "It's open every day, including holidays." She looks up expectantly.

"King Tut's tomb?" I say. "In the Valley of the Kings?"

"Yes," she says, and starts to read. "'It was found intact in 1922 by Howard Carter. It contained—'"

All the belongings necessary for the deceased's journey to the afterworld, I think. Sandals and clothes and *Egypt Made Easy.*

"I'd rather have a drink," Lissa's husband says.

"And a nap," Zoe's husband says. "You go on, and we'll meet you at the hotel."

"I don't think you should go off on your own," I say. "I think we should keep together."

"It will be crowded if we wait," Zoe says. "I'm going now. Are you coming, Lissa?"

Lissa looks appealingly up at Neil. "I don't think I'd better walk that far. My ankle's starting to hurt again."

Neil looks helplessly at Zoe. "I guess we'd better pass."

"What about you?" Zoe's husband says to me. "Are you going with Zoe or do you want to come with us?"

"Before, you said death was the same everywhere," I say to him, "and I said, 'Which is what?' and then Zoe interrupted us and you never did answer me. What were you going to say?"

"I've forgotten," he says, looking at Zoe as if he hopes she will interrupt us again, but she is intent on the guidebook.

"You said death is the same everywhere," I persist, "and I said, 'Which is what?' What did you think death would be like?"

"I don't know . . . unexpected, I guess. And probably pretty damn unpleasant." He laughs nervously. "If we're going to the hotel, we'd better get started. Who else is coming?"

I toy with the idea of going with them, of sitting safely in the hotel bar with ceiling fans and palms, drinking zibib while we wait. That's what the people on the ship did. And in spite of Lissa, I want to stay with Neil.

I look at the expanse of sand back toward the east. There is no sign of Cairo from here, or of the terminal, and far off there is a flicker of movement, like something running.

I shake my head. "I want to see King Tut's tomb." I go over to Neil.

"I think we should go with Zoe," I say, and put my hand on his arm. "After all, she's our guide."

Neil looks helplessly at Lissa and then back at me. "I don't know . . ."

"The three of you can go back to the hotel," I say to Lissa, gesturing to include the other men, "and Zoe and Neil and I can meet you there after we've been to the tomb."

Neil moves away from Lissa. "Why can't you and Zoe just go?" he whispers at me.

"I think we should keep together," I say. "It would be so easy to get separated."

"How come you're so stuck on going with Zoe anyway?" Neil says. "I thought you said you hated being led around by the nose all the time."

I want to say, Because she has the book, but Lissa has come over and is watching us, her eyes bright behind her sunglasses. "I've always wanted to see the inside of a tomb," I say.

"King Tut?" Lissa says. "Is that the one with the treasure, the necklaces and the gold coffin and stuff?" She puts her hand on Neil's arm. "I've always wanted to see that."

"Okay," Neil says, relieved. "I guess we'll go with you, Zoe."

Zoe looks expectantly at her husband.

"Not me," he says. "We'll meet you in the bar."

"We'll order drinks for you," Lissa's husband says. He waves goodbye, and they set off as if they know where they were going, even though Zoe hasn't told them the name of the hotel.

"The Valley of the Kings is located in the hills west of Luxor," Zoe says and starts off across the sand the way she did at the airport. We follow her.

I wait until Lissa gets a shoeful of sand and she and Neil fall behind while she empties it.

"Zoe," I say quietly. "There's something wrong."

"Umm," she says, looking up something in the guidebook's index.

"The Valley of the Kings is four hundred miles south of Cairo," I say. "You can't walk there from the Pyramids."

She finds the page. "Of course not. We have to take a boat."

She points, and I see we have reached a stand of reeds, and beyond it is the Nile. Nosing out from the rushes is a boat, and I am afraid it will be made of gold, but it is only one of the Nile cruisers. And I am so relieved that the Valley of the Kings is not within walking distance that I do not recognize the boat until we have climbed on board and are standing on the canopied deck next to the wooden paddle wheel. It is the steamer from *Death on the Nile*.

Chapter 5: Cruises, Day Trips, and Guided Tours

Lissa is sick on the boat. Neil offers to take her below, and I expect her to say yes, but she shakes her head. "My ankle hurts," she says, and sinks down in one of the deck chairs. Neil kneels by her feet and examines a bruise no bigger than a piaster.

"Is it swollen?" she asks anxiously. There is no sign of swelling, but Neil eases her sandal off and takes her foot tenderly, caressingly, in both hands. Lissa closes her eyes and leans back against the deck chair, sighing.

I toy with the idea that Lissa's husband couldn't take any more of this, either, and that he murdered us all and then killed himself.

"Here we are on a ship," I say, "like the dead people in that movie."

"It's not a ship, it's a steamboat," Zoe says. "'The Nile steamer is the most pleasant way to travel in Egypt and one of the least expensive. Costs range from $180 to $360 per person for a four-day cruise.'"

Or maybe it was Zoe's husband, finally determined to shut Zoe up so he could finish a conversation, and then he had to murder the rest of us one after the other to keep from being caught.

"We're all alone on the ship," I say, "just like they were."

"How far is it to the Valley of the Kings?" Lissa asks.

"'Three and a half miles (5 km.) west of Luxor,'" Zoe says, reading. "'Luxor is four hundred miles south of Cairo.'"

"If it's that far, I might as well read my book," Lissa says, pushing her sunglasses up on top of her head. "Neil, hand me my bag."

He fishes *Death on the Nile* out of her bag and hands it to her, and she flips through it for a moment, like Zoe looking for exchange rates, and then begins to read.

"The wife did it," I say. "She found out her husband was being unfaithful."

Lissa glares at me. "I already knew that," she says carelessly. "I saw the movie," but after another half-page she lays the open book facedown on the empty deck chair next to her.

"I can't read," she says to Neil. "The sun's too bright." She squints up at the sky, which is still hidden by its gauzelike haze.

"'The Valley of the Kings is the site of the tombs of sixty-four pharaohs,'" Zoe says. "'Of these, the most famous is Tutankhamun's.'"

I go over to the railing and watch the Pyramids recede, slipping slowly out of sight behind the rushes that line the shore. They look flat, like yellow triangles stuck up in the sand, and I remember how in Paris, Zoe's husband wouldn't believe the *Mona Lisa* was the real thing. "It's a fake," he insisted before Zoe interrupted. "The real one's much larger."

And the guidebook said, "Prepare to be disappointed," and the Valley of the Kings is four hundred miles from the Pyramids like it's supposed to be, and Middle Eastern airports are notorious for their lack of security. That's how all those bombs get on planes in the first place, because they don't make people go through customs. I shouldn't watch so many movies.

"'Among its treasures, Tutankhamun's tomb contained a golden boat, by which the soul would travel to the world of the dead,'" Zoe says.

I lean over the railing and look into the water. It is not muddy, like I thought it would be, but a clear waveless blue, and in its depths the sun is shining brightly.

"'The boat was carved with passages from *The Book of the Dead*,'" Zoe reads, "'to protect the deceased from monsters and demigods who might try to destroy him before he reached the Hall of Judgment.'"

There is something in the water. Not a ripple, not even enough of a movement to shudder the image of the sun, but I know there is something there.

"'Spells were also written on papyruses buried with the body,'" Zoe says.

It is long and dark, like a crocodile. I lean over farther, gripping the rail, trying to see into the transparent water, and catch a glint of scales. It is swimming straight toward the boat.

"'These spells took the form of commands,'" Zoe reads. "'Get back, you evil one! Stay away! I adjure you in the name of Anubis and Osiris.'"

The water glitters, hesitating.

"'Do not come against me,'" Zoe says. "'My spells protect me. I know the way.'"

The thing in the water turns and swims away. The boat follows it, nosing slowly in toward the shore.

"There it is," Zoe says, pointing past the reeds at a distant row of cliffs. "The Valley of the Kings."

"I suppose this'll be closed, too," Lissa says, letting Neil help her off the boat.

"Tombs are never closed," I say, and look north, across the sand, at the distant Pyramids.

Chapter 6: Accommodations

The Valley of the Kings is not closed. The tombs stretch along a sandstone cliff, black openings in the yellow rock, and there are no chains across the stone steps that lead down to them. At the south end of the valley a Japanese tour group is going into the last one.

"Why aren't the tombs marked?" Lissa asks. "Which one is King Tut's?" and Zoe leads us to the north end of the valley, where the cliff dwindles into a low wall. Beyond it, across the sand, I can see the Pyramids, sharp against the sky.

Zoe stops at the very edge of a slanting hole dug into the base of the rocks. There are steps leading down into it. "Tutankhamun's tomb was found when a workman accidentally uncovered the top step," she says.

Lissa looks down into the stairwell. All but the top two steps are in shadow, and it is too dark to see the bottom. "Are there snakes?" she asks.

"No," Zoe, who knows everything, says. "Tutankhamun's tomb is the smallest of the pharaohs' tombs in the valley." She fumbles in her bag for her flashlight. "The tomb consists of three rooms—an antechamber, the burial chamber containing Tutankhamun's coffin, and the Hall of Judgment."

There is a slither of movement in the darkness below us, like a slow uncoiling, and Lissa steps back from the edge. "Which room is the stuff in?"

"Stuff?" Zoe says uncertainly, still fumbling for her flashlight. She opens her guidebook. "Stuff?" she says again, and flips to the back of it, as if she is going to look "stuff" up in the index.

"*Stuff,*" Lissa says, and there is an edge of fear in her voice. "All the furniture and vases and stuff they take with them. You said the Egyptians buried their belongings with them."

"King Tut's treasure," Neil says helpfully.

"Oh, the *treasure,*" Zoe says, relieved. "The belongings buried with Tutankhamun for his journey into the afterworld. They're not here. They're in Cairo in the museum."

"In Cairo?" Lissa says. "They're in Cairo? Then what are we doing here?"

"We're dead," I say. "Arab terrorists blew up our plane and killed us all."

"I *came* all the way out here because I wanted to see the treasure," Lissa says.

"The coffin is here," Zoe says placatingly, "and there are wall paintings in the antechamber," but Lissa has already led Neil away from the steps, talking earnestly to him.

"The wall paintings depict the stages in the judgment of the soul, the weighing of the soul, the recital of the deceased's confession," Zoe says.

The deceased's confession. I have not taken that which belongs to another. I have not caused any pain. I have not committed adultery.

Lissa and Neil come back, Lissa leaning heavily on Neil's arm. "I think we'll pass on this tomb thing," Neil says apologetically. "We want to get to the museum before it closes. Lissa had her heart set on seeing the treasure."

"'The Egyptian Museum is open from nine A.M. to four P.M. daily, nine to eleven-fifteen A.M. and one-thirty to four P.M. Fridays,'" Zoe says, reading from the guidebook. "'Admission is three Egyptian pounds.'"

"It's already four o'clock," I say, looking at my watch. "It will be closed before you get there." I look up.

Neil and Lissa have already started back, not toward the boat but across the sand in the direction of the Pyramids. The light behind the Pyramids is beginning to fade, the sky going from white to gray-blue.

"Wait," I say, and run across the sand to catch up with them. "Why don't you wait and we'll all go back together? It won't take us very long to see the tomb. You heard Zoe, there's nothing inside."

They both look at me.

"I think we should stay together," I finish lamely.

Lissa looks up alertly, and I realize she thinks I am talking about divorce, that I have finally said what she has been waiting for.

"I think we should all keep together," I say hastily. "This is Egypt. There are all sorts of dangers, crocodiles and snakes and . . . It won't take us very long to see the tomb. You heard Zoe, there's nothing inside."

"We'd better not," Neil says, looking at me. "Lissa's ankle is starting to swell. I'd better get some ice on it."

I look down at her ankle. Where the bruise was there are two little puncture marks, close together, like a snakebite, and around them the ankle is starting to swell.

"I don't think Lissa's up to the Hall of Judgment," he says, still looking at me.

"You could wait at the top of the steps," I say. "You wouldn't have to go in."

Lissa takes hold of his arm, as if anxious to go, but he hesitates. "Those people on the ship," he says to me. "What happened to them?"

"I was just trying to frighten you," I say. "I'm sure there's a logical explanation. It's too bad Hercule Poirot isn't here—he'd be able to explain everything. The Pyramids were probably closed for some Muslim holiday Zoe didn't know about, and that's why we didn't have to go through customs, either, because it was a holiday."

"What happened to the people on the ship?" Neil says again.

"They got judged," I say, "but it wasn't nearly as bad as they'd thought. They were all afraid of what was going to happen, even the clergyman, who hadn't committed any sins, but the judge turned out to be somebody he knew. A bishop. He wore a white suit, and he was very kind, and most of them came out fine."

"Most of them," Neil says.

"Let's go," Lissa says, pulling on his arm.

"The people on the ship," Neil says, ignoring her. "Had any of them committed some horrible sin?"

"My ankle hurts," Lissa says. "Come on."

"I have to go," Neil says, almost reluctantly. "Why don't you come with us?"

I glance at Lissa, expecting her to be looking daggers at Neil, but she is watching me with bright, lidless eyes.

"Yes. Come with us," she says, and waits for my answer.

I lied to Lissa about the ending of Death on the Nile. It was the wife they killed. I toy with the idea that they have committed some horrible sin, that I am lying in my hotel room in Athens, my temple black with blood and powder burns. I would be the only one here, then, and Lissa and Neil would be demigods disguised to look like them. Or monsters.

"I'd better not," I say, and back away from them.

"Let's go, then," Lissa says to Neil, and they start off across the sand. Lissa is limping badly, and before they have gone very far, Neil stops and takes off his shoes.

The sky behind the Pyramids is purple-blue, and the Pyramids stand out flat and black against it.

"Come on," Zoe calls from the top of the steps. She is holding the flashlight and looking at the guidebook. "I want to see the weighing of the soul."

Chapter 7: Off the Beaten Track

Zoe is already halfway down the steps when I get back, shining her flashlight on the door below her. "When the tomb was discovered, the door was plastered over and stamped with the seals bearing the cartouche of Tutankhamun," she says.

"It'll be dark soon," I call down to her. "Maybe we should go back to the hotel with Lissa and Neil." I look back across the desert, but they are already out of sight.

Zoe is gone, too. When I look back down the steps, there is nothing but darkness. "Zoe!" I shout and run down the sand-drifted steps after her. "Wait!"

The door to the tomb is open, and I can see the light from her flashlight bobbing on rock walls and ceiling far down a narrow corridor.

"Zoe!" I shout, and start after her. The floor is uneven, and I trip and put my hand on the wall to steady myself. "Come back! You have the book!"

The light flashes on a section of carved-out wall, far ahead, and then vanishes, as if she has turned a corner.

"Wait for me!" I shout and stop because I cannot see my hand in front of my face.

There is no answering light, no answering voice, no sound at all. I stand very still, one hand still on the wall, listening for footsteps, for quiet padding, for the sound of slithering, but I can't hear anything, not even my own heart beating.

"Zoe," I call out, "I'm going to wait for you outside," and turn around, holding on to the wall so I don't get disoriented in the dark, and go back the way I came.

The corridor seems longer than it did coming in, and I toy with the idea that it will go on forever in the dark, or that the door will be locked, the opening plastered over and the ancient seals affixed, but there is a line of light under the door, and it opens easily when I push on it.

I am at the top of a stone staircase leading down into a long wide hall. On either side the hall is lined with stone pillars, and between the pillars I can see that the walls are painted with scenes in sienna and yellow and bright blue.

It must be the anteroom because Zoe said its walls were painted with scenes from the soul's journey into death, and there is Anubis weighing the soul, and, beyond it, a baboon devouring something, and, opposite where I am standing on the stairs, a painting of a boat crossing the blue Nile. It is made of gold, and in it four souls squat in a line, their kohl-outlined eyes looking ahead at the shore. Beside them, in the transparent water, Sebek, the crocodile demigod, swims.

I start down the steps. There is a doorway at the far end of the hall, and if this is the anteroom, then the door must lead to the burial chamber.

Zoe said the tomb consists of only three rooms, and I saw the map myself on the plane, the steps and straight corridor and then the unimpressive rooms leading one into another, anteroom and burial chamber and Hall of Judgment, one after another.

So this is the anteroom, even if it is larger than it was on the map, and Zoe has obviously gone ahead to the burial chamber and is standing by Tutankhamun's coffin, reading aloud from the travel guide. When I come in, she will look up and say, "The quartzite sarcophagus is carved with passages from *The Book of the Dead*."

I have come halfway down the stairs, and from here I can see the painting of the weighing of the soul. Anubis, with his jackal's head, standing on one side of the yellow scales, and the deceased on the other, reading his confession from a papyrus.

I go down two more steps, till I am even with the scales, and sit down.

Surely Zoe won't be long—there's nothing in the burial chamber except the coffin—and even if she has gone on ahead to the Hall of Judgment, she'll have to come back this way. There's only one entrance to the tomb. And she can't get turned around because she has a flashlight. And the book. I clasp my hands around my knees and wait.

I think about the people on the ship, waiting for judgment. "It wasn't as bad as they thought," I told Neil, but now, sitting here on the steps, I remember that the bishop, smiling kindly in his white suit, gave them sentences appropriate to their sins. One of the women was sentenced to being alone forever.

The deceased in the painting looks frightened, standing by the scale, and I wonder what sentence Anubis will give him, what sins he has committed.

Maybe he has not committed any sins at all, like the clergyman, and is worried over nothing, or maybe he is merely frightened at finding himself in this strange place, alone. Was death what he expected?

"Death is the same everywhere," Zoe's husband said. "Unexpected." And nothing is the way you thought it would be. Look at the *Mona Lisa*. And Neil. The people on the ship had planned on something else altogether, pearly gates and angels and clouds, all the modern refinements. Prepare to be disappointed.

And what about the Egyptians, packing their clothes and wine and sandals for their trip? Was death, even on the Nile, what they expected?

Or was it not the way it had been described in the travel guide at all? Did they keep thinking they were alive, in spite of all the clues?

The deceased clutches his papyrus and I wonder if he has committed some horrible sin. Adultery. Or murder. I wonder how he died.

The people on the ship were killed by a bomb, like we were. I try to remember the moment it went off—Zoe reading out loud and then the sudden shock of light and decompression, the travel guide blown out of Zoe's hands and Lissa falling through the blue air, but I can't. Maybe it didn't happen on the plane. Maybe the terrorists blew us up in the airport in Athens, while we were checking our luggage.

I toy with the idea that it wasn't a bomb at all, that I murdered Lissa and then killed myself, like in *Death on the Nile*. Maybe I reached into my bag, not for my paperback but for the gun I bought in Athens, and shot Lissa while she was looking out the window. And Neil bent over her, solicitous, concerned, and I raised the gun again, and Zoe's husband tried to wrestle it out of my hand, and the shot went wide and hit the gas tank on the wing.

I am still frightening myself. If I'd murdered Lissa, I would remember it, and even Athens, notorious for its lack of security, wouldn't have let me on board a plane with a gun. And you could hardly commit some horrible crime without remembering it, could you?

The people on the ship didn't remember dying, even when someone told them, but that was because the ship was so much like a real one, the railings and the water and the deck. And because of the bomb. People never remember being blown up. It's the concussion or something, it knocks the memory out of you. But I would surely have remembered murdering someone. Or being murdered.

I sit on the steps a long time, watching for the splash of Zoe's flashlight in the doorway. Outside it will be dark, time for the *Son et Lumière* show at the Pyramids.

It seems darker in here, too. I have to squint to see Anubis and the yellow scales and the deceased, awaiting judgment. The papyrus he is holding is covered with long, bordered columns of hieroglyphics and I hope they are magic spells to protect him and not a list of all the sins he has committed.

I have not murdered another, I think. I have not committed adultery. But there are other sins.

It will be dark soon, and I do not have a flashlight. I stand up. "Zoe!" I call, and go down the stairs and between the pillars. They are carved with animals—cobras and baboons and crocodiles.

"It's getting dark," I call, and my voice echoes hollowly among the pillars. "They'll be wondering what happened to us."

The last pair of pillars is carved with a bird, its sandstone wings outstretched. A bird of the gods. Or a plane.

"Zoe?" I say, and stoop to go through the low door. "Are you in here?"

Chapter Eight: Special Events

Zoe isn't in the burial chamber. It is much smaller than the anteroom, and there are no paintings on the rough walls or above the door that leads to the Hall of Judgment. The ceiling is scarcely higher than the door, and I have to hunch down to keep from scraping my head against it.

It is darker in here than in the anteroom, but even in the dimness I can see that Zoe isn't here. Neither is Tutankhamun's sarcophagus, carved with *The Book of the Dead*. There is nothing in the room at all, except for a pile of suitcases in the corner by the door to the Hall of Judgment.

It is our luggage. I recognize my battered Samsonite and the carry-on bags of the Japanese tour group. The flight attendants' navy blue overnight cases are in front of the pile, strapped like victims to their wheeled carriers.

On top of my suitcase is a book, and I think, It's the travel guide, even though I know Zoe would never have left it behind, and I hurry over to pick it up.

It is not *Egypt Made Easy*. It is my *Death on the Nile*, lying open and facedown the way Lissa left it on the boat, but I pick it up anyway and open it to the last pages, searching for the place where Hercule Poirot explains all the strange things that have been happening, where he solves the mystery.

I cannot find it. I thumb back through the book, looking for the map. There is always a map in Agatha Christie, showing who had what stateroom on the ship, showing the stairways and the doors and the unimpressive rooms leading one into another, but I cannot find that, either. The pages are covered with long unreadable columns of hieroglyphics.

I close the book. "There's no point in waiting for Zoe," I say, looking past the luggage at the door to the next room. It is lower than the one I came through, and dark beyond. "She's obviously gone on to the Hall of Judgment."

I walk over to the door, holding the book against my chest. There are stone steps leading down. I can see the top one in the dim light from the burial chamber. It is steep and very narrow.

I toy briefly with the idea that it will not be so bad after all, that I am dreading it like the clergyman, and it will turn out to be not judgment but someone I know, a smiling bishop in a white suit, and mercy is not a modern refinement after all.

"I have not murdered another," I say, and my voice does not echo. "I have not committed adultery."

I take hold of the doorjamb with one hand so I won't fall on the stairs. With the other I hold the book against me. "Get back, you evil ones," I say. "Stay away. I adjure you in the name of Osiris and Poirot. My spells protect me. I know the way."

I begin my descent.

Afterword for "Death on the Nile"

When people ask me if I like horror, I usually say no, because they mean Elm Street and murderers that refuse to die and impalings and beheadings and disembowelings, accompanied by buckets and buckets of blood.

But it's not really true that I don't like horror—I love horror, just not that kind. I love stories where nothing frightening that you can put your finger on is happening, but the hairs on the back of your neck are still standing straight up, stories that don't have any monsters or internal organs or sharp objects, that have instead a nice, friendly small town and a white dress and a ball of yarn, or an oddly deserted ocean liner crossing the Atlantic during wartime without any running lights, or a woman standing perfectly still, watching you from the other side of the lake.

Or a number you keep seeing—on an apartment door, on a taxi, on an airline flight.

You might recognize that last one. It's from possibly the scariest *Twilight Zone* episode I ever saw. The woman on the far side of the lake is of course from Henry James's *The Turn of the Screw.* The ball of yarn and the white dress are from Kit Reed's "The Wait," and the deserted deck is from *Between Two Worlds,* the movie the heroine of "Death on the Nile" kept talking about when she was trying to frighten Lissa.

I saw that movie on TV when I was a teenager, and loved it (and not just because it was set in the London Blitz), but I had no idea what it was called or who was in it, so I had no chance of finding it again till I had the bright idea of asking at a science-fiction convention. (Science-fiction fans know everything.)

But even though I hadn't seen it since I was a kid, it had stuck with me all those years, just as "The Wait" and the *Twilight Zone* episode have stayed with me, just as the movie *The Others* and Shirley Jackson's novel *The Haunting of Hill House* and Daphne DuMaurier's short story "Don't Look Now!" have, in spite of the fact that there's not a machete or a drop of blood in any of them.

Or maybe because of that. I've always thought that slasher-type horror had the same problem as Victorian interior decoration, with all its cushions, knickknacks, whatnot cabinets, and ottomans, and its penchant for putting tassels and fringes and ruffles and lace on everything. They're both wildly cluttered—one with tea cozies and doilies, the other with severed heads and psychopaths—so crowded that the terror can't figure out a way to maneuver its way through.

But I also think it's because the stuff we have in our heads is way scarier than anything H. P. Lovecraft or a WetaWorks special effects team can invent. The movie *Alien* was absolutely terrifying right up to the moment you saw the monster, and I've always thought the best thing that ever happened to *Jaws* was that they couldn't get the mechanical sharks to work. They kept sinking and/or exploding when they hit the water, and that's why they had to resort to the buoys, which were *far* more frightening, and the shadowy, undefined "something" under the water.

It's that undefined something we're really afraid of—the flicker of movement we don't quite catch out of the corner of our eye, the bad dream we can't quite remember when we wake up, the sound of a door opening downstairs we thought we heard. And worst of all, the things we're not sure even happened, the things that we might just have imagined, that might mean we're going mad, all those nameless, nebulous things we can't quite put our finger on and can only guess at.

That's why death is the scariest thing of all. Nobody living has ever caught sight of it, and in spite of centuries' worth of claims of hauntings and messages from beyond the grave, nobody has ever come back to tell us what it was like. And we not only can't imagine what it's like, we can't even imagine how to imagine it.

But we keep trying. So we tell ghost stories about somebody coming to get your liver, and go to slasher movies, and read zombie novels, though none of them are really scary. What's *really* scary is looking up at the clock on the wall of the railway station and seeing that it has no hands.

Or realizing that you've seen the people in the ship's lounge before—right before they were killed by a bomb.

THE SOUL SELECTS HER OWN SOCIETY: INVASION AND REPULSION: A CHRONOLOGICAL REINTERPRETATION OF TWO OF EMILY DICKINSON'S POEMS: A WELLSIAN PERSPECTIVE

Until recently it was thought that Emily Dickinson's poetic output ended in 1886, the year she died. Poems 186B and 272?, however, suggest that not only did she write poems at a later date, but she was involved in the "great and terrible events"[1] of 1897.

The poems in question originally came to light in 1991[2], while Nathan Fleece was working on his doctorate. Fleece, who found the poems[3] under a hedge in the Dickinsons' backyard, classified the poems

---

[1] For a full account, see H. G. Wells, *The War of the Worlds*, Oxford University Press, 1898.

[2] The details of the discovery are recounted in *Desperation and Discovery: The Unusual Number of Lost Manuscripts Located by Doctoral Candidates,* by J. Marple, Reading Railway Press, 1993.

[3] Actually a poem and a poem fragment consisting of a four-line stanza and a single word fragment* from the middle of the second stanza.

*Or word. See later on in this paper.

as belonging to Dickinson's Early or Only Slightly Eccentric Period, but a recent examination of the works[4] has yielded up an entirely different interpretation of the circumstances under which the poems were written.

The sheets of paper on which the poems were written are charred around the edges, and that of Number 272? has a large round hole burnt in it. Martha Hodge-Banks claims that said charring and hole were caused by "a pathetic attempt to age the paper and forgetting to watch the oven,"[5] but the large number of dashes makes it clear they were written by Dickinson, as well as the fact that the poems are almost totally indecipherable. Dickinson's unreadable handwriting has been authenticated by any number of scholars, including Elmo Spencer in *Emily Dickinson: Handwriting or Hieroglyphics?* and M. P. Cursive, who wrote, "Her *a*'s look like *c*'s, her *e*'s look like 2's, and the whole thing looks like chicken scratches."[6]

The charring seemed to indicate that the poems had been written either while smoking[7] or in the midst of some catastrophe, and I began examining the text for clues. Fleece had deciphered Number 272? as beginning, "I never saw a friend— / I never saw a moom—," which made no sense at all,[8] and on closer examination I saw that the stanza actually read:

> *I never saw a fiend—*
> *I never saw a bomb—*

---

[4]   While I was working on *my* dissertation.

[5]   Dr. Banks's assertion that "the paper was manufactured in 1990 and the ink was from a Flair tip pen" is merely airy speculation.*

   *See "Carbon Dating Doesn't Prove Anything," by Jeremiah Habakkuk, in *Creation Science for Fun and Profit*, Golden Slippers Press, 1974.

[6]   The pathetic nature of her handwriting is also addressed in *Impetus to Reform: Emily Dickinson's Effect on the Palmer Method*, and in "Depth, Dolts, and Teeth: An Alternate Translation of Emily Dickinson's Death Poems," in which it is argued that Number 712 actually begins, "Because I could not stoop for darts," and recounts an arthritic evening at the local pub.

[7]   Dickinson is not known to have smoked, except during her Late or Downright Peculiar Period.

[8]   Of course, neither does "How pomp surpassing ermine." Or "A dew sufficed itself."

And yet of both of them I dreamed—
While in the—dreamless tomb—

a much more authentic translation, particularly in regard to the rhyme scheme. "Moom" and "tomb" actually rhyme, which is something Dickinson hardly ever did, preferring near-rhymes such as "mat/gate," "tune/sun," and "balm/hermaphrodite."

The second stanza was more difficult, as it occupied the area of the round hole, and the only readable portion was a group of four letters farther down that read "ulla."[9] This was assumed by Fleece to be part of a longer word such as "bullary" (a convocation of popes),[10] or possibly "dullard" or "hullabaloo."[11]

I, however, immediately recognized "ulla" as the word H. G. Wells had reported hearing the dying Martians utter, a sound he described as "a sobbing alternation of two notes[12] . . . a desolating cry."

"Ulla" was a clear reference to the 1897 invasion by the Martians, previously thought to have been confined to England, Missouri, and the University of Paris.[13] The poem fragment, along with 186B, clearly indicated that the Martians had landed in Amherst and that they had met Emily Dickinson.

At first glance, this seems an improbable scenario due to both the Martians' and Emily Dickinson's dispositions. Dickinson was a recluse who didn't meet anybody, preferring to hide upstairs when neighbors came to call and to float notes down on them.[14] Various theories have been advanced for her self-imposed hermitude, including Bright's Disease, an unhappy love affair, eye trouble, and bad skin. T. L. Mensa

---

[9]   Or possibly "ciee." Or "vole."

[10]   Unlikely, considering her Calvinist upbringing.

[11]   Or the Australian city Ulladulla. Dickinson's poems are full of references to Australia. W. G. Mathilda has theorized from this that "the great love of Dickinson's life was neither Higginson nor Judge Lord, but Mel Gibson." See *Emily Dickinson: The Billabong Connection*, by C. Dundee, Outback Press, 1985.

[12]   See Rod McKuen.

[13]   Where Jules Verne was working on *his* doctorate.

[14]   The notes contained charming, often enigmatic sentiments such as, "Which shall it be— Geraniums or Tulips?" and "Go away—and Shut the door When—you Leave."

suggests the simpler theory that all the rest of the Amherstonians were morons.[15]

None of these explanations would have made it likely that she would like Martians any better than Amherstates, and there is the added difficulty that, having died in 1886, she would also have been badly decomposed.

The Martians present additional difficulties. The opposite of recluses, they were in the habit of arriving noisily, attracting reporters, and blasting at everybody in the vicinity. There is no record of their having landed in Amherst, though several inhabitants mention unusually loud thunderstorms in their diaries,[16] and Louisa May Alcott, in nearby Concord, wrote in her journal, "Wakened suddenly last night by a loud noise to the west. Couldn't get back to sleep for worrying. Should have had Jo marry Laurie. To Do: Write sequel in which Amy dies. Serve her right for burning manuscript."

There is also indirect evidence for the landing. Amherst, frequently confused with Lakehurst, was obviously the inspiration for Orson Welles's setting the radio version of "War of the Worlds" in New Jersey.[17] In addition, a number of the tombstones in West Cemetery are tilted at an angle, and, in some cases, have been knocked down, making it clear that the Martians landed not only in Amherst, but in West Cemetery, very near Dickinson's grave.

Wells describes the impact of the shell[18] as producing "a blinding glare of vivid green light" followed by "such a concussion as I have

---

[15] See *Halfwits and Imbeciles: Poetic Evidence of Emily Dickinson's Opinion of Her Neighbors*, by I. Smart, Intelligentsia Press, 1991.

[16] Virtually everyone in Amherst kept a diary, containing entries such as "Always knew she'd turn out to be a great poet," and "Full moon last night. Caught a glimpse of her out in her garden planting peas. Completely deranged."

[17] The inability of people to tell Orson Welles and H. G. Wells apart lends credence to Dickinson's opinion of humanity. (See Footnote 15.)

[18] Not the one at the beginning of the story, which everybody knows about, the one that practically landed on him in the middle of the book which everybody missed because they'd already turned off the radio and were out running up and down the streets screaming, "The end is here! The Martians are coming!"*

* Thus proving again that Emily was right in her assessment of the populace.

never heard before or since." He reports that the surrounding dirt "splashed," creating a deep pit and exposing drainpipes and house foundations. Such an impact in West Cemetery would have uprooted the surrounding coffins and broken them open, and the resultant light and noise clearly would have been enough to "wake the dead," including the slumbering Dickinson.

That she was thus awakened, and that she considered the event an invasion of her privacy, is made clear in the longer poem, Number 186B, of which the first stanza reads:

> I scarce was settled in the grave—
> When came—unwelcome guests—
> Who pounded on my coffin lid—
> Intruders—in the dust—[19]

Why the "unwelcome guests" did not hurt her,[20] in light of their usual behavior, and how she was able to vanquish them are less apparent, and we must turn to H. G. Wells's account of the Martians for answers.

On landing, Wells tells us, the Martians were completely helpless due to Earth's greater gravity, and remained so until they were able to build their fighting machines. During this period they would have posed no threat to Dickinson except that of company.[21]

Secondly, they were basically big heads. Wells describes them as having eyes, a beak, some tentacles, and "a single large tympanic drum" at the back of the head which functioned as an ear. Wells theorized that the Martians were "descended from beings not unlike ourselves, by a gradual development of brain and hands . . . at the expense of the body." He concluded that, without the body's vulnerability and senses, the

---

[19]   See *Sound, Fury, and Frogs: Emily Dickinson's Seminal Influence on William Faulkner*, by W. Snopes, Yoknapatawpha Press, 1955.
[20]   She was, of course, already dead, which meant the damage they could inflict was probably minimal.
[21]   Which she considered a considerable threat. "If the butcher boy should come now, I would jump into the flour barrel,"* she wrote in 1873.
   * If she was in the habit of doing this, it may account for her always appearing in white.

brain would become "selfish and cruel" and take up mathematics,[22] but Dickinson's effect on them suggests that the overenhanced development of their neocortexes had turned them instead into poets.

The fact that they picked off people with their heat rays, sucked human blood, and spewed poisonous black smoke over entire counties would seem to contraindicate poetic sensibility, but look how poets act. Take Shelley, for instance, who went off and left his first wife to drown herself in the Serpentine so he could marry a woman who wrote monster movies. Or Byron. The only people who had a kind word to say about him were his dogs.[23] Take Robert Frost.[24]

The Martians' identity as poets is corroborated by the fact that they landed seven shells in Great Britain, three in the Lake District,[25] and none at all in Liverpool. It may have determined their decision to land in Amherst.

But they had reckoned without Dickinson's determination and literary technique, as Number 186B makes clear.[26] Stanza Two reads:

> I wrote a letter—to the fiends—
> And bade them all be—gone—
> In simple words—writ plain and clear—
> "I vant to be alone."

"Writ plain and clear" is obviously an exaggeration, but it is manifest that Dickinson wrote a note and delivered it to the Martians, as the next line makes even more evident:

> They (indecipherable)[27] it with an awed dismay—

---

[22]   Particularly nonlinear differential equations.
[23]   See *Lord Byron's Don Juan: The Mastiff as Muse* by C. Harold.
[24]   He didn't like people, either. See "Mending Wall," *The Complete Works*, Random House. Frost preferred barbed wire fences with spikes on top to walls.
[25]   See "Semiotic Subterfuge in Wordsworth's 'I Wandered Lonely as a Cloud': A Dialectic Approach," by N. Compos Mentis, Postmodern Press, 1984.
[26]   Sort of.
[27]   The word is either "read" or "heard" or possibly "pacemaker."

Dickinson may have read it aloud or floated the note down to them in their landing pit in her usual fashion, or she may have unscrewed the shell and tossed it in, like a hand grenade.

Whatever the method of delivery, however, the result was "awed dismay" and then retreat, as the next line indicates:

They—promptly took—their leave—

It has been argued that Dickinson would have had no access to writing implements in the graveyard, but this fails to take into consideration the Victorian lifestyle. Dickinson's burial attire was a white dress, and all Victorian dresses had pockets.[28]

During the funeral, Emily's sister, Lavinia, placed two heliotropes in her sister's hand, whispering that they were for her to take to the Lord. She may also have slipped a pencil and some Post-its into the coffin, or Dickinson, in the habit of writing and distributing notes, may simply have planned ahead.[29]

In addition, grave poems[30] are a well-known part of literary tradition. Dante Gabriel Rossetti, in the throes of grief after the death of his beloved Elizabeth Siddell, entwined poems in her auburn hair as she lay in her coffin.[31]

However the writing implements came to be there, Dickinson obviously made prompt and effective use of them. She scribbled down several stanzas and sent them to the Martians, who were so distressed at them that they decided to abort their mission and return to Mars.

The exact cause of this deadly effect has been much debated, with

---

[28]   Also pleats, tucks, ruching, flounces, frills, ruffles, and passementerie.*
         *See *Pockets as Political Statement: The Role of Clothing in Early Victorian Feminism*, by E. and C. Pankhurst, Angry Women's Press, 1978.
[29]   A good writer is never without pencil and paper.*
         *Or laptop.
[30]   See "Posthumous Poems" in *Literary Theories That Don't Hold Water* by H. Houdini.
[31]   Two years later, no longer quite so grief-stricken and thinking of all that lovely money, he dug her up and got them back.*
         *I told you poets behaved badly.

several theories being advanced. Wells was convinced that microbes killed the Martians landed in England, who had no defense against Earth's bacteria, but such bacteria would have taken several weeks to infect the Martians, and it was obviously Dickinson's poems which caused them to leave, not dysentery.

Spencer suggests that her illegible handwriting led the Martians to misread her message and take it as some sort of ultimatum. A. Huyfen argues that the advanced Martians, being good at punctuation, were appalled by her profligate use of dashes and random capitalizing of letters. S. W. Lubbock proposes the theory that they were unnerved by the fact that all of her poems can be sung to the tune of "The Yellow Rose of Texas."[32]

It seems obvious, however, that the most logical theory is that the Martians were wounded to the heart by Dickinson's use of near-rhymes, which all advanced civilizations rightly abhor. Number 186B contains two particularly egregious examples: "gone/alone" and "guests/dust," and the burnt hole in 272? may indicate something even worse.

The near-rhyme theory is corroborated by H. G. Wells's account of the damage done to London, a city in which Tennyson ruled supreme, and by an account of a near-landing in Ong, Nebraska, recorded by Muriel Addleson:

> We were having our weekly meeting of the Ong Ladies Literary Society when there was a dreadful noise outside, a rushing sound, like something falling off the Grange Hall. Henrietta Muddie was reading Emily Dickinson's "I Taste a Liquor Never Brewed," out loud, and we all raced to the window but couldn't see anything except a lot of dust,[33] so Henrietta started reading

[32]   Try it. No, really. "Be-e-e-cause I could not stop for Death, He kindly stopped for me-e-e." See?*

    *Not all of Dickinson's poems can be sung to "The Yellow Rose of Texas."** Numbers 2, 18, and 1411 can be sung to "The Itsy-Bitsy Spider."

    **Could her choice of tunes be a coded reference to the unfortunate Martian landing in Texas? See "The Night of the Cooters" by Howard Waldrop.

[33]   Normal to Ong, Nebraska.

again and there was a big whoosh, and a big round metal thing
like a cigar[34] rose straight up in the air and disappeared.

It is significant that the poem in question is Number 214, which
rhymes[35] "pearl" and "alcohol."[36]

Dickinson saved Amherst from Martian invasion and then, as she
says in the final two lines of 186B, "rearranged" her "grassy bed— / And
Turned—and went To sleep." She does not explain how the poems got
from the cemetery to the hedge, and we may never know for sure,[37] as
we may never know whether she was being indomitably brave or merely
crabby.

What we do know is that these poems, along with a number of her
other poems,[38] document a heretofore unguessed-at Martian invasion.
Poems 186B and 272?, therefore, should be reassigned to the Very Late
or Deconstructionist Period, not only to give them their proper place as
Dickinson's last and most significant poems, but also so that the full
symbolism intended by Dickinson can be seen in their titles. The properly placed poems will be Numbers 1775 and 1776, respectively, a clear
Dickinsonian reference to the Fourth of July[39], and to the second Inde-

---

[34] See Freud.
[35] Sort of.
[36] The near-rhyme theory also explains why Dickinson responded with such fierceness when
Thomas Wentworth Higginson changed "pearl" to "jewel." She knew, as he could not, that the
fate of the world might someday rest on her inability to rhyme.
[37] For an intriguing possibility, see "The Literary Litterbug: Emily Dickinson's Note-
Dropping as a Response to Thoreau's Environmentalism," by P. Walden, *Transcendentalist Re-*
view, 1990.
[38] Number 187's "awful rivet" is clearly a reference to the Martian cylinder. Number 258's
"There's a certain slant of light" echoes Wells's "blinding glare of vivid green light," and its "af-
fliction / Sent us of the air" obviously refers to the landing. Such allusions indicate that as many
as fifty-five * of the poems were written at a later date than originally supposed, and that the
entire chronology and numbering system of the poems needs to be reconsidered.
  *Significantly enough, the age Emily Dickinson was when she died.
[39] A holiday Dickinson did not celebrate because of its social nature, although she was spotted
in 1881 lighting a cherry bomb on Mabel Dodd's porch and running away.*
  *Which may be why the Martian landing attracted so little attention. The Amherstodes
may have assumed it was Em up to her old tricks again.

pendence Day she brought about by banishing[40] the Martians from Amherst.

NOTE: It is unfortunate that Wells didn't know about the deadly effect of near-rhymes. He could have grabbed a copy of the *Poems*, taken it to the landing pit, read a few choice lines of "The Bustle in a House," and saved everybody a lot of trouble.

---

[40]   There is compelling evidence that the Martians, thwarted in New England, went to Long Island. This theory will be the subject of my next paper,* "The Green Light at the End of Daisy's Dock: Evidence of Martian Invasion in F. Scott Fitzgerald's *The Great Gatsby*."

*   I'm up for tenure.

Afterword for "The Soul Selects Her Own Society"

People are always surprised and disturbed by Emily Dickinson's "reclusive" lifestyle and come up with all sorts of theories to explain her staying in her room, doing her gardening at night, and vanishing upstairs whenever visitors came to call: depression, a skin condition that wouldn't let her out in the sun, lupus, a love affair that ended badly and that she never got over, agoraphobia, epilepsy, etc.

I, however, find her behavior completely understandable. She lived in *Amherst, Massachusetts,* for God's sake.

She had a mind that could connect buggy rides with death, books with sailing ships, and winter light with "the weight of cathedral tunes." She could write lines like "Tell all the Truth but tell it slant" and "Parting is all we know of heaven and all we need of hell," and "And then the windows failed, and then I could not see to see." She was funny, ironic, and *very* smart, and she was stuck in a small town where people's top concerns were bread baking and antimacassar crocheting, where they liked poems that rhymed and had opinions on everything and everybody—and breathlessly repeated them to everybody else. "Did you *hear* what that Dickinson girl *said*?"

I see Amherst as sort of a cross between Avonlea (without Anne of Green Gables), Yonkers (without Dolly Levi), Gopher Prairie, Minnesota, and River City, Iowa, a small all-American town where the entire populace consists of Mrs. Rachel Lynde, Horace Vandergelder, and Eulalie Mackechnie Shinn.

I'd have stayed in my room, too.

FIRE WATCH

---

*History hath triumphed over time, which besides it nothing but
eternity hath triumphed over.*

—Sir Walter Raleigh

September 20—Of course the first thing I looked for was the fire
watch stone. And of course it wasn't there yet. It wasn't dedicated
until 1951, accompanying speech by the Very Reverend Dean Walter
Matthews, and this is only 1940. I knew that. I went to see the fire watch
stone only yesterday, with some kind of misplaced notion that seeing
the scene of the crime would somehow help. It didn't.

The only things that would have helped were a crash course in "London During the Blitz" and a little more time. I had not gotten either.

"Traveling in time is not like taking the Tube, Mr. Bartholomew," the esteemed Dunworthy had said, blinking at me through those antique spectacles of his. "Either you report on the twentieth or you don't go at all."

"But I'm not ready," I'd said. "Look, it took me four years to get ready to travel with St. Paul. *St. Paul.* Not St. Paul's. You can't expect me to get ready for London in the Blitz in two days."

"Yes," Dunworthy had said. "We can." End of conversation.

"Two days!" I had shouted at my roommate Kivrin. "All because some computer adds an apostrophe *s.*

"And the esteemed Dunworthy doesn't even bat an eye when I tell him. 'Time travel is not like taking the Tube, young man,' he says. 'I'd suggest you get ready. You're leaving day after tomorrow.' The man's a total incompetent."

"No," she said. "He isn't. He's the best there is. He wrote the book on St. Paul's. Maybe you should listen to what he says."

I had expected Kivrin to be at least a little sympathetic. She had been practically hysterical when her practicum got changed from fifteenth- to fourteenth-century England, and how did either century qualify as a practicum? Even counting infectious diseases, they couldn't have been more than a five. The Blitz is an eight, and St. Paul's itself is, with my luck, a ten.

"You think I should go see Dunworthy again?" I said.

"Yes."

"And then what? I've got two days. I don't know the money, the language, the history. Nothing."

"He's a good man," Kivrin said. "I think you'd better listen to him while you can." Good old Kivrin. Always the sympathetic ear.

The good man was responsible for my standing just inside the propped-open west doors, gawking like the country boy I was supposed to be, looking for a stone that wasn't there. Thanks to the good man, I was about as unprepared for my practicum as it was possible for him to make me.

I couldn't see more than a few feet into the church. I could see a candle gleaming feebly a long way off and a closer blur of white moving toward me. A verger, or possibly the Very Reverend Dean himself. I pulled out the letter from my clergyman uncle in Wales that was supposed to gain me access to the Dean, and patted my back pocket to make sure I hadn't lost the microfiche *Oxford English Dictionary, Revised, with Historical Supplements* I'd smuggled out of the Bodleian. I couldn't pull it out in the middle of the conversation, but with luck I could muddle through the first encounter by context and look up the words I didn't know later.

"Are you from the ayarpee?" he said. He was no older than I am, a head shorter and much thinner. Almost ascetic-looking. He reminded me of Kivrin. He was not wearing white, but clutching it to his chest. In other circumstances I would have thought it was a pillow. In other circumstances I would know what was being said to me, but there had been no time to unlearn sub-Mediterranean Latin and Jewish law and learn Cockney and air-raid procedures.

Two days, and the esteemed Dunworthy, who wanted to talk about the sacred burdens of the historian instead of telling me what the ayarpee was.

"Are you?" he demanded again.

I considered whipping out the OED after all on the grounds that Wales was a foreign country, but I didn't think they had microfiche in 1940. Ayarpee. It could be anything, including a nickname for the fire watch, in which case the impulse to say no was not safe at all. "No," I said.

He lunged suddenly toward and past me and peered out the open doors. "Damn," he said, coming back to me. "Where are they, then? Bunch of lazy bourgeois tarts!" And so much for getting by on context.

He looked at me closely, suspiciously, as if he thought I was only pretending not to be with the ayarpee. "The church is closed," he said finally.

I held up the envelope and said, "My name's Bartholomew. Is Dean Matthews in?"

He looked out the door a moment longer as if he expected the lazy bourgeois tarts at any moment and intended to attack them with the white bundle, then he turned and said, as if he were guiding a tour, "This way, please," and took off into the gloom.

He led me to the right and down the south aisle of the nave. Thank God I had memorized the floor plan or, at that moment, heading into total darkness, led by a raving verger, the whole bizarre metaphor of my situation would have been enough to send me out the west doors and back to St. John's Wood. It helped a little to know where I was. We should have been passing number twenty-six: Hunt's painting *The Light of the World*—Jesus with his lantern—but it was too dark to see it. We could have used the lantern ourselves.

He stopped abruptly ahead of me, still raving. "We weren't asking for the bloody savoy, just a few cots. Nelson's better off than we are—at least he's got a pillow provided." He brandished the white bundle like a torch in the darkness. It was a pillow, after all. "We asked for them over a fortnight ago, and here we still are, sleeping on the bleeding generals from Trafalgar because those bitches want to play tea and crumpets with the tommies at victoria and the hell with us!"

He didn't seem to expect me to answer his outburst, which was good, because I had understood perhaps one key word in three. He stomped on ahead, moving out of sight of the one pathetic altar candle and stopping again at a black hole. Number twenty-five: stairs to the Whispering Gallery, the dome, the library (not open to the public.)

Up the stairs, down a hall, stop again at a medieval door and knock. "I've got to go wait for them," he said. "If I'm not there they'll likely take them over to the abbey. Tell the Dean to ring them up again, will you?" and he took off down the stone steps, still holding his pillow like a shield against him.

He had knocked, but the door was at least a foot of solid oak, and it was obvious the Very Reverend Dean had not heard. I was going to have to knock again. Yes, well, and the man holding the pinpoint had to let go of it, too, but even knowing it will all be over in a moment and you won't feel a thing doesn't make it any easier to say, "Now!"

So I stood in front of the door, cursing the history department and the esteemed Dunworthy and the computer that had made the mistake and brought me here to this dark door with only a letter from a fictitious uncle whom I trusted no more than I trusted the rest of them.

Even the old reliable Bodleian had let me down. The batch of research stuff I'd cross-ordered through Balliol and the main terminal is probably sitting in my room right now, a century out of reach. And Kivrin, who had already done her practicum and should have been bursting with advice, walked around as silent as a saint until I begged her to help me.

"Did you go to see Dunworthy?" she said.

"Yes. You want to know what priceless bit of information he had for me? 'Silence and humility are the sacred burdens of the historian.' He also told me I would love St. Paul's. Golden gems from the Master. Unfortunately, what I need to know are the times and places of the bombs so one doesn't fall on me." I flopped down on the bed. "Any suggestions?"

"How good are you at memory retrieval?" she said.

I sat up. "I'm pretty good. You think I should assimilate?"

"There isn't time for that," she said. "I think you should put everything you can directly into long-term."

"You mean endorphins?" I said.

The biggest problem with using memory-assistance drugs to put information into your long-term memory is that it never sits, even for a microsecond, in your short-term memory, and that makes retrieval complicated, not to mention unnerving. It gives you the most unsettling sense of *déjà vu* to suddenly know something you're positive you've never seen or heard before.

The main problem, though, is not eerie sensations but retrieval. Nobody knows exactly how the brain gets what it wants out of storage, but short-term is definitely involved. That brief, sometimes microscopic, time information spends in short-term is apparently used for something besides tip-of-the-tongue availability. The whole complex sort-and-file process of retrieval is apparently centered in short-term, and without it, and without the help of the drugs that put it there or artificial substitutes, information can be impossible to retrieve. I'd used endorphins for examinations and never had any difficulty with retrieval, and it looked like it was the only way to store all the information I needed in anything approaching the time I had left, but it also meant that I would *never* have known any of the things I needed to know, even for long enough to have forgotten them. If and when I could retrieve the information, I would know it. Till then I was as ignorant of it as if it were not stored in some cobwebbed corner of my mind at all.

"You can retrieve without artificials, can't you?" Kivrin said, looking skeptical.

"I guess I'll have to."

"Under stress? Without sleep? Low body endorphin levels?" What exactly had her practicum been? She had never said a word about it, and undergraduates are not supposed to ask. Stress factors in the Middle Ages? I thought everybody slept through them.

"I hope so," I said. "Anyway, I'm willing to try this idea if you think it will help."

She looked at me with that martyred expression and said, "Nothing will help." Thank you, St. Kivrin of Balliol.

But I tried it anyway. It was better than sitting in Dunworthy's rooms having him blink at me through his historically accurate eyeglasses and tell me I was going to love St. Paul's. When my Bodleian requests didn't come, I overloaded my credit and bought out Blackwell's. Tapes on World War II, Celtic literature, history of mass transit, tourist guidebooks, everything I could think of. Then I rented a high-speed recorder and shot up. When I came out of it, I was so panicked by the feeling of not knowing any more than I had when I started that I took the Tube to London and raced up Ludgate Hill to see if the fire watch stone would trigger any memories.

It didn't.

"Your endorphin levels aren't back to normal yet," I told myself and tried to relax, but that was impossible with the prospect of the practicum looming up before me. And those are real bullets, kid. Just because you're a history undergraduate doing his practicum doesn't mean you can't get killed.

I read history books all the way home on the Tube and right up until Dunworthy's flunkies came to take me to St. John's Wood this morning. Then I jammed the microfiche OED in my back pocket and went off feeling as if I would have to survive by my native wit and hoping I could get hold of artificials in 1940. Surely I could get through the first day without mishap, I thought, and now here I was, stopped cold by almost the first word that had been spoken to me.

Well, not quite. In spite of Kivrin's advice that I not put anything in short-term, I'd memorized the British money, a map of the tube system, a map of my own Oxford. It had gotten me this far. Surely I would be able to deal with the Dean.

Just as I had almost gotten up the courage to knock, he opened the door, and as with the pinpoint, it really was over quickly and without pain. I handed him my letter and he shook my hand and said something understandable like, "Glad to have another man, Bartholomew."

He looked strained and tired and as if he might collapse if I told him the Blitz had just started. I know, I know: Keep your mouth shut. The sacred silence, etc.

He said, "We'll get Langby to show you round, shall we?" I assumed that was my Verger of the Pillow, and I was right. He met us at the foot of the stairs, puffing a little, but jubilant.

"The cots came," he said to Dean Matthews. "You'd have thought they were doing us a favor. All high heels and hoity-toity. 'You made us miss our tea, luv,' one of them said to me. 'Yes, well, and a good thing, too,' I said. 'You look as if you could stand to lose a stone or two.'"

Even Dean Matthews looked as though he did not completely understand him. He said, "Did you set them up in the crypt?" and then introduced us. "Mr. Bartholomew's just got in from Wales," he said. "He's come to join our volunteers." Volunteers, not fire watch.

Langby showed me around, pointing out various dimnesses in the general gloom, and then dragged me down to see the ten folding canvas cots set up among the tombs in the crypt, also, in passing, Lord Nelson's black marble sarcophagus. He told me I don't have to stand a watch the first night and suggested I go to bed, since sleep is the most precious commodity in the raids. I could well believe it. He was clutching that silly pillow to his breast like his beloved.

"Do you hear the sirens down here?" I asked, wondering if he buried his head in it.

He looked round at the low stone ceilings. "Some do, some don't. Brinton has to have his Horlick's. Bence-Jones would sleep if the roof fell in on him. I must have a pillow. The important thing is to get your eight in no matter what. If you don't, you turn into one of the walking dead. And then you get killed."

On that cheering note he went off to post the watches for tonight, leaving his pillow on one of the cots with orders for me to let nobody touch it. So here I sit, waiting for my first air-raid siren and trying to get all this down before I turn into one of the walking or non-walking dead.

I've used the stolen OED to decipher a little Langby. Middling success. A tart is either a pastry or a prostitute (I assume the latter, although I was wrong about the pillow). "Bourgeois" is a catchall term for all the faults of the middle class. A Tommy's a soldier. Ayarpee I could not find under any spelling and I had nearly given up when something in longterm about the use of acronyms and abbreviations in wartime popped forward (bless you, St. Kivrin) and I realized it must be an abbreviation. ARP. Air-Raid Precautions. Of course. Where else would you get the bleeding cots from?

September 21—Now that I'm past the first shock of being here, I realize that the history department neglected to tell me what I'm supposed to do in the three-odd months of this practicum. They handed me this journal, the letter from my uncle, and a ten-pound note, and sent me packing into the past. The ten pounds (already depleted by train and tube fares) is supposed to last me until the end of December and get me back to St. John's Wood for pickup when the second letter calling me back to Wales to my ailing uncle's bedside comes.

Till then I live here in the crypt with Nelson, who, Langby tells me, is pickled in alcohol inside his coffin. If we take a direct hit, will he burn like a torch or simply trickle out in a decaying stream onto the crypt floor, I wonder. Board is provided by a gas ring, over which are cooked wretched tea and indescribable kippers. To pay for all this luxury I am to stand on the roofs of St. Paul's and put out incendiaries.

I must also accomplish the purpose of this practicum, whatever it may be. Right now the only purpose I care about is staying alive until the second letter from Uncle arrives and I can go home.

I am doing make-work until Langby has time to "show me the ropes." I've cleaned the skillet they cook the foul little fishes in, stacked wooden folding chairs at the altar end of the crypt (flat instead of standing because they tend to collapse like bombs in the middle of the night) and tried to sleep.

I am apparently not one of the lucky ones who can sleep through the raids. I spent most of the night wondering what St. Paul's risk rating is. Practica have to be at least a six. Last night I was convinced this was a ten, with the crypt as ground zero, and that I might as well have applied for Denver.

The most interesting thing that's happened so far is that I've seen a cat. I am fascinated, but trying not to appear so since they seem commonplace here.

September 22—Still in the crypt. Langby comes dashing through periodically cursing various government agencies (all abbreviated) and promising to take me up on the roofs. In the meantime, I've run out of make-work and taught myself to work a stirrup pump. Kivrin was overly concerned about my memory retrieval abilities. I have not had any trouble so far. Quite the opposite. I called up firefighting information and got the whole manual with pictures, including instructions on the use of the stirrup pump. If the kippers set Lord Nelson on fire, I shall be a hero.

Excitement last night. The sirens went early and some of the chars who clean offices in the City sheltered in the crypt with us. One of them woke me out of a sound sleep, going like an air-raid siren. Seems she'd seen a mouse. We had to go whacking at tombs and under the cots with a rubber boot to persuade her it was gone. Obviously what the history department had in mind: murdering mice.

September 24—Langby took me on rounds. Into the choir, where I had to learn the stirrup pump all over again, assigned rubber boots and a tin helmet. Langby says Commander Allen is getting us asbestos firemen's coats, but hasn't yet, so it's my own wool coat and muffler and very cold on the roofs even in September. It feels like November and looks it, too, bleak and cheerless with no sun. Up to the dome and onto the roofs, which should be flat but in fact are littered with towers, pinnacles, gutters, statues, all designed expressly to catch and hold incendiaries out of reach. Shown how to smother an incendiary with sand before it burns through the roof and sets the church on fire. Shown the ropes (literally) lying in a heap at the base of the dome in case somebody has to go up one of the west towers or over the top of the dome. Back inside and down to the Whispering Gallery.

Langby kept up a running commentary through the whole tour, part practical instruction, part church history. Before we went up into the Gallery he dragged me over to the south door to tell me how Christopher Wren stood in the smoking rubble of Old St. Paul's and asked a workman to bring him a stone from the graveyard to mark the cornerstone. On the stone was written in Latin, "I shall rise again," and Wren was so impressed by the irony that he had the word inscribed above the door. Langby looked as smug as if he had not told me a story every first-year history student knows, but I suppose without the impact of the fire watch stone, the other is just a nice story.

Langby raced me up the steps and onto the narrow balcony circling the Whispering Gallery. He was already halfway round to the other side, shouting dimensions and acoustics at me. He stopped facing the wall opposite and said softly, "You can hear me whispering because of the shape of the dome. The sound waves are reinforced around the perimeter of the dome. It sounds like the very crack of doom up here during a raid. The dome is one hundred and seven feet across. It is eighty feet above the nave."

I looked down. The railing went out from under me and the black and white marble floor came up with dizzying speed. I hung on to something in front of me and dropped to my knees, staggered and sick at heart. The sun had come out, and all of St. Paul's seemed drenched in gold. Even the carved wood of the choir, the white stone pillars, the leaden pipes of the organ, all of it golden, golden.

Langby was beside me, trying to pull me free. "Bartholomew," he shouted, "what's wrong? For God's sake, man."

I knew I must tell him that if I let go, St. Paul's and all the past would fall in on me, and that I must not let that happen because I was an historian. I said something, but it was not what I intended because Langby merely tightened his grip. He hauled me violently free of the railing and back onto the stairway, then let me collapse limply on the steps and stood back from me, not speaking.

"I don't know what happened in there," I said. "I've never been afraid of heights before."

"You're shaking," he said sharply. "You'd better lie down." He led me back to the crypt.

September 25—Memory retrieval: ARP manual. Symptoms of bombing victims. Stage one—shock; stupefaction; unawareness of injuries; words may not make sense except to victim. Stage two—shivering; nausea; injuries, losses felt; return to reality. Stage three—talkativeness that cannot be controlled; desire to explain shock behavior to rescuers.

Langby must surely recognize the symptoms, but how does he account for the fact there was no bomb? I can hardly explain my shock behavior to him, and it isn't just the sacred silence of the historian that stops me.

He has not said anything, in fact assigned me my first watches for tomorrow night as if nothing had happened, and he seems no more preoccupied than anyone else. Everyone I've met so far is jittery (one thing I had in short-term was how calm everyone was during the raids) and the raids have not come near us since I got here. They've been mostly over the East End and the docks.

There was a reference tonight to a UXB, and I have been thinking about the Dean's manner and the church being closed, when I'm almost sure I remember reading it was open through the entire Blitz. As soon as I get a chance, I'll try to retrieve the events of September. As to retrieving anything else, I don't see how I can hope to remember the right information until I know what it is I am supposed to do here, if anything.

There are no guidelines for historians, and no restrictions, either. I could tell everyone I'm from the future if I thought they would believe me. I could murder Hitler if I could get to Germany. Or could I? Time paradox talk abounds in the history department, and the graduate students back from their practica don't say a word one way or the other. Is there a tough, immutable past? Or is there a new past every day and do we, the historians, make it? And what are the consequences of what we do, if there are consequences? And how do we dare do anything without knowing them? Must we interfere boldly, hoping we do not bring about all our downfalls? Or must we do nothing at all, not interfere, stand by and watch St. Paul's burn to the ground if need be so that we don't change the future?

All those are fine questions for a late-night study session. They do not matter here. I could no more let St. Paul's burn down than I could kill Hitler. No, that is not true. I found that out yesterday in the Whispering Gallery. I could kill Hitler if I caught him setting fire to St. Paul's.

September 26—I met a young woman today. Dean Matthews has opened the church, so the watch have been doing duties as chars and people have started coming in again. The young woman reminded me of Kivrin, though Kivrin is a good deal taller and would never frizz her hair like that. She looked as if she had been crying. Kivrin has looked like that since she got back from her practicum. The Middle Ages were too much for her. I wonder how she would have coped with this. By pouring out her fears to the local priest, no doubt, as I sincerely hoped her look-alike was not going to do to me.

"May I help you?" I said, not wanting in the least to help. "I'm a volunteer."

She looked distressed. "You're not paid?" she said, and wiped at her reddened nose with a handkerchief. "I read about St. Paul's and the fire watch and all and I thought, perhaps there's a position there for me. In the canteen, like, or something. A paying position." There were tears in her red-rimmed eyes.

"I'm afraid we haven't a canteen," I said as kindly as I could, considering how impatient Kivrin always makes me, "and it's not actually a real shelter. Some of the watch sleep in the crypt. I'm afraid we're all volunteers, though."

"That won't do, then," she said. She dabbed at her eyes with the handkerchief. "I love St. Paul's, but I can't take on volunteer work, not with my little brother Tom back from the country."

I was not reading this situation properly. For all the outward signs of distress she sounded quite cheerful and no closer to tears than when she had come in.

"I've got to get us a proper place to stay. With Tom back, we can't go on sleeping in the Tube."

A sudden feeling of dread, the kind of sharp pain you get sometimes from involuntary retrieval, went over me. "The Tube?" I said, trying to get at the memory.

"Marble Arch, usually," she went on. "My brother Tom saves us a place early and I go . . ." She stopped, held the handkerchief close to her nose, and exploded into it. "I'm sorry," she said, "this awful cold!"

Red nose, watering eyes, sneezing. Respiratory infection. It was a wonder I hadn't told her not to cry. It's only by luck that I haven't made some unforgivable mistake so far, and this is not because I can't get at the long-term memory. I don't have half the information I need even stored: cats and colds and the way St. Paul's looks in full sun. It's only a matter of time before I am stopped cold by something I do not know. Nevertheless, I am going to try for retrieval tonight after I come off watch. At least I can find out whether and when something is going to fall on me.

I have seen the cat once or twice. He is coal-black with a white patch on his throat that looks as if it were painted on for the blackout.

September 27—I have just come down from the roofs. I am still shaking.

Early in the raid the bombing was mostly over the East End. The view was incredible. Searchlights everywhere, the sky pink from the fires and reflecting in the Thames, the exploding shells sparkling like fireworks. There was a constant, deafening thunder broken by the occasional droning of the planes high overhead, then the repeating stutter of the ack-ack guns.

About midnight the bombs began falling quite near with a horrible sound like a train running over me. It took every bit of will I had to keep from flinging myself flat on the roof, but Langby was watching. I didn't want to give him the satisfaction of watching a repeat performance of my behavior in the dome. I kept my head up and my sand bucket firmly in hand and felt quite proud of myself.

The bombs stopped roaring down about three, and there was a lull of about half an hour, and then a clatter like hail on the roofs. Everybody except Langby dived for shovels and stirrup pumps. He was watching me. And I was watching the incendiary.

It had fallen only a few meters from me, behind the clock tower. It was much smaller than I had imagined, only about thirty centimeters long. It was sputtering violently, throwing greenish-white fire almost to where I was standing. In a minute it would simmer down into a molten mass and begin to burn through the roof. Flames and the frantic shouts of firemen, and then the white rubble stretching for miles, and nothing, nothing left, not even the fire watch stone.

It was the Whispering Gallery all over again. I felt that I had said something, and when I looked at Langby's face he was smiling crookedly.

"St. Paul's will burn down," I said. "There won't be anything left."

"Yes," Langby said. "That's the idea, isn't it? Burn St. Paul's to the ground? Isn't that the plan?"

"Whose plan?" I said stupidly.

"Hitler's, of course," Langby said. "Who did you think I meant?" and, almost casually, picked up his stirrup pump.

The page of the ARP manual flashed suddenly before me. I poured the bucket of sand around the still sputtering bomb, snatched up another bucket and dumped that on top of it. Black smoke billowed up in such a cloud that I could hardly find my shovel. I felt for the smothered bomb with the tip of it and scooped it into the empty bucket, then shoveled the sand in on top of it. Tears were streaming down my face from the acrid smoke. I turned to wipe them on my sleeve and saw Langby.

He had not made a move to help me. He smiled. "It's not a bad plan, actually. But of course we won't let it happen. That's what the fire watch is here for. To see that it doesn't happen. Right, Bartholomew?"

I know now what the purpose of my practicum is. I must stop Langby from burning down St. Paul's.

September 28—I try to tell myself I was mistaken about Langby last night, that I misunderstood what he said. Why would he want to burn down St. Paul's unless he is a Nazi spy? How can a Nazi spy have gotten on the fire watch? I think about my faked letter of introduction and shudder.

How can I find out? If I set him some test, some fatal thing that only a loyal Englishman in 1940 would know, I fear I am the one who would be caught out. I must get my retrieval working properly.

Until then, I shall watch Langby. For the time being at least, that should be easy. Langby has just posted the watches for the next two weeks. We stand every one together.

September 30—I know what happened in September. Langby told me.

Last night in the choir, putting on our coats and boots, he said, "They've already tried once, you know."

I had no idea what he meant. I felt as helpless as that first day when he asked me if I was from the ayarpee.

"The plan to destroy St. Paul's. They've already tried once. The tenth of September. A high-explosive bomb. But of course you didn't know about that. You were in Wales."

I was not even listening. The minute he had said "high-explosive bomb," I had remembered it all. It had burrowed in under the road and lodged on the foundations. The bomb squad had tried to defuse it, but there'd been a leaking gas main. They'd decided to evacuate St. Paul's, but Dean Matthews had refused to leave, and they'd got it out after all and exploded it in Barking Marshes. Instant and complete retrieval.

"The bomb squad saved her that time," Langby was saying. "It seems there's always somebody about."

"Yes," I said. "There is," and walked away from him.

October 1—I thought last night's retrieval of the events of September tenth meant some sort of breakthrough, but I have been lying here on my cot most of the night trying for Nazi spies in St. Paul's and getting nothing. Do I have to know exactly what I'm looking for before I can remember it? What good does that do me?

Maybe Langby is not a Nazi spy. Then what is he? An arsonist? A madman? The crypt is hardly conducive to thought, being not at all as silent as a tomb. The chars talk most of the night and the sound of the bombs is muffled, which somehow makes it worse. I find myself straining to hear them. When I did get to sleep this morning, I dreamed about one of the tube shelters being hit, broken mains, drowning people.

October 4—I tried to catch the cat today. I had some idea of persuading it to dispatch the mouse that has been terrifying the chars. I also wanted to see one up close. I took the water bucket I had used with the stirrup pump last night to put out some burning shrapnel from one of the anti-aircraft guns. It still had a bit of water in it, but not enough to drown the cat, and my plan was to clamp the bucket over him, reach under and pick him up, then carry him down to the crypt and point him at the mouse. I did not even come close to him.

I swung the bucket, and as I did so, perhaps an inch of water splashed out. I thought I remembered that the cat was a domesticated animal, but I must have been wrong about that. The cat's wide complacent face pulled back into a skull-like mask that was absolutely terrifying, vicious claws extended from what I had thought were harmless paws, and the cat let out a sound to top the chars.

In my surprise I dropped the bucket and it rolled against one of the pillars. The cat disappeared. Behind me, Langby said, "That's no way to catch a cat."

"Obviously," I said, and bent to retrieve the bucket.

"Cats hate water," he said, still in that expressionless voice.

"Oh," I said, and started in front of him to take the bucket back to the choir. "I didn't know that."

"Everybody knows it. Even the stupid Welsh."

October 8—We have been standing double watches for a week— bomber's moon. Langby didn't show up on the roofs, so I went looking for him in the church. I found him standing by the west doors talking to an old man. The man had a newspaper tucked under his arm and he handed it to Langby, but Langby gave it back to him. When the man saw me, he ducked out. Langby said, "Tourist. Wanted to know where the Windmill Theatre is. Read in the paper the girls are starkers."

I know I looked as if I didn't believe him because he said, "You look rotten, old man. Not getting enough sleep, are you? I'll get somebody to take the first watch for you tonight."

"No," I said coldly. "I'll stand my own watch. I like being on the roofs," and added silently, Where I can watch you.

He shrugged and said, "I suppose it's better than being down in the crypt. At least on the roofs you can hear the one that gets you."

October 10—I thought the double watches might be good for me, take my mind off my inability to retrieve. The watched pot idea. Actually, it sometimes works. A few hours of thinking about something else, or a good night's sleep, and the fact pops forward without any prompting, without any artificials.

The good night's sleep is out of the question. Not only do the chars talk constantly, but the cat has moved into the crypt and sidles up to everyone, making siren noises and begging for kippers. I am moving my cot out of the transept and over by Nelson before I go on watch. He may be pickled, but he keeps his mouth shut.

October 11—I dreamed Trafalgar, ships' guns and smoke and falling plaster and Langby shouting my name. My first waking thought was that the folding chairs had gone off. I could not see for all the smoke.

"I'm coming," I said, limping toward Langby and pulling on my boots. There was a heap of plaster and tangled folding chairs in the transept. Langby was digging in it. "Bartholomew!" he shouted, flinging a chunk of plaster aside. "Bartholomew!"

I still had the idea it was smoke. I ran back for the stirrup pump and then knelt beside him and began pulling on a splintered chair back. It resisted, and it came to me suddenly, There is a body under here. I will reach for a piece of the ceiling and find it is a hand. I leaned back on my heels, determined not to be sick, then went at the pile again.

Langby was going far too fast, jabbing with a chair leg. I grabbed his hand to stop him, and he struggled against me as if I were a piece of rubble to be thrown aside. He picked up a large flat square of plaster, and under it was the floor. I turned and looked behind me. Both chars huddled in the recess by the altar. "Who are you looking for?" I said, keeping hold of Langby's arm.

"Bartholomew," he said, and swept the rubble aside, his hands bleeding through the coating of smoky dust.

"I'm here," I said. "I'm all right." I choked on the white dust. "I moved my cot out of the transept."

He turned sharply to the chars and then said quite calmly, "What's under here?"

"Only the gas ring," one of them said timidly from the shadowed recess, "and Mrs. Galbraith's pocketbook." He dug through the mess until he had found them both. The gas ring was leaking at a merry rate, though the flame had gone out.

"You've saved St. Paul's and me after all," I said, standing there in my underwear and boots, holding the useless stirrup pump. "We might all have been asphyxiated."

He stood up. "I shouldn't have saved you," he said.

Stage one: shock, stupefaction, unawareness of injuries, words may not make sense except to victim. He would not know his hand was bleeding yet. He would not remember what he had said. He had said he shouldn't have saved my life.

"I shouldn't have saved you," he repeated. "I have my duty to think of."

"You're bleeding," I said sharply. "You'd better lie down." I sounded just like Langby in the Gallery.

October 13—It was a high-explosive bomb. It blew a hole in the choir roof, and some of the marble statuary is broken, but the ceiling of the crypt did not collapse, which is what I thought at first. It only jarred some plaster loose.

I do not think Langby has any idea what he said. That should give me some sort of advantage, now that I am sure where the danger lies, now that I am sure it will not come crashing down from some other direction. But what good is all this knowing, when I do not know what he will do? Or when?

Surely I have the facts of yesterday's bomb in long-term, but even falling plaster did not jar them loose this time. I am not even trying for retrieval now. I lie in the darkness waiting for the roof to fall in on me. And remembering how Langby saved my life.

October 15—The girl came in again today. She still has the cold, but she has gotten her paying position. It was a joy to see her. She was wearing a smart uniform and open-toed shoes, and her hair was in an elaborate frizz around her face. We are still cleaning up the mess from the bomb, and Langby was out with Allen getting wood to board up the choir, so I let the girl chatter at me while I swept. The dust made her sneeze, but at least this time I knew what she was doing.

She told me her name is Enola and that she's working for the WVS, running one of the mobile canteens that are sent to the fires. She came, of all things, to thank me for the job. She said that after she told the WVS that there was no proper shelter with a canteen for St. Paul's, they gave her a run in the City. "So I'll just pop in when I'm close and let you know how I'm making out, won't I just?"

She and her brother Tom are still sleeping in the Tube. I asked her if that was safe and she said probably not, but at least down there you couldn't hear the one that got you and that was a blessing.

October 18—I am so tired I can hardly write this. Nine incendiaries tonight and a land mine that looked as though it was going to catch on the dome till the wind drifted its parachute away from the church. I put out two of the incendiaries. I have done that at least twenty times since I got here and helped with dozens of others, and still it is not enough. One incendiary, one moment of not watching Langby, could undo it all.

I know that is partly why I feel so tired. I wear myself out every night trying to do my job and watch Langby, making sure none of the incendiaries falls without my seeing it. Then I go back to the crypt and wear myself out trying to retrieve something, anything, about spies, fires, St. Paul's in the fall of 1940, anything. It haunts me that I am not doing enough, but I do not know what else to do. Without the retrieval, I am as helpless as these poor people here, with no idea what will happen tomorrow.

If I have to, I will go on doing this till I am called home. He cannot burn down St. Paul's so long as I am here to put out the incendiaries. "I have my duty," Langby said in the crypt.

And I have mine.

October 21—It's been nearly two weeks since the blast and I just now realized we haven't seen the cat since. He wasn't in the mess in the

crypt. Even after Langby and I were sure there was no one in there, we
sifted through the stuff twice more. He could have been in the choir,
though.

Old Bence-Jones says not to worry. "He's all right," he said. "The
jerries could bomb London right down to the ground and the cats
would waltz out to greet them. You know why? They don't love anybody. That's what gets half of us killed. Old lady out in Stepney got
killed the other night trying to save her cat. Bloody cat was in the
Anderson."

"Then where is he?"

"Someplace safe, you can bet on that. If he's not around St. Paul's,
it means we're for it. That old saw about the rats deserting a sinking
ship, that's a mistake, that is. It's cats, not rats."

October 25—Langby's tourist showed up again. He cannot still be looking for the Windmill Theatre. He had a newspaper under his arm again
today, and he asked for Langby, but Langby was across town with Allen,
trying to get the asbestos firemen's coats. I saw the name of the paper. It
was *The Worker*. A Nazi newspaper?

November 2—I've been up on the roofs for a week straight, helping
some incompetent workmen patch the hole the bomb made. They're
doing a terrible job. There's still a great gap on one side a man could fall
into, but they insist it'll be all right because, after all, you wouldn't fall
clear through but only as far as the ceiling, and "the fall can't kill you."
They don't seem to understand it's a perfect hiding place for an incendiary.

And that is all Langby needs. He does not even have to set a fire to
destroy St. Paul's. All he needs to do is let one burn uncaught until it is
too late.

I could not get anywhere with the workmen. I went down into the church to complain to Matthews, and saw Langby and his tourist behind a pillar, close to one of the windows. Langby was holding a newspaper and talking to the man. When I came down from the library an hour later, they were still there. So is the gap. Matthews says we'll put planks across it and hope for the best.

November 5—I have given up trying to retrieve. I am so far behind on my sleep I can't even retrieve information on a newspaper whose name I already know. Double watches the permanent thing now. Our chars have abandoned us altogether (like the cat), so the crypt is quiet, but I cannot sleep.

If I do manage to doze off, I dream. Yesterday I dreamed Kivrin was on the roofs, dressed like a saint. "What was the secret of your practicum?" I said. "What were you supposed to find out?"

She wiped her nose with a handkerchief and said, "Two things. One, that silence and humility are the sacred burdens of the historian. Two"—she stopped and sneezed into the handkerchief—"don't sleep in the Tube."

My only hope is to get hold of an artificial and induce a trance. That's a problem. I'm positive it's too early for chemical endorphins and probably hallucinogens. Alcohol is definitely available, but I need something more concentrated than ale, the only alcohol I know by name. I do not dare ask the watch. Langby is suspicious enough of me already. It's back to the OED, to look up a word I don't know.

November 11—The cat's back. Langby was out with Allen again, still trying for the asbestos coats, so I thought it was safe to leave St. Paul's. I went to the grocer's for supplies, and hopefully, an artificial. It was late, and the sirens sounded before I had even gotten to Cheapside, but the raids do not usually start until after dark. It took a while to get all the groceries and to get up my courage to ask whether he had any alcohol—he told me to go to a pub—and when I came out of the shop, it was as if I had pitched suddenly into a hole.

I had no idea where St. Paul's lay, or the street, or the shop I had just come from. I stood on what was no longer the sidewalk, clutching my brown-paper parcel of kippers and bread with a hand I could not have seen if I held it up before my face. I reached up to wrap my muffler closer about my neck and prayed for my eyes to adjust, but there was no reduced light to adjust to. I would have been glad of the moon, for all St. Paul's watch cursed it and called it a fifth columnist. Or a bus, with its shuttered headlights giving just enough light to orient myself by. Or a searchlight. Or the kickback flare of an ack-ack gun. Anything.

Just then I did see a bus, two narrow yellow slits a long way off. I started toward it and nearly pitched off the curb. Which meant the bus was sideways in the street, which meant it was not a bus. A cat meowed, quite near, and rubbed against my leg. I looked down into the yellow lights I had thought belonged to the bus. His eyes were picking up light from somewhere, though I would have sworn there was not a light for miles, and reflecting it flatly up at me.

"A warden'll get you for those lights, old tom," I said, and then as a plane droned overhead, "Or a jerry."

The world exploded suddenly into light, the searchlights and a glow along the Thames seeming to happen almost simultaneously, lighting my way home.

"Come to fetch me, did you, old tom?" I said gaily. "Where've you been? Knew we were out of kippers, didn't you? I call that loyalty." I talked to him all the way home and gave him half a tin of the kippers for saving my life. Bence-Jones said he smelled the milk at the grocer's.

November 13—I dreamed I was lost in the blackout. I could not see my hands in front of my face, and Dunworthy came and shone a pocket torch at me, but I could only see where I had come from and not where I was going.

"What good is that to them?" I said. "They need a light to show them where they're going."

"Even the light from the Thames? Even the light from the fires and the ack-ack guns?" Dunworthy said.

"Yes. Anything is better than this awful darkness." So he came closer to give me the pocket torch. It was not a pocket torch after all, but Christ's lantern from the Hunt picture in the south nave. I shone it on the curb before me so I could find my way home, but it shone instead on the fire watch stone and I hastily put the light out.

November 20—I tried to talk to Langby today. "I've seen you talking to the old gentleman," I said. It sounded like an accusation. I meant it to. I wanted him to think it was and stop whatever he was planning.

"Reading," he said. "Not talking." He was putting things in order in the choir, piling up sandbags.

"I've seen you reading, then," I said belligerently, and he dropped a sandbag and straightened.

"What of it?" he said. "It's a free country. I can read to an old man if I want, same as you can talk to that little WVS tart."

"What do you read?" I said.

"Whatever he wants. He's an old man. He used to come home from his job, have a bit of brandy, and listen to his wife read the papers to him. She got killed in one of the raids. Now I read to him. I don't see what business it is of yours."

It sounded true. It didn't have the careful casualness of a lie, and I almost believed him, except that I had heard the tone of truth from him before. In the crypt. After the bomb.

"I thought he was a tourist looking for the Windmill," I said.

He looked blank only a second, and then he said, "Oh, yes, that. He came in with the paper and asked me to tell him where it was. I looked it up to find the address. Clever, that. I didn't guess he couldn't read it for himself." But it was enough. I knew that he was lying.

He heaved a sandbag almost at my feet. "Of course you wouldn't understand a thing like that, would you? A simple act of human kindness?"

"No," I said coldly. "I wouldn't."

None of this proves anything. He gave away nothing, except perhaps the name of an artificial, and I can hardly go to Dean Matthews and accuse Langby of reading aloud.

I waited till he had finished in the choir and gone down to the crypt. Then I lugged one of the sandbags up to the roof and over to the chasm. The planking has held so far, but everyone walks gingerly around it, as if it were a grave. I cut the sandbag open and spilled the loose sand into the bottom. If it has occurred to Langby that this is the perfect spot for an incendiary, perhaps the sand will smother it.

November 21—I gave Enola some of "Uncle's" money today and asked her to get me the brandy. She was more reluctant than I thought she'd be, so there must be societal complications I am not aware of, but she agreed.

I don't know what she came for. She started to tell me about her brother and some prank he'd pulled in the Tube that got him in trouble with the guard, but after I asked her about the brandy, she left without finishing the story.

November 25—Enola came today, but without bringing the brandy. She is going to Bath for the holidays to see her aunt. At least she will be away from the raids for a while. I will not have to worry about her. She finished the story of her brother and told me she hopes to persuade this aunt to take Tom for the duration of the Blitz but is not at all sure the aunt will be willing.

Young Tom is apparently not so much an engaging scapegrace as a near-criminal. He has been caught twice picking pockets in the Bank tube shelter, and they have had to go back to Marble Arch. I comforted her as best I could, told her all boys were bad at one time or another. What I really wanted to say was that she needn't worry at all, that young Tom strikes me as a true survivor type, like my own tom, like Langby, totally unconcerned with anybody but himself, well equipped to survive the Blitz and rise to prominence in the future.

Then I asked her whether she had gotten the brandy.

She looked down at her open-toed shoes and muttered unhappily, "I thought you'd forgotten all about that."

I made up some story about the watch taking turns buying a bottle, and she seemed less unhappy, but I am not convinced she will not use this trip to Bath as an excuse to do nothing. I will have to leave St. Paul's and buy it myself, and I don't dare leave Langby alone in the church. I made her promise to bring the brandy today before she leaves. But she is still not back, and the sirens have already gone.

November 26—No Enola, and she said their train left at noon. I suppose I should be grateful that at least she is safely out of London. Maybe in Bath she will be able to get over her cold.

Tonight one of the ARP girls breezed in to borrow half our cots and tell us about a mess over in the East End where a surface shelter was hit. Four dead, twelve wounded. "At least it wasn't one of the tube shelters!" she said. "Then you'd see a real mess, wouldn't you?"

November 30—I dreamed I took the cat to St. John's Wood. "Is this a rescue mission?" Dunworthy said.

"No, sir," I said proudly. "I know what I was supposed to find in my practicum. The perfect survivor. Tough and resourceful and selfish. This is the only one I could find. I had to kill Langby, you know, to keep him from burning down St. Paul's. Enola's brother has gone to Bath, and the others will never make it. Enola wears open-toed shoes in the winter and sleeps in the tubes and puts her hair up on metal pins so it will curl. She cannot possibly survive the Blitz."

Dunworthy said, "Perhaps you should have rescued her instead. What did you say her name was?"

"Kivrin," I said, and woke up cold and shivering.

December 5—I dreamed Langby had the pinpoint bomb. He carried it under his arm like a brown-paper parcel, coming out of St. Paul's Station and up Ludgate Hill to the west doors.

"This is not fair," I said, barring his way with my arm. "There is no fire watch on duty."

He clutched the bomb to his chest like a pillow. "That is your fault," he said, and before I could get to my stirrup pump and bucket, he tossed it in the door.

The pinpoint was not even invented until the end of the twentieth century, and it was another ten years before the dispossessed communists got hold of it and turned it into something that could be carried under your arm. A parcel that could blow a quarter-mile of the City into oblivion. Thank God that is one dream that cannot come true.

It was a sunlit morning in the dream, and this morning when I came off watch the sun was shining for the first time in weeks. I went down to the crypt and then came up again, making the rounds of the roofs twice more, then of the steps and the grounds and all the treacherous alleyways between where an incendiary could be missed. I felt better after that, but when I got to sleep I dreamed again, this time of fire and Langby watching it, smiling.

December 15—I found the cat this morning. Heavy raids last night, but most of them over toward Canning Town and nothing on the roofs to speak of. Nevertheless the cat was quite dead. I found him lying on the steps this morning when I made my own private rounds. Concussion. There was not a mark on him anywhere except the white blackout patch on his throat, but when I picked him up, he was all jelly under the skin.

I could not think what to do with him. I thought for one mad moment of asking Matthews if I could bury him in the crypt. Honorable death in war or something. Trafalgar, Waterloo, London, died in battle. I ended by wrapping him in my muffler and taking him down Ludgate Hill to a building that had been bombed out and burying him in the rubble. It will do no good. The rubble will be no protection from dogs or rats, and I shall never get another muffler. I have gone through nearly all of Uncle's money.

I should not be sitting here. I haven't checked the alleyways or the rest of the steps, and there might be a dud or a delayed incendiary or something that I missed.

When I came here, I thought of myself as the noble rescuer, the savior of the past. I am not doing very well at the job. At least Enola is out of it. I wish there were some way I could send St. Paul's to Bath for safekeeping. There were hardly any raids last night. Bence-Jones said cats can survive anything. What if he was coming to get me, to show me the way home? All the bombs were over Canning Town.

December 16—Enola has been back a week. Seeing her, standing on the west steps where I found the cat, sleeping in Marble Arch and not safe at all, was more than I could absorb. "I thought you were in Bath," I said stupidly.

"My aunt said she'd take Tom but not me as well. She's got a houseful of evacuated children, and what a noisy lot. Where is your muffler?" she said. "It's dreadful cold up here on the hill."

"I . . ." I said, unable to answer, "I lost it."

"You'll never get another one," she said. "They're going to start rationing clothes. And wool, too. You'll never get another one like that."

"I know," I said, blinking at her.

"Good things just thrown away," she said. "It's absolutely criminal, that's what it is."

I don't think I said anything to that, just turned and walked away with my head down, looking for bombs and dead animals.

December 20—Langby isn't a Nazi. He's a communist. I can hardly write this. A communist.

One of the chars found *The Worker* wedged behind a pillar and brought it down to the crypt as we were coming off the first watch.

"Bloody communists," Bence-Jones said. "Helping Hitler, they are. Talking against the king, stirring up trouble in the shelters. Traitors, that's what they are."

"They love England same as you," the char said.

"They don't love nobody but themselves, bloody selfish lot. I wouldn't be surprised to hear they were ringing Hitler up on the telephone," Bence-Jones said. "'Ello, Adolf, here's where to drop the bombs."

The kettle on the gas ring whistled. The char stood up and poured the hot water into a chipped teapot, then sat back down. "Just because they speak their minds don't mean they'd burn down old St. Paul's, does it now?"

"Of course not," Langby said, coming down the stairs. He sat down and pulled off his boots, stretching his feet in their wool socks. "Who wouldn't burn down St. Paul's?"

"The communists," Bence-Jones said, looking straight at him, and I wondered if he suspected Langby, too.

Langby never batted an eye. "I wouldn't worry about them if I were you," he said. "It's the jerries that are doing their bloody best to burn her down tonight. Six incendiaries so far, and one almost went into that great hole over the choir." He held out his cup to the char, and she poured him a cup of tea.

I wanted to kill him, smashing him to dust and rubble on the floor of the crypt while Bence-Jones and the char looked on in helpless surprise, shouting warnings to them and the rest of the watch. "Do you know what the communists did?" I wanted to shout. "Do you? We have to stop him." I even stood up and started toward him as he sat with his feet stretched out before him and his asbestos coat still over his shoulders.

And then the thought of the Gallery drenched in gold, the communist coming out of the tube station with the package so casually under his arm, made me sick with the same staggering vertigo of guilt and helplessness, and I sat back down on the edge of my cot and tried to think what to do.

They do not realize the danger. Even Bence-Jones, for all his talk of traitors, thinks they are capable only of talking against the king. They do not know, cannot know, what the communists will become. Stalin is an ally. Communists mean Russia. They have never heard of the USSR or Karinsky or the New Russia or any of the things that will make "communist" into a synonym for "monster." They will never know it. By the time the communists become what they became, there will be no fire watch. Only I know what it means to hear the name "communist" uttered here, so carelessly, in St. Paul's.

A communist. I should have known. I should have known.

December 22—Double watches again. I have not had any sleep and I am getting very unsteady on my feet. I nearly pitched into the chasm this morning, only saved myself by dropping to my knees. My endorphin levels are fluctuating wildly, and I know I must get some sleep soon or I will become one of Langby's walking dead, but I am afraid to leave him alone on the roofs, alone in the church with his communist party leader, alone anywhere. I have taken to watching him when he sleeps.

If I could just get hold of an artificial, I think I could induce a trance in spite of my poor condition. But I cannot even go out to a pub. Langby is on the roofs constantly, waiting for his chance. When Enola comes again, I must convince her to get the brandy for me. There are only a few days left.

December 28—Enola came this morning while I was on the west porch, picking up the Christmas tree. It has been knocked over three nights running by concussion. I righted the tree and was bending down to pick up the scattered tinsel when Enola appeared suddenly out of the fog like some cheerful saint. She stooped quickly and kissed me on the cheek. Then she straightened up, her nose red from her perennial cold, and handed me a box wrapped in colored paper.

"Merry Christmas," she said. "Go on, then, open it. It's a gift."

My reflexes are almost totally gone. I knew the box was far too shallow for a bottle of brandy. Nevertheless, I believed she had remembered, had brought me my salvation. "You darling," I said, and tore it open.

It was a muffler. Gray wool. I stared at it for fully half a minute without realizing what it was. "Where's the brandy?" I said.

She looked shocked. Her nose got redder and her eyes started to blur. "You need this more. You haven't any clothing coupons and you have to be outside all the time. It's been so dreadful cold."

"I needed the brandy," I said angrily.

"I was only trying to be kind," she started, and I cut her off.

"Kind?" I said. "I asked you for brandy. I don't recall ever saying I needed a muffler." I shoved it back at her and began untangling a string of colored lights that had shattered when the tree fell.

She got that same holy martyr look Kivrin is so wonderful at. "I worry about you all the time up here," she said in a rush. "They're *trying* for St. Paul's, you know. And it's so close to the river. I didn't think you should be drinking. I . . . it's a crime when they're trying so hard to kill us all that you won't take care of yourself. It's like you're in it with them. I worry someday I'll come up to St. Paul's and you won't be here."

"Well, and what exactly am I supposed to do with a muffler? Hold it over my head when they drop the bombs?"

She turned and ran, disappearing into the gray fog before she had gone down two steps. I started after her, still holding the string of broken lights, tripped over it, and fell almost all the way to the bottom of the steps.

Langby picked me up. "You're off watches," he said grimly.

"You can't do that," I said.

"Oh, yes, I can. I don't want any walking dead on the roofs with me."

I let him lead me down here to the crypt, make me a cup of tea, put me to bed, all very solicitous. No indication that this is what he has been waiting for. I will lie here till the sirens go. Once I am on the roofs he will not be able to send me back without seeming suspicious. Do you know what he said before he left, asbestos coat and rubber boots, the dedicated fire watcher? "I want you to get some sleep." As if I could sleep with Langby on the roofs. I would be burned alive.

December 30—The sirens woke me yesterday, and old Bence-Jones said, "That should have done you some good. You've slept the clock round."

"What day is it?" I said, going for my boots.

"The twenty-ninth," he said, and as I dived for the door, "No need to hurry. They're late tonight. Maybe they won't come at all. That'd be a blessing, that would. The tide's out."

I stopped by the door to the stairs, holding on to the cool stone. "Is St. Paul's all right?"

"She's still standing," he said. "Have a bad dream?"

"Yes," I said, remembering the bad dreams of all the past weeks—the dead cat in my arms in St. John's Wood, Langby with his parcel and his

Worker under his arm, the fire watch stone garishly lit by Christ's lantern. Then I remembered I had not dreamed at all. I had slept the kind of sleep I had prayed for, the kind of sleep that would help me remember.

Then I remembered. Not St. Paul's, burned to the ground by the communists. A headline from the dailies. "Marble Arch hit. Eighteen killed by blast." The date was not clear except for the year. 1940. There were exactly two more days left in 1940. I grabbed my coat and muffler and ran up the stairs and across the marble floor.

"Where the hell do you think you're going?" Langby shouted to me. I couldn't see him.

"I have to save Enola," I said, and my voice echoed in the dark sanctuary. "They're going to bomb Marble Arch."

"You can't leave now," he shouted after me, standing where the fire watch stone would be. "The tide's out. You dirty . . ."

I didn't hear the rest of it. I had already flung myself down the steps and into a taxi. It took almost all the money I had, the money I had so carefully hoarded for the trip back to St. John's Wood. Shelling started while we were still in Oxford Street, and the driver refused to go any farther. He let me out into pitch-blackness, and I saw I would never make it in time.

Blast. Enola crumpled on the stairway down to the Tube, her open-toed shoes still on her feet, not a mark on her. And when I try to lift her, jelly under the skin. I would have to wrap her in the muffler she gave me, because I was too late. I had gone back a hundred years to be too late to save her.

I ran the last blocks, guided by the gun emplacement that had to be in Hyde Park, and skidded down the steps into Marble Arch. The woman in the ticket booth took my last shilling for a ticket to St. Paul's Station. I stuck it in my pocket and raced toward the stairs.

"No running," she said placidly. "To your left, please." The door to the right was blocked off by wooden barricades, the metal gates beyond pulled to and chained. The board with names on it for the stations was

X-ed with tape, and a new sign that read ALL TRAINS was nailed to the barricade, pointing left.

Enola was not on the stopped escalators or sitting against the wall in the hallway. I came to the first stairway and could not get through. A family had set out, just where I wanted to step, a communal tea of bread and butter, a little pot of jam sealed with waxed paper, and a kettle on a ring like the one Langby and I had rescued out of the rubble, all of it spread on a cloth embroidered at the corners with flowers. I stood staring down at the layered tea, spread like a waterfall down the steps.

"I . . . Marble Arch . . ." I said. Another twenty killed by flying tiles. "You shouldn't be here."

"We've as much right as anyone," the man said belligerently, "and who are you to tell us to move on?"

A woman lifting saucers out of a cardboard box looked up at me, frightened. The kettle began to whistle.

"It's you that should move on," the man said. "Go on, then." He stood off to one side so I could pass. I edged past the embroidered cloth apologetically.

"I'm sorry," I said. "I'm looking for someone. On the platform."

"You'll never find her in there, mate," the man said, thumbing in that direction. I hurried past him, nearly stepping on the tea cloth, and rounded the corner into hell.

It was not hell. Shopgirls folded coats and leaned back against them, cheerful or sullen or disagreeable, but certainly not damned. Two boys scuffled for a shilling and lost it on the tracks. They bent over the edge, debating whether to go after it, and the station guard yelled to them to back away. A train rumbled through, full of people. A mosquito landed on the guard's hand and he reached out to slap it and missed. The boys laughed. And behind and before them, stretching in all directions down the deadly tile curves of the tunnel like casualties, backed into the entranceways and onto the stairs, were people. Hundreds and hundreds of people.

I stumbled back into the hall, knocking over a teacup. It spilled like a flood across the cloth.

"I told you, mate," the man said cheerfully. "It's hell in there, ain't it? And worse below."

"Hell," I said. "Yes." I would never find her. I would never save her. I looked at the woman mopping up the tea, and it came to me that I could not save her, either. Enola or the cat or any of them, lost here in the endless stairways and cul-de-sacs of time. They were already dead a hundred years, past saving. The past is beyond saving. Surely that was the lesson the history department sent me all this way to learn. Well, fine, I've learned it. Can I go home now?

Of course not, dear boy. You have foolishly spent all your money on taxicabs and brandy, and tonight is the night the Germans burn the City. (Now it is too late, I remember it all. Twenty-eight incendiaries on the roofs.) Langby must have his chance, and you must learn the hardest lesson of all and the one you should have known from the beginning. You cannot save St. Paul's.

I went back out onto the platform and stood behind the yellow line until a train pulled up. I took my ticket out and held it in my hand all the way to St. Paul's Station. When I got there, smoke billowed toward me like an easy spray of water. I could not see St. Paul's.

"The tide's out," a woman said in a voice devoid of hope, and I went down in a snake pit of limp cloth hoses. My hands came up covered with rank-smelling mud, and I understood finally (and too late) the significance of the tide. There was no water to fight the fires.

A policeman barred my way and I stood helplessly before him with no idea what to say. "No civilians allowed up there," he said. "St. Paul's is for it." The smoke billowed like a thundercloud, alive with sparks, and the dome rose golden above it.

"I'm fire watch," I said, and his arm fell away, and then I was on the roofs.

My endorphin levels must have been going up and down like an air-raid siren—I do not have any short-term from then on, just moments that do not fit together: the people in the church when we brought Langby down, huddled in a corner playing cards, the whirlwind of burning scraps of wood in the dome, the ambulance driver who wore open-toed shoes like Enola and smeared salve on my burned hands. And in the center, the one clear moment when I went after Langby on a rope and saved his life.

I stood by the dome, blinking against the smoke. The City was on fire and it seemed as if St. Paul's would ignite from the heat, would crumble from the noise alone. Bence-Jones was by the northwest tower, hitting at an incendiary with a spade. Langby was too close to the patched place where the bomb had gone through, looking toward me. An incendiary clattered behind him. I turned to grab a shovel, and when I turned back, he was gone.

"Langby!" I shouted, and could not hear my own voice. He had fallen into the chasm and nobody had seen him or the incendiary. Except me. I do not remember how I got across the roof. I think I called for a rope. I got a rope. I tied it around my waist, gave the ends of it into the hands of the fire watch, and went over the side. The fires lit the walls of the hole almost all the way to the bottom. Below me I could see a pile of whitish rubble. He's under there, I thought, and jumped free of the wall. The space was so narrow there was nowhere to throw the rubble. I was afraid I would inadvertently stone him, and I tried to toss the pieces of planking and plaster over my shoulder, but there was barely room to turn. For one awful moment I thought he might not be there at all, that the pieces of splintered wood would brush away to reveal empty pavement, as they had in the crypt.

I was numbed by the indignity of crawling over him. If he was dead I did not think I could bear the shame of stepping on his helpless body. Then his hand came up like a ghost's and grabbed my ankle, and within seconds I had whirled and had his head free.

He was the ghastly white that no longer frightens me. "I put the bomb out," he said. I stared at him, so overwhelmed with relief I could not speak. For one hysterical moment I thought I would even laugh, I was so glad to see him. I finally realized what it was I was supposed to say.

"Are you all right?" I said.

"Yes," he said, and tried to raise himself on one elbow. "So much the worse for you."

He could not get up. He grunted with pain when he tried to shift his weight to his right side and lay back, the uneven rubble crunching sickeningly under him. I tried to lift him gently so I could see where he was hurt. He must have fallen on something.

"It's no use," he said, breathing hard. "I put it out."

I spared him a startled glance, afraid that he was delirious, and went back to rolling him onto his side.

"I know you were counting on this one," he went on, not resisting me at all. "It was bound to happen sooner or later with all these roofs. Only I went after it. What'll you tell your friends?"

His asbestos coat was torn down the back in a long gash. Under it his back was charred and smoking. He had fallen on the incendiary. "Oh, my God," I said, trying frantically to see how badly he was burned without touching him. I had no way of knowing how deep the burns went, but they seemed to extend only in the narrow space where the coat had torn. I tried to pull the bomb out from under him, but the casing was as hot as a stove. It was not melting, though. My sand and Langby's body had smothered it. I had no idea if it would start up again when it was exposed to the air. I looked around, a little wildly, for the bucket and stirrup pump Langby must have dropped when he fell.

"Looking for a weapon?" Langby said, so clearly it was hard to believe he was hurt at all. "Why not just leave me here? A bit of exposure and I'd be done for by morning. Or would you rather do your dirty work in private?"

I stood up and yelled to the men on the roof above us. One of them shone a pocket torch down at us, but its light didn't reach.

"Is he dead?" somebody shouted down to me.

"Send for an ambulance," I said. "He's been burned."

I helped Langby up, trying to support his back without touching the burn. He staggered a little and then leaned against the wall, watching me as I tried to bury the incendiary, using a piece of the planking as a scoop. The rope came down and I tied Langby to it. He had not spoken since I helped him up. He let me tie the rope around his waist, still looking steadily at me. "I should have let you smother in the crypt," he said.

He stood leaning easily, almost relaxed against the cold supports, his hands holding him up. I put his hands on the slack rope and wrapped it once around them for the grip I knew he didn't have. "I've been on to you since that day in the Gallery. I knew you weren't afraid of heights. You came down here without any fear of heights when you thought I'd ruined your precious plans. What was it? An attack of conscience? Kneeling there like a baby, whining, 'What have we done? What have we done?' You made me sick. But you know what gave you away first? The cat. Everybody knows cats hate water. Everybody but a dirty Nazi spy."

There was a tug on the rope. "Come ahead," I said, and the rope tautened.

"That WVS tart? Was she a spy, too? Supposed to meet you in Marble Arch? Telling me it was going to be bombed. You're a rotten spy, Bartholomew. Your friends already blew it up in September. It's open again."

The rope jerked suddenly and began to lift Langby. He twisted his hands to get a better grip. His right shoulder scraped the wall. I put up my hands and pushed him gently so that his left side was to the wall. "You're making a big mistake, you know," he said. "You should have killed me. I'll tell."

I stood in the darkness, waiting for the rope. Langby was unconscious when he reached the roof. I walked past the fire watch to the dome and down to the crypt.

This morning the letter from my uncle came and with it a five-pound note.

———

December 31—Two of Dunworthy's flunkies met me in St. John's Wood to tell me I was late for my exams. I did not even protest. I shuffled obediently after them without even considering how unfair it was to give an exam to one of the walking dead. I had not slept in—how long? Since yesterday, when I went to find Enola. I had not slept in a hundred years.

Dunworthy was at his desk, blinking at me. One of the flunkies handed me a test paper and the other one called time. I turned the paper over and left an oily smudge from the ointment on my burns. I stared uncomprehendingly at them. I had grabbed at the incendiary when I turned Langby over, but these burns were on the backs of my hands. The answer came to me suddenly in Langby's unyielding voice. "They're rope burns, you fool. Don't they teach you Nazi spies the proper way to come down a rope?"

I looked down at the test. It read, "Number of incendiaries that fell on St. Paul's. Number of land mines. Number of high-explosive bombs. Method most commonly used for extinguishing incendiaries. Land mines. High-explosive bombs. Number of volunteers on first watch. Second watch. Casualties. Fatalities." The questions made no sense. There was only a short space, long enough for the writing of a number, after any of the questions. Method most commonly used for extinguishing incendiaries. How would I ever fit what I knew into that narrow space? Where were the questions about Enola and Langby and the cat?

I went up to Dunworthy's desk. "St. Paul's almost burned down last night," I said. "What kind of questions are these?"

"You should be answering questions, Mr. Bartholomew, not asking them."

"There aren't any questions about the people," I said. The outer casing of my anger began to melt.

"Of course there are," Dunworthy said, flipping to the second page of the test. "Number of casualties, 1940. Blast, shrapnel, other."

"Other?" I said. At any moment the roof would collapse on me in a shower of plaster dust and fury. "*Other?* Langby put out a fire with his own body. Enola has a cold that keeps getting worse. The cat . . ." I snatched the paper back from him and scrawled "one cat" in the narrow space next to "blast." "Don't you care about them at all?"

"They're important from a statistical point of view," he said, "but as individuals, they are hardly relevant to the course of history."

My reflexes were shot. It was amazing to me that Dunworthy's were almost as slow. When I hit him, I grazed the side of his jaw and knocked his glasses off. "Of course they're relevant!" I shouted. "They *are* the history, not all these bloody numbers!"

The reflexes of the flunkies were very fast. They did not let me start another swing at him before they had me by both arms and were hauling me out of the room.

"They're back there in the past with nobody to save them," I shouted. "They can't see their hands in front of their faces and there are bombs falling down on them and you tell me they aren't important? You call that being an historian?"

The flunkies dragged me out the door and down the hall. "Langby saved St. Paul's. How much more important can a person get? You're no historian! You're nothing but a . . ." I wanted to call him a terrible name, but the only curses I could summon up were Langby's. "You're nothing but a dirty Nazi spy!" I bellowed. "You're nothing but a lazy bourgeois tart!"

They dumped me on my hands and knees outside the door and slammed it in my face. "I wouldn't be an historian if you paid me!" I shouted, and went to see the fire watch stone.

December 31—I am having to write this in bits and pieces. My hands are in pretty bad shape, and Dunworthy's boys didn't help matters much. Kivrin comes in periodically, wearing her Saint Joan look, and smears so much salve on my hands that I can't hold a pencil.

St. Paul's Station is not there, of course, so I got out at Holborn and walked, thinking about my last meeting with Dean Matthews on the morning after the burning of the City. This morning.

"I understand you saved Langby's life," he said. "I also understand that between you, you saved St. Paul's last night."

I showed him the letter from my uncle and he stared at it as if he could not think what it was. "Nothing stays saved forever," he said, and for a terrible moment I thought he was going to tell me Langby had died. "We shall have to keep on saving St. Paul's until Hitler decides to bomb something else."

The raids on London are almost over, I wanted to tell him. He'll start bombing the countryside in a matter of weeks. Canterbury, Bath, aiming always at the cathedrals. You and St. Paul's will both outlast the war and live to dedicate the fire watch stone.

"I am hopeful, though," he said. "I think the worst is over."

"Yes, sir." I thought of the stone, its letters still readable after all this time. No, sir, the worst is not over.

I managed to keep my bearings almost to the top of Ludgate Hill. Then I lost my way completely, wandering about like a man in a grave-yard. I had not remembered that the rubble looked so much like the white plaster dust Langby had tried to dig me out of. I could not find the stone anywhere. In the end I nearly fell over it, jumping back as if I had stepped on a grave.

It is all that's left. Hiroshima is supposed to have had a handful of untouched trees at ground zero, Denver the capitol steps. Neither of them says, "Remember men and women of St. Paul's Watch who by the grace of God saved this cathedral." The grace of God.

Part of the stone is sheared off. Historians argue there was another line that said, "for all time," but I do not believe that, not if Dean Matthews had anything to do with it. And none of the watch it was dedicated to would have believed it for a minute. We saved St. Paul's every time we put out an incendiary, and only until the next one fell. Keeping watch on the danger spots, putting out the little fires with sand and stirrup pumps, the big ones with our bodies, in order to keep the whole vast complex structure from burning down. Which sounds to me like a course description for History Practicum 401. What a fine time to discover what historians are for when I have tossed my chance for being one out the windows as easily as they tossed the pinpoint bomb in! No, sir, the worst is not over.

There are flash burns on the stone, where legend says the Dean of St. Paul's was kneeling when the bomb went off. Totally apocryphal, of course, since the front door is hardly an appropriate place for prayers. It is more likely the shadow of a tourist who wandered in to ask the whereabouts of the Windmill Theatre, or the imprint of a girl bringing a volunteer his muffler. Or a cat.

Nothing is saved forever, Dean Matthews, and I knew that when I walked in the west doors that first day, blinking into the gloom, but it is pretty bad nevertheless. Standing here knee-deep in rubble out of which I will not be able to dig any folding chairs or friends, knowing that Langby died thinking I was a Nazi spy, knowing that Enola came one day and I wasn't there. It's pretty bad.

But it is not as bad as it could be. They are both dead, and Dean Matthews, too, but they died without knowing what I knew all along, what sent me to my knees in the Whispering Gallery, sick with grief and guilt: that in the end none of us saved St. Paul's. And Langby cannot turn to me, stunned and sick at heart, and say, "Who did this? Your friends the Nazis?" And I would have to say, "No, the communists." That would be the worst.

I have come back to the room and let Kivrin smear more salve on my hands. She wants me to get some sleep. I know I should pack and get gone. It will be humiliating to have them come and throw me out, but I do not have the strength to fight her. She looks so much like Enola.

January 1—I have apparently slept not only through the night, but through the morning mail drop as well. When I woke up just now, I found Kivrin sitting on the end of the bed holding an envelope. "Your exam results came," she said.

I put my arm over my eyes. "They can be marvelously efficient when they want to, can't they?"

"Yes," Kivrin said.

"Well, let's see it," I said, sitting up. "How long do I have before they come and throw me out?"

She handed the flimsy computer envelope to me. I tore it along the perforation. "Wait," she said. "Before you open it, I want to say something." She put her hand gently on my burns. "You're wrong about the history department. They're very good."

It was not exactly what I expected her to say. " 'Good' is not the word I'd use to describe Dunworthy," I said and yanked the inside slip free.

Kivrin's look did not change, not even when I sat there with the printout on my knees where she could surely see it.

"Well," I said.

The slip was hand-signed by the esteemed Dunworthy. I have taken a first. With honors.

January 2—Two things came in the mail today. One was Kivrin's assignment. The history department thinks of everything—even to keeping her here long enough to nursemaid me, even to coming up with a pre-fabricated trial by fire to send their history majors through.

I think I wanted to believe that was what they had done, Enola and Langby only hired actors, the cat a clever android with its clockwork innards taken out for the final effect, not so much because I wanted to believe Dunworthy was not good at all, but because then I would not have this nagging pain at not knowing what had happened to them.

"You said your practicum was England in 1300?" I said, watching her as suspiciously as I had watched Langby.

"1348," she said, and her face went slack with memory. "The plague year."

"My God," I said. "How could they do that? The plague's a ten."

"I have a natural immunity," she said, and looked at her hands.

Because I could not think of anything to say, I opened the other piece of mail. It was a report on Enola. Computer-printed, facts and dates and statistics, all the numbers the history department so dearly loves, but it told me what I thought I would have to go without knowing: that she had gotten over her cold and survived the Blitz. Young Tom had been killed in the Baedeker raids on Bath, but Enola had lived until 2015, the year before they blew up St. Paul's.

I don't know whether I believe the report or not, but it does not matter. It is, like Langby's reading aloud to the old man, a simple act of human kindness. They think of everything.

Not quite. They did not tell me what happened to Langby. But I find as I write this that I already know: I saved his life. It does not seem to matter that he might have died in hospital next day, and I find, in spite of all the hard lessons the history department has tried to teach me, I do not quite believe this one: that nothing is saved forever. It seems to me that perhaps Langby is.

January 3—I went to see Dunworthy today. I don't know what I intended to say—some pompous drivel about my willingness to serve in the fire watch of history, standing guard against the falling incendiaries of the human heart, silent and saintly.

But he blinked at me nearsightedly across his desk, and it seemed to me that he was blinking at that last bright image of St. Paul's in sunlight before it was gone forever and that he knew better than anyone that the past cannot be saved, and I said instead, "I'm sorry that I broke your glasses, sir."

"How did you like St. Paul's?" he said, and like my first meeting with Enola, I felt I must be somehow reading the signals all wrong, that he was not feeling loss, but something quite different.

"I loved it, sir," I said.

"Yes," he said. "So do I."

Dean Matthews is wrong. I have fought with memory my whole practicum only to find that it is not the enemy at all, and being an historian is not some saintly burden after all. Because Dunworthy is not blinking against the fatal sunlight of the last morning, but into the gloom of that first afternoon, looking in the great west doors of St. Paul's at what is, like Langby, like all of it, every moment, in us, saved forever.

Afterword for "Fire Watch"

Like John Bartholomew, I fell in love with St. Paul's Cathedral the moment I stepped through the west door and saw the church in all its sunny, high-arched golden glory.

I had heard about the fire watch, but didn't know all that much about it. The note I'd written in the notebook I took with me on the trip said simply, "The priests used to sleep in the crypt of St. Paul's during the Blitz to put out the fires as they started," and underneath it the words "Here we lie," the first line of a poem I had thought I might write from the viewpoint of the earlier heroes who lay buried in St. Paul's—Nelson and Wellington and General Gordon—commenting on their modern-day counterparts.

But when I actually saw the cathedral and learned how near it had come to being destroyed, I knew I had to write the story that eventually became "Fire Watch."

"Go away," I told my husband and the friends we'd come to England with. "Go have tea or something. I need to get this all down," and for the next two hours frantically took notes on everything I might possibly need: the layout of the crypt, the number of steps up to the Whispering Gallery, the locations of the chapels and *The Light of the World* and Nelson's tomb. And then I went home and researched everything I could find about the war and the cathedral and the fire watchers.

I used to tell people that this was when I fell in love with the London Blitz, too, but a few years ago I happened upon a book and realized that that wasn't true, that my fascination with the Blitz had actually begun much earlier.

The book was Rumer Godden's *An Episode of Sparrows*, which my eighth-grade teacher, Mrs. Werner, had read aloud to us every day after lunch. It's not really a YA sort of book, and I have no idea why she read it to us, except probably for the best of all reasons—because she liked it herself. And I have no memory of how the other kids in the class responded to it. But I loved it.

It's the story of a little girl, Lovejoy Mason, who plants a garden in the bombed-out rubble of a London church, and many years and readings later, it finally dawned on me that it's a modern retelling of Frances Hodgson Burnett's *A Secret Garden.*

It's a great book—although, as I say, not exactly one you'd expect to be read to eighth-graders. Lovejoy's a juvenile delinquent. She's also illegitimate, her mother's not exactly a role model, and the book treats of very adult issues like neglect and bankruptcy and unhappy marriages and cancer and death.

But it's a wonderful book, full of peril and kindness where you'd least expect it. And hope. The best thing about it, though, was that it gave me my first glimpse of the Blitz, that it planted that first seed. A seed just like the cornflower seeds in Lovejoy's garden, only this one didn't germinate till the day I walked into the sun of St. Paul's.

Moral: Teachers, read to your students. Parents, read to your kids. But not what you think they should read or what everybody's reading or what's age- and subject-matter-appropriate. Read inappropriate stuff, and stuff other people might think is boring. Stuff you like. You may be planting seeds that will germinate for a really long time. And burst into bloom twenty years later.

INSIDE JOB

Nobody ever went broke underestimating the intelligence of the American people.

—H. L. Mencken

"It's me, Rob," Kildy said when I picked up the phone. "I want you to go with me to see somebody Saturday."

Usually when Kildy calls, she's bubbling over with details. "You've *got* to see this psychic cosmetic surgeon, Rob," she'd crowed the last time. "His specialty is liposuction, and you can *see* the tube coming out of his sleeve. And that's not all. The fat he's supposed to be suctioning out of their thighs is that goop they use in McDonald's milk shakes. You can smell the vanilla! It wouldn't fool a five-year-old, so of course half the women in Hollywood are buying it hook, line, and sinker. We've *got* to do a story on him, Rob!"

I usually had to say, "Kildy—Kildy—Kildy!" before I could get her to shut up long enough to tell me where said scammer was performing.

But this time all she said was, "The seminar's at one o'clock at the Beverly Hills Hilton. I'll meet you in the parking lot," and hung up before I could ask her if the somebody she wanted me to see was a pet channeler or a vedic-force therapist, and how much it was going to cost.

I called her back.

"The tickets are on me," she said.

If Kildy had her way, the tickets would always be on her, and she can more than afford it. Her father's a director at Dreamworks, her current stepmother heads her own production company, and her mother's a two-time Oscar winner. And Kildy's rich in her own right—she only acted in four films before she quit the business for a career in debunking, but one of them was the surprise top grosser of the year, and she'd opted for shares instead of a salary.

But she's ostensibly my employee, even though I can't afford to pay her enough to keep her in toenail polish. The least I can do is spring for expenses, and a barely known channeler shouldn't be too bad. Medium Charles Fred, the current darling of the Hollywood set, was only charging two hundred a séance.

"*The Jaundiced Eye* is paying for the tickets," I said firmly. "How much?"

"Seven hundred and fifty apiece for the group seminar," she said. "Fifteen hundred for a private enlightenment audience."

"The tickets are on you," I said.

"Great," she said. "Bring the Sony vidcam."

"Not the little one?" I asked. Most psychic events don't allow recording devices—they make it too easy to spot the earpieces and wires— and the Hasaka is small enough to be smuggled in.

"No," she said, "bring the Sony. See you Saturday, Rob. 'Bye."

"Wait," I said. "You haven't told me what this guy does."

"Woman. She's a channeler. She channels an entity named Isis," Kildy said and hung up again.

I was surprised. We don't usually waste our time on channelers. They're no longer trendy. Right now mediums like Charles Fred and Yogi Magaputra and assorted sensory therapists (aroma-, sonic, auratic) are the rage.

It's also an exercise in frustration, since there's no way to prove whether someone's channeling or not, unless they claim to be channeling Abraham Lincoln (like Randall Mars) or Nefertiti (like Hanh Nah). In that case you can challenge their facts—Nefertiti could *not* have had an affair with Alexander the Great, who wasn't born till a thousand years later, and she was *not* Cleopatra's cousin—but most of them channel hundred-thousand-year-old sages or high priests of Lemuria, and there are no physical manifestations.

They've learned their lesson from the Victorian spiritualists (who kept getting caught), so there's no ectoplasm or ghostly trumpets or double-exposed photographic plates. Just a deep, hollow voice that sounds like a cross between Obi-Wan Kenobi and Basil Rathbone. Why is it that channeled "entities" all have British accents? And speak King James Bible English?

And why was Kildy willing to waste fifteen hundred bucks—correction, twenty-two fifty; she'd already been to the seminar once—to have me see this Isis? The channeler must have a new gimmick. I'd noticed a couple of people advertising themselves as "angel channelers" in the local psychic rag, but Isis wasn't an angel name. Egyptian channeler? Goddess conduit?

I looked "Isis channeler" up on the Net. At first I couldn't find any references, even using Google. I tried skeptics.org and finally Marty Rumboldt, who runs a website that tracks psychics.

"You're spelling it wrong, Rob," he e-mailed me back. "It's Isus."

Which should have occurred to me. The channelers of Lazaris,

Kochise, and Merlynn all use variations on historical names (probably from some fear of spiritual slander lawsuits), and more than one channeler's prone to "inventive" spelling: Joye Wildde. And Emmanual.

I Googled "Isus." He—bad sign, the channeler didn't even know Isis was female—was the "spirit entity" channeled by somebody named Ariaura Keller. She'd started in Salem, Massachusetts (a breeding ground for psychics), moved to Sedona (another one), and then headed west and worked her way down the coast, appearing in Seattle, the other Salem, Eugene, Berkeley, and now Beverly Hills. She had six afternoon seminars and two weeklong "spiritual immersions" scheduled for L.A., along with private "individually scheduled enlightenment audiences" with Isus. She'd written two books, *The Voice of Isus* and *On the Receiving End* (with links to Amazon.com), and you could read her bio: "I knew from childhood that I was destined to be a channel for the Truth," and extracts from her speeches: "The earth is destined to witness a transforming spiritual event," online. She sounded just like every other channeler I'd ever heard.

And I'd sat through a bunch of them. Back at the height of their popularity (and before I knew better), *The Jaundiced Eye* had done a six-part series on them, starting with M. Z. Lord and running on through Joye Wildde, Todd Phoenix, and Taryn Kryme, whose "entity" was a giggly four-year-old kid from Atlantis. It was the longest six months of my life. And it didn't have any impact at all on the business. It was tax evasion and mail fraud charges that had put an end to the fad, not my hard-hitting exposés.

Ariaura Keller didn't have a criminal record (at least under that name), and there weren't many articles about her. And no mention of any gimmick. "The electric, amazing Isus shares his spiritual wisdom and helps you find your own inner-centeredness and soul-unenfoldment." Nothing new there.

Well, whatever it was that had gotten Kildy interested in her, I'd find out on Saturday. In the meantime, I had an article on Charles Fred to write for the December issue, a book on intelligent design (the latest

ploy for getting creationism into the schools and evolution out) to re-
view, and a past-life chiropractor to go see. He claimed his patients'
backaches came from hauling blocks of stone to Stonehenge and/or the
Pyramids. (The Pyramids had in fact been a big job, but over the course
of three years in business he'd told over two thousand patients they'd
gotten their herniated discs at Stonehenge, every single one of them
while setting the altar stone in place.)

And he was actually credible compared to Charles Fred, who was
having amazing success communicating highly specific messages from
the dead to their grieving relatives. I was convinced he was using something besides the usual cold reading and shills to get the millions he
was raking in, but so far I hadn't been able to figure out what, and every
lead I managed to come up with went nowhere.

I didn't think about the "electric, amazing Isus" again till I was
driving over to the Hilton on Saturday. Then it occurred to me that I
hadn't heard from Kildy since her phone call. Usually she drops by the
office every day, and if we're going somewhere calls three or four times
to reconfirm where and when we're meeting. I wondered if the seminar
was still on, or if she'd forgotten all about it. Or suddenly gotten tired of
being a debunker and gone back to being a movie star.

I'd been waiting for that to happen ever since the day just over eight
months ago when, just like the gorgeous dame in a Bogie movie, she'd
walked into my office and asked if she could have a job.

There are three cardinal rules in the skeptic business. The first one
is "Extraordinary claims require extraordinary evidence," and the second one is "If it seems too good to be true, it probably is." And if anything was ever too good to be true, it's Kildy. She's not only rich and
movie-star beautiful, but intelligent, and, unlike everyone else in Hollywood, a complete skeptic, even though, as she told me the first day,
Shirley MacLaine had dandled her on her knee and her own mother
would believe anything, "no matter how ridiculous, which is probably
why her marriage to my father lasted nearly six years."

She was now on Stepmother Number Four, who had gotten her the role in the surprise top grosser, "which made almost as much money as *Lord of the Rings* and enabled me to take early retirement."

"Retirement?" I'd said. "Why would you want to retire? You could have—"

"Starred in *The Hulk IV*," she said, "and been on the cover of the *Globe* with Ben Affleck. Or with my lawyer in front of a rehab center. I know, it was tough to give all that up."

She had a point, but that didn't explain why she'd want to go to work for a barely-making-it magazine like *The Jaundiced Eye*. Or why she'd want to go to work at all.

I said so.

"I've already tried the whole 'fill your day with massages and lunch at Ardani's and sex with your trainer' scene, Rob," she said. "It was even worse than *The Hulk*. Plus, the lights and makeup *destroy* your complexion."

I found that hard to believe. She had skin like honey.

"And then my mother took me to this luminescence reading, she's into all those things, psychics and past-life regression and intuitive healing, and the guy doing the reading—"

"Lucius Windfire," I'd said. I'd been working on an exposé of him for the last two months.

"Yes, Lucius Windfire," she'd said. "He claimed he could read your mind by determining your vedic fault lines, which consisted of setting candles all around you and 'reading' the wavering of the flames. It was obvious he was a fake—you could see the earpiece he was getting his information about the audience over—but everybody there was eating it up, especially my mother. He'd already talked her into private sessions that set her back ten thousand dollars. And I thought, Somebody should put him out of business, and then I thought, That's what I want to do with my life, and I looked up 'debunkers' online and found your magazine, and here I am."

I'd said, "I can't possibly pay you the kind of money you're—"

"Your going rate for articles is fine," she'd said and flashed me her better-than-Julia-Roberts smile. "I just want the chance to do something useful and sensible with my life."

And for the last eight months she'd been working with me on the magazine. She was wonderful—she knew everybody in Hollywood, which meant she could get us into invitation-only stuff, and heard about new spiritual fads even before I did. She was also willing to do anything, from letting herself be hypnotized to stealing chicken guts from psychic surgeons to proofreading galleys. And fun to talk to, and gorgeous, and much too good for a small-time skeptic.

And I knew it was just a matter of time before she got bored with debunking—and me—and went back to going to premieres and driving around in her Jaguar, but she didn't. "Have you ever *worked* with Ben Affleck?" she'd said when I told her she was too beautiful not to still be in the movies. "You couldn't *pay* me to go back to that."

She wasn't in the parking lot, and neither was her Jaguar, and I wondered, as I did every day, if this was the day she'd decided to call it quits. No, there she was, getting out of a taxi. She was wearing a honey-colored pantsuit the same shade as her hair, and designer sunglasses, and she looked, as always, too good to be true. She saw me and waved, and then reached back into the taxi for two big throw pillows.

Shit. That meant we were going to have to sit on the floor again. These people made a fortune scamming people out of their not-so-hard-earned cash. You'd think they could afford chairs.

I walked over to her. "I take it we're going in together," I said, since the pillows were a matching pair, purple brocade jobs with tassels at the corners.

"Yes," Kildy said. "Did you bring the Sony?"

"Yeah," I said. "I still think I should have brought the Hasaka."

She shook her head. "They're doing body checks. I don't want to give them an excuse to throw us out. When they fill out the nametags, give them your real name."

"We're not using a cover?" I asked. Psychics often use skeptics in the audience as an excuse for failure: The negative vibrations made it impossible to contact the spirits, etc. A couple of them had even banned me from their performances, claiming I disturbed the cosmos with my nonbelieving presence. "Do you think that's a good idea?"

"We don't have any choice," she said. "When I came last week, I was with my publicist, so I had to use my own name, and I didn't think it mattered—we never do channelers. Besides, the ushers recognized me. So our cover is, I was so impressed with Ariaura that I talked you into coming to see her."

"Which is pretty much the truth," I said. "What exactly is her gimmick, that you thought I should see her?"

"I don't want to prejudice you beforehand." She glanced at her Vera Wang watch and handed me one of the pillows. "Let's go."

We went into the lobby and over to a table under a lilac-and-silver banner proclaiming PRESENTING ARIAURA AND THE WISDOM OF ISUS and under it, BELIEVE AND IT WILL HAPPEN. Kildy told the woman at the table our names.

"Oh, I loved you in that movie, Miss Ross," she said and handed us lilac-and-silver nametags and motioned us toward another table next to the door, where a Russell Crowe type in a lilac polo shirt was doing security checks.

"Any cameras, tape recorders, videocams?" he asked us.

Kildy opened her bag and took out an Olympus. "Can't I take *one* picture?" she pleaded. "I won't use the flash or anything. I just wanted to get a photo of Ariaura."

He plucked the Olympus neatly from her fingers. "Autographed eight-by-ten glossies can be purchased in the waiting area."

"Oh, *good*," she said. She really should have stayed in acting.

I relinquished the videocam. "What about videos of today's performance?" I said after he finished frisking me.

He stiffened. "Ariaura's communications with Isus are not performances. They are unique glimpses into a higher plane. You can order videos of today's experience in the waiting area," he said, pointing toward a pair of double doors.

The "waiting area" was a long hall lined with tables full of books, videos, audiotapes, chakra charts, crystal balls, aromatherapy oils, amulets, Zuni fetishes, wisdom mobiles, healing stones, singing crystal bowls, amaryllis roots, aura cleansers, pyramids, and assorted other New Age junk, all with the lilac-and-silver Isus logo.

The third cardinal rule of debunking, and maybe the most important, is "Ask yourself, what do they get out of it?" or, as the Bible (source of many scams) puts it, "By their fruits shall ye know them."

And if the prices on this stuff were any indication, Ariaura was getting a hell of a lot out of it. The 8x10 glossies were $28.99, or $35 with Ariaura's signature. "And if you want it signed by Isus," the blond guy behind the table said, "it's a hundred. He's not always willing to sign."

I could see why. His signature (done in Magic Marker) was a string of complicated symbols that looked like a cross between Elvish runes and Egyptian hieroglyphics, whereas Ariaura's was a script A followed by a formless scrawl.

Videotapes of her previous seminars—Volumes 1–20—cost a cool sixty apiece, and Ariaura's "sacred amulet" (which looked like something you'd buy on the Home Shopping Network) cost nine hundred and fifty (box extra). People were snapping them up like hotcakes, along with Celtic pentacles, meditation necklaces, dreamcatcher earrings, worry beads, and toe rings with your zodiac sign on them.

Kildy bought one of the outrageously priced stills (no signature) and three of the videos, cooing, "I just *loved* her last seminar," gave the guy selling them her autograph, and we went into the auditorium.

It was hung with rose, lilac, and silver chiffon floor-length banners and a state-of-the-art lighting system. Stars and planets rotated overhead, and comets occasionally whizzed by. The stage end of the auditorium was hung with gold Mylar, and in the center of the stage was a black pyramid-backed throne. Apparently Ariaura did not intend to sit on the floor like the rest of us.

At the door, ushers clad in mostly unbuttoned lilac silk shirts and tight pants took our tickets. They all looked like Tom Cruise, which would be par for the course even if this weren't Hollywood.

Sex has been a mainstay of the psychic business since Victorian days. Half the appeal of early table-rapping had been the filmy-draperies-and-nothing-else-clad female "spirits" who drifted tantalizingly among the male séance goers, fogging up their spectacles and preventing them from thinking clearly. Sir William Crookes, the famous British chemist, had been so besotted by an obviously fake medium's sexy daughter that he'd staked his scientific reputation on the medium's dubious authenticity, and nowadays it's no accident that most channelers are male and given to chest-baring Rudolph Valentino–like robes. Or, if they're female, have buff, handsome ushers to distract the women in the audience. If you're drooling over them, you're not likely to spot the wires and chicken guts or realize what they're saying is nonsense. It's the oldest trick in the book.

One of the ushers gave Kildy a Tom Cruise smile and led her to the end of a cross-legged row on the very hard-looking floor. I was glad Kildy had brought the pillows.

I plopped mine down next to hers and sat down on it. "This had better be good," I said.

"Oh, it will be," said a fiftyish redhead wearing the sacred amulet and a diamond as big as my fist. "I've seen Ariaura, and she's wonderful." She reached into one of the three lilac shopping bags she'd stuck between us and pulled out a lavender needlepoint pillow that said, "Believe and It Will Happen."

I wondered if that applied to her believing her pillow was large enough to sit on, because it was about the same size as the rock on her finger, but as soon as they'd finished organizing the rows, the ushers came around bearing stacks of plastic-covered cushions (the kind rented at football games, only lilac) for ten bucks apiece.

The woman next to me took three, and I counted ten other people in our row, and eleven in the row ahead of us, shelling out for them. Eighty rows times ten, to be conservative. A cool eight thousand bucks, just to sit down, and who knows how much profit in all those lilac shopping bags. "By their fruits shall ye know them."

I looked around. I couldn't see any signs of shills or a wireless setup, but unlike psychics and mediums, channelers don't need them. They give out general advice, couched in New Age terms.

"Isus is absolutely astonishing," my neighbor confided. "He's so *wise*! Much better than Romtha. He's responsible for my deciding to leave Randall. 'To thine inner self be true,' Isus said, and I realized Randall had been *blocking* my spiritual ascent—"

"Were you at last Saturday's seminar?" Kildy leaned across me to ask.

"*No*. I was in Cancun, and I was just decimated when I realized I'd missed it. I made Tio bring me back early so I could come today. I desperately need Isus's wisdom about the divorce. Randall's claiming Isus had nothing to do with my decision, that I left him because the prenup had expired, and he's threatening to call Tio as—"

But Kildy had lost interest and was leaning across *her* to ask a pencil-thin woman in the full lotus position if she'd seen Ariaura before. She hadn't, but the one on her right had.

"Last Saturday?" Kildy asked.

She hadn't. She'd seen her six weeks ago in Eugene.

I leaned toward Kildy and whispered, "What happened last Saturday?"

"I think they're starting, Rob," she said, pointing at the stage, where absolutely nothing was happening, and got off her pillow and onto her knees.

"What are you doing?" I whispered.

She didn't answer that, either. She reached inside her pillow, pulled out an orange pillow the same size as the "Believe and It Will Happen" cushion, handed it to me, and arranged herself gracefully on the large tasseled one. As soon as she was cross-legged, she took the orange pillow back from me and laid it across her knees.

"Comfy?" I asked.

"Yes, thank you," she said, turning her movie-star smile on me.

I leaned toward her. "You sure you don't want to tell me what we're doing here?"

"Oh, look, they're starting," she said, and this time they were.

A Brad Pitt look-alike stepped out onstage holding a hand mike and gave us the ground rules. No flash photos (even though they'd confiscated all the cameras). No applause (it breaks Ariaura's concentration). No bathroom breaks. "The cosmic link with Isus is extremely fragile," Brad explained, "and movement or the shutting of a door can break that connection."

Right. Or else Ariaura had learned a few lessons from EST, including the fact that people who are distracted by their bladders are less likely to spot gobbledygook, like the stuff Brad was spouting right now:

"Eighty thousand years ago Isus was a high priest of Atlantis. He lived for three hundred years before he departed this earthly plane and acquired the wisdom of the ages—"

What ages? The Paleolithic and Neolithic? Eighty thousand years ago we were still living in trees.

"—he spoke with the oracle at Delphi, he delved into the Sacred Writings of Rosicrucian—"

Rosicrucian?

"Now watch as Ariaura calls him from the Cosmic All to share his wisdom with you."

The lights deepened to rose, and the chiffon banners began to blow in, as if there were a breeze behind them. Correction, state-of-the-art lighting *and* fans.

The gale intensified, and for a moment I wondered if Ariaura was going to swoop in on a wire, but then the gold Mylar parted, revealing a curving black stairway, and Ariaura, in a purple velvet caftan and her sacred amulet, descended it to the strains of Holst's *Planets* and went to stand dramatically in front of her throne.

The audience paid no attention to the "no applause" edict, and Ariaura seemed to expect it. She stood there for at least two minutes, regally

surveying the crowd. Then she raised her arms as if delivering a benediction and lowered them again, quieting the crowd. "Welcome, Seekers after Divine Truth," she said in a peppy, Oprah-type voice, and there
was more applause. "We're going to have a wonderful spiritual experience together here today and achieve a new plane of enlightenment."

More applause.

"But you mustn't applaud me. I am only the conduit through which
Isus passes, the vessel he fills. Isus first came to me, or, rather, I should
say, *through* me, five years ago, but I was afraid. I didn't want to believe
it. It took me nearly a whole year to accept that I had become the focus
for cosmic energies beyond the reality we know. It's the wisdom of his
highly evolved spirit you'll hear today, not mine. If . . ." a nice theatrical
pause here, ". . . he deigns to come to us. For Isus is a sage, not a servant
to be bidden. He comes when he wills. Mayhap he will be among us
this afternoon, mayhap not."

In a pig's eye. These women weren't going to shell out seven hundred and fifty bucks for a no-show, even if this was Beverly Hills. I'd bet
the house Isus showed up right on cue.

"Isus will come only if our earthly plane is in alignment with the
cosmic," Ariaura said, "if the auratic vibrations are right." She looked
sternly out at the audience. "If any of you are harboring negative vibrations, contact cannot be made."

Uh-oh, here it comes, I thought, and waited for her to look straight
at the two of us and tell us to leave, but she didn't. She merely said, "Are
all of you thinking positive thoughts, feeling positive emotions? Are you
all believing?"

You bet.

"I sense that every one of you is thinking positive thoughts," Ariaura said. "Good. Now, to bring Isus among us, you must help me. You
must each calm your center." She closed her eyes. "You must concentrate on your inner soul-self."

I glanced around the audience. Over half of the women had their
eyes shut, and many had folded their hands in an attitude of prayer.

Some swayed back and forth, and the woman next to me was droning, "Om." Kildy had her eyes closed, her orange pillow clasped to her chest.

"Align ... align ..." Ariaura chanted, and then with finality, "Align." There was another theatrical pause.

"I will now attempt to contact Isus," she said. "The focusing of the astral energy is a dangerous and difficult operation. I must ask that you remain perfectly quiet and still while I am preparing myself."

The woman next to me obediently stopped chanting "Om," and everyone opened their eyes. Ariaura closed hers and leaned back in her throne, her ring-covered hands draped over the ends of the arms. The lights went down and the music came up, the theme from Holst's "Mars." Everyone, including Kildy, watched breathlessly.

Ariaura jerked suddenly as if she were being electrocuted and clutched the arms of the throne. Her face contorted, her mouth twisting and her head shaking.

The audience gasped.

Her body jerked again, slamming back against the throne, and she went into a series of spasms and writhings, with more shaking. This went on for a full minute, while "Mars" built slowly behind her and the spotlight morphed to pink. The music cut off, and she slumped lifelessly back against the throne.

She remained there for a nicely timed interval, and then sat up stiffly, staring straight ahead, her hands lying loosely on the throne's arms. "I am Isus!" she said in a booming voice that was a dead ringer for "Who dares to approach the great and powerful Oz?"

"I am the Enlightened One, a servant unto that which is called the Text and the First Source. I have come from the ninth level of the astral plane," she boomed, "to aid you in your spiritual journeys."

So far it was an exact duplicate of Romtha, right down to the pink light and the number of the astral plane level, but next to me Kildy was leaning forward expectantly.

"I have come to speak the truth," Isus boomed, "to reveal to thou thine higher self."

I leaned over to Kildy and whispered, "Why is it they never learn how to use 'thee' and 'thou' correctly on the astral plane?"

"Shh," Kildy hissed, intent on what Isus was saying.

"I bring you the long-lost wisdom of the kingdom of Lemuria and the prophecies of Antinous to aid thee in these troubled days, for thou livest in a time of tribulation. The last days these are of the Present Age, days filled with anxiety and terrorist attacks and dysfunctional relationships. But I say unto ye, thou must not look without but within, for thee alone are responsible for your happiness, and if that means getting out of a bad relationship, make it so. Seek you must your own inner isness and create thou must thine own inner reality. Thee art the universe."

I don't know what I'd been expecting. *Something*, at least, but this was just the usual New Age nonsense, a mush of psychobabble, self-help tips, pseudo-scripture, and Chicken Soup for the Soul.

I sneaked a glance at Kildy. She was sitting forward, still clutching her pillow tightly to her chest, her beautiful face intent, her mouth slightly open. I wondered if she could actually have been taken in by Ariaura. It's always a possibility, even with skeptics. Kildy wouldn't be the first one to be fooled by a cleverly done illusion.

But this wasn't cleverly done. It wasn't even original. The Lemuria stuff was Richard Zephyr, the "Thou art the universe" stuff was Shirley MacLaine, and the syntax was pure Yoda.

And this was Kildy we were talking about. Kildy, who never fell for anything, not even that vedic levitator. She had to have had a good reason for shelling out over two thousand bucks for this, but so far I was stumped. "What exactly is it you wanted me to see?" I murmured.

"Shhh."

"But fear not," Ariaura said, "for a New Age is coming, an age of peace, of spiritual enlightenment, when you—doing here listening to this confounded claptrap?"

I looked up sharply. Ariaura's voice had changed in mid-sentence from Isus's booming bass to a gravelly baritone, and her manner had, too. She leaned forward, hands on her knees, scowling at the audience. "It's a lot of infernal gabble," she said belligerently.

I glanced at Kildy. She had her eyes fixed on the stage.

"This hokum is even worse than the pretentious bombast you hear in the Chautauqua," the voice croaked.

Chautauqua? I thought. What the—?

"But there you sit, with your mouths hanging open, like the rubes at an Arkansas camp meeting, listening to a snake-charming preacher, waiting for her to fix up your romances and cure your gallstones—"

The woman next to Kildy glanced questioningly at us and then back at the stage. Two of the ushers standing along the wall exchanged frowning glances, and I could hear whispering from somewhere in the audience.

"Have you yaps actually fallen for this mystical mumbo-jumbo? Of course you have. This is America, home of the imbecile and the ass!" the voice said, and the whispering became a definite murmur.

"What in the—?" a woman behind us said, and the woman next to me gathered up her bags, stuffed her "Believe" pillow into one of them, stood up, and began to step over people to get to the door.

One of the ushers signaled someone in the control booth, and the lights and Holst's "Venus" began to come up. The emcee took a hesitant step out onto the stage.

"You sit there like a bunch of gaping primates, ready to buy anyth—" Ariaura said, and her voice changed abruptly back to the basso of Isus, "—but the Age of Spiritual Enlightenment cannot begin until each of thou beginnest thy own journey."

The emcee stopped in mid-step, and so did the murmuring. And the woman who'd been next to me and who was almost to the door. She stood there next to it, holding her bags and listening.

"And believe. All of you, casteth out the toxins of doubt and skepticism now. *Believe* and it will happen."

She must be back on script. The emcee gave a sigh of relief, and retreated back into the wings, and the woman who'd been next to me sat down where she'd been standing, bags and pillows and all. The music faded, and the lights went back to rose.

"Believe in thine inner soul-self," Ariaura/Isus said. "Believe, and let your spiritual unfoldment begin." She paused, and the ushers looked up nervously. The emcee poked his head out from the gold Mylar drapes.

"I grow weary," she said. "I must return now to that higher reality from whence I cameth. Fear not, for though I no longer share this earthly plane with thee, still I am with thou." She raised her arm stiffly in a benediction / Nazi salute, gave a sharp shudder, and then slumped forward in a swoon that would have done credit to Gloria Swanson. Holst's "Venus" began again, and she sat up, blinking, and turned to the emcee, who had come out onstage again.

"Did Isus speak?" she asked him in her original voice.

"Yes, he did," the emcee said, and the audience burst into thunderous applause, during which he helped her to her feet and handed her over to two of the ushers, who walked her, leaning heavily on them, up the black stairway and out of sight.

As soon as she was safely gone, the emcee quieted the applause and said, "Copies of Ariaura's books and videotapes are available outside in the waiting area. If you wish to arrange for a private audience, see me or one of the ushers," and everyone began gathering up their pillows and heading for the door.

"Wasn't he *wonderful?*" a woman ahead of us in the exodus said to her friend. "So authentic!"

Is Los Angeles the worst town in America, or only next to the worst? The skeptic, asked the original question, will say yes, the believer will say no. There you have it.

—H. L. MENCKEN

Kildy and I didn't talk till we were out of the parking lot and on Wilshire, at which point Kildy said, "Now do you understand why I wanted you to see it for yourself, Rob?"

"It was interesting, all right. I take it she did the same thing at the seminar you went to last week?"

She nodded. "Only last week two people walked out."

"Was it the exact same spiel?"

"No. It didn't last quite as long—I don't know how long exactly, it caught me by surprise—and she used slightly different words, but the message was the same. And it happened the same way—no warning, no contortions, her voice just changed abruptly in mid-sentence. So what do you think's going on, Rob?"

I turned onto La Brea. "I don't know, but lots of channelers do more than one 'entity.' Joye Wildde does two, and before Hans Lightfoot went to jail, he did half a dozen."

Kildy looked skeptical. "Her promotional material doesn't say anything about multiple entities."

"Maybe she's tired of Isus and wants to switch to another spirit. When you're a channeler, you can't just announce, 'Coming soon: Isus II.' You've got to make it look authentic. So she introduces him with a few words one week, a couple of sentences the next, etcetera."

"She's introducing a new and improved spirit who yells at the audience and calls them imbeciles and rubes?" she said incredulously.

"It's probably what channelers call a 'dark spirit,' a so-called bad entity that tries to lead the unwary astray. Todd Phoenix used to have a nasty voice break in in the middle of White Feather's spiel and make heckling comments. It's a useful trick. It reinforces the idea that the psychic's actually channeling, and anything inconsistent or controversial the channeler says can be blamed on the bad spirit."

"But Ariaura didn't even seem to be aware there *was* a bad spirit, if that's what it was supposed to be. Why would it tell the audience to go home and stop giving their money to a snake-oil vendor like Ariaura?"

A snake-oil vendor? That sounded vaguely familiar, too. "Is that what she said last week? Snake-oil vendor?"

"Yes," she said. "Why? Do you know who she's channeling?"

"No," I said, frowning, "but I've heard that phrase somewhere. And the line about the Chautauqua."

"So it's obviously somebody famous," Kildy said.

But the historical figures channelers did were always instantly recognizable. Randall Mars's Abraham Lincoln began every sentence with "Four score and seven years ago," and the others were all equally obvious. "I wish I'd gotten Ariaura's little outburst on tape," I said.

"We did," Kildy said, reaching over the backseat and grabbing her orange pillow. She unzipped it, reached inside, and brought out a micro-vidcam. "Ta-da! I'm sorry I didn't get last week's. I didn't realize they were frisking people."

She fished in the pillow again and brought out a sheet of paper. "I had to run to the bathroom and scribble down what I could remember."

"I thought they didn't let people go to the bathroom."

She grinned at me. "I gave an Oscar-worthy performance of an actress they'd let out of rehab too soon."

I glanced at the list at the next stoplight. There were only a few phrases on it: the one she'd mentioned, and "I've never seen such shameless bilge," and "You'd have to be a pack of deluded half-wits to believe something so preposterous."

"That's all?"

She nodded. "I told you, it didn't last nearly as long last time. And since I wasn't expecting it, I missed most of the first sentence."

"That's why you were asking at the seminar about buying the video-tape?"

"Uh-huh, although I doubt if there's anything on it. I've watched her last three videos, and there's no sign of Entity Number Two."

"But it happened at the seminar you went to and at this one. Has it occurred to you it might have happened *because* we were there?" I pulled into a parking space in front of the building where *The Jaundiced Eye* has its office.

"But—" she said.

"The ticket-taker could have alerted her that we were there," I said.

I got out and opened her door for her, and we started up to the office. "Or she could have spotted us in the audience—you're not the only one who's famous. My picture's on every psychic wanted poster on the West Coast—and she decided to jazz up the performance a little by adding another entity. To impress us."

"That can't be it."

I opened the door. "Why not?"

"Because it's happened at least twice before," she said, walking in and sitting down in the only good chair. "In Berkeley and Seattle."

"How do you know?"

"My publicist's ex-boyfriend's girlfriend saw her in Berkeley—that's how my publicist found out about Ariaura—so I got her number and called her and asked her, and she said Isus was talking along about tribulation and thee being the universe, and all of a sudden this other voice said, 'What a bunch of boobs!' She said that's how she knew Ariaura was really channeling, because if it was fake she'd hardly have called the audience names."

"Well, there's your answer. She does it to make her audiences believe her."

"You saw them, they already believe her," Kildy said. "And if that's what she's doing, why isn't it on the Berkeley videotape?"

"It isn't?"

She shook her head. "I watched it six times. Nothing."

"And you're sure your publicist's ex-boyfriend's girlfriend really saw it? That you weren't leading her when you asked her questions?"

"I'm sure," she said indignantly. "Besides, I asked my mother."

"She was there, too?"

"No, but two of her friends were, and one of them knew someone who saw the Seattle seminar. They all said basically the same thing, except the part about it making them believe her. In fact, one of them said, 'I think her cue cards were out of order,' and told me not to waste my money, that the person I should go see was Angelina Black Feather."

She grinned at me and then went serious. "If Ariaura was doing it on purpose, why would she edit it out? And why did the emcee and the ushers look so uneasy?"

So she'd noticed that, too.

"Maybe she didn't warn them she was going to do it. Or, more likely, it's all part of the act, to make people believe it's authentic."

Kildy shook her head doubtfully. "I don't think so. I think it's something else."

"Like what? You don't think she's really channeling this guy?"

"No, of *course* not, Rob," she said indignantly. "It's just that . . . you say she's doing it to get publicity and bigger crowds, but as you told me, the first rule of success in the psychic business is to tell people what they want to hear, not to call them boobs. You saw the woman next to you—she was all ready to walk out, and I watched her afterward. She didn't sign up for a private enlightenment audience, and neither did very many other people, and I heard the emcee telling someone there were lots of tickets still available for the next seminar. Last week's was sold out a month in advance. Why would she do something to hurt her business?"

"She's got to do something to up the ante, to keep the customers coming back, and this new spirit is to create buzz. You watch, next week she'll be advertising 'The Battle of the Ancients.' It's a gimmick, Kildy."

"So you don't think we should go see her again."

"No. That's the worst thing we could possibly do. We don't want to give her free publicity, and if she did do it to impress us, though it doesn't sound like it, we'd be playing right into her hands. If she's not, and the spirit *is* driving customers away, like you say, she'll dump it and come up with a different one. Or put herself out of business. Either way, there's no need for us to do anything. It's a non-story. You can forget all about her."

Which just goes to show you why I could never make it as a psychic. Because before the words were even out of my mouth, the office door banged open, and Ariaura roared in and grabbed me by the lapels.

"I don't know what you're doing or how you're doing it," she screamed, "but I want you to stop it *right now!*"

He has a large and extremely uncommon capacity for
provocative utterance . . .

—H. L. Mencken

I hadn't given Ariaura's acting skills enough credit. Her portrayal of Isus might be wooden and fakey, but she gave a pretty convincing portrayal of a hopping-mad psychic.

"How *dare* you!" she shrieked. "I'll sue you for everything you own!"

She had changed out of her flowing robes and into a lilac-colored suit Kildy told me later was a Zac Posen, and her diamond-studded necklace and earrings rattled. She was practically vibrating with rage, though not the positive vibrations she'd said were necessary for the appearance of spirits.

"I just watched the video of my seminar," she shrieked, her face two inches from mine. "How *dare* you hypnotize me and make me look like a complete fool in front of—"

"Hypnotize?" Kildy said. (I was too busy trying to loosen her grip on my lapels to say anything.) "You think Rob hypnotized you?"

"Oh, don't play the innocent with me," Ariaura said, wheeling on her. "I saw you two out there in the audience today, and I know all about you and your nasty, sneering little magazine. I know you nonbelievers will stop at nothing to keep us from spreading the Higher Truth, but I didn't think you'd go this far, hypnotizing me against my will and making me say those things! Isus told me I shouldn't let you stay in the auditorium, that he sensed danger in your presence, but I said, 'No, let the unbeliever stay and experience your reality. Let them know you come from the Existence Beyond to help us, to bring us words of Higher Wisdom.' But Isus was right, you were up to no good."

She removed one hand from my lapel long enough to shake a lilac-lacquered fingernail at me. "Well, your little hypnotism scheme won't work. I've worked too hard to get where I am, and I'm not going to let a pair of narrow-minded little unbelievers like you get in my way. I have no intention—Higher Wisdom, my foot!" she snorted. "Higher Humbug is what I call it."

Kildy glanced, startled, at me.

"Oh, the trappings are a lot gaudier, I'll give you that," Ariaura said in the gravelly voice we'd heard at the seminar.

As before, the change had come without a break and in mid-sentence. One minute she had had me by the lapels, and the next she'd let go and was pacing around the room, her hands behind her back, musing, "That auditorium's a lot fancier, and it's a big improvement over a courthouse lawn, and a good forty degrees cooler." She sat down on the couch, her hands on her spread-apart knees. "And those duds she wears would make a Grand Worthy bow-wow of the Knights of Zoroaster look dowdy, but it's the same old line of buncombe and the same old Boobus Americanus drinking it in."

Kildy took a careful step toward my desk, reached for her handbag and did something I couldn't see, and then went back to where she'd been standing, keeping her eyes the whole time on Ariaura, who was holding forth about the seminar.

"I never saw such an assortment of slack-jawed simians in one place! Except for the fact that the yokels have to sit on the floor—*and* pay for the privilege!—it's the spitting image of a Baptist tent revival. Tell 'em what they want to hear, do a couple of parlor tricks, and then pass the collection plate. And they're still falling for it!"

She stood up and began pacing again. "I knew I should've stuck around. It's just like that time in Dayton—I think it's all over and leave, and look what happens! You let the quacks and the crooks take over, like this latter-day Aimee Semple McPherson. She's no more a seer than—of allowing you to ruin everything I've worked for! I . . ." Ariaura looked around bewilderedly. ". . . what? . . . I . . ." She faltered to a stop.

I had to hand it to her. She was good. She'd switched back into her own voice without missing a beat, and then given an impressive impersonation of someone who had no idea what was going on.

She looked confusedly from me to Kildy and back. "It happened again, didn't it?" she asked, a quaver in her voice, and turned to appeal to Kildy. "He did it again, didn't he?" and began backing toward the door. "*Didn't* he?"

She pointed accusingly at me. "You keep *away* from me!" she shrieked. "And you keep away from my seminars! If you so much as *try* to come near me again, I'll get a restraining order against you!" She roared out, slamming the door behind her.

"Well," Kildy said after a minute. "That was interesting."

"Yes," I said, looking at the door. "Interesting."

Kildy went over to my desk and pulled the Hasaka out from behind her handbag. "I got it all," she said, taking out the disk, sticking it in the computer dock, and sitting down in front of the monitor. "There were a lot more clues this time." She began typing in commands. "There should be more than enough for us to be able to figure out who it is."

"I know who it is," I said.

Kildy stopped in mid-keystroke. "Who?"

"The High Priest of Irreverence."

"*Who?*"

"The Holy Terror from Baltimore, the Apostle of Common Sense, the Scourge of Con Men, Creationists, Faith Healers, and the Booboisie," I said. "Henry Louis Mencken."

In brief, it is a fraud.

—H. L. MENCKEN

"H. L. Mencken?" Kildy said. "The reporter who covered the Scopes trial?" (I told you she was too good to be true.)

"But why would Ariaura channel him?" she asked after we'd checked the words and phrases we'd listed against Mencken's writings. They all checked out, from "buncombe" to "slack-jawed simians" to "home of the imbecile and the ass."

"What did he mean about leaving Dayton early? Did something happen in Ohio?"

I shook my head. "Tennessee. Dayton, Tennessee, was where the Scopes trial was held."

"And Mencken left early?"

"I don't know," I said, and went over to the bookcase to look for *The Great Monkey Trial*, "but I know it got so hot during the trial they moved it outside."

"That's what that comment about the courthouse lawn and its being forty degrees cooler meant," Kildy said.

I nodded. "It was a hundred and five degrees and ninety percent humidity the week of the trial. It's definitely Mencken. He invented the term 'Boobus Americanus.'"

"But why would Ariaura channel H. L. Mencken, Rob? He *hated* people like her, didn't he?"

"He certainly did." He'd been the bane of charlatans and quacks all through the twenties, writing scathing columns on all kinds of scams, from faith healing to chiropractic to creationism, railing incessantly against all forms of "hocus-pocus" and on behalf of science and rational thought.

"Then why would she channel him?" Kildy asked. "Why not somebody sympathetic to psychics, like Edgar Cayce or Madame Blavatsky?"

"Because they'd obviously be suspect. By channeling an enemy of psychics, she makes it seem more credible."

"But nobody's ever heard of him."

"You have. I have."

"But nobody else in Ariaura's audience has."

"Exactly," I said, still looking for *The Great Monkey Trial*.

"You mean you think she's doing it to impress us?"

"Obviously," I said, scanning the titles. "Why else would she have come all the way over here to give that little performance?"

"But—what about the Seattle seminar? Or the one in Berkeley?"

"Dry runs. Or she was hoping we'd hear about them and go see her. Which we did."

"I didn't," Kildy said. "I went because my publicist wanted me to."

"But you go to lots of spiritualist events, and you talk to lots of people. Your publicist was there. Even if you hadn't gone, she'd have told you about it."

"But what would be the point? You're a skeptic. You don't believe in channeling. Would she honestly think she could convince you Mencken was real?"

"Maybe," I said. "She's obviously gone to a lot of trouble to make the spirit sound like him. And think what a coup that would be. 'Skeptic Says Channeled Spirit Authentic'? Have you ever heard of Uri Geller? He made a splash back in the seventies by claiming to bend spoons with his mind. He got all kinds of attention when a pair of scientists from the Stanford Research Institute said it wasn't a trick, that he was actually doing it."

"Was he?"

"No, of course not, and eventually he was exposed as a fraud. By Johnny Carson. Geller made the mistake of going on *The Tonight Show* and doing it in front of him. He'd apparently forgotten Carson had been a magician in his early days. But the point is, he made it onto *The Tonight Show*. And what made him a celebrity was having the endorsement of reputable scientists."

"And if you endorsed Ariaura, if you said you thought it was really Mencken, she'd be a celebrity, too."

"Exactly."

"So what do we do?"

"Nothing."

"Nothing? You're not going to try to expose her as a fake?"

"Channeling isn't the same as bending spoons. There's no inde-pendently verifiable evidence." I looked at her. "It's not worth it, and we've got bigger fish to fry. Like Charles Fred. He's making *way* too much money for a medium who only charges two hundred a perfor-mance, and he has way too many hits for a cold-reader. We need to find out how he's doing it, and where the money's coming from."

"But shouldn't we at least go to Ariaura's next seminar to see if it happens again?" Kildy persisted.

"And have to explain to the *L.A. Times* reporter who just happens to be there why we're so interested in Ariaura?" I said. "And why you came back three times?"

"I suppose you're right. But what if some other skeptic endorses her? Or some English professor?"

I hadn't thought of that. Ariaura had dangled the bait at four semi-nars we knew of. She might have been doing it at more, and *The Skep-tical Mind* was in Seattle, Carlyle Drew was in San Francisco, and there were any number of amateur skeptics who went to spiritualist events.

And they would all know who Mencken was. He was the critical thinker's favorite person, next to the Amazing Randi and Houdini. He'd not only been fearless in his attacks on superstition and fraud, he could write "like a bat out of hell." And, unlike the rest of us skeptics, people had actually listened to what he said.

I'd liked him ever since I'd read about him chatting with somebody in his office at the Baltimore *Sun* and then suddenly looking out the window, saying, "The sons of bitches are gaining on us!" and frantically beginning to type. That was how I felt about twice a day, and more than once I'd muttered to myself, "Where the hell is Mencken when we need him?"

And I'd be willing to bet there were other people who felt the same way I did, who might be seduced by Mencken's language and the fact that Ariaura was telling them exactly what they wanted to hear.

"You're right," I said. "We need to look into this, but we should send somebody else to the seminar."

"How about my publicist? She said she wanted to go again."

"No, I don't want it to be anybody connected with us."

"I know just the person," Kildy said, snatching up her cell phone. "Her name's Riata Starr. She's an actress."

With a name like that, what else could she be?

"She's between jobs right now," Kildy said, punching in a number, "and if I tell her there's likely to be a casting director there, she'll definitely do it for us."

"Does she believe in channelers?"

She looked pityingly at me. "Everyone in Hollywood believes in channelers, but it won't matter." She put the phone to her ear. "I'll put a videocam on her, and a recorder," she whispered. "And I'll tell her an undercover job would look great on her acting résumé. Hello?" she said in a normal voice. "I'm trying to reach Riata Starr. Oh. No, no message."

She pushed "end." "She's at a casting call at Miramax." She stuck the phone in her bag, fished her keys out of its depths, and slung the bag over her shoulder. "I'm going to go out there and talk to her. I'll be back," she said, and went out.

Definitely too good to be true, I thought, watching her leave, and called up a friend of mine in the police department and asked him what they had on Ariaura.

He promised he'd call me back, and while I was waiting I looked for and found *The Great Monkey Trial*. I looked up Mencken in the index and started through the references to see when Mencken had left Dayton. I doubted that he would have left before the trial was over. He'd been having the time of his life, pillorying William Jennings Bryan and the creationists. Maybe the reference was to Mencken's having left before Bryan's death.

Bryan had died five days after the trial ended, presumably from a heart attack, but more likely from the humiliation he'd suffered at the hands of Clarence Darrow, who'd put him on the stand and fired questions at him about the Bible. Darrow had made him—and creationism—look ridiculous, or rather, he'd made himself look ridiculous. The cross-examination had been the high point of the trial, and it had killed him.

Mencken had written a deadly, unforgiving obituary of Bryan, and he might very well have been sorry he hadn't been in at the kill, but I couldn't imagine Ariaura knowing that, even if she had taken the trouble to look up "Boobus Americanus" and "unmitigated bilge" and research Mencken's gravelly voice and explosive delivery.

Of course she might have read it. In this very book, even. I read the chapter on Bryan's death, looking for references to Mencken, but I couldn't find any. I backtracked, and there it was. And I couldn't believe it.

Mencken hadn't left after the trial. When Darrow's expert witnesses had all been disallowed, he'd assumed it was all over but assorted legal technicalities and had gone back to Baltimore. He hadn't seen Darrow's withering cross-examination. He'd missed Bryan saying man wasn't a mammal, missed his insisting the sun could stand still without throwing the earth out of orbit. He'd definitely left too soon. And I was willing to bet he'd never forgiven himself for it.

To me, the scientific point of view is completely satisfying, and it has been so as long as I remember. Not once in this life have I ever been inclined to seek a rock and refuge elsewhere.

—H. L. MENCKEN

"But how could Ariaura know that?" Kildy said when she got back from the casting call.

"The same way I know it. She read it in a book. Did your friend Riata agree to go to the seminar?"

"Yes, she said she'd go. I gave her the Hasaka, but I'm worried they might confiscate it, so I've got an appointment with this props guy at Universal who worked on the last Bond movie to see if he's got any ideas."

"Uh, Kildy . . . those gadgets James Bond uses aren't real. It's a movie."

She shot me her Julia-Roberts-plus smile. "I said *ideas.* Oh, and I got Riata's ticket. When I called, I asked if they were sold out, and the guy I talked to said, 'Are you kidding?' and told me they'd only sold about half what they usually do. Did you find out anything about Ariaura?"

"No," I said. "I'm checking out some leads."

But my friend at the police department didn't have any dope on Ariaura, not even a possible alias. "She's clean," he said when he finally called back the next morning. "No mail fraud, not even a parking ticket."

I couldn't find anything on her in *The Skeptical Mind* or on the Scamwatch website. It looked like she made her money the good old American way, by telling her customers a bunch of nonsense and selling them chakra charts.

I told Kildy as much when she came in, looking gorgeous in a casual shirt and jeans that had probably cost as much as *The Jaundiced Eye*'s annual budget.

"Ariaura's obviously not her real name, but so far I haven't been able to find out what it is," I said. "Did you get a James Bond secret videocam from your buddy Q?"

"Yes," she said, setting the tote bag down. "And I have an idea for proving Ariaura's a fraud." She handed me a sheaf of papers. "Here are the transcripts of everything Mencken said. We check them against Mencken's writings, and—" She stopped. "What?"

I was shaking my head. "This is channeling. When I wrote an exposé about Swami Vishnu Jammi's fifty-thousand-year-old entity, Yogati, using phrases like 'totally awesome' and 'funky' and talking about cell phones, he said he 'transliterated' Yogati's thoughts into his own words."

"Oh." Kildy bit her lip. "Rob, what about a computer match? You know, one of those things where they compare a manuscript with Shakespeare's plays to see if they were written by the same person."

"Too expensive," I said. "Besides, they're done by universities, who I doubt would want to risk their credibility by running a check on a channeler. And even if they did match, all it would prove is that it's Mencken's words, not that it's Mencken."

"Oh." She sat on the corner of my desk swinging her long legs for a minute, and then stood up, walked over to the bookcase, and began pulling down books.

"What are you doing?" I asked, going over to see what she was doing. She was holding a copy of Mencken's *Heathen Days*. "I told you," I said, "Mencken's phrases won't—"

"I'm not looking up his phrases," she said, handing me *Prejudices* and Mencken's biography. "I'm looking for questions to ask him."

"*Him?* He's not Mencken, Kildy. He's a concoction of Ariaura's."

"I know," she said, handing me *The Collectible Mencken*. "That's why we need to question him—I mean Ariaura. We need to ask him—her—questions like, 'What was your wife's maiden name?' and 'What was the first newspaper you worked for?' and—are any of these paperbacks on the bottom shelf here by Mencken?"

"No, they're mysteries mostly. Chandler and Hammett and James M. Cain."

She quit looking at them and straightened to look at the middle shelves. "Questions like, 'What did your father do for a living?'"

"He made cigars," I said. "The first newspaper he worked for wasn't the Baltimore *Sun*, it was the *Morning Herald*, and his wife's maiden name was Sara Haardt. With a *d* and two *a*'s. But that doesn't mean I'm Mencken."

"No," Kildy said, "but if you didn't know them, it would prove you weren't."

She handed me *A Mencken Chrestomathy*. "If we ask Ariaura questions Mencken would know the answers to, and she gets them wrong, it proves she's faking."

She had a point. Ariaura had obviously researched Mencken fairly thoroughly to be able to mimic his language and mannerisms, and probably well enough to answer basic questions about his life, but she would hardly have memorized every detail. There were dozens of books about him, let alone his own work and his diaries. Plus *Inherit the Wind* and all the other plays and books and treatises that had been written about the Scopes trial. I'd bet there were close to a hundred Mencken things in print, and that didn't include the stuff he'd written for the Baltimore *Sun*.

And if we could catch her not knowing something Mencken would know, it would be a simple way to prove conclusively that she was faking, and we could move on to the much more important question of why. *If* Ariaura would let herself be questioned.

"How do you plan to get Ariaura to agree to this?" I said. "My guess is she won't even let us in to see her."

"If she doesn't, then that's proof, too," she said imperturbably.

"All right," I said, "but forget about asking what Mencken's father did. Ask what he drank. Rye, by the way."

Kildy grabbed a notebook and started writing.

"Ask what the name of his first editor at the *Sun* was," I said, picking up *The Great Monkey Trial*. "And ask who Sue Hicks was."

"Who was she?" Kildy asked.

"He. He was one of the defense lawyers at the Scopes trial."

"Should we ask him—her what the Scopes trial was about?"

"No, too easy. Ask him . . ." I said, trying to think of a good question. "Ask him what he ate while he was there covering the trial, and ask him where he sat in the courtroom."

"Where he sat?"

"It's a trick question. He stood on a table in the corner. Oh, and ask where he was born."

She frowned. "Isn't that too easy? Everyone knows he's from Baltimore."

"I want to hear him say it."

"Oh," Kildy said, nodding. "Did he have any kids?"

I shook my head. "He had a sister and two brothers. Gertrude, Charles, and August."

"Oh, good, those aren't names you'd be able to come up with just by guessing. Did he have any hobbies?"

"He played the piano. Ask about the Saturday Night Club. He and a bunch of friends got together to play music."

We worked on the questions the rest of the day and the next morning, writing them down on index cards so they could be asked out of order.

"What about some of his sayings?" Kildy asked.

"You mean like, 'Puritanism is the haunting fear that someone, somewhere, may be happy'? No. They're the easiest thing of all to memorize, and no real person speaks in aphorisms."

Kildy nodded and bent her beautiful head over the book again. I looked up Mencken's medical history—he suffered from ulcers and had had an operation on his throat to remove his uvula—and went out and got us sandwiches for lunch and made copies of Mencken's "History of the Bathtub" and a fake handbill he'd passed out during the Scopes trial announcing "a public demonstration of healing, casting out devils, and prophesying" by a made-up evangelist. Mencken had crowed that not a single person in Dayton had spotted the fake.

Kildy looked up from her book. "Did you know Mencken dated Lillian Gish?" she asked, sounding surprised.

"Yeah. He dated a lot of actresses. He had an affair with Anita Loos and nearly married Aileen Pringle. Why?"

"I'm impressed he wasn't intimidated by the fact that they were movie stars, that's all."

I didn't know if that was directed at me or not.

"Speaking of actresses," I said, "what time is Ariaura's seminar?"

"Two o'clock," she said, glancing at her watch. "It's a quarter till two right now. It should be over around four. Riata said she'd call as soon as the seminar was done."

We went back to looking through Mencken's books and his biographies, looking for details Ariaura was unlikely to have memorized. He'd loved baseball. He had stolen Gideon Bibles from hotel rooms and then given them to his friends, inscribed, "Compliments of the Author." He'd been friends with lots of writers, including Theodore Dreiser and F. Scott Fitzgerald, who'd gotten so drunk at a dinner with Mencken he'd stood up at the dinner table and pulled his pants down.

The phone rang. I reached for it, but it was Kildy's cell phone. "It's Riata," she told me, looking at the readout.

"Riata?" I glanced at my watch. It was only two-thirty. "Why isn't she in the seminar?"

Kildy shrugged and put the phone to her ear. "Riata? What's going on? . . . You're kidding! . . . Did you get it? Great . . . no, meet me at Spago's, like we agreed. I'll be there in half an hour."

She hit "end," stood up, and took out her keys, all in one graceful motion. "Ariaura did it again, only this time as soon as she started, they stopped the seminar, yanked her offstage, and told everybody to leave. Riata got it on tape. I'm going to go pick it up. Will you be here?"

I nodded absently, trying to think of a way to ask about Mencken's two-fingered typing, and Kildy waved good-bye and went out.

If I asked, "How do you write your stories?" I'd get an answer about the process of writing, but if I asked, "Do you touch-type?" Ariaura—

Kildy reappeared in the doorway, sat down, and picked up her notebook again. "What are you doing?" I asked, "I thought you were going—"

She put her finger to her lips. "She's here," she mouthed, and Ariaura came in.

She was still wearing her purple robes and her stage makeup, so she must have come here straight from her seminar, but she didn't roar in angrily the way she had before. She looked frightened.

"What are you doing to me?" she asked, her voice trembling. "And don't say you're not doing anything. I saw the videotape. You're—that's what I want to know, too," the gravelly voice demanded. "What the hell have you been doing? I thought you ran a magazine that worked to put a stop to the kind of bilgewater this high priestess of blather spews out. She was at it again today, calling up spirits and rooking a bunch of mysticism-besotted fools out of their cold cash, and where the hell were you? I didn't see you there, cracking heads."

"We didn't go because we didn't want to encourage her if she was—" Kildy hesitated. "We're not sure what . . . I mean, who we're dealing with here . . ." she faltered.

"Ariaura," I said firmly. "You pretend to channel spirits from the astral plane for a living. Why should we believe you're not pretending to channel H. L. Mencken?"

"Pretending?" she said, sounding surprised. "You think I'm something that two-bit Jezebel's confabulating?"

She sat down heavily in the chair in front of my desk and grinned wryly at me. "You're absolutely right. I wouldn't believe it, either. A skeptic after my own heart."

"Yes," I said. "And as a skeptic, I need to have some proof you're who you say you are."

"Fair enough. What kind of proof?"

"We want to ask you some questions," Kildy said.

Ariaura slapped her knees. "Fire away."

"All right," I said. "Since you mentioned fires, when was the Baltimore fire?"

"Aught-four," she said promptly. "February. Cold as hell." She grinned. "Best time I ever had."

Kildy glanced at me. "What did your father drink?" she asked.

"Rye."

"What did *you* drink?" I asked.

"From 1919 on, whatever I could get."

"Where are you from?" Kildy asked.

"The most beautiful city in the world."

"Which is?" I said.

"Which *is*?" she roared, outraged. "Bawlmer!"

Kildy shot me a glance.

"What's the Saturday Night Club?" I snapped out.

"A drinking society," she said, "with musical accompaniment."

"What instrument did you play?"

"Piano."

"What's the Mann Act?"

"Why?" she said, winking at Kildy. "You planning on taking her across state lines? Is she underage?"

I ignored that. "If you're really Mencken, you hate charlatans, so why have you inhabited Ariaura's body?"

"Why do people go to zoos?"

She was good, I had to give her that. And fast. She spat out answers as fast as I could ask her questions about the *Sun* and *The Smart Set* and William Jennings Bryan.

"Why did you go to Dayton?"

"To see a three-ring circus. And stir up the animals."

"What did you take with you?"

"A typewriter and four quarts of Scotch. I should have taken a fan. It was hotter than the seventh circle of hell, with the same company."

"What did you eat while you were there?" Kildy asked.

"Fried chicken and tomatoes. At every meal. Even breakfast."

I handed him the bogus evangelist handbill Mencken had handed out at the Scopes trial. "What's this?"

She looked at it, turned it over, looked at the other side. "It appears to be some sort of circular."

And there's all the proof we need, I thought smugly. Mencken would have recognized that instantly. "Do you know who wrote this handbill?" I started to ask and thought better of it. The question itself might give the answer away. And better not use the word "handbill."

"Do you know the event this circular describes?" I asked instead.

"I'm afraid I can't answer that," she said.

Then you're not Mencken, I thought. I shot a triumphant glance at Kildy.

"But I would be glad to," Ariaura said, "if you would be so good as to read what is written on it to me."

She handed the handbill back to me, and I stood there looking at it and then at her and then at it again.

"What is it, Rob?" Kildy said. "What's wrong?"

"Nothing," I said. "Never mind about the circular. What was your first published news story about?"

"A stolen horse and buggy," she said, and proceeded to tell the whole story, but I wasn't listening.

He didn't know what the handbill was about, I thought, because he couldn't read. Because he'd had an aphasic stroke in 1948 that had left him unable to read and write.

I had a nice clean place to stay, madam, and I left it to come here.

—INHERIT THE WIND

"It doesn't prove anything," I told Kildy after Ariaura was gone. She'd come out of her Mencken act abruptly after I'd asked her what street she lived on in Baltimore, looked bewilderedly at me and then Kildy, and bolted without a word. "Ariaura could have found out about Mencken's stroke the same way I did," I said, "by reading it in a book."

"Then why did you go white like that?" Kildy said. "I thought you were going to pass out. And why wouldn't she just answer the question? She knew the answers to all the others."

"Probably she didn't know that one and that was her fallback response," I said. "It caught me off guard, that's all. I was expecting her to have memorized pat answers, not—"

"Exactly," Kildy cut in. "Somebody faking it would have said they had an aphasic stroke if you asked them a direct question about it, but they wouldn't have . . . and that wasn't the only instance. When you asked him about the Baltimore fire, he said it was the best time he'd ever had. Someone faking it would have told you what buildings burned or how horrible it was."

And he'd said, not "1904" or "oh-four," but "aught-four." Nobody talked like that nowadays, and it wasn't something that would have been in Mencken's writings. It was something people said, not wrote, and Ariaura couldn't possibly—

"It doesn't prove he's Mencken," I said and realized I was saying "he." And shouting.

I lowered my voice. "It's a very clever trick, that's all. And just because we don't know how the trick's being done doesn't mean it's not a trick. She could have been coached in the part, *including* telling her how to pretend she can't read if she's confronted with anything written. Or she could be hooked up to somebody with a computer."

"I looked. She wasn't wearing an earpiece, and if somebody was looking up the answers and feeding them to her, she'd be slower answering them, wouldn't she?"

"Not necessarily. She might have a photographic memory."

"But then wouldn't she be doing a mind-reading act instead of channeling?"

"Maybe she did. We don't know what she was doing before Salem," I said, but Kildy was right. Someone with a photographic memory could make a killing as a fortune-teller or a medium, and there were no signs of a photographic memory in Ariaura's channeling act—she spoke only in generalities.

"Or she might be coming up with the answers some other way," I said.

"What if she isn't, Rob? What if she's really channeling the spirit of Mencken?"

"Kildy, channels are fakes. There are no spirits, no sympathetic vibrations, there's no astral plane."

"I know," she said, "but his answers were so—" She shook her head. "And there's something about him, his voice and the way he moves—"

"It's called acting."

"But Ariaura's a terrible actress. You saw her do Isus."

"All right," I said. "Let's suppose for a minute it is Mencken, and that instead of being in the family plot in Loudon Park Cemetery, his spirit's floating in the ether somewhere, why would he come back at this particular moment? Why didn't he come back when Uri Geller was bending spoons all over the place, or when Shirley MacLaine was on every talk show in the universe? Why didn't he come back in the fifties when Virginia Tighe was claiming to be Bridey Murphy?"

"I don't know," Kildy admitted.

"And why would he choose to make his appearance through the 'channel' of a third-rate mountebank like Ariaura? He *hated* charlatans like her."

"Maybe that's why he came back, because people like her are still around and he hadn't finished what he set out to do. You heard him—he said he left too early."

"He was talking about the Scopes trial."

"Maybe not. You heard him, he said, 'You let the quacks and the crooks take over.' Or maybe—" she stopped.

"Maybe what?"

"Maybe he came back to help you, Rob. That time you were so frustrated over Charles Fred, I heard you say, 'Where the hell is H. L. Mencken when we need him?' Maybe he heard you."

"And decided to come all the way back from an astral plane that doesn't exist to help a skeptic nobody's ever heard of."

"It's not *that* inconceivable that someone would be interested in you," Kildy said. "I . . . I mean, the work you're doing is really important, and Mencken—"

"*Kildy*," I said, "I don't believe this."

"I don't, either—I just . . . you have to admit, it's a very convincing illusion."

"Yes, so was the Fox sisters' table-rapping and Virginia Tighe's past life as an Irish washerwoman in 1880s Dublin, but there was a logical explanation for both of them, and it may not even be that complicated. The details Bridey Murphy knew all turned out to have come from Virginia Tighe's Irish nanny. The Fox sisters were cracking their *toes*, for God's sake."

"You're right," Kildy said, but she didn't sound completely convinced, and that worried me. If Ariaura's Mencken imitation could fool Kildy, it could fool anybody, and "I'm sure it's a trick. I just don't know how she's doing it" wasn't going to cut it when the networks called me for a statement. I had to figure this out fast.

"Ariaura has to be getting her information about Mencken from someplace," I said. "We need to find out where. We need to check with bookstores and the library. And the Internet," I said, hoping that wasn't what she was using. It would take forever to find out what sites she'd visited.

"What do you want me to do?" Kildy asked.

"I want you to go through the transcripts like you suggested and find out where the quotes came from so we'll know the particular works we're dealing with," I told her. "And I want you to talk to your publicist and anybody else who's been to the seminars and find out if any of them had a private enlightenment audience with Ariaura. I want to know what goes on in them. Is she using Mencken for some purpose we don't know about? See if you can find out."

"I could ask Riata to get an audience," she suggested.

"That's a good idea," I said.

"What about questions? Do you want me to try to come up with some harder ones than the ones we asked him—I mean, her?"

I shook my head. "Asking harder questions won't help. If she's got a photographic memory, she'll know anything we throw at her, and if she doesn't, and we ask her some obscure question about one of the reporters Mencken worked with at the *Morning Herald*, or one of his *Smart Set* essays, she can say she doesn't remember, and it won't prove anything. If you asked me what was in articles I wrote for *The Jaundiced Eye* five years ago, I couldn't remember, either."

"I'm not talking about facts and figures, Rob," Kildy said. "I'm talking about the kinds of things people don't forget, like the first time Mencken met Sara."

I thought of the first time I met Kildy, looking up from my desk to see her standing there, with her honey-blond hair and that movie-star smile. "Unforgettable" was the word, all right.

"Or how his mother died," Kildy was saying, "or how he found out about the Baltimore fire. The paper called him and woke him out of a sound sleep. There's no way you could forget that, or the name of a dog you had as a kid, or the nickname the other kids called you in grade school."

Nickname. That triggered something. Something Ariaura wouldn't know. About a baby. Had Mencken had a nickname when he was a baby? No, that wasn't it—

"Or what he got for Christmas when he was ten," Kildy said. "We need to find a question Mencken would absolutely know the answer to, and if he doesn't, it proves it's Ariaura."

"And if he does, it still doesn't prove it's Mencken. Right?"

"I'll go talk to Riata about getting a private audience," she said, stuffed the transcripts in her tote, and put on her sunglasses. "And I'll pick up the videotape. I'll see you tomorrow morning."

"Right, Kildy?" I insisted.

"Right," she said, her hand on the door. "I guess."

In the highest confidence there is always a flavor of doubt—a feeling, half instinctive and half logical, that, after all, the scoundrel may have something up his sleeve.

—H. L. MENCKEN

After Kildy left, I called up a computer-hacker friend of mine and put him to work on the problem and then phoned a guy I knew in the English department at UCLA.

"Inquiries about Mencken?" he said. "Not that I know of, Rob. You might try the journalism department."

The guy at the journalism department said, "Who?" and, when I explained, suggested I call Johns Hopkins in Baltimore.

And what had I been thinking? Kildy said Ariaura had started doing Mencken in Seattle. I needed to be checking there, or in Salem or—where had she gone after that? Sedona. I spent the rest of the day (and evening) calling bookstores and reference librarians in all three places. Five of them responded "Who?" and all of them asked me how to spell "Mencken," which might or might not mean they hadn't heard the name lately, and only seven of the thirty bookstores stocked any books on him. Half of those were the latest Mencken biography, which for an excited moment I thought might have answered the question, "Why Mencken?"—the title of it was *Skeptic and Prophet*—but it had only been out two weeks. None of the bookstores could give me any information on orders or recent purchases, and the public libraries couldn't give me any information at all.

I tried their electronic card catalogues, but they only showed currently checked-out books. I called up the L.A. Public Library's catalogue. It showed four Mencken titles checked out, all from the Beverly Hills branch.

"Which looks promising," I told Kildy when she came in the next morning.

"No, it doesn't," she said. "I'm the one who checked them out, to compare the transcripts against." She pulled a sheaf of papers out of her designer tote. "I need to talk to you about the transcripts. I found something interesting. I know," she said, anticipating my objection, "you said all it proved was that Ariaura—"

"Or whoever's feeding this stuff to her."

She acknowledged that with a nod. "—all it proved was that whoever was doing it was reading Mencken, and I agree, but you'd expect her to quote him back verbatim, wouldn't you?"

"Yes," I said, thinking of Randall Mars's Lincoln and his "Four score and seven . . ."

"But she doesn't. Look, here's what she said when we asked him about William Jennings Bryan: 'Bryan! I don't even want to hear that mangy old mountebank's name mentioned. That scoundrel had a malignant hatred of science and sense.'"

"And he didn't say that?"

"Yes and no. Mencken called him a 'walking malignancy' and said he was 'mangy and flea-bitten' and had 'an almost pathological hatred of all learning.' And the rest of the answers, and the things she said at the seminars, are like that, too."

"So she mixed and matched his phrases," I said, but what she'd found was disturbing. Someone trying to pull off an impersonation would stick to the script, since any deviations from Mencken's actual words could be used as proof it wasn't him.

And the annotated list Kildy handed me was troubling in another way. The phrases hadn't been taken from one or two sources. They were from all over the map—"complete hooey" from *Minority Report*, "buncombe" from *The New Republic*, "as truthful as Lydia Pinkham's Vegetable Compound" from an article on pedagogy in the *Sun*.

"Could they all have been in a Mencken biography?"

She shook her head. "I checked. I found a couple of sources that had several of them, but no one source that had them all."

"That doesn't mean there isn't one," I said, and changed the subject. "Was your friend able to get a private audience with Ariaura?"

"Yes," she said, glancing at her watch. "I have to go meet her in a few minutes. She also got tickets to the seminar Saturday. They didn't cancel it like I thought they would, but they did cancel a local radio interview she was supposed to do last night and the weeklong spiritual immersion she had scheduled for next week."

"Did Riata give you the recording of Ariaura's last seminar?"

"No, she'd left it at home. She said she'd bring it when we meet before her private audience. She said she got some really good footage of the emcee. She swears from the way he looked that he's not in on the scam. And there's something else. I called Judy Helzberg, who goes to every psychic event there is. Remember? I interviewed her when we did the piece on shamanic astrologers. And she said Ariaura called her and asked her for Wilson Amboy's number."

"Wilson Amboy?"

"Beverly Hills psychiatrist."

"It's all part of the illusion," I said, but even I sounded a little doubtful. It was an awfully good deception for a third-rate channeler like Ariaura.

There's somebody else in on it, I thought, and not just somebody feeding her answers. A partner. A mastermind.

After Kildy left I called Marty Rumboldt and asked him if Ariaura had had a partner in Salem. "Not that I know of," he said. "Prentiss just did a study on witchcraft in Salem. She might know somebody who would know. Hang on. Hey, Prentiss!" I could hear him call. "Jamie!"

Jamie, I thought. That had been James M. Cain's nickname, and Mencken had been good friends with him. Where had I read that?

"She said to call Madame Orima," Marty said, getting back on the phone, and gave me the number.

I started to dial it and then stopped and looked up "Cain, James M." in Mencken's biography. It said he and Mencken had worked on the Baltimore *Sun* together, that they had been good friends, that Mencken had helped him get his first story collection published: *The Baby in the Icebox.*

I went over to the bookcase, squatted down, and started through the row of paperbacks on the bottom shelf . . . Chandler, Hammett . . . It had a red cover, with a picture of a baby in a high chair and a . . . Chandler, Cain . . .

But no red. I scanned the titles—*Double Indemnity, The Postman Always Rings Twice* . . . Here it was, stuck behind *Mildred Pierce* and not red at all. *The Baby in the Icebox.* It was a lurid orange and yellow, and had pictures of a baby in its mother's arms and a cigarette-smoking lug in front of a gas station. I hoped I remembered the inside better than the outside.

I did. The introduction was by Roy Hoopes, and it was not only a Penguin edition, but one that had been out of print for at least twenty years. Even if Ariaura's researcher had bothered to check out Cain, it would hardly be this edition.

And the introduction was full of stuff about Cain that was perfect— the fact that everyone who knew him called him Jamie, the fact that he'd spent a summer in a tuberculosis sanitarium and that he hated Baltimore, Mencken's favorite place.

Some of the information was in the Mencken books—Mencken's introducing him to Alfred A. Knopf, who'd published that first collection, the *Sun* connection, their rivalry over movie star Aileen Pringle.

But most of the facts in the introduction weren't, and they were exactly the kind of thing a friend would know. And Ariaura wouldn't, because they were details about Cain's life, not Mencken's. Even a mastermind wouldn't have memorized every detail of Cain's life or those of Mencken's other famous friends. If there wasn't anything here I could use, there might be something in Dreiser's biography, or F. Scott Fitzgerald's. Or Lillian Gish's.

But there was plenty here, like the fact that James M. Cain's brother Boydie had died in a tragic accident after the Armistice, and his statement that all his writing was modeled on *Alice in Wonderland*. That was something no one would ever guess from reading Cain's books, which were all full of crimes and murderers and beautiful, calculating women who seduced the hero into helping her with a scam and then turned out to be working a scam of her own.

Not exactly the kind of thing Ariaura would read, and definitely the kind of thing Mencken *would* have. He'd bought *The Baby in the Icebox* for *The American Mercury* and told Cain it was one of the best things he'd ever written. Which meant it would make a perfect source for a question, and I knew just what to ask. To anyone who hadn't heard of the story, the question wouldn't even make sense. Only somebody who'd read the story would know the answer. Like Mencken.

And if Ariaura knew it, I'd—what? Believe she was actually channeling Mencken?

Right. And Charles Fred was really talking to the dead and Uri Geller was really bending spoons. It was a trick, that was all. She had a photographic memory, or somebody was feeding her the answers.

Feeding her the answers.

I thought suddenly of Kildy saying, "Who *was* Sue Hicks?"—of her insisting I go with her to see Ariaura—of her saying, "But why would Ariaura channel a spirit who yells at her audiences?"

I looked down at the orange and yellow paperback in my hand. "A beautiful, calculating woman who seduces the hero into helping her with a scam," I murmured, and thought about Ariaura's movie-star-handsome ushers and about scantily clad Victorian spirits and about Sir William Crookes.

Sex. Get the chump emotionally involved and he won't see the wires. It was the oldest trick in the book.

I'd said Ariaura wasn't smart enough to pull off such a complicated scam, and she wasn't. But Kildy was. So you get her on the inside where she can see the shelf full of Mencken books, where she can hear the chump mutter, "Where the hell is Mencken when we need him?" You get the chump to trust her, and if he falls in love with her, so much the better. It'll keep him off balance and he won't get suspicious.

And it all fit. It was Kildy who'd set up the contact—I never did channelers, and Kildy knew that. It was Kildy who'd said we couldn't go incognito, Kildy who'd said to bring the Sony, knowing it would be confiscated, Kildy who'd taken a taxi to the seminar instead of coming in her Jaguar so she'd be at the office when Ariaura came roaring in.

But she'd gotten the whole thing on tape. And she hadn't had any idea who the spirit was. I was the one who'd figured out it was Mencken.

With Kildy feeding me clues from the seminar she'd gone to before, and I only had her word that Ariaura had channeled him that

time. And that it had happened in Berkeley and Seattle. And that the
tapes had been edited.

And she was the one who'd kept telling me it was really Mencken,
the one who'd come up with the idea of asking him questions that
would prove it—questions I'd conveniently told her the answers to—the
one who'd suggested a friend of hers go to the seminar and videotape it,
a videotape I'd never seen. I wondered if it—or Riata—even existed.

The whole thing, from beginning to end, had been a setup.

And I had never tumbled to it. Because I'd been too busy looking
at her legs and her honey-colored hair and that smile. Just like Crookes.

I don't believe it, I thought. Not Kildy, who'd worked side by side
with me for nearly a year, who'd stolen chicken guts and pretended to
be hypnotized and let Jean-Pierre cleanse her aura, who'd come to work
for me in the first place because she hated scam artists like Ariaura.

Right. Who'd come to work for a two-bit magazine when she could
have been getting five million a movie and dating Viggo Mortensen.
Who'd been willing to give up premieres and summers in Tahiti and
deep massages for me. Skeptics' Rule Number Two: If it seems too good
to be true, it is. And how often have you said she's a good actress?

No, I thought, every bone in my body rebelling. It can't be true.

And that's what the chump always says, isn't it, even when he's
faced with the evidence? "I don't believe it. She wouldn't do that to
me."

And that was the whole point—to get you to trust her, to make you
believe she was on your side. Otherwise you'd have insisted on checking
those tapes of Ariaura's seminars for yourself to see if they'd been edited, you'd have demanded independently verifiable evidence that Ariaura had really canceled those seminars and asked about a psychiatrist.

Independently verifiable evidence. That's what I needed, and I
knew exactly where to look.

"My mother took me to Lucius Windfire's luminescence reading,"
Kildy had said, and I had the guest lists for those readings. They were
part of the court records, and I'd gotten them when I'd done the story

on his arrest. Kildy had come to see me on May tenth and he'd only had two seminars that month.

I called up the lists for both seminars and for the two before that and typed in Kildy's name.

Nothing.

She said she went with her mother, I thought, and typed her mom's name in. Nothing. And nothing when I printed out the lists and went through them by hand, nothing when I went through the lists for March and April. And June. And no ten-thousand-dollar donation on any of Windfire, Inc.'s financial statements.

Half an hour later Kildy showed up smiling, beautiful, full of news. "Ariaura's canceled all the private sessions she scheduled and the rest of her tour."

She leaned over my shoulder to look at what I was doing. "Did you come up with a foolproof question for Mencken?"

"No," I said, sliding *The Baby in the Icebox* under a file folder and sticking them both in a drawer. "I came up with a theory about what's going on, though."

"Really?" she said.

"Really. You know, one of my big problems all along has been Ariaura. She's just not smart enough to have come up with all this—the 'aught-four' thing, the not being able to read, the going to see a psychiatrist. Which either meant she was actually channeling Mencken, or there was some other factor. And I think I've got it figured out."

"You have?"

"Yeah. Tell me what you think of this: Ariaura wants to be big. Not just seven-hundred-and-fifty-a-pop seminars and sixty-dollar video-tapes, but *Oprah,* the *Today* show, *Larry King,* the whole works. But to do that it's not enough to have audiences who believe her. She needs to have somebody with credibility say she's for real, a scientist, say, or a professional skeptic."

"Like you," she said cautiously.

"Like me. Only I don't believe in astral spirits. Or channelers. And

I certainly wouldn't fall for the spirit of an ancient priest of Atlantis. It's going to have to be somebody a charlatan would never dream of channeling, somebody who'll say what I want to hear. And somebody I know a lot about so I'll recognize the clues being fed to me, somebody custom-tailored for me."

"Like H. L. Mencken," Kildy said. "But how would she have known you were a fan of Mencken's?"

"She didn't have to," I said. "That was her partner's job."

"Her part—"

"Partner, sidekick, shill, whatever you want to call it. Somebody I'd trust when she said it was important to go see some channeler."

"Let me get this straight," she said. "You think I went to Ariaura's seminar and her imitation of Isus was so impressive I immediately became a Believer with a capital *B* and fell in with her nefarious scheme, whatever it is?"

"No," I said. "I think you were in it with her from the beginning, from the very first day you came to work for me."

She really was a good actress. The expression in those beautiful blue eyes looked exactly like stunned hurt. "You believe I set you up," she said wonderingly.

I shook my head. "I'm a skeptic, remember? I deal in independently verifiable evidence. Like this," I said, and handed her Lucius Windfire's attendance list.

She looked at it in silence.

"Your whole story about how you found out about me was a fake, wasn't it? You didn't look up 'debunkers' in the phone book, did you? You didn't go see a luminescence therapist with your mother?"

"No."

No.

I hadn't realized till she admitted it how much I had been counting on her saying, "There must be some mistake, I was there," on her having some excuse, no matter how phony: "Did I say the fourteenth? I meant the twentieth," or "My publicist got the tickets for us. It would be in her name." Anything. Even flinging the list dramatically at me and sobbing, "I can't believe you don't trust me."

But she just stood there, looking at the incriminating list and then at me, not a tantrum or a tear in sight.

"You concocted the whole story," I said finally.

"Yes."

I waited for her to say, "It's not the way it looks, Rob, I can explain," but she didn't say that, either. She handed the list back to me and picked up her cell phone and her bag, fishing for her keys and then slinging her bag over her shoulder as casually as if she were on her way to go cover a new moon ceremony or a tarot reading, and left.

And this was the place in the story where the private eye takes a bottle of Scotch out of his bottom drawer, pours himself a nice stiff drink, and congratulates himself on his narrow escape.

I'd almost been made a royal chump of, and Mencken (the real one, not the imitation Kildy and Ariaura had tried to pass off as him) would never have forgiven me.

So good riddance. And what I needed to do now was write up the whole sorry scam as a lesson to other skeptics for the next issue.

But I sat there a good fifteen minutes, thinking about Kildy and her exit, and knowing that, in spite of its offhandedness, I was never going to see her again.

What I need is a miracle.

—Inherit the Wind

I told you I'd make a lousy psychic. The next morning Kildy walked in carrying an armload of papers and file folders. She dumped them in front of me on my desk, picked up my phone, and began punching in numbers.

"What the hell do you think you're doing? And what's all this?" I said, gesturing at the stack of papers.

"Independently verifiable evidence," she said, still punching in numbers, and put the phone to her ear. "Hello, this is Kildy Ross. I need to speak to Ariaura." There was a pause. "She's not taking calls? All right, tell her I'm at the *Jaundiced Eye* office, and I need to speak to her as soon as possible. Tell her it's urgent. Thank you." She hung up.

"What the hell do you think you're doing, calling Ariaura on my phone?" I said.

"I wasn't," she said. "I was calling Mencken." She pulled a file out of the middle of the stack. "I'm sorry it took me so long. Getting Ariaura's phone records was harder than I thought."

"Ariaura's phone records?"

"Yeah. Going back four years," she said, pulling a file folder out of the middle of the stack and handing it to me.

I opened it up. "How did you get her phone records?"

"I know this computer guy at Pixar. We should do an issue on how easy it is to get hold of private information and how mediums are using it to convince their people they're talking to their dead relatives," she said, fishing through the stack for another folder.

"And here are my phone records." She handed it to me. "The cell's on top, and then my home number and my car phone. And my mom's. And my publicist's cell phone."

"Your publicist's cell—?"

She nodded. "In case you think I used her phone to call Ariaura. She doesn't have a regular phone, just a cell. And here are my dad's and my stepmother's. I can get my other stepmothers', too, but it'll take a couple more days, and Ariaura's big seminar is tonight."

She handed me more files. "This is a list of all my trips—airline tickets, hotel bills, rental car records. Credit card bills, with annotations," she said, and went over to her tote bag and pulled out three fat Italian-leather notebooks with a bunch of Post-its sticking out the sides.

"These are my day planners, with notes as to what the abbreviations mean, and my publicist's log."

"And this is supposed to prove you were at Lucius Windfire's luminescence reading with your mother?"

"No, Rob, I told you, I lied about the seminar," she said, looking earnestly through the stack, folder by folder. "These are to prove I didn't call Ariaura, that she didn't call me, that I wasn't in Seattle or Eugene or any of the other cities she was in, and I never went to Salem."

She pulled a folder out of the pile and began handing items to me. "Here's the program for Yogi Magaputra's matinee performance for May nineteenth. I couldn't find the ticket stubs and I didn't buy the tickets, the studio did, but here's a receipt for the champagne cocktail I had at intermission. See? It's got the date and it was at the Roosevelt, and here's a schedule of Magaputra's performances, showing he was at the Roosevelt on that day. And a flyer for the next session they gave out as we left."

I had one of those flyers in my file on mediums, and I was pretty sure I'd been at that séance. I'd gone to three, working on a piece on his use of funeral home records to obtain information on his victims' dead relatives. I'd never published it—he'd been arrested on tax evasion charges before I finished it. I looked questioningly at Kildy.

"I was there researching a movie I was thinking about doing," Kildy said, "a comedy about a medium. It was called *Medium Rare*. Here's the screenplay."

She handed me a thick bound manuscript. "I wouldn't read the whole thing. It's terrible. Anyway, I saw you there, talking to this guy with hair transplants—"

Magaputra's personal manager, who I'd suspected was feeding him info from the audience. I'd been trying to see if I could spot his concealed mike.

"I saw you talking to him, and I thought you looked—"

"Gullible?"

Her jaw tightened. "No. Interesting. Cute. Not the kind of guy I expected to see at one of the yogi's séances. I asked who you were, and somebody said you were a professional skeptic, and I thought, Well, thank goodness! Magaputra was *patently* fake, and everyone was buying it, lock, stock, and barrel."

"Including your mother," I said.

"No, I made that up, too. My mother's even more of a skeptic than I am, especially after being married to my father. She's partly why I was interested—she's always after me to date guys from outside the movie business—so I bought a copy of *The Jaundiced Eye* and got your address and came to see you."

"And lied."

"Yes," she said. "It was a dumb thing to do. I knew it as soon as you started talking about how you shouldn't take anything anyone tells you on faith and how important independently verifiable evidence is, but I was afraid if I told you I was doing research for a movie you wouldn't want me tagging along, and if I told you I was attracted to you, you wouldn't believe me. You'd think it was a reality show or some kind of Hollywood fad thing everybody was doing right then, like opening a boutique or knitting or checking into Betty Ford."

"And you fully intended to tell me," I said, "you were just waiting for the right moment. In fact, you were all set to when Ariaura came along—"

"You don't have to be sarcastic," she said. "I thought if I went to work for you and you got to know me, you might stop thinking of me as a movie star and ask me out—"

"And incidentally pick up some good acting tips for your medium movie."

"Yes," she said angrily. "If you want to know the truth, I also thought if I kept going to those stupid past-life regression sessions and covens and soul retrieval circles, I might get over the stupid crush I had on you, but the better I got to know you, the worse it got."

She looked up at me. "I know you don't believe me, but I didn't set you up. I'd never seen Ariaura before I went to that first seminar with my publicist, and I'm not in any kind of scam with her. And that story I told you the first day is the only thing I've ever lied to you about. Everything else I told you—about hating psychics and Ben Affleck and wanting to get out of the movie business and wanting to help you debunk charlatans and loathing the idea of ending up in rehab or in *The Hulk IV*—was true."

She rummaged in the pile and pulled out an olive-green-covered script. "They really did offer me the part."

"Of the Hulk?"

"No," she said and held the script out to me. "Of the love interest."

She looked up at me with those blue eyes of hers, and if anything had ever been too good to be true, it was Kildy, standing there with that bilious green script and the office's fluorescent light on her golden hair. I had always wondered how all those chumps sitting around séance tables and squatting on lilac-colored cushions could believe such obvious nonsense. Well, now I knew.

Because standing there right then, knowing it all had to be a scam, that the *Hulk IV* script and the credit card bills and the phone bills didn't prove a thing, that they could easily have been faked and I was nothing more than a prize chump being set up for the big finale by a couple of pros, I still wanted to believe it. And not just the researching-a-movie alibi, but the whole thing—that H. L. Mencken had come back from the grave, that he was here to help me crusade against charlatans, that if I grabbed the wrist holding that script and pulled Kildy toward me and kissed her, we would live happily ever after.

And no wonder Mencken, railing against creationists and chiropractic and Mary Baker Eddy, hadn't gotten anywhere. What chance do facts and reason possibly have against what people desperately need to believe?

Only Mencken hadn't come back. A third-rate channeler was only pretending to be him, and Kildy's protestations of love, much as I wanted to hear them, were the oldest trick in the book.

"Nice try," I said.

"But you don't believe me," she said bleakly, and Ariaura walked in.

"I got your message," she said to Kildy in Mencken's gravelly voice. "I came as soon as I could." She plunked down in a chair facing me. "Those goons of Ariaura's—"

"You can knock off the voices, Ariaura," I said. "The jig, as Mencken would say, is up."

Ariaura looked inquiringly at Kildy.

"Rob thinks Ariaura's a fake," Kildy said.

Ariaura switched her gaze to me. "You just figured that out? Of course she's a fake, she's a bamboozling mountebank, an oleaginous—"

"He thinks you're not real," Kildy said. "He thinks you're just a voice Ariaura does, like Isus, that your disrupting her seminars is a trick to convince him she's an authentic channeler, and he thinks I'm in on the plot with you, that I helped you set him up."

Here it comes, I thought. Shocked outrage. Affronted innocence. Kildy's a total stranger, I've never seen her before in my life!

"He thinks that you—?" Ariaura hooted and banged the arms of the chair with glee. "Doesn't the poor fish know you're in love with him?"

"He thinks that's part of the scam," Kildy said earnestly. "The only way he'll believe I am is if he believes there *is* no scam, if he believes you're really Mencken."

"Well, then," Ariaura said and grinned, "I guess we'll have to convince him." He slapped his knees and turned expectantly to me. "What do you want to know, sir? I was born in 1880 at nine P.M., right before the police went out and raided ten or twenty saloons, and went to work at the *Morning Herald* at the tender age of eighteen—"

"Where you laid siege to the editor Max Ways for four straight weeks before he gave you an assignment," I said, "but my knowing that doesn't any more make me Henry Lawrence Mencken than it does you."

"Henry *Louis*," Ariaura said, "after an uncle of mine who died when he was a baby. All right, you set the questions."

"It's not that simple," Kildy said. She pulled a chair up in front of

Ariaura and sat down, facing her. She took both hands in hers. "To prove you're Mencken you can't just answer questions. The skeptic's first rule is: 'Extraordinary claims require extraordinary evidence.' You've got to do something extraordinary."

"And independently verifiable," I said.

"Extraordinary," Ariaura said, looking at Kildy. "I presume you're not talking about handling snakes. Or speaking in tongues."

"No," I said.

"The problem is, if you prove you're Mencken," Kildy said earnestly, "then you're also proving that Ariaura's really channeling astral spirits, which means she's not—"

"—the papuliferous poser I know her to be."

"Exactly," Kildy said, "and her career will skyrocket."

"Along with that of every other channeler and psychic and medium out there," I said.

"Rob's put his entire life into trying to debunk these people," Kildy said. "If you prove Ariaura's really channeling—"

"The noble calling of skepticism will be dealt a heavy blow," Ariaura said thoughtfully, "hardly the outcome a man like Mencken would want. So the only way I can prove who I am is to keep silent and go back to where I came from."

Kildy nodded.

"But I came to try and stop her. If I return to the ether, Ariaura will go right back to spreading her pernicious astral-plane-Higher-Wisdom hokum and bilking her benighted audiences out of their cash."

Kildy nodded again. "She might even pretend she's channeling you."

"*Pretend!*" Ariaura said, outraged. "I won't allow it! I'll—" and then stopped. "But if I speak out, I'm proving the very thing I'm trying to debunk. And if I don't—"

"Rob will never trust me again," Kildy said.

"So," Ariaura said, "it's—"

A catch-22, I thought, and then, if she says that, I've got her—the book wasn't written till 1961, five years after Mencken had died. And "catch-22" was the kind of thing, unlike "Bible Belt" or "booboisie," that even Kildy wouldn't have thought of, it had become such an ingrained part of the language. I listened, waiting for Ariaura to say it.

"—a conundrum," she said.

"A what?" Kildy said.

"A puzzle with no solution, a hand there's no way to win, a hellacious dilemma."

"You're saying it's impossible," Kildy said hopelessly.

Ariaura shook her head. "I've had tougher assignments than this. There's bound to be something—" She turned to me. "She said something about 'the skeptic's first rule.' Are there any others?"

"Yes," I said. "If it seems too good to be true, it is."

"And 'By their fruits shall ye know them,'" Kildy said. "It's from the Bible."

"The Bible . . ." Ariaura said, narrowing her eyes thoughtfully. "The Bible . . . how much time have we got? When's Ariaura's next show?"

"Tonight," Kildy said, "but she canceled the last one. What if she—"

"What time?" Ariaura cut in.

"Eight o'clock."

"Eight o'clock," she repeated, and made a motion toward her midsection for all the world as if she was reaching for a pocket watch. "You two be out there, front row center."

"What are you doing to do?" Kildy asked hopefully.

"I dunno," Ariaura said. "Sometimes you don't have to do a damned thing—they do it to themselves. Look at that High Muckitymuck of Hot Air, Bryan." She laughed. "Either of you know where I can get some rope?"

She didn't wait for an answer. "I'd better get on it. There's only a couple hours to deadline—" She slapped her knees. "Front row center," she said to Kildy. "Eight o'clock."

"What if she won't let us in?" Kildy asked. "Ariaura said she was going to get a restraining order against—"

"She'll let you in. Eight o'clock."

Kildy nodded. "I'll be there, but I don't know if Rob—"

"Oh, I wouldn't miss this for the world," I said.

Ariaura ignored my tone. "Bring a notebook," she ordered. "And in the meantime, you'd better get busy on your charlatan debunking. The sons of bitches are gaining on us."

One sits through long sessions . . . and then suddenly there comes a show so gaudy and hilarious, so melodramatic and obscene, so unimaginably exhilarating and preposterous that one lives a gorgeous year in an hour.

—H. L. MENCKEN

An hour later, a messenger showed up with a manila envelope. In it was a square vellum envelope sealed with pink sealing wax and embossed with Isus's hieroglyphs. Inside that were a lilac card printed in silver with "The pleasure of your company is requested . . ." and two tickets to the seminar.

"Is the invitation signed?" Kildy asked.

She'd refused to leave after Ariaura, still acting the part of Mencken, had departed. "I'm staying right here with you till the seminar," she'd said, perching herself on my desk. "It's the only way I can prove I'm not off somewhere with Ariaura cooking up some trick. And here's my phone," she'd handed me her cell phone, "so you won't think I'm sending her secret messages via text message or something. Do you want to check me to see if I'm wired?"

"No."

"Do you need any help?" she'd asked, picking up a pile of proofs. "Do you want me to go over these, or am I fired?"

"I'll let you know after the seminar."

She'd given me a Julia-Roberts-radiant smile and retreated to the far end of the office with the proofs, and I'd called up Charles Fred's file and started through it, looking for leads and trying not to think about Ariaura's parting shot.

I was positive I'd never told Kildy that story about Mencken saying, "The sons of bitches are gaining on us," and it wasn't in Daniels's biography, or Hobson's. The only place I'd ever seen it was in an article in *The Atlantic Monthly*. I looked it up in Bartlett's, but it wasn't there. I Googled "Mencken bitches." Nothing.

Which didn't prove anything. Ariaura—or Kildy—could have read it in *The Atlantic Monthly* just like I had. And since when had H. L. Mencken looked to the Bible for inspiration? That remark alone proved it wasn't Mencken, didn't it?

On the other hand, he hadn't said "catch-22," although "conundrum" wasn't nearly as precise a word. And he hadn't said William Jennings Bryan, he'd said "that High Muckitymuck of Hot Air, Bryan," which I hadn't read anywhere, but which sounded like something he would have put in that scathing obituary he'd written of Bryan.

And this wasn't going anywhere. There was nothing, short of a heretofore undiscovered manuscript or a will in his handwriting leaving everything to Lillian Gish—no, that wouldn't work. The aphasic stroke, remember?—that would prove it was Mencken. And both of those could be faked, too.

And there wasn't anything that could do what Kildy had told him he—correction, told Ariaura *she*—had to do: Prove he was real without proving Ariaura was legit. Which she clearly wasn't.

I'd gotten out Ariaura's transcripts and read through them, looking for I wasn't sure what, until the tickets had come.

"Is the card signed?" Kildy asked again.

"No," I said and handed it to her.

"'The pleasure of your company is requested' is printed on," she said, turning the invitation over to look at the back. "What about the address on the envelope?"

"There isn't one," I said, seeing where she was going with this.

"But just because it's not handwritten, that doesn't prove it's from Mencken."

"I know. 'Extraordinary claims.' But at least it's consistent with its being Mencken."

"It's also consistent with the two of you trying to convince me it's Mencken so I'll go to that seminar tonight."

"You think it's a trap?" Kildy said.

"Yes," I said, but standing there staring at the tickets, I had no idea what kind. Ariaura couldn't possibly still be hoping I'd stand up and shout, "By George, she's the real thing! She's channeling Mencken!" no matter what anecdote she quoted. I wondered if her lawyers might be intending to slap me with a restraining order or a subpoena when I walked in, but that made no sense. She knew my address—she'd been here this very afternoon, and I'd been here most of the past two days. Besides, if she had me arrested, the press would be clamoring to talk to me, and she wouldn't want me voicing my suspicions of a con game to the *L.A. Times.*

When Kildy and I left for the seminar an hour and a half later (on our way out, I'd pretended I forgot my keys and left Kildy standing in the hall while I went back in, bound *The Baby in the Icebox* with Scotch tape, and hid it down behind the bookcase), I still hadn't come up with a plausible theory, and the Santa Monica Hilton, where the seminar was being held, didn't yield any clues.

It had the same "Believe and It Will Happen" banner, the same Tom Cruiseish bodyguards, the same security check. They confiscated my Olympus and my digital recorder and Kildy's Hasaka (and asked for her autograph), and we went through the same crystal/pyramid/amulet-crammed waiting area into the same lilac-and-rose-draped ballroom. With the same hard, bare floor.

"Oh, I forgot to bring pillows, I'm sorry," Kildy said and started toward the ushers and stacks of lilac plastic cushions at the rear. Halfway there she turned around and came back. "I don't want to have had an opportunity to send some kind of secret message to Ariaura," she said. "If you want to come with me . . ."

I shook my head. "The floor'll be good," I said, lowering myself to the wooden surface. "It may actually keep me in touch with reality."

Kildy sat down effortlessly beside me, opened her bag, and fumbled in it for her mirror. I looked around. The crowd seemed a little sparser, and somewhere behind us, I heard a woman say, "It was *so* bizarre. Romtha never did anything like that. I wonder if she's drinking."

The lights went pink, the music swelled, and Brad Pitt came out, went through the same spiel (no flash photography, no applause, no bathroom breaks) and the same intro (Atlantis, Oracle of Delphi, Cosmic All), and revealed Ariaura, standing at the top of the same black stairway.

She was exactly the same as she had been at that first seminar, dramatically regal in her purple robes and amulets, serene as she acknowledged the audience's applause. The events of the past few days—her roaring into my office, asking frightenedly, "What's happening? Where am I?" and slapping her knees and exploding with laughter—might never have happened.

And obviously were a fake, I thought grimly. I glanced at Kildy. She was still fishing unconcernedly in her bag.

"Welcome, Seekers after Divine Truth," Ariaura said. "We're going to have a wonderful spiritual experience together here today. It's a very special day. This is my one hundredth 'Believe and It Will Happen' seminar."

Lots of applause, which after a couple of minutes she motioned to stop.

"In honor of the anniversary, Isus and I want to do something a little different today."

More applause. I glanced at the ushers. They were looking nervously at each other, as if they expected her to start spouting Menckenese, but the voice was clearly Ariaura's and so was the Oprah-perky manner.

"My—*our*—seminars are usually pretty structured. They have to be—if the auratic vibrations aren't exactly right beforehand, the spirits cannot come, and after I've channeled, I'm physically and spiritually exhausted, so I rarely have the opportunity to just *talk* to you. But to-day's a special occasion. So I'd like the tech crew"—she looked up at the control booth—"to bring up the lights—"

There was a pause, as if the tech crew was debating whether to fol-low orders, and then the lights came up.

"Thanks, that's perfect, you can have the rest of the day off," Ari-aura said. She turned to the emcee. "That goes for you, too, Ken. And my fabulous ushers—Derek, Jared, Tad—let's hear it for the great job they do."

She led a round of applause and then, since the ushers continued to stand there at the doors, looking warily at each other and at the emcee, she made shooing motions with her hands. "Go on. Scoot. I want to talk to these people in private," and when they still hesitated, "You'll still get paid for the full seminar. Go on."

She walked over to the emcee and said something to him, smiling, and it must have reassured him because he nodded to the ushers and then up at the control room, and the ushers went out.

I looked over at Kildy. She was calmly applying lipstick. I looked back at the stage.

"Are you sure—?" I could see the emcee whisper to Ariaura.

"I'm *fine*," she mouthed back at him.

The emcee frowned and then stepped off the stage and over to the side door, and the cameraman at the back began taking his videocam off its tripod. "No, no, Ernesto, not you," Ariaura said. "Keep filming."

She waited as the emcee pulled the last door shut behind him and then walked to the front of the stage and stood there completely silent, her arms stiffly at her sides.

Kildy leaned close to me, her lipstick still in her hand. "Are you thinking the prom scene in *Carrie*?"

I nodded, gauging our distance to the emergency exit. There was a distant sound of a door shutting above us—the control room—and Ari-aura clasped her hands together. "Alone at last," she said, smiling. "I thought they'd *never* leave."

Laughter.

"And now that they're gone, I have to say this—" She paused dramatically. "Aren't they *gorgeous?*"

Laughter, applause, and several whistles. Ariaura waited till the noise had died down and then asked, "How many of you were at my seminar last Saturday?"

The mood changed instantly. Several hands went up, but tentatively, and two hoop-earringed women looked at each other with the same nervous glance as the ushers had had.

"Or at the one two weeks ago?" Ariaura asked.

Another couple of hands.

"Well, for those of you who weren't at either, let's just say that lately my seminars have been rather . . . interesting, to put it mildly."

Scattered nervous laughter.

"And those of you familiar with the spirit world know that's what can happen when we try to make contact with energies beyond our earthly plane. The astral plane can be a dangerous place. There are spirits there beyond our control, false spirits who seek to keep us from enlightenment."

False spirits is right, I thought.

"But I fear them not, for my weapon is the Truth." She somehow managed to say it with a capital *T.*

I looked over at Kildy. She was leaning forward the way she had at that first seminar, intent on Ariaura's words. She was still holding her mirror and lipstick.

"What's she up to?" I whispered to Kildy.

She shook her head, still intent on the stage. "It's not her."

"What?"

"She's channeling."

"Chan—?" I said and looked at the stage.

"No spirit, no matter how dark," Ariaura said, "no matter how dishonest, can stand between me and that Higher Truth."

Applause, more enthusiastic.

"Or keep me from bringing that Truth to all of you." She smiled and spread out her arms. "I'm a fraud, a charlatan, a fake," she said cheerfully. "I've never channeled a cosmic spirit in my life. Isus is something I made up back in 1996, when I was running a pyramid scheme in Dayton, Ohio. The feds were closing in on us, and I'd already been up on charges of mail fraud in '94, so I changed my name—my real name's Bonnie Friehl, by the way, but I was using Doreen Manning in Dayton—and stashed the money in a bank in Chickamauga, Virginia, my hometown, and then moved to Miami Beach and did fortune-telling while I worked on perfecting Isus's voice."

I fumbled for my notebook and pen. Bonnie Friehl, Chickamauga, Miami Beach—

"I did fortune-telling, curses mostly—'Pay me and I'll remove the curse I see hanging over you'—till I had my Isus impersonation ready and then I contacted this guy I knew in Vegas—"

There was an enormous crash from the rear. Ernesto had dropped his shoulder-held video camera and was heading for the door. And this needed to be on film. But I didn't want to miss anything while I tried to figure out how the camera worked.

I glanced over at Kildy, hoping she was taking notes, but she seemed transfixed by what was happening onstage, her forgotten mirror and lipstick still in her hands, her mouth open. I would have to risk missing a few words. I scrambled to my feet.

"Where are you going?" Kildy whispered.

"I've got to get this on tape."

"We are," she said calmly, and nodded imperceptibly at the lipstick and then the mirror, "Audio . . . and video."

"I love you," I said.

She nodded. "You'd better get those names down, just in case the police confiscate my makeup as evidence," she said.

"His name was Chuck Venture," Ariaura was saying. "He and I had worked together on a chain-letter scheme. His real name's Harold Vogel, but you probably know him by the name he uses out here, Charles Fred."

Jesus. I scribbled the names down: Harold Vogel, Chuck Venture—

"We'd worked a couple of chain-letter scams together," Ariaura said, "so I told him I wanted him to take me to Salem and set me up in the channeling business."

There was a clank and a thud as Ernesto made it to the door and out. It slammed shut behind him.

"Harold always did have a bad habit of writing everything down," Ariaura said chattily. " 'You can't blackmail me, Doreen,' he said. 'Wanna bet?' I said. 'It's all in a safety deposit box in Dayton with instructions to open it if anything happens to me.' "

She leaned confidingly forward. "It's not, of course. It's in the safe in my bedroom behind the portrait of Isus. The combination's twelve left, six right, fourteen left." She laughed brightly. "So anyway, he taught me all about how you soften the chumps up in the seminars so they'll tell Isus all about their love life in the private audiences and then send them copies of the videotapes—"

There were several audible gasps behind me and then the beginnings of a murmur, or possibly a growl, but Ariaura paid no attention.

"—and he introduced me to one of the orderlies at New Beginnings Rehab Center, and the deep masseuse at the Willowsage Spa for personal details Isus can use to convince them he knows all, sees all—"

The growl was becoming a roar, but it was scarcely audible over the shouts from outside and the banging on the doors, which were apparently locked from the inside.

"—and how to change my voice and expression to make it look like I'm actually channeling a spirit from beyond—"

It sounded as though the emcee and ushers had found a battering ram. The banging had become shuddering thuds.

"—although I don't think learning all that junk about Lemuria and stuff was necessary," Ariaura said. "I mean, it's obvious you people will believe *anything*."

She smiled beatifically at the audience, as if expecting applause, but the only sound (beside the thuds) was of cell phone keys being hit and women shouting into them. When I glanced back, everybody except Kildy had a phone clapped to their ear.

"Are there any questions?" Ariaura asked brightly.

"Yes," I said. "Are you saying you're the one doing the voice of Isus?"

She smiled pleasedly down at me. "Of course. There's no such thing as channeling spirits from the Great Beyond. Other questions?" She looked past me to the other wildly waving hands. "Yes? The woman in blue?"

"How could you lie to us, you—?"

I stepped adroitly in front of her. "Are you saying Todd Phoenix is a fake, too?"

"Oh, yes," Ariaura said. "They're all fakes—Todd Phoenix, Joye Wildde, Randall Mars. Next question? Yes, Miss Ross?"

Kildy stepped forward, still holding the compact and lipstick. "When was the first time you met me?" she asked.

"You don't have to do this," I said.

"Just for the record," she said, flashing me her radiant smile and then turning back to the stage. "Ariaura, had you ever met me before last week?"

"No," she said. "I saw you at Ari—at my seminar, but I didn't meet you till afterward at the office of *The Jaundiced Eye*, a fine magazine, by the way. I suggest you all take out subscriptions."

"And I'm not your shill?" Kildy persisted.

"No, though I do have them," she said. "The woman in green back there in the sixth row is one," she said, pointing at a plump brunette. "Stand up, Lucy."

Lucy was already scuttling to the door, and so were a thin redhead in a rainbow caftan and an impeccably tailored sixty-year-old in an Armani suit, with a large number of the audience right on their tails.

"Janine's one, too," Ariaura said, pointing at the redhead. "And Doris. They all help gather personal information for Isus to tell them, so it looks like he 'knows all, sees all.'" She laughed delightedly. "Come up onstage and take a bow, girls."

The "girls" ignored her. Doris, a pack of elderly women on her heels, pushed open the middle door and shouted, "You've got to stop her!"

The emcee and ushers began pushing their way through the door and toward the stage. The audience was even more determined to get out than they were to get in, but I still didn't have much time. "Are all the psychics you named using blackmail like you?" I asked.

"Ariaura!" the emcee shouted, halfway to the stage and caught in the flood of women. "Stop talking. Anything you say can be held against you."

"Oh, hi, Ken," she said. "Ken's in charge of laundering all our money. Take a bow, Ken! And you, too, Derek and Tad and Jared," she said, indicating the ushers. "The boys pump the audience for information and feed it to me over this," she said, holding up her sacred amulet.

She looked back at me. "I forgot what you asked."

"Are all the pyschics you named using blackmail like you?"

"No, not all of them. Swami Vishnu Jammi uses post-hypnotic suggestion, and Nadrilene's always used extortion."

"What about Charles Fred? What's his scam?"

"Invest—" Ariaura's pin-on mike went suddenly dead. I looked back at the melee. One of the ushers was proudly holding up an unplugged cord.

"Investment fraud," Ariaura shouted, her hands cupped around her mouth. "Chuck tells his marks their dead relations want them to invest in certain stocks. I'd suggest you—"

One of the ushers reached the stage. He grabbed Ariaura by one arm and tried to grab the other.

"—suggest you check out Metra—" Ariaura shouted, flailing at him. "Metracon, Spirilink—"

A second usher appeared, and the two of them managed to pinion her arms. "Crystalcom, Inc.," she said, kicking out at them, "and Universis. Find out—" She aimed a kick at the groin of one of the ushers that made me flinch. "Get your paws off me."

The emcee stepped in front of her. "That concludes Ariaura's presentation," he said, avoiding her kicking feet. "Thank you all for coming. Videos of—" he said, and then thought better of it, "—personally autographed copies of Ariaura's book, *Believe and—*"

"Find out who the majority stockholder is," Ariaura shrieked, struggling. "And ask Chuck what he knows about a check forgery scam Zolita's running in Reno."

"—*It Will Happen* are on sale in the . . ." the emcee said, and gave up. He grabbed for Ariaura's feet. The three of them wrestled her toward the wings.

"One last question!" I shouted, but it was too late. They already had her off the stage. "Why was the baby in the icebox?"

. . . this is the last time you'll see me . . .

—H. L. MENCKEN

"It still doesn't prove it was Mencken," I told Kildy. "The whole thing could have been a manifestation of Ariaura's—excuse me, Bonnie Friehl's—subconscious, produced by her guilt."

"*Or*," Kildy said, "there could have been a scam just like the one you postulated, only one of the swindlers fell in love with you and decided she couldn't go through with it."

"Nope, that won't work," I said. "She might have been able to talk Ariaura into calling off the scam, but not into confessing all those crimes."

"If she really committed them," Kildy said. "We don't have any independently verifiable evidence that she is Bonnie Friehl yet."

But the fingerprints on her Ohio driver's license matched, and every single lead she'd given us checked out.

We spent the next two months following up on all of them and putting together a massive special issue on "The Great Channeling Swindle." It looked like we were going to have to testify at Ariaura's preliminary hearing, which could have proved awkward, but she and her lawyers got in a big fight over whether or not to use an insanity defense, since she was claiming she'd been possessed by the Spirit of Evil and Darkness, and she ended up firing them and turning state's evidence against Charles Fred, Joye Wildde, and several other psychics she hadn't gotten around to mentioning, and it began to look like the magazine might fold because there weren't any scams left to write about.

Fat chance. Within weeks, new mediums and psychics, advertising themselves as "Restorers of Cosmic Ethics" and "the spirit entity you can trust," moved in to fill the void, and a new weight-loss-through-meditation program began packing them in, promising Low-Carb Essence, and Kildy and I were back in business.

"He didn't make any difference at all," Kildy said disgustedly after a standing-room-only seminar on psychic Botox treatments.

"Yeah, he did," I said. "Charles Fred's up on insider trading charges, attendance is down at the Temple of Cosmic Exploration, and half of L.A.'s psychics are on the lam. And it'll take everybody a while to come up with new methods for separating people from their money."

"I thought you said it wasn't Mencken."

"I said it didn't *prove* it was Mencken. Rule Number One: Extraordinary claims require extraordinary evidence."

"And you don't think what happened on that stage was extraordinary?"

I had to admit it was. "But it could have been Ariaura herself. She didn't say anything she couldn't have known."

"What about her telling us the combination of her safe? And ordering everybody to subscribe to *The Jaundiced Eye*?"

"It still doesn't prove it was Mencken. It could have been some sort of Bridey Murphy phenomenon. Ariaura could have had a babysitter who read the Baltimore *Sun* out loud to her when she was a toddler."

Kildy laughed. "You don't believe that."

"I don't believe anything without proof," I said. "I'm a skeptic, remember? And there's nothing that happened on that stage that couldn't be explained rationally."

"Exactly," Kildy said.

"What do you mean, exactly?"

"By their fruits shall ye know them."

"What?"

"I mean it has to have been Mencken because he did exactly what we asked him to do: Prove it wasn't a scam and he wasn't a fake and Ariaura was. And do it without proving he was Mencken because if he did, then that proved she was on the level. Which *proves* it was Mencken."

There was no good answer to that kind of crazy illogic except to change the subject, which I did. I kissed her.

And then sent the transcripts of Ariaura's outbursts to UCLA to have the language patterns compared to Mencken's writing. Independently verifiable evidence. And got the taped *The Baby in the Icebox* out of its hiding place down behind the bookcase while Kildy was out of the office, took it home, wrapped it in tinfoil, stuck it inside an empty Lean Cuisine box, and hid it—where else?—in the icebox. Old habits die hard.

UCLA sent the transcripts back, saying it wasn't a big enough sample for a conclusive result. So did Caltech. And Duke. So that was that. Which was too bad. It would have been nice to have Mencken back in the fray, even for a little while. He had definitely left too soon.

So Kildy and I would have to pick up where he left off, which meant not only putting "The sons of bitches are gaining on us" on the masthead of *The Jaundiced Eye*, but trying to channel his spirit into every page.

And that didn't just mean exposing shysters and con men. Mencken hadn't been the important force he was because of his rants against creationism and faith healers and patent medicine, but because of what he'd stood for: the truth. That's why he'd hated ignorance and superstition and dishonesty so much, because he loved science and reason and logic, and he'd communicated that love, that passion, to his readers with every word he wrote.

That was what we had to do with *The Jaundiced Eye*. It wasn't enough just to expose Ariaura and Swami Vishnu and psychic dentists and meditation Atkins diets. We also had to make our readers as passionate about science and reason as they were about Romtha and luminescence readings. We had to not only tell the truth, but make our readers want to believe it.

So, as I say, we were pretty busy for the next few months, revamping the magazine, cooperating with the police, and following up on all the leads Ariaura had given us. We went to Vegas to research the chain-letter scam she and Chuck Venture / Charles Fred had run, after which I came home to put the magazine to bed and Kildy went to Dayton and then to Chickamauga to follow up on Ariaura's criminal history.

She called last night. "It's me, Rob," she said, sounding excited. "I'm in Chattanooga."

"Chattanooga, *Tennessee*?" I said. "What are you doing there?"

"The prosecutor working on the pyramid scheme case is on a trip to Roanoke, so I can't see him till Monday, and the school board in Zion—that's a little town near here—is trying to pass a law requiring intelligent design to be taught in the public schools. This Zion thing's part of a nationwide program that's going to introduce intelligent design state by state. So, anyway, since I couldn't see the prosecutor, I thought I'd drive over—it's only about fifty miles from Chickamauga—and interview some of the science teachers for that piece on 'The Scopes Trial Eighty Years Out' you were talking about doing."

"And?" I said warily.

"*And*, according to the chemistry teacher, something peculiar happened at the school board meeting. It might be nothing, but I thought I'd better call so you could be looking up flights to Chattanooga, just in case."

Just in case.

"One of the school board members, a Mr.—" she paused as if consulting her notes, "Horace Didlong, was talking about the lack of scientific proof for Darwin's theory, when he suddenly started ranting at the crowd."

"Did the chemistry teacher say what he said?" I asked, hoping I didn't already know.

"She couldn't remember all of it," Kildy said, "but the basketball coach said some of the students had said they intended to tape the meeting and send it to the ACLU, and he'd try to find out if they did and get me a copy. He said it was 'a very odd outburst, almost like he was possessed.'"

"Or drunk," I said. "And neither of them remembers what he said?"

"No, they both do, just not everything. Didlong apparently went on for several minutes. He said he couldn't believe there were still addle-pated ignoramuses around who didn't believe in evolution, and what the hell had they been teaching in the schools all this time. The chemistry teacher said the rant went on like that for about five minutes and then broke off, right in the middle of a word, and Didlong went back to talking about Newton's Second Law making evolution physically impossible."

"Have you interviewed Didlong?"

"No. I'm going over there as soon as we finish talking, but the chemistry teacher said she heard Didlong's wife ask him what happened, and he looked like he didn't have any idea."

"That doesn't prove it's Mencken," I said.

"I know," she said, "but it *is* Tennessee, and it *is* evolution. And it would be nice if it was him, wouldn't it?"

Nice. H. L. Mencken loose in the middle of Tennessee in the middle of a creationism debate.

"Yeah," I said and grinned, "it would, but it's much more likely Horace Didlong has been smoking something he grew in his backyard. Or is trying to stir up some publicity, à la Judge Roy Moore and his Ten Commandments monument. Do they remember anything else he said?"

"Yes, um . . . where is it?" she said. "Oh, here it is. He called the other board members a gang of benighted rubes . . . and then he said he'd take a monkey any day over a school board whose cerebellums were all paralyzed from listening to too much theological bombast . . . and right at the end, before he broke off, the chemistry teacher said he said, 'I never saw much resemblance to Alice myself.'"

"Alice?" I said. "They're sure he said Alice and not August?"

"Yes, because the chemistry teacher's name is Alice, and she thought he was talking to her, and the chairman of the school board did, too, because he looked at her and said, 'Alice? What the heck does Alice have to do with intelligent design?' and Didlong said, 'Jamie sure could write, though, even if the bastard did steal my girl. You better be careful I don't steal yours.' Do you know what that means, Rob?"

"Yes," I said. "How long does it take to get a marriage license in Tennessee?"

"I'll find out," Kildy said, sounding pleased, "and then the chairman said, 'You cannot use language like that,' and, according to the chemistry teacher, Didlong said . . . wait a minute, I need to read it to you so I get it right—it really didn't make any sense—he said, 'You'd be surprised at what I can do. Like stir up the animals. Speaking of which, that's why the baby was stashed in the icebox. Its mother stuck it inside to keep the tiger from eating it.'"

"I'll be right there," I said.

Afterword for "Inside Job"

I *really* miss H. L. Mencken. I have spent the last forty years (since Nixon and Watergate) following politics, observing my fellow humans, and saying, "*Where* is Mencken when we need him?" And wishing desperately that he'd come back from the grave to say all those things that desperately need saying.

Like:

"The whole aim of practical politics is to keep the populace alarmed (and hence clamorous to be led to safety) by an endless series of hobgoblins, most of them imaginary."

And:

"In this world of sin and sorrow there is always something to be thankful for. As for me, I rejoice that I am not a Republican."

And:

"It may be hard for the average man to believe he is descended from an ape . . . Nevertheless, it is even harder for the average ape to believe that he has descended from man."

I also miss him because he loved language. His book *The American Language* is a masterpiece, and he was the first to document what Mark Twain had understood, that "American" is not "English" but a language all its own.

Most of all, I miss the Mencken who loved women and music and a good, stiff drink and who wrote: *"Life may not be exactly pleasant, but it is at least not dull. Heave yourself into Hell today, and you may miss, tomorrow or next day, another Scopes trial, or another War to End War, or perchance a rich and buxom widow with all her first husband's clothes. There are always more Hardings hatching. I advocate hanging on as long as possible."*

I wish he *had* hung on a bit longer.

But at least we still have his books. And the occasional not-quite-as-phony-as-she-thought channeler.

EVEN THE QUEEN

The phone sang as I was looking over the defense's motion to dismiss. "It's the universal ring," my law clerk Bysshe said, reaching for it. "It's probably the defendant. They don't let you use signatures from jail."

"No, it's not," I said. "It's my mother."

"Oh." Bysshe reached for the receiver. "Why isn't she using her signature?"

"Because she knows I don't want to talk to her. She must have found out what Perdita's done."

"Your daughter Perdita?" he asked, holding the receiver against his chest. "The one with the little girl?"

"No, that's Viola. Perdita's my younger daughter. The one with no sense."

"What's she done?"

"She's joined the Cyclists."

Bysshe looked inquiringly blank, but I was not in the mood to enlighten him. Or in the mood to talk to Mother. "I know exactly what

Mother will say," I told him. "She'll ask me why I didn't tell her, and then she'll demand to know what I'm going to do about it, and there is nothing I *can* do about it, or I obviously would have done it already."

Bysshe looked bewildered. "Do you want me to tell her you're in court?"

"No." I reached for the receiver. "I'll have to talk to her sooner or later." I took it from him. "Hello, Mother," I said.

"Traci," Mother said dramatically, "Perdita has become a Cyclist."

"I know."

"Why didn't you tell me?"

"I thought Perdita should tell you herself."

"Perdita!" She snorted. "She wouldn't tell me. She knows what I'd have to say about it. I suppose you told Karen."

"Karen's not here. She's in Iraq." The only good thing about this whole debacle was that thanks to Iraq's eagerness to show it was a responsible world community member, and its previous penchant for self-destruction, my mother-in-law was in the one place on the planet where the phone service was bad enough that I could claim I'd tried to call her but couldn't get through, and she'd have to believe me.

The Liberation has freed us from all sorts of indignities and scourges, including assorted Saddams, but mothers-in-law aren't one of them, and I was almost happy with Perdita for her excellent timing. When I didn't want to kill her.

"What's Karen doing in Iraq?" Mother asked.

"Negotiating a Palestinian homeland."

"And meanwhile her granddaughter is ruining her life," she said irrelevantly. "Did you tell Viola?"

"I *told* you, Mother. I thought Perdita should tell all of you herself."

"Well, she didn't. And this morning one of my patients, Carol Chen, called me and demanded to know what I was keeping from her. I had no idea what she was talking about."

"How did Carol Chen find out?"

"From her daughter, who almost joined the Cyclists last year. *Her* family talked her out of it," she said accusingly. "Carol was convinced the medical community had discovered some terrible side effect of ammenerol and was covering it up. I cannot believe you didn't tell me, Traci."

And I cannot believe I didn't have Bysshe tell her I was in court, I thought. "I told you, Mother. I thought it was Perdita's place to tell you. After all, it's her decision."

"Oh, Traci!" Mother said. "You cannot mean that!"

In the first fine flush of freedom after the Liberation, I had entertained hopes that it would change everything—that it would somehow do away with inequality and patriarchal dominance and those humorless women determined to eliminate the word "manhole" and third person singular pronouns from the language.

Of course it didn't. Men still make more money, "herstory" is still a blight on the semantic landscape, and my mother can still say, "Oh, *Traci!*" in a tone that reduces me to pre-adolescence.

"*Her* decision!" Mother said. "Do you mean to tell me you plan to stand idly by and allow your daughter to make the mistake of her life?"

"What can I do? She's twenty-two years old and of sound mind."

"If she were of sound mind she wouldn't be doing this. Didn't you try to talk her out of it?"

"Of course I did, Mother."

"And?"

"And I didn't succeed. She's determined to become a Cyclist."

"Well, there must be something we can do. Get an injunction or hire a deprogrammer or sue the Cyclists for brainwashing. You're a judge. There must be some law you can invoke—"

"The law is called personal sovereignty, Mother, and since it was what made the Liberation possible in the first place, it can hardly be used against Perdita. Her decision meets all the criteria for a case of personal sovereignty: It's a personal decision, it was made by a sovereign adult, it affects no one else—"

"What about my practice? Carol Chen is convinced shunts cause cancer."

"Any effect on your practice is considered an indirect effect. Like secondary smoke. It doesn't apply. Mother, whether we like it or not, Perdita has a perfect right to do this, and we don't have any right to interfere. A free society has to be based on respecting others' opinions and leaving each other alone. We have to respect Perdita's right to make her own decisions."

All of which was true. It was too bad I hadn't said any of it to Perdita when she called. What I had said, in a tone that sounded exactly like my mother's, was "Oh, *Perdita*!"

"This is all your fault, you know," Mother said. "I *told* you you shouldn't have let her get that tattoo over her shunt. And don't tell me it's a free society. What good is a free society when it allows my granddaughter to ruin her life?" She hung up.

I handed the receiver back to Bysshe.

"I really liked what you said about respecting your daughter's right to make her own decisions," he said. He held out my robe. "And about not interfering in her life."

"I want you to research the precedents on deprogramming for me," I said, sliding my arms in the sleeves. "And find out if the Cyclists have been charged with any free choice violations—brainwashing, intimidation, coercion."

The phone sang, another universal. "Hello, who's calling?" Bysshe said cautiously. His voice became suddenly friendlier. "Just a minute." He put his hand over the receiver. "It's your daughter Viola."

I took the receiver. "Hello, Viola."

"I just talked to Grandma," she said. "You will not believe what Perdita's done now. She's joined the Cyclists."

"I know," I said.

"You *know*? And you didn't tell me? I can't believe this. You never tell me anything."

"I thought Perdita should tell you herself," I said tiredly.

"Are you kidding? She never tells me anything, either. That time she had eyebrow implants she didn't tell me for three weeks, and when she got the laser tattoo she didn't tell me at all. Twidge told me. You should have called me. Did you tell Grandma Karen?"

"She's in Baghdad," I said.

"I know," Viola said. "I called her."

"Oh, Viola, you didn't!"

"Unlike you, Mom, I believe in telling members of our family about matters that concern them."

"What did she say?" I asked, a kind of numbness settling over me now that the shock had worn off.

"I couldn't get through to her. The phone service over there is terrible. I got somebody who didn't speak English, and then I got cut off, and when I tried again they said the whole city was down."

Thank you, I breathed silently. Thank you, thank you, thank you.

"Grandma Karen has a right to know, Mother. Think of the effect this could have on Twidge. She thinks Perdita's wonderful. When Perdita got the eyebrow implants, Twidge glued LEDs to hers, and I almost never got them off. What if Twidge decides to join the Cyclists, too?"

"Twidge is only nine. By the time she's supposed to get her shunt, Perdita will have long since quit." I hope, I added silently. Perdita had had the tattoo for a year and a half now and showed no signs of tiring of it. "Besides, Twidge has more sense."

"It's true. Oh, Mother, how could Perdita do this? Didn't you tell her about how awful it was?"

"Yes," I said. "And inconvenient. And unpleasant and unbalancing and painful. None of it made the slightest impact on her. She told me she thought it would be fun."

Bysshe was pointing to his watch and mouthing, "Time for court."

"Fun!" Viola said. "When she saw what I went through that time? Honestly, Mother, sometimes I think she's completely brain-dead. Can't you have her declared incompetent and locked up or something?"

"No," I said, trying to zip up my robe with one hand. "Viola, I have to go. I'm late for court. I'm afraid there's nothing we can do to stop her. She's a rational adult."

"Rational!" Viola said. "Her eyebrows light up, Mother. She has Custer's Last Stand lased on her arm."

I handed the phone to Bysshe. "Tell Viola I'll talk to her tomorrow." I zipped up my robe. "And then call Baghdad and see how long they expect the phones to be out."

I started into the courtroom. "And if there are any more universal calls, make sure they're local before you answer."

Bysshe couldn't get through to Baghdad, which I took as a good sign, and my mother-in-law didn't call. Mother did, in the afternoon, to ask if lobotomies were legal.

She called again the next day. I was in the middle of my Personal Sovereignty class, explaining the inherent right of citizens in a free society to make complete jackasses of themselves. My students weren't buying it.

"I think it's your mother," Bysshe whispered to me as he handed me the phone. "She's still using the universal. But it's local. I checked."

"Hello, Mother," I said.

"It's all arranged," Mother said. "We're having lunch with Perdita at McGregor's. It's on the corner of Twelfth Street and Larimer."

"I'm in the middle of class," I said.

"I know. I won't keep you. I just wanted to tell you not to worry. I've taken care of everything."

I didn't like the sound of that. "What have you done?"

"Invited Perdita to lunch with us. I told you. At McGregor's."

"Who is 'us,' Mother?"

"Just the family," she said innocently. "You and Viola."

Well, at least she hadn't brought in the deprogrammer. Yet. "What are you up to, Mother?"

"Perdita said the same thing. Can't a grandmother ask her granddaughters to lunch? Be there at twelve-thirty."

"Bysshe and I have a court calendar meeting at three."

"Oh, we'll be done by then. And bring Bysshe with you. He can provide a man's point of view." She hung up.

"You'll have to go to lunch with me, Bysshe," I said. "Sorry."

"Why? What's going to happen at lunch?"

"I have no idea."

On the way over to McGregor's, Bysshe told me what he'd found out about the Cyclists. "They're not a cult. There's no religious connection. They seem to have grown out of a pre-Liberation women's group," he said, looking at his notes, "although there are also links to the pro-choice movement, the University of Wisconsin, and the Museum of Modern Art."

"What?"

"They call their group leaders 'docents.' Their philosophy seems to be a mix of pre-Liberation radical feminism and the environmental primitivism of the eighties. They're floratarians and they don't wear shoes."

"Or shunts," I said. We pulled up in front of McGregor's and got out of the car. "Any mind control convictions?" I asked hopefully.

"No. A bunch of civil suits against individual members, all of which they won."

"On grounds of personal sovereignty."

"Yeah. And a criminal case brought by a member whose family tried to deprogram her. The deprogrammer was sentenced to twenty years, and the family got twelve."

"Be sure to tell Mother about that one," I said, and opened the door to McGregor's.

It was one of those restaurants with a morning glory vine twining around the maître d's desk and garden plots between the tables.

"Perdita suggested it," Mother said, guiding Bysshe and me past the onions to our table. "She told me a lot of the Cyclists are floratarians."

"Is she here?" I asked, sidestepping a cucumber frame.

"Not yet." She pointed past a rose arbor. "There's our table."

Our table was a wicker affair under a mulberry tree. Viola and Twidge were seated on the far side next to a trellis of runner beans, looking at menus.

"What are you doing here, Twidge?" I asked. "Why aren't you in school?"

"I am," she said, holding up her LCD slate. "I'm remoting today."

"I thought she should be part of this discussion," Viola said. "After all, she'll be getting her shunt soon."

"My friend Kensy says she isn't going to get one, like Perdita," Twidge said.

"I'm sure Kensy will change her mind when the time comes," Mother said. "Perdita will change hers, too. Bysshe, why don't you sit next to Viola?"

Bysshe slid obediently past the trellis and sat down in the wicker chair at the far end of the table. Twidge reached across Viola and handed him a menu. "This is a great restaurant," she said. "You don't have to wear shoes." She held up a bare foot to illustrate. "And if you get hungry while you're waiting, you can just pick something."

She twisted around in her chair, picked two of the green beans, gave one to Bysshe, and bit into the other one. "I bet Kensy doesn't. She says a shunt hurts worse than braces."

"It doesn't hurt as much as not having one," Viola said, shooting me a Now-Do-You-See-What-My-Sister's-Caused? look.

"Traci, why don't you sit across from Viola?" Mother said to me. "And we'll put Perdita next to you when she comes."

"*If* she comes," Viola said.

"I told her one o'clock," Mother said, sitting down at the near end. "So we'd have a chance to plan our strategy before she gets here. I talked to Carol Chen—"

"Her daughter nearly joined the Cyclists last year," I explained to Bysshe and Viola.

"*She* said they had a family gathering, like this, and simply talked to her daughter, and she decided she didn't want to be a Cyclist after all." She looked around the table. "So I thought we'd do the same thing with Perdita. I think we should start by explaining the significance of the Liberation and the days of dark oppression that preceded it—"

"*I* think," Viola interrupted, "we should try to talk her into just going off the ammenerol for a few months instead of having the shunt removed. If she comes. Which she won't."

"Why not?"

"Would you? I mean, it's like the Inquisition. Her sitting here while all of us 'explain' at her. Perdita may be crazy, but she's not stupid."

"It's hardly the Inquisition," Mother said. She looked anxiously past me toward the door. "I'm sure Perdita—" She stopped, stood up, and plunged off suddenly through the asparagus.

I turned around, half-expecting Perdita with light-up lips or a full-body tattoo, but I couldn't see through the leaves. I pushed at the branches.

"Is it Perdita?" Viola said, leaning forward.

I peered around the mulberry tree. "Oh, my God," I said.

It was my mother-in-law, wearing a black abayah and a silk yarmulke. She swept toward us through a pumpkin patch, robes billowing and eyes flashing. Mother hurried in her wake of trampled radishes, looking daggers at me.

I turned them on Viola. "It's your grandmother Karen," I said accusingly. "You told me you didn't get through to her."

"I didn't," she said. "Twidge, sit up straight. And put your slate down."

There was an ominous rustling in the rose arbor, as of leaves shrinking back in terror, and my mother-in-law arrived.

"Karen!" I said, trying to sound pleased. "What on earth are you doing here? I thought you were in Baghdad."

"I came back as soon as I got Viola's message," she said, glaring at everyone in turn. "Who's this?" she demanded, pointing at Bysshe. "Viola's new live-in?"

"No!" Bysshe said, looking horrified.

"This is my law clerk, Mother," I said. "Bysshe Adams-Hardy."

"Twidge, why aren't you in school?"

"I *am*," Twidge said. "I'm remoting." She held up her slate. "See? Math."

"I see," she said, turning to glower at me. "It's a serious enough matter to require my great-grandchild's being pulled out of school *and* the hiring of legal assistance, and yet you didn't deem it important enough to notify *me*. Of course, you *never* tell me anything, Traci."

She swirled herself into the end chair, sending leaves and sweet pea blossoms flying and decapitating the broccoli centerpiece. "I didn't get Viola's cry for help until yesterday. Viola, you should never leave messages with Hassim. His English is virtually nonexistent. I had to get him to hum me your ring. I recognized your signature, but the phones were out, so I flew home. In the middle of negotiations, I might add."

"How *are* negotiations going, Grandma Karen?" Viola asked.

"They *were* going extremely well. The Israelis have given the Palestinians half of Jerusalem, and they've agreed to time-share the Golan Heights." She turned to glare momentarily at me. "*They* know the importance of communication." She turned back to Viola. "So why are they picking on you, Viola? Don't they like your new live-in?"

"I am *not* her live-in," Bysshe protested.

I have often wondered how on earth my mother-in-law became a mediator and what she does in all those negotiation sessions with Serbs and Catholics and North and South Koreans and Protestants and Croats. She takes sides, jumps to conclusions, misinterprets everything you say, refuses to listen. And yet she talked South Africa into a Mandelan government and would probably get the Palestinians to observe Yom Kippur. Maybe she just bullies everyone into submission. Or maybe they have to band together to protect themselves against her.

Bysshe was still protesting. "I never even met Viola till today. I've only talked to her on the phone a couple of times."

"You must have done something," Karen said to Viola. "They're obviously out for your blood."

"Not mine," Viola said. "Perdita's. She's joined the Cyclists."

"The Cyclists? I left the West Bank negotiations because you don't approve of Perdita joining a biking club? How am I supposed to explain this to the president of Iraq? She will *not* understand, and neither do I. A biking club!"

"The Cyclists do not ride bicycles," Mother said.

"They menstruate," Twidge said.

There was a dead silence of at least a minute, and I thought, It's finally happened. My mother-in-law and I are actually going to be on the same side of a family argument.

"All this fuss is over Perdita's having her shunt removed?" Karen said finally. "She's of age, isn't she? And this is obviously a case where personal sovereignty applies. You should know that, Traci. After all, you're a judge."

I should have known it was too good to be true.

"You mean you approve of her setting back the Liberation twenty years?" Mother said.

"I hardly think it's that serious," Karen said. "There are anti-shunt groups in the Middle East, too, you know, but no one takes them seriously. Not even the Iraqis, and they still wear the veil."

"Perdita is taking them seriously."

Karen dismissed Perdita with a wave of her black sleeve. "They're a trend, a fad. Like microskirts. Or those dreadful electronic eyebrows. A few women wear silly fashions like that for a little while, but you don't see women as a whole giving up pants or going back to wearing hats."

"But Perdita . . ." Viola said.

"If Perdita wants to have her period, I say let her. Women functioned perfectly well without shunts for thousands of years."

Mother brought her fist down on the table. "Women also functioned *perfectly well* with concubinage, cholera, and corsets," she said, emphasizing each word with her fist. "But that is no reason to take them on voluntarily, and I have no intention of allowing Perdita—"

"Speaking of Perdita, where is the poor child?" Karen said.

"She'll be here any minute," Mother said. "I invited her to lunch so we could discuss this with her."

"Ha!" Karen said. "So you could browbeat her into changing her mind, you mean. Well, I have no intention of collaborating with you. *I* intend to listen to the poor thing's point of view with interest and an open mind. Respect, that's the key word, and one you all seem to have forgotten. Respect and common courtesy."

A barefoot young woman wearing a flowered smock and a red scarf tied around her left arm came up to the table with a sheaf of pink folders.

"It's about time," Karen said, snatching one of the folders away from her. "Your service here is dreadful. I've been sitting here ten minutes." She snapped the folder open. "I don't suppose you have Scotch."

"My name is Evangeline," the young woman said. "I'm Perdita's docent." She took the folder away from Karen. "She wasn't able to join you for lunch, but she asked me to come in her place and explain the Cyclist philosophy to you."

She sat down in the wicker chair next to me.

"The Cyclists are dedicated to freedom," she said. "Freedom from artificiality, freedom from body-controlling drugs and hormones, freedom from the male patriarchy that attempts to impose them on us. As you probably already know, we do not wear shunts."

She pointed to the red scarf around her arm. "Instead, we wear this as a badge of our freedom and our femaleness. I'm wearing it today to announce that my time of fertility has come."

"We had that, too," Mother said, "only we wore it on the back of our skirts."

I laughed.

The docent glared at me. "Male domination of women's bodies began long before the so-called 'Liberation,' with government regulation of abortion and fetal rights, scientific control of fertility, and finally the development of ammenerol, which eliminated the reproductive cycle altogether. This was all part of a carefully planned takeover of women's bodies, and by extension, their identities, by the male patriarchal regime."

"What an interesting point of view!" Karen said enthusiastically.

It certainly was. In point of fact, ammenerol hadn't been invented to eliminate menstruation at all. It had been developed for shrinking malignant tumors, and its uterine-lining-absorbing properties had only been discovered by accident.

"Are you trying to tell us," Mother said, "that men forced shunts on women? We had to *fight* everyone to get it approved by the FDA!"

It was true. What surrogate mothers and anti-abortionists and the fetal rights issue had failed to do in uniting women, the prospect of not having to menstruate did. Women had organized rallies, circulated petitions, elected senators, passed amendments, been excommunicated, and gone to jail, all in the name of Liberation.

"Men were *against* it," Mother said, getting rather red in the face. "And so were the religious right and the tampon manufacturers, and the Catholic Church—"

"They knew they'd have to allow women priests," Viola said.

"Which they did," I said.

"The Liberation hasn't freed you," the docent said loudly. "Except from the natural rhythms of your life, the very wellspring of your femaleness."

She leaned over and picked a daisy that was growing under the table. "We in the Cyclists celebrate the onset of our menses and rejoice in our bodies," she said, holding the daisy up. "Whenever a Cyclist comes into blossom, as we call it, she is honored with flowers and poems and songs. Then we join hands and tell what we like best about our menses."

"Water retention," I said.

"Or lying in bed with a heating pad for three days a month," Mother said.

"*I* think I like the anxiety attacks best," Viola said. "When I went off the ammenerol, so I could have Twidge, I'd have these days where I was convinced the space station was going to fall on me."

A middle-aged woman in overalls and a straw hat had come over while Viola was talking and was standing next to Mother's chair. "I had these mood swings," she said. "One minute I'd feel cheerful and the next like Lizzie Borden."

"Who's Lizzie Borden?" Twidge asked.

"She killed her parents," Bysshe said. "With an ax."

Karen and the docent glared at both of them. "Aren't you supposed to be working on your math, Twidge?" Karen said.

"I've always wondered if Lizzie Borden had PMS," Viola said, "and that was why—"

"No," Mother said. "It was having to live before tampons and ibuprofen. An obvious case of justifiable homicide."

"I hardly think this sort of levity is helpful," Karen said, glowering at everyone.

"Are you our waitress?" I asked the straw-hatted woman hastily.

"Yes," she said, producing a slate from her overalls pocket.

"Do you serve wine?" I asked.

"Yes. Dandelion, cowslip, and primrose."

"We'll take them all."

"A bottle of each?"

"For now. Unless you have them in kegs."

"Our specials today are watermelon salad and *choufleur gratiné*," she said, smiling at everyone. Karen and the docent did not smile back. "You hand-pick your own cauliflower from the patch up front. The floratarian special is sautéed lily buds with marigold butter."

There was a temporary truce while everyone ordered. "I'll have the sweet peas," the docent said, "and a glass of rose water."

Bysshe leaned over to Viola. "I'm sorry I sounded so horrified when your grandmother asked if I was your live-in," he said.

"That's okay," Viola said. "Grandma Karen can be pretty scary."

"I just didn't want you to think I didn't like you. I do. Like you, I mean."

"Don't they have soyburgers?" Twidge asked.

As soon as the waitress left, the docent began passing out the pink folders she'd brought with her. "These will explain the working philosophy of the Cyclists," she said, handing me one, "along with practical information on the menstrual cycle." She handed Twidge one.

"It looks just like those books we used to get in junior high," Mother said, looking at hers. "'A Special Gift,' they were called, and they had all these pictures of girls with pink ribbons in their hair, playing tennis and smiling. Blatant misrepresentation."

She was right. There was even the same drawing of the fallopian tubes I remembered from my middle-school movie, a drawing that had always reminded me of *Alien* in the early stages.

"Oh, yuck," Twidge said. "This is disgusting."

"Do your math," Karen said.

Bysshe looked sick. "Did women really *do* this stuff?"

The wine arrived, and I poured everyone a large glass. The docent pursed her lips disapprovingly and shook her head. "The Cyclists do not use the artificial stimulants or hormones that the male patriarchy has forced on women to render them docile and subservient."

"How long do you menstruate?" Twidge asked.

"Forever," Mother said.

"Four to six days," the docent said. "It's there in the booklet."

"No, I mean, your whole life or what?"

"A woman has her menarche at twelve years old on the average and ceases menstruating at age fifty-five."

"I had my first period at eleven," the waitress said, setting a bouquet down in front of me. "At school."

"I had my last one on the day the FDA approved ammenerol," Mother said.

"Three hundred and sixty-five divided by twenty-eight," Twidge said, writing on her slate. "Times forty-three years," She looked up. "That's five hundred and fifty-nine periods."

"That can't be right," Mother said, taking the slate away from her. "It's at least five thousand."

"And they all start on the day you leave on a trip," Viola said.

"Or get married," the waitress said.

Mother began writing on the slate. I took advantage of the cease-fire to pour everyone some more dandelion wine.

Mother looked up from the slate. "Do you realize with a period of five days, you'd be menstruating for nearly three thousand days? That's over eight solid years."

"And in between there's PMS," the waitress said, delivering flowers.

"What's PMS?" Twidge asked.

"Premenstrual syndrome was the name the male medical establishment fabricated for the natural variation in hormonal levels that signal the onset of menstruation," the docent said. "This mild and entirely normal fluctuation was exaggerated by men into a debility." She looked at Karen for confirmation.

"I used to cut my hair," Karen said.

The docent looked uneasy.

"Once I chopped off one whole side," Karen went on. "Bob had to hide the scissors every month. And the car keys. I'd start to cry every time I hit a red light."

"Did you swell up?" Mother asked, pouring Karen another glass of dandelion wine.

She nodded. "I looked just like Orson Welles."

"Who's Orson Welles?" Twidge asked.

"Your comments reflect the self-loathing thrust on you by the patriarchy," the docent said. "Men have brainwashed women into thinking menstruation is evil and unclean. Women even called their menses 'the curse' because they accepted men's judgment."

"I called it the curse because I thought a witch must have laid a curse on me," Viola said. "Like in 'Sleeping Beauty.'"

Everyone looked at her.

"Well, I did," she said. "It was the only reason I could think of for such an awful thing happening to me." She handed the folder back to the docent. "It still is."

"I think you were awfully brave," Bysshe said to Viola, "going off the ammenerol to have Twidge."

"It was awful," Viola said. "You can't imagine."

Mother sighed. "When I got my period, I asked my mother if Annette had it, too."

"Who's Annette?" Twidge said.

"A Mouseketeer," Mother said and added, at Twidge's uncomprehending look. "On TV."

"High-res," Viola said.

"*The Mickey Mouse Club,*" Mother said.

"There was a high-rezzer called *The Mickey Mouse Club?*" Twidge said incredulously.

"They were days of dark oppression in many ways," I said.

Mother glared at me. "Annette was every young girl's ideal," she said to Twidge. "Her hair was curly, she had actual breasts, her pleated skirt was always pressed, and I could not imagine that she could have anything so *messy* and undignified. Mr. Disney would never have allowed it. And if Annette didn't have one, I wasn't going to have one, either. So I asked my mother—"

"What did she say?" Twidge cut in.

"She said every woman had periods," Mother said. "So I asked her, 'Even the Queen of England?' And she said, 'Even the Queen.'"

"Really?" Twidge said. "But she's so old!"

"She isn't having it now," the docent said irritatedly. "I told you, menopause occurs at age fifty-five."

"And then you have hot flashes," Karen said, "and osteoporosis and so much hair on your upper lip you look like Mark Twain."

"Who's—?" Twidge asked.

"You are simply reiterating negative male propaganda," the docent interrupted, looking very red in the face.

"You know what I've always wondered?" Karen said, leaning conspiratorially close to Mother. "If Maggie Thatcher's menopause was responsible for the Falklands War."

"Who's Maggie Thatcher?" Twidge asked.

The docent, who was now as red in the face as the scarf on her arm, stood up. "It is clear there is no point in trying to talk to you. You've all been completely brainwashed by the male patriarchy." She began grabbing up her folders. "You're blind, all of you! You don't even see that you're victims of a male conspiracy to deprive you of your biological identity, of your very womanhood. The Liberation wasn't a liberation at all. It was only another kind of slavery!"

"Even if that were true," I said, "even if it had been a conspiracy to bring us under male domination, it would have been worth it."

"She's right, you know," Karen said to Mother. "Traci's absolutely right. There are some things worth giving up anything for, even your freedom, and getting rid of your period is definitely one of them."

"Victims!" the docent shouted. "You've been stripped of your femininity, and you don't even care!" She stomped out, destroying several squash and a row of gladiolas in the process.

"You know what I hated most before the Liberation?" Karen said, pouring the last of the dandelion wine into her glass. "Sanitary belts."

"And those cardboard tampon applicators," Mother said.

"I'm never going to join the Cyclists," Twidge said.

"Good," I said.

"Can I have dessert?"

I called the waitress over, and Twidge ordered sugared violets.

"Anyone else want dessert?" the waitress asked. "Or more primrose wine?"

"I think it's wonderful the way you're trying to help your sister," Bysshe said, leaning close to Viola.

"And those Modess ads," Mother said. "You remember, with those glamorous women in satin brocade evening dresses and long white gloves, and below the picture was written, 'Modess, because . . .' I thought Modess was a perfume."

Karen giggled. "I thought it was a brand of *champagne!*"

"I don't think we'd better have any more wine," I said.

The phone started singing the minute I got to my chambers the next morning, the universal ring.

"Karen went back to Iraq, didn't she?" I asked Bysshe.

"Yeah," he said. "Viola said there was some snag over whether to put Disneyland on the West Bank or not."

"When did Viola call?"

Bysshe looked sheepish. "I had breakfast with her and Twidge this morning."

"Oh." I picked up the phone. "It's probably Mother with a plan to kidnap Perdita. Hello?"

"This is Evangeline, Perdita's docent," the voice on the phone said. "I hope you're happy. You've bullied Perdita into surrendering to the enslaving male patriarchy."

"I have?" I said.

"You've obviously employed mind control, and I want you to know we intend to file charges." She hung up.

The phone rang again immediately, another universal. "What is the good of signatures when no one ever uses them?" I said, and picked up the phone.

"Hi, Mom," Perdita said. "I thought you'd want to know I've changed my mind about joining the Cyclists."

"Really?" I said, trying not to sound jubilant.

"I found out they wear this red scarf thing on their arm. It covers up Sitting Bull's horse."

"That is a problem," I said.

"Well, that's not all. My docent told me about your lunch. Did Grandma Karen really tell you you were right?"

"Yes."

"Gosh! I didn't believe that part. Well, anyway, my docent said you wouldn't listen to her about how great menstruating is, that you all kept talking about the negative aspects of it, like bloating and cramps and crabbiness, and I said, 'What are cramps?' and she said, 'Menstrual bleeding frequently causes headaches and depression,' and I said, 'Bleeding? Nobody ever said anything about bleeding!' Why didn't you tell me there was blood involved, Mother?"

I had, but I felt it wiser to keep silent.

"And you didn't say a word about its being painful. And all the hormone fluctuations! Anybody'd have to be crazy to want to go through that when they didn't have to! How did you stand it before the Liberation?"

"They were days of dark oppression," I said.

"I *guess*! Well, anyway, I quit and now my docent is really mad. But I told her it was a case of personal sovereignty, and she has to respect my decision. I'm still going to become a floratarian, though, and I don't want you to try to talk me out of it."

"I wouldn't dream of it," I said.

"You know, this whole thing is really your fault, Mom! If you'd told me about the pain part in the first place, none of this would have happened. Viola's right! You never tell us *anything*!"

Afterword for "Even the Queen"

Over the years, a *lot* of people (mostly guys) have asked me, "*Where* did you get the idea for "Even the Queen"? And I usually say something like "You're kidding me, right?" Or "Wish fulfillment, pure wish fulfillment."

But it was actually more complicated than that. The initial idea came from several places. The first was those "Modess, because . . ." ads I talk about in the story. As a kid, I loved those ads because they had full-page photos of women wearing long white gloves and gorgeous evening gowns by Schiaparelli and Yves St. Laurent.

I used to cut those pictures out and put them in a scrapbook. They seemed to me to epitomize glamour. Just like the women in the story, I had no idea what "Modess" was. I assumed it was a brand name for a perfume, or for a brand of jewelry, like Tiffany. I still remember the shock and betrayal I felt when I finally figured it out. (For you guys out there, think Ralphie and the Little Orphan Annie / Ovaltine decoder ring episode.)

The second place "Even the Queen" came from was something my grandmother had said to me. As a teenager, I had a thing for *Anne of Green Gables* and *Little Women* and the "olden days" when girls got to wear long skirts and petticoats, and one day I was waxing rhapsodic about how much *fun* it must have been to have lived back then, and my grandmother said, "I have two words for you: Kleenex and tampons."

The third was a conversation I had in an elevator at Clarion West with some of my students. Everyone in the elevator was female, and somebody asked if anybody had any ibuprofen she could borrow for her cramps, and a lively discussion ensued in which we all agreed that if guys had periods, the person who'd invented ibuprofen would have been a cinch to win the Nobel Prize.

But the episode that *really* convinced me I needed to write about this came when I was on a panel at a certain feminist science-fiction convention that shall remain nameless. (You know who you are.) I don't remember what the panel was about, but I *do* remember that one of the panel members said that women only thought of their menstrual cycle as a "curse" because the male-dominated patriarchy had taught them to, and that left on their own, women would welcome and embrace their menses.

I thought then (and think now) that this was one of the most idiotic things I had *ever* heard. In the first place, no one had had to say anything to me to make me despise menstruation, and in the second, nobody in my generation ever called it "the curse." Yet when I finally encountered the term (probably in one of those olden days / long skirts books I was always reading), I thought the name was *perfect*.

After the panel, I did some research and found out this theory was not just the ravings of one lunatic but actually pretty common in feminist circles, and then I talked to every young woman I could find (just in case attitudes had changed), and they were all as outraged and/or gobsmacked as I had been. And horrified to learn that tampons hadn't been around forever.

Plus, some of my fellow women science-fiction writers had been on my case because I wrote stories about time-travelers and old movies and the end of the world instead of writing stories about "women's issues."

So I decided to write one.

THE WINDS OF MARBLE ARCH

Cath refused to take the Tube.

"You loved it the last time we were here," I said, rummaging through my suitcase for a tie.

"Correction. *You* loved it," she said, brushing her short hair. "*I* thought it was dirty and smelly and dangerous."

"You're thinking of the New York subway. This is the London Underground." The tie wasn't there. I unzipped the side pocket and jammed my hand down it. "You rode the Tube the last time we were here."

"I also carried my suitcase up five flights of stairs at that awful bed and breakfast we stayed at. I have no intention of doing that, either."

She wouldn't have to. The Connaught had a lift *and* a bellman.

"I *hated* the Tube," she said. "I only took it because we couldn't afford taxis. And now we can."

We certainly could. We could also afford a hotel with carpet on the floor and a bathroom in our room instead of down the hall. A far cry from the—what was it called? It had had brown linoleum floors you hadn't wanted to walk on in your bare feet, and you'd had to put coins in a meter above the bathtub to get hot water.

"What was the name of that place we stayed at?" I asked Cath.

"I've repressed it," she said. "All I remember is that the tube station had the name of a cemetery."

"Marble Arch," I said, "and it wasn't named after a cemetery. It was named after the copy of the Roman arch of Constantine in Hyde Park."

"Well, it sounded like a cemetery."

"The Royal Hernia!" I said, suddenly remembering.

Cath grinned. "The Royal *Heritage.*"

"The Royal Hernia of Marble Arch," I said. "We should go visit it, just for old times' sake."

"I doubt if it's still there," she said, putting on her earrings. "It's been twenty years."

"Of course it's still there," I said. "Scummy showers and all. Do you remember those narrow beds? They were just like coffins, only at least coffins have sides so you don't roll off."

The tie wasn't there. I started taking shirts out of the suitcase and piling them on the bed. "These beds aren't much better. It makes you wonder how the British have managed to reproduce all these years."

"We seemed to manage all right," Cath said, putting on her shoes. "What time does the conference start?"

"Ten," I said, dumping socks and underwear onto the bed. "What time are you meeting Sara?"

"Nine-thirty," she said, looking at her watch. "Will you have time to pick up the tickets for the play?"

"Sure," I said. "The Old Man won't show up before eleven."

"Good," she said. "Sara and Elliott can only go Saturday. They've got something tomorrow night, and we've got dinner with Milford Hughes's widow and her sons Friday night. Is Arthur going with us to the play? Did you get in touch with him?"

"No, but I know the Old Man'll want to go. What are we seeing?" I asked, giving up on the tie.

"*Ragtime,* if we can get tickets. It's at the Adelphi. If not, try to get *The Tempest* or *Sunset Boulevard,* and if they're sold out, *Endgames.* Hayley Mills is in it."

"*Kismet* isn't playing?"

She grinned again. "*Kismet* isn't playing."

"Which tube stop does it say for the Adelphi?"

"Charing Cross," she said, consulting the map. "*Sunset Boulevard's* at the Old Vic, and *The Tempest's* at the Duke of York. On Shaftesbury Avenue. You could get the tickets through a ticket agent. It would be a lot faster than going to the theaters."

"Not on the Tube, it won't," I said. "It's a snap to go anywhere. And ticket agents are for tourists."

She looked skeptical. "Get third row if you can, but not on the sides. And no farther back than the dress circle."

"Not the balcony?" I asked. The farthest, highest seats had been all we could afford the first time we were here, so high up all you could see was the tops of the actors' heads. When we'd gone to *Kismet,* the Old Man had spent the entire time leaning forward to look down the front of the well-endowed Lalume's Arabian costume through a pair of rental binoculars.

"*Not* the balcony," Cath said, sticking the guidebook in her bag. "Put it on the American Express, if they'll take it. If not, the Visa."

"Are you sure the third row's a good idea?" I said. "Remember, the Old Man nearly got us thrown out of the upper balcony the last time, and there wasn't even anybody else up there."

Cath stopped putting things in her bag. "Tom," she said, looking worried. "It's been twenty years, and you haven't seen Arthur in over five."

"And you think the Old Man will have grown up in the meantime?" I said. "Not a chance. This is the guy who got us thrown out of Graceland five years ago. He'll still be the same."

Cath looked like she was going to say something else, and then began putting stuff in her bag again. "What time is the cocktail party tonight?"

"Sherry party," I said. "They have sherry parties here. Six. I'll meet you back here, okay? Or is that enough time for you and Sara to buy out the town and catch up on—what is it?—three years' gossip?"

I'd seen Elliott and Sara last year in Atlanta and the year before that in Barcelona, but Cath hadn't come with me to either conference. "Where are you doing all this shopping?"

"Harrods," she said. "Remember the tea set I bought the first time we were here? I'm going to buy the matching china. And a scarf at Liberty's and a cashmere cardigan, all the things we couldn't afford last time." She looked at her watch again. "And I'd better get going. The traffic's going to be bad in this rain."

"The Tube would be faster," I said. "And drier. You take the Piccadilly Line to Knightsbridge, and you're right there. You don't even have to go outside. There's an entrance to Harrods right in the tube station."

"I am not maneuvering shopping bags up and down those awful escalators," she said. "They're broken half the time. Besides, there are rats."

"You saw *one* mouse in Piccadilly Circus *one* time, and it was down on the tracks," I said.

"It's been twenty years," she said, coming over to the bed and deftly pulling my tie out of the mess. "There are probably thousands of rats down there now." She kissed me on the cheek. "Good luck presenting your paper." She grabbed up an umbrella. "*You* take the Tube," she said, going out the door. "You're the one who's crazy about it."

"I intend to," I called after her, but the lift had already closed.

In spite of Cath's dire predictions, the Tube was exactly the same as it had been twenty years ago. Well, maybe not exactly. There were ticket machines now, and automated stiles that sucked up my five-day pass and spat it out to me again. And most of the escalators were metal now instead of wooden. But they were as steep as ever, and the posters for musicals and plays that lined them had hardly changed at all. *Kismet* and *Cats* had been playing then. Now it was *Showboat* and *Cats*.

Cath was right—I did love the Tube. It's the best underground system in the world. Boston's "T" is old and decrepit, Tokyo's subway system is a sardine can, and Washington's Metro looks like it was designed as a bomb shelter. The Métro's not bad, but it has the handicap of being in Paris. BART's in San Francisco, but it doesn't go anywhere.

The Tube goes everywhere, all the way to Heathrow and Hampton Court and beyond, to obscure suburban stops like Cockfosters and Mudchute. There's a stop at every tourist attraction, and it's impossible to get lost.

But it isn't just an efficient way of getting from the Tower to Westminster Abbey to Buckingham Palace. It's a place in itself, a wonderful underground warren of tunnels and stairs and corridors, as colorful as the billboard-sized theater posters on the walls of the platforms, as the maps posted on every pillar and wall and forking of the tunnels.

I stopped in front of one, studying the crisscrossing green and blue and red lines. Charing Cross. I needed the gray line. What was that? Jubilee.

I followed the signs down a curving platform and out onto the eastbound platform. A train was pulling out. An LED sign above the tracks said NEXT TRAIN 6 MIN. The train started into the narrow tunnel, and I waited for the blast of wind that would follow it, pushing the air in front of it as the train disappeared.

It came, smelling faintly of diesel and dust, ruffling the hair of the woman standing next to me, rippling her skirt. NEXT TRAIN 3 MIN., the sign said.

I filled the time by watching a pair of newlyweds holding hands and reading the posters on the tunnel walls for *Sunset Boulevard* and *Sliding Doors* and Harrods. "A Blast from the Past," the one on the end said. "Experience the London Blitz at the Imperial War Museum. Elephant and Castle Tube Station."

"Train approaching," a voice said from nowhere, and I stepped forward to the yellow line.

The familiar MIND THE GAP sign was still painted on the edge of the platform. Cath had always refused to stand anywhere near the edge. She had stood nervously against the tiled wall as if she expected the train to suddenly leap off the tracks and plow into us.

The train pulled in. Right on time, shining chrome and plastic, no gum on the floor, no unknown substances on the orange plush seats.

"I beg your pardon," the woman next to me said, shifting her shopping bag so I could sit down.

Even the people who rode the Tube were more polite than people on any other subway. And better read. The man opposite me was reading Dickens's *Bleak House.*

The train slowed. "Regent's Park," the flat voice announced.

Regent's Park. The last time we were here, the Old Man had shouted "To the head!" and vaulted off the train at this station.

He had been taking us on a riotous tour of Sir Thomas More's body. We had gone to the Tower of London to see the Crown Jewels, and Cath, reading her Frommer's *England on $40 a Day* while we stood in line, had said, "Sir Thomas More is buried in the church here. You know, *A Man for All Seasons*," and we had all trooped over to see his grave.

"Want to see the rest of him?" the Old Man had said.

"The rest of him?" Sara had asked.

"Only his body's buried there," the Old Man had said. "You need to see his head!" and had led us off to London Bridge, where More's head had been stuck on a pike, and the Chelsea garden, where his daughter Margaret had buried it after she took it down, and then off to Canterbury, with the Old Man turned around and talking to us as he drove, to the small church where the head was buried now.

"Thomas More's Remains: The World Tour," he had said, driving us back at breakneck speed.

"Except for Lake Havasu," Elliott had said. "Isn't that where the original London Bridge is?" And when the annual conference was in San Diego, the Old Man had roared up in a rental car and hijacked us all on an overnight jaunt to Arizona to see it.

I couldn't wait to see him. There was no telling what wild sightseeing he had in mind this time. This was, after all, the man who had gotten us thrown out of Alcatraz.

He hadn't been at the last four conferences—he'd been off in Nepal for the first one and finishing a book the last three—and I was eager to hear what he'd been up to.

"Oxford Circus," the flat voice said. Two more stops to Charing Cross.

I leaned out to look at the station as we stopped. Each station has its own distinctive design, its own identifying color: St. Pancras green edged with navy, Euston Square black and orange, Bond Street red. Oxford Circus had a blue chutes and ladders design that was new since the first time we'd been here.

The train pulled out, picked up speed. I would be there in five minutes and to the Adelphi in ten, a lot faster than Cath in her taxi, and at least as comfortable.

I was there in eight, up the escalators and out in the rain, up the Strand to the Adelphi in twenty. It would have been fifteen, but I had to wait ten (huddled under an awning and wishing I'd taken Cath's advice about an umbrella) to cross the Strand. Black London taxis, bumper to bumper, and double-decker buses, and minis, all going nowhere fast.

Ragtime was sold out. I got a theater map from the rack in the lobby and looked to see where the Duke of York was. It was over on Shaftesbury, with the nearest tube stop Leicester Square. I went back to Charing Cross, and went down the escalator and into the passage that led to the Northern Line. I still had half an hour, which would be cutting it close, but not impossible.

I started down the left-hand tunnel toward the trains, keeping pace with the crowd, straining to hear the rumble of a train pulling in over the muffled din of voices, the crisp clatter of high heels.

People began to walk faster. The high heels beat a quicker tattoo. I got the tube map out of my back pocket. I could take the Piccadilly Line to South Kensington and change to the District and—

The wind hit me like the blast from an explosion. I reeled back, nearly losing my balance. My head snapped back sharply like I'd been punched in the jaw. I groped wildly for the tiled wall.

The IRA's blown up a train! I thought.

But there was no sound accompanying the sudden blast of searing air, only a dank, horrible smell.

Sarin gas, I thought, and reflexively put my hand over my nose and mouth, but I could still smell it. Sulfur and a wet earthy smell, and something else. Gunpowder? Dynamite? I sniffed at the air, trying to identify it.

But whatever it was, it was already over. The wind had stopped as abruptly as it had hit me, and so had the smell. Not even a trace of it lingered in the dry, stuffy air.

And it must not have been an explosion, or poison gas, because no one else had even slackened their steps. The sound of high heels retained its brisk, even clatter down the tiled passage. Two German teenagers with backpacks hurried past, giggling, and a businessman in a gray topcoat, the *Times* tucked under his arm, and a young woman in floppy sandals, all of them oblivious.

Hadn't any of them felt it? Or was it a usual occurrence in Charing Cross Station and they were used to it?

How could anybody possibly get used to a blast like that? They must not have felt it.

Had *I* felt it?

It was like an earthquake back home in California, a jolt, and then before you could even register it, it was over, and you weren't sure it had really happened. The only way you could tell for sure was by asking Cath or the kids, "Did you feel that?" or by the picture tilted on the wall.

The only pictures on the walls down here were pasted on, and the

German students, the businessman, had already told me the answer to "Did you feel that?"

But I did feel it, I thought, and tried to reconstruct it.

Heat, and the sharp tang of sulfur and wet dirt. But that wasn't what had made me lose my balance, what had sent me staggering against the wall. It was the smell of panic and of people screaming, of a bomb going off.

But it couldn't be a bomb. The IRA was in peace negotiations with the British, there hadn't been an incident for over a year, and bombs didn't stop in mid-blast. There had been bombs in the Tube before— the mechanical voice would be saying, "Please exit up the escalator immediately," not "Mind the gap."

But if it wasn't a bomb, what was it? And where had it come from? I looked up at the roof of the passage, but there wasn't a grate or a vent, no water pipes running along the ceiling. I walked along the tunnel, sniffing the air, but there were only the usual smells—dust and damp wool and cigarette smoke, and, where the passage went up a short flight of stairs, a strong smell of oil.

A train rumbled in somewhere down the passage. The train. There had been one pulling in when it hit. It must be causing the wind somehow. I went out onto the platform and stood there looking down the tunnel, half-hoping, half-dreading it would happen again.

The train pulled in and stopped, and a handful of people got off. "Mind the gap!" the computerized voice said. The doors whooshed shut, and the train pulled out. A wind picked up the scraps of paper on the track and whirled them into the side walls, and I braced myself, my feet apart, but it was just an ordinary breeze, smelling of nothing in particular.

I went back out in the passage and examined the walls for doors, felt along the tiles for drafts, stood in the same place as before, waiting for another train to come in.

But there was nothing, and I was in the way. People going around me murmured "Sorry" over and over, which I have never been able to get used to, even though I know it's merely the British equivalent of "Excuse me." It still sounded like they were apologizing, when I was the one blocking traffic. And I needed to get to the conference.

And whatever had caused the wind, it was probably just a fluke. The passages connecting the trains and the different lines and levels were like a rabbit warren. The wind could have come from anywhere. Maybe somebody on the Jubilee Line had been transporting a carton of rotten eggs. Or blood samples. Or both.

I went up to the Northern Line, caught a train that had just pulled in, and made it to the conference in time for the eleven o'clock session, but the episode must have unnerved me more than I'd admitted to myself. As I stood in the lobby pinning on my registration badge, the outside door opened, letting in a blast of air.

I flinched away from it and then stood there, staring blindly at the door, until the woman at the registration table asked, "Are you all right?"

I nodded. "Have the Old Man or Elliott Templeton registered yet?"

"An old man?" the woman said, bewilderedly.

"Not *an* old man, *the* Old Man," I said impatiently. "Arthur Birdsall."

"The morning session's already started," she said, looking through the ranked badges. "Have you looked in the ballroom?"

The Old Man had never attended a session in his life.

"Mr. Templeton's here," she said, still looking. "No, Mr. Birdsall hasn't registered yet."

"Daniel Drecker's here," Marjorie O'Donnell said, descending on me. "You heard about his daughter, didn't you?"

"No," I said, scanning the room for Elliott.

"She's in an institution," she said. "Schizophrenia."

I wondered if she was telling me this because she thought I was acting unbalanced, too, but she added, "So, for heaven's sake, don't ask him about her. And don't ask Peter Jamieson if Leslie's here. They're separated."

"I won't," I said and escaped to the first session. Elliott wasn't in the audience, or at lunch. I sat down next to John McCord, who lived in London, and said, without preamble, "I was in the Tube this morning."

"Wretched, isn't it?" McCord said. "And so expensive. What's a day pass now? Two pounds fifty?"

"While I was in Charing Cross Station, there was this strange wind."

McCord nodded knowingly. "The trains cause them. When they pull out of a station, they push the air in front of them," he said, illustrating the pushing with this hands, "and because they fill the tunnel, it creates a slight vacuum in the train's wake, and air rushes in behind to fill the vacuum, and it creates a wind. The same thing happens in reverse as trains pull into the station."

"I know," I said impatiently. "But this one was like an explosion, and it smelled—"

"It's all the dirt down there. And the beggars. They sleep in the passages, you know. Some of them even urinate on the walls. I'm afraid the Underground's deteriorated considerably in the past few years."

"Everything in London has," the woman across the table said. "Did you know there's a Disney store in Regent Street?"

"And a Gap," McCord said.

"Mind the Gap," I said, but they were off on the subject of the Decline and Fall of London. I said I needed to go look for Elliott.

He was nowhere to be found. The afternoon session was starting. I sat down next to John and Irene Watson.

"You haven't seen Arthur Birdsall or Elliott Templeton, have you?" I said, scanning the ballroom.

"Elliott was here before the morning session," John said. "Stewart's here."

Irene leaned across John. "You heard about his surgery, didn't you? Colon cancer."

"The doctors say they got it all," John said.

"I hate coming to these things anymore," Irene said, leaning confidingly across John again. "Everybody's either gotten old or sick or divorced. You heard Hari Srinivasau died, didn't you? Heart attack."

"I see somebody over there I need to talk to," I said. "I'll be right back." I started up the aisle.

And ran straight into Stewart.

"Tom!" he said. "How have you been?"

"How have *you* been?" I said. "I heard you've been ill."

"I'm fine. The doctors tell me they caught it in time, that they got it all," he said. "It isn't so much the cancer coming back that worries me as knowing this is the kind of thing in store for us as we get older. You heard about Paul Wurman?"

"No," I said. "Look, I have to go make a phone call before the session starts." And before he could fill me in on the Decline and Fall of Everybody.

I took off for the lobby. "Where have you been?" Elliott said, clapping a hand on my shoulder. "I've been looking all over for you."

"Where have *I* been?" I said, like a shipwreck victim who'd been on a raft for days. "You have no idea how glad I am to see you," I said, looking happily at him. He looked just the same as ever, tall, in shape, his hairline not even receding. "Everyone else is falling apart."

"Including you," he said, grinning. "You look like you need a drink."

"Is the Old Man with you?" I asked, looking around for him.

"No," he said. "Do you have any notion where the bar is in this place?"

"In there." I pointed.

"Lead the way," he said. "I've got all sorts of things to tell you. I've just talked Evers and Associates into a new project. I'll tell you all about it over a couple of pints."

He did, and then told me about what he and Sara had been doing since the last conference.

"I thought the Old Man would be here today," I said. "He'll be here tonight, though?"

"I think so," Elliott said. "Or tomorrow."

"He's all right, isn't he?" I said, looking across the bar to where Stewart stood talking. "He's not sick or anything?"

"I don't think so," Elliott said, looking reassuringly surprised. "He lives in Cambridge now, you know. And Sara and I won't be there, either. Evers and Associates are taking us out to dinner to celebrate. We'll stop by for a few minutes on our way, though. Sara insisted. She wants to see you. She's been so excited about your visit. She's talked of nothing else for weeks. She couldn't wait to go shopping with Cath." He went over to the bar and got us two more pints. "Speaking of which, Sara said I'm to tell you we're definitely on for the play and supper Saturday. What are we going to see? Please tell me it's not *Sunset Boulevard*."

"Oh, my God!" I said. "It's not anything. I forgot to get the tickets." I glanced hastily at my watch. Three forty-five. "Do you think the box offices will be open now?"

He nodded.

"Good." I snatched up my coat and started for the lobby.

"And not *Cats*!" Elliott called after me.

I would be lucky if I got anything, I thought, sprinting down to the tube station and pushing my way through the turnstile, including a train at this hour. The escalators were so jammed I had trouble getting the list of theaters out of my pocket. *The Tempest* was at the Duke of York. Leicester Square. I pulled my tube map out—Piccadilly Line.

The passage to the Piccadilly Line was even more crowded than the escalator, and slower. The elderly woman ahead of me, in a gray head scarf and an ancient brown coat, was shuffling at a snail's pace, clutching her coat collar to her throat with a blue-veined hand, her head down and her body hunched forward as if she were struggling against a hurricane.

I tried to get around her, but the way was blocked by more teenagers with backpacks, Spanish this time, walking four abreast and discussing *una visita a la Torre de Londres*.

I missed the train and had to wait for the next one, checking the

NEXT TRAIN 4 MIN. sign every fifteen seconds and listening to the American couple behind me bitterly arguing.

"I *told* you it started at four," the woman said. "Now we'll be late."

"Who was the one who had to take one more picture?" the man said. "You've already taken five hundred pictures, but oh, no, you had to take one more."

"I wanted to have something to remember our vacation by," she said bitterly. "Our happy, happy vacation."

The train came in, and I mashed my way on and grabbed a pole and then stood there, squashed, reading my list. The Wyndham was near Leicester Square, too. What was at the Wyndham?

Cats.

No good. But *Death of a Salesman* was at the Prince Edward, which was only a few blocks over. And there was a whole row of theaters on Shaftesbury.

"Leicester Square," the automated voice said, and I forced my way off the train, down the passage, and up the escalators and into Leicester Square.

The traffic up top was even worse, and it took me nearly twenty minutes to get to the Duke of York, only to find that its box office was closed until six. The Prince Edward was open, but it only had two sets of single seats fifteen rows apart for *Death of a Salesman*. "The soonest I can get you five seats all together," the black-lipsticked girl said, tapping keys on a computer, "is March fifteenth."

The Ides of March, I thought. How fitting, since Cath would kill me if I came home without the tickets.

"Where's the nearest ticket agent?" I asked the girl.

"There's one on Cannon Street," she said vaguely.

Cannon Street. That was the name of a tube station. I consulted my tube map. District and Circle Line. I could take the Northern Line down to Embankment and catch the District and Circle from there.

I looked at my watch. It was already four-thirty. We were supposed to be at the sherry party at six. I would be cutting it close. I sprinted back to Leicester Square, down to the Northern Line, and onto a train. It was even more jammed, but everyone was still polite. They held their books above the fray and continued to read in spite of the crush. *Madame Bovary* and Geoff Ryman's *253* and Charles Williams's *Descent into Hell*.

"Cannon Street," the computer voice said, and I pushed my way off and headed for the exit.

I was halfway down the passage when it hit again, the same violent blast as before, the same smell. No, not the same, I thought, regaining my footing, watching unconcerned commuters walk past. There had been the same sharp smell of sulfur and explosives, but no musty wetness. And this time there was the smell of smoke.

But no fire alarms had gone off, no sprinkler system been activated. No one had even noticed it.

Maybe it's one of those things where it's so common the locals don't even notice it, I thought, they can't even smell it anymore. Like a lumber mill or chemical plant. We had gone to see Cath's uncle in Nebraska one time, and I'd asked him if he minded the smell from the feedlots.

"What smell?" he'd said.

But manure didn't smell like violence, like panic. And the smell from the feedlots had been everywhere. If this was a persistent, pervasive smell, why hadn't I smelled it in Piccadilly Circus or Leicester Square?

I was all the way to South Kensington before I realized I had gone back down the passage without even being aware of it, boarded a train, ridden seven stops. And not gotten the tickets.

I got off the train, half-intending to go back, and then stood there on the platform uncertainly. This was no carton of rotten eggs, or blood samples, no localized phenomenon of Charing Cross. So what was it?

A woman got off the train, glancing irritatedly at her watch. I looked at mine. Five-thirty. It was too late to go back to the ticket agent's, too late to do anything but figure out which line to take to get home.

I felt a rush of relief that I wouldn't have to go back to Cannon Street, wouldn't have to face that wind again. What were they, I wondered, pulling out my tube map, that they produced such a feeling of fear?

I thought about it all the way back to the hotel, wondering if I should tell Cath. It would only confirm her in her opinion of the Tube, and she would hardly be in the mood for wild stories about winds in the Tube, not if she'd been waiting for me to show up. Cath hated being late to things, and it was already after six. By the time I made it back to the hotel it would be nearly six-thirty.

It was six forty-five. I pushed unavailingly on the lift button for five minutes and then took the stairs. Maybe she was running late, too. When she and Sara started shopping, they lost all track of time. I fished the room key out of my pants pocket.

Cath opened the door.

"I'm late, I know," I said, unpinning my nametag and peeling my jacket off. "Give me five minutes. Are you ready?"

"Yes," she said. She walked over and sat down on the bed, watching me.

"How was Harrods?" I said, unbuttoning my shirt. "Did you get your china?"

"No," she said, looking down at her folded hands.

I grabbed a clean shirt out of my suitcase and pulled it on. "But you and Sara had a good time?" I said, buttoning it. "What did you buy? Elliott said he was afraid you'd clean out Harrods between the two of you." I stopped, looking at her. "What's wrong?" I said. "Did the kids call? Has something happened?"

"The kids are fine," she said.

"But something happened," I said. "The taxi you and Sara took had an accident."

She shook her head. "Nothing happened," and then, still looking down at her hands, "Sara's having an affair."

"What?" I said stupidly.

"She's having an affair."

"*Sara?*" I said, disbelieving. Not Sara, affectionate, loyal Sara.

Cath nodded, still looking at her hands.

I sat down on my bed. "Did she tell you she was?"

"No, of course not," Cath said, standing up and walking over to the mirror.

"Then how do you know?" I asked, but I knew how. The same way she had known that the kids were getting chicken pox, that her sister was engaged, that her father was worried about his business. Cath always noticed things before anybody else—she was equipped with some kind of super-sensitive radar that picked up on subliminal signs or vibrations in the air or something. And she was always right.

But Sara and Elliott had been married as long as we had. They were the couple at the top of our "Marriage Is Still a Viable Institution" list.

"Are you sure?" I said.

"I'm sure."

I wanted to ask her how she knew, but there wasn't any point. When Ashley had gotten the chicken pox, she'd said, "Her eyes always look bright when she has a fever, and, besides, Lindsay had it two weeks ago," but most of the time she could only shake her short blond hair, unable to say how she'd reached her conclusion.

But she was always right. Always right.

"But—I saw Elliott today," I said. "He was fine. He didn't—" I thought back over everything he had said, wondering if there had been some indication in it that he was worried or unhappy. He had said Sara and Cath would spend a lot of money, but he always said that. "He sounded fine."

"Put your tie on," she said.

"But if she— We don't have to go if you don't want to," I said.

"No," she said, shaking her head. "No. No, we have to go."

"Maybe you misinterpreted—"

"I didn't," she said and went into the bathroom and shut the door.

———

We had trouble getting a taxi. The Connaught's doorman seemed to have disappeared, and all of the black boxy London cabs ignored my frantic waving. Even when one finally stopped, it took us forever to get to the party. "Theatergoers," the cabbie explained cheerfully of the traffic. "You two plan to see any plays while you're here?"

I wondered if Cath would still want to go to a play, convinced as she was that Sara was having an affair, but as we passed the Savoy, its neon sign for *Miss Saigon* blazing, she asked, "What play did you get tickets for?"

"I didn't," I said. "I ran out of time." I started to say that I intended to get them tomorrow, but she wasn't listening.

"Harrods didn't have my china," she said, and her tone sounded as hopeless as it had telling me about Sara. "They discontinued the pattern four years ago."

We were nearly an hour and a half late for the party. Elliott and Sara have probably long since left for dinner, I thought, and was secretly relieved.

"Cath!" Marjorie said as we walked in the door and hurried over with her nametag. "You look wonderful! I have so much to tell you!"

"I'm going to go look for the Old Man," I said. "I'll see if he wants to go to dinner afterward." He would probably drag us off to Soho or Hampstead Heath. He always knew some out-of-the-way place that had eel pie or authentic English stout.

I set off through the crowd. You could usually locate the Old Man by the crowd of people gathered around, and the laughter. And the proximity to the bar, I thought, spotting a huddle of people in that direction.

I waded toward them through the crush, grabbing a glass of wine off a tray as I went, but it wasn't the Old Man. It was the people who'd been at lunch. They were discussing, of all things, the Beatles, but at least it wasn't the Decline and Fall.

"The three of them were talking about a reunion tour," McCord was saying. "I suppose that's all off now."

"The Old Man took us on a Beatles tour," I said. "Has anybody seen him? He insisted we re-create all the album covers. We nearly got killed crossing Abbey Road."

"I don't think he's coming down from Cambridge till tomorrow," McCord said. "It's a long drive."

The Old Man had driven us four hundred miles to see London Bridge. I peered over their heads, trying to spot the Old Man. I couldn't see him, but I did spot Evers, which meant Sara and Elliott were still here. Cath was over by the door with Marjorie.

"It was just so *sad* about Linda McCartney," the Disney woman said.

I took a swig of my wine and remembered too late this was a sherry party.

"How old was she?" McCord was asking.

"Fifty-three."

"I know three women who've been diagnosed with breast cancer," the Gap woman said. "*Three.* It's dreadful."

"One keeps wondering who's next," the other woman said.

"Or *what's* next," McCord said. "You heard about Stewart, didn't you?"

I handed my sherry glass to the Disney woman, who looked at me, annoyed, and started through the crowd toward Cath, but now I couldn't see her, either. I stopped, craning my neck to see over the crowd.

"*There* you are, you handsome thing!" Sara said, coming up behind me and putting her arm around my waist. "We've been looking all over for you!"

She kissed me on the cheek. "Elliott's been fretting that you were going to make us all go see *Cats*. He loathes *Cats*, and everyone who comes to visit drags us to it. And you know how he frets over things. You didn't, did you? Get tickets for *Cats*?"

"No," I said, staring at her. She looked the same as always—her dark hair still tucked behind her ears, her eyebrows still arched mischievously. This was the same old Sara who'd gone with us to *Kismet*, to Lake Havasu, to Abbey Road.

Cath was wrong. She might pick up subliminal signals about other people, but this time she was wrong. Sara wasn't acting guilty or uneasy, wasn't avoiding my eyes, wasn't avoiding Cath.

"Where *is* Cath?" she asked, standing on tiptoe to peer over the crowd. "I have something I've got to tell her."

"What?"

"About her china. We couldn't find it today, did she tell you? Well, after I got home, I thought, 'I'll wager they have it at Selfridge's.' They're always years behind the times. Oh, there she is." She waved frantically. "I want to tell her before we leave," she said, and took off through the crowd. "Find Elliott and tell him I'll only be a sec. And tell him we aren't seeing *Cats*," she called back to me. "I don't want him stewing all night. He's over there somewhere." She waved vaguely in the direction of the door, and I pushed my way between people till I found him, standing by the front door.

"You haven't seen Sara, have you?" he said. "Evers is bringing his car round."

"She's talking to Cath," I said. "She said she'll be here in a minute."

"Are you kidding? When those two get together—" He shook his head indulgently. "Sara said they had a wonderful time today."

"Is the Old Man here yet?" I said.

"He called and said he couldn't make it tonight. He said to tell you he'll see us tomorrow. I'm looking forward to it. We've scarcely seen him since he moved to Cambridge. We're down in Wimbledon, you know."

"And he hasn't swooped down and kidnapped you to go see Dickens's elbow or something?"

"Not lately. Oh, God, do you remember that time Sara mentioned Arthur Conan Doyle, and he dragged us up and down Baker Street, looking for Sherlock Holmes's missing flat?"

I laughed, remembering him knocking on doors, demanding,

"What have you done with 221B, madam?" and deciding we needed to call in Scotland Yard.

"And then demanding to know what they'd done with the yard," Elliott said, laughing.

"Did you tell him we're all going to a play together Saturday?"

"Yes. You didn't get tickets for *Cats*, did you?"

"I didn't get tickets for anything," I said. "I ran out of time."

"Well, *don't* get tickets for *Cats*. Or *Phantom*."

Sara came running up, flushed and breathless. "I'm sorry. Cath and I got to talking," she said. She gave me a smacking kiss on the lips. "Good-bye, you adorable hunk. See you Saturday."

"Come *on*," Elliott said. "You can kiss him all you like on Saturday." He hustled her out the door. "And not *Les Miz!*" he shouted back to me.

I stood, smiling after them. You're wrong, Cath, I thought. Look at them. Not only would Sara never have kissed me like that if she were having an affair, but Elliott wouldn't have looked on complacently like that, and neither of them would have been talking about china, about *Cats*.

Cath had made a mistake. Her radar, usually so infallible, had messed up this time. Sara and Elliott's marriage was fine. Nobody was having an affair, and we'd all have a great time Saturday night.

The mood persisted through the rest of the evening, in spite of Marjorie's latching onto me and telling me all about the Decline and Fall of her father, who she was going to have to put in a nursing home, and our finding out that the pub that had had such great fish and chips the first time we'd been here had burned down.

"It doesn't matter," Cath said, standing on the corner where it had been. "Let's go to the Lamb and Crown. I know it's still there. I saw it on the way to Harrods this morning."

"That's on Wilton Place, isn't it?" I said, pulling out my tube map. "That's right across from Hyde Park Corner Station. We can take—"

"A taxi," Cath said.

———

Cath didn't say anything else about the affair she thought Sara was having, except to tell me they were going shopping again the next day. "Selfridge's first, and then Reject China . . ." and I wondered if she had realized, seeing Sara at the party, that she'd made a mistake.

But in the morning, as I was leaving, she said, "Sara called and canceled while you were in the shower."

"They can't go to the play with us Saturday?"

"No," Cath said. "She isn't going shopping with me today. She said she had a headache."

"She must have drunk some of that awful sherry," I said. "So what are you going to do? Do you want to come have lunch with me?"

"I think it's someone at the conference."

"Who?" I said, lost.

"The man Sara's having an affair with," she said, picking up her guidebook. "If it was someone who lived here, she wouldn't risk seeing him while we're here."

"She's *not* having an affair," I said. "I saw her. I saw Elliott. He—"

"Elliott doesn't know." She jammed the guidebook savagely into her bag. "Men never notice anything."

She began stuffing things into her bag—her sunglasses, her umbrella. "We're having dinner with the Hugheses tonight at seven. I'll meet you back here at five-thirty." She picked up her umbrella.

"You're wrong," I said. "They've been married longer than we have. She's crazy about Elliott. Why would somebody with that much to lose risk it all by having an affair?"

She turned and looked at me, still holding the umbrella. "I don't know," she said bleakly.

"Look," I said, suddenly sorry for her, "why don't you come and have lunch with the Old Man and me? He'll probably get us thrown out like he did at that Indian restaurant. It'll be fun."

She shook her head. "You and Arthur will want to catch up, and I don't want to wait on Selfridge's." She looked up at me.

"When you see Arthur—" She paused, looking the way she did when she was thinking about Sara.

"You think he's having an affair, too, oh Madame Knows-All, Sees-All?"

"No," she said. "He was older than us."

"Which was why we called him the Old Man," I said, "and you think he'll have gotten a cane and grown a long white beard?"

"No," she said, and slung her bag over her shoulder. "I think if they have my china at Selfridge's, I'll buy twelve place settings."

She was wrong, and I would prove it to her. We would have a great time at the play, and she would realize Sara couldn't be having an affair. If I could get the tickets. *Ragtime* had been sold out, which meant *The Tempest* was likely to be, too, and there weren't a lot of other choices, since Elliott had said no to *Sunset Boulevard*. And *Cats*, I thought, looking at the theater posters as I went down the escalator. And *Les Miz*.

The Tempest and the Hayley Mills thing, *Endgames*, were both at theaters close to Leicester Square. If I couldn't get tickets at either, there was a ticket agent in Lisle Street.

The Tempest was sold out, as I'd expected. I walked over to the Albery.

Endgames had five seats in the third row center of the orchestra. "Great," I said, and slapped down my American Express, thinking how much things had changed.

In the old days I would have been asking if they didn't have anything in the sherpa section, seats so steep we had to clutch the arms of our seats to keep from plummeting to our deaths and we had to rent binoculars to even see the stage.

And in the old days, I thought grimly, Cath would have been at my side, making rapid calculations to see if our budget could afford even the cheap seats. And now I was getting tickets in third row center, and not even asking the price, and Cath was on her way to Selfridge's in a taxi.

The girl handed me the tickets. "What's the nearest tube station?" I asked.

"Tottenham Court Road," she said.

I looked at my tube map. I could take the Central Line over to Holborn and then a train straight to South Kensington. "How do I get there?"

She waved an arm full of bracelets vaguely north. "You go up St. Martin's Lane."

I went up St. Martin's Lane, and up Monmouth, and up Mercer and Shaftesbury and New Oxford. There clearly had to be closer stations than Tottenham Court Road, but it was too late to do anything about it now. And I wasn't about to take a taxi.

It took me half an hour to make the trek, and another ten to reach Holborn, during which I figured out that the Lyric had been less than four blocks from Piccadilly Circus. I'd forgotten how deep the station was, how long the escalators were. They seemed to go down for miles. I rattled down the slatted wooden rungs and down the passage, glancing at my watch as I walked.

Nine-thirty. I'd make it to the conference in plenty of time. I wondered when the Old Man would get there. He had to drive down from Cambridge, I thought, going down a short flight of steps behind a man in a tweed jacket, which was an hour and a—

I was on the bottom step when the wind hit. This time it was not so much a blast as a sensation of a door opening onto a cold room.

A cellar, I thought, groping for the metal railing. No. Colder. Deathly cold. A meat locker. A frozen food storage vault. With a sharp, unpleasant chemical edge, like disinfectant. A sickening smell.

No, not a refrigerated vault, I thought, a biology lab, and recognized the smell as formaldehyde. And something under it. I shut my mouth, held my breath, but the sweet, sickening stench was already in my nostrils, in my throat. Not a biology lab, I thought in horror. A charnel house.

It was over, the door shutting as suddenly as it had opened, but the bite of the icy air was still in my nostrils, the nasty taste of formaldehyde still in my mouth. Of corruption and death and decay.

I stood there on the bottom step taking shallow, swallowing breaths, while people walked around me. I could see the man in the tweed jacket, rounding the corner in the passage ahead. He *must* have felt it, I thought. He was right in front of me. I started after him, dodging around a pair of children, an Indian woman in a sari, a housewife with a string bag, finally catching up to him as he turned out onto the crowded platform.

"Did you feel that wind?" I asked, taking hold of his sleeve. "Just now, in the tunnel?"

He looked alarmed, and then, as I spoke, tolerant. "You're from the States, aren't you? There's always a slight rush of air as a train enters one of the tunnels. It's perfectly ordinary. Nothing to be alarmed about." He looked pointedly at my hand on his sleeve.

"But this one was ice-cold," I persisted. "It—"

"Ah, yes, well, we're very near the river here," he said, looking less tolerant. "If you'll excuse me." He freed his arm. "Have a pleasant holiday," he said and walked away through the crowd to the farthest end of the platform.

I let him go. He clearly hadn't felt it. But he had to, I thought. He was right in front of me.

Unless it wasn't real, and I was experiencing some bizarre form of hallucination.

"Finally," a woman said, looking down the track, and I saw a train was approaching. Wind fluttered a flyer stuck on the wall and then the blond hair of the woman standing closest to the edge. She turned unconcernedly toward the man next to her, saying something to him, shifting the leather strap of her bag on her shoulder.

It hit again, an onslaught of cold and chemicals and corruption, a stench of decay.

He has to have felt that, I thought, looking down the platform, but he was unconcernedly boarding the train, the tourists next to him were looking up at the train and back down at their tube maps, unaware.

They have to have felt it, I thought, and saw the elderly black man. He was halfway down the platform, wearing a plaid jacket. He shuddered as the wind hit, and then hunched his gray grizzled head into his shoulders like a turtle withdrawing into its shell.

He felt it, I thought, and started toward him, but he was already getting on the train, the doors were already starting to close. Even running, I wouldn't reach him.

I bounded onto the nearest car as the doors whooshed shut and stood there just inside the door, waiting for the next station. As soon as the doors opened I jumped out, holding on to the edge of the door, to see if he got off. He didn't, or at the next station, and Bond Street was easy. Nobody got off.

"Marble Arch," the disembodied voice said, and the train pulled into the tiled station.

What the hell was at Marble Arch? There had never been this many people when Cath and I stayed at the Royal Hernia.

Everybody on the train was getting off.

But was the old man? I leaned out from the door, trying to see if he'd gotten off.

I couldn't see him for the crowd. I stepped forward and was immediately elbowed aside by an equally large herd of people getting on.

I headed down the platform toward his car, craning my neck to spot his plaid jacket, his grizzled head in the exodus.

"The doors are closing," the voice of the Tube said, and I turned just in time to see the train pull out, and the old man sitting inside, looking out at me.

And now what? I thought, standing on the abruptly deserted platform. Go back to Holborn and see if it happened again and somebody else felt it? Somebody who wasn't getting on a train.

Certainly nothing was going to happen here. This was our station, the one we had set out from every morning, come home to every night, the first time we were here, and there hadn't been any strange winds. The Royal Hernia was only three blocks away, and we had run up the drafty stairs, holding hands, laughing about what the Old Man had said to the verger in Canterbury when he had shown us Thomas More's grave—

The Old Man. He would know what was causing the winds, or how to find out. He loved mysteries. He had dragged us to Greenwich, the British Museum, and down into the crypt of St. Paul's, trying to find out what had happened to the arm Nelson lost in one of his naval battles. If anybody could, he'd find out what was causing these winds.

And he should be here by now, I thought, looking at my watch. Good God. It was nearly one. I went over to the tube map on the wall to find the best way over to the conference. Go to Notting Hill Gate and take the District and Circle Line. I looked up at the sign above the platform to see how long it would be till the next train, so that when the wind hit, I didn't have time to hunch down the way the old man had, to flinch away from the blow. My neck was fully extended, like Sir Thomas More's on the block.

And it was like a blade, slicing through the platform with killing force. No charnel house smell this time, no heat. Nothing but blast and the smell of salt and iron. The scent of terror and blood and sudden death.

What *is* it? I thought, clutching blindly for the tiled wall. What *are* they?

The Old Man, I thought again. I have to find the Old Man.

I took the Tube to South Kensington and ran all the way to the conference, half-afraid he wouldn't be there, but he was. I could hear his voice when I came in. The usual admiring group was clustered around him. I started across the lobby toward them.

Elliott detached himself from the group and came over to me.

"I need to see the Old Man," I said.

He put a restraining hand on my arm. "Tom—" he said.

He looked like Cath had, sitting on the bed, telling me Sara was having an affair.

"What's wrong?" I asked, dreading the answer.

"Nothing," he said, glancing back toward the lounge. "Arthur—nothing." He let go of my arm. "He'll be overjoyed to see you. He's been asking for you."

The Old Man was sitting in an easy chair, holding court. He looked exactly the same as he had twenty years ago, his frame still lanky, his light hair still falling boyishly over his forehead.

See, Cath, I thought. No long white beard. No cane.

He broke off as soon as he saw us and stood up. "Tom, you young reprobate!" he said, and his voice sounded as strong as ever. "I've been waiting for you to get here all morning. Where were you?"

"In the Tube," I said. "Something happened. I—"

"In the *Tube*? What were you doing down in the Tube?"

"I was—"

"Never use the Tube anymore," he said. "It's gone completely to hell ever since Tony Blair got into office. Like everything else."

"I want you to come with me," I said. "I want to show you something."

"Come where?" he said. "Down in the Tube? Not on your life." He sat back down. "I *loathe* the Tube. Smelly, dirty . . ."

He sounded like Cath.

"Look," I said, wishing there weren't all these people around. "Something peculiar happened to me in Charing Cross Station yesterday. You know the winds that blow through the tunnels when the trains come in?"

"I certainly do. Dreadful drafty places—"

"Exactly," I said. "It's the drafts I want you to see. Feel. They—"

"And catch my death of cold? No, thank you."

"You don't understand," I said. "These weren't ordinary drafts. I was heading for the Northern Line platform, and—"

"You can tell me about it at lunch." He turned back to the others. "Where shall we go?"

He had never, ever, in all the years I'd known him, asked anybody where to go for lunch. I blinked stupidly at him.

"How about the Bangkok House?" Elliott said.

The Old Man shook his head. "Their food's too spicy. It always makes me bloat."

"There's a sushi place round the corner," one of the admiring circle volunteered.

"*Sushi!*" he said, in a tone that put an end to the discussion.

I tried again. "Yesterday I was in Charing Cross Station, and this wind, this *blast* hit me that smelled like sulfur. It—"

"It's the damned smog," the Old Man said. "Too many cars. Too many people. It's got nearly as bad as it was in the old days, when there were coal fires."

Coal, I thought. Could that have been the smell I couldn't identify? Coal smelled of sulfur.

"The inversion layer makes it worse," the admirer who'd suggested sushi said.

"Inversion layer?" I said.

"Yes," he said, pleased to have been noticed. "London's in a shallow depression that causes inversion layers. That's when a layer of warm air above the ground traps the surface air under it, so the smoke and particulates collect—"

"I thought we were going to lunch," the Old Man said petulantly.

"Remember the time we tried to find out what had happened to Sherlock Holmes's address?" I said. "This is an even stranger mystery."

"That's *right*," he said. "221B Baker Street. I'd forgotten that. Do you remember the time I took you on a tour of Sir Thomas More's head? Elliott, tell them what Sara said in Canterbury."

Elliott told them, and they roared with laughter, the Old Man included. I half-expected somebody to say, "Those were the days."

"Tom, tell everybody about that time we went to see *Kismet*," the Old Man said.

"We've got tickets for *Endgames* for the five of us for tomorrow night," I said, even though I knew what was coming.

He was already shaking his head. "I never go to plays anymore. The theater's gone to hell like everything else. Lot of modernist nonsense." He smacked his hands on the arms of the easy chair. "Lunch! Did we decide where we're going?"

"What about the New Delhi Palace?" Elliott said.

"Can't handle Indian food," the Old Man, who had once gotten us thrown out of the New Delhi Palace by dancing with the Tandoori chicken, said. "Isn't there anywhere that serves plain, ordinary food?"

"Wherever we're going, we need to make up our minds," the admirer said. "The afternoon session starts at two."

"We can't miss that," the Old Man said. He looked around the circle. "So where are we going? Tom, are you coming to lunch with us?"

"I can't," I said. "I wish you'd come with me. It would be like old times."

"Speaking of old times," the Old Man said, turning back to the group, "I still haven't told you about the time I got thrown out of *Kismet*. What was that harem girl's name, Elliott?"

"Lalume," Elliott said, turning to look at the Old Man, and I made my escape.

An inversion layer. Holding the air down so it couldn't escape, trapping it belowground so that smoke and particulates, and smells, became concentrated, intensified.

I took the Tube back to Holborn and went down to the Central Line to look at the ventilation system. I found a couple of wall grates no larger than the size of a theater handbill and a louvered vent two-thirds of the way down the westbound passage, but no fans, nothing that moved the air or connected it with the outside.

There had to be one. The deep stations went down hundreds of feet. They couldn't rely on nature recirculating the air, especially with diesel fumes and carbon monoxide from the traffic up above. There must be ventilation. But some of these tube stations had been built as long ago as the 1880s, and Holborn looked like it hadn't been repaired since then.

I went out into the large room containing the escalators and stood looking up. It was open all the way to the ticket machines at the top, and the station had wide doors on three sides, all open to the outside.

Even without ventilation, the air would eventually make its way up and out onto the streets of London. Wind would blow in from outside, and rain, and the movement of the people hurrying through the station, up the escalators, down the passages, would circulate it. But if there was an inversion layer, trapping the air close to the ground, keeping it from escaping—

Pockets of carbon monoxide and deadly methane accumulated in coal mines. The Tube was a lot like a mine, with the complicated bendings and turnings of its tunnels. Could pockets of air have accumulated in the train tunnels, becoming more concentrated, more lethal, as time went by?

The inversion layer would explain why there were winds, but not what had caused them in the first place. An IRA bombing, like I had thought when I felt the first one? That would explain the blast and the smell of explosives, but not the formaldehyde. Or the stifling smell of dirt in Charing Cross.

A collapse of one of the tunnels? Or a train accident?

I made the long trek back up to the station and asked the guard next to the ticket machines, "Do these tunnels ever collapse?"

"Oh, no, sir, they're quite safe." He smiled reassuringly. "There's no need to worry."

"But there must be accidents occasionally," I said.

"I assure you, sir, the London Underground is the safest in the world."

"What about bombings?" I asked. "The IRA—"

"The IRA has signed the peace agreement," he said, looking at me suspiciously.

A few more questions, and I was likely to find myself arrested as an IRA bomber. I would have to ask the Old—Elliott. And in the meantime, I could try to find out if there were winds in all the stations or just a few.

"Can you show me how to get to the Tower of London?" I asked him, extending my tube map like a tourist.

"Yes, sir, you take the Central Line, that's this red line, to Bank," he said, tracing his finger along the map, "and then change to the District and Circle. And don't worry. The London Underground is perfectly safe."

Except for the winds, I thought, getting on the escalator. I got out a pen and marked an X on the stations I'd been to as I rode down. Marble Arch, Charing Cross, Sloane Square.

I hadn't been to Russell Square. I rode there and waited in the passages and then on both platforms through two trains.

There wasn't anything at Russell Square, but on the Metropolitan Line at St. Pancras there was the same shattering blast as at Charing Cross—heat and the acrid smells of sulfur and violent destruction.

There wasn't anything at Barbican, or Aldgate, and I thought I knew why. At both of them the tracks were aboveground, with the platform open to the air. The winds would disperse naturally instead of being trapped, which meant I could eliminate most of the suburban stations.

But St. Paul's and Chancery Lane were both underground, with deep, drafty tunnels, and there was nothing in either of them except a faint scent of diesel and mildew. There must be some other factor at work.

It isn't the line they're on, I thought, riding toward Warren Street.

Marble Arch and Holborn were on the Central Line, but Charing Cross wasn't, and neither was St. Pancras. Maybe it was the convergence of them. Chancery Lane, St. Paul's, and Russell Square all had only one line. Holborn had two lines, and Charing Cross had three. St. Pancras had five.

Those are the stations I should be checking, I thought, the ones where multiple lines meet, the ones honeycombed with tunnels and passages and turns. Monument, I thought, looking at the circles where green and purple and red lines converged. Baker Street and Moorgate.

Baker Street was closest, but hard to get to. Even though I was only two stops away, I'd have to switch over at Euston, take the Northern going the other way back to St. Pancras, and catch the Bakerloo. I was glad Cath wasn't here to say, "I thought you said it was easy to get anywhere on the Tube."

Cath! I'd forgotten all about meeting her at the hotel so we could go to dinner with the Hugheses.

What time was it? Only five, thank God. I looked hastily at the map. Good. Northern down to Leicester Square and then the Piccadilly Line, and who says it isn't easy to get anywhere on the Tube? I'd be to the Connaught in less than half an hour.

And when I got there I'd tell Cath about the winds, even if she did hate the Tube. I'd tell her about all of it, the Old Man and the charnel house smell and the old man in the plaid jacket.

But she wasn't there. She'd left a note on the pillow of my bed. "Meet you at Grimaldi's. 7 P.M."

No explanation. Not even a signature, and the note looked hasty, scribbled. What if Sara called? I wondered, a thought as chilly as the wind in Marble Arch. What if Cath had been right about her, the way she'd been right about the Old Man?

But when I got to Grimaldi's, it turned out she'd only been shopping. "The woman in the china department at Fortnum and Mason's told me about a place in Bond Street that specialized in discontinued patterns."

Bond Street. It was a wonder we hadn't run into each other. But she wasn't in the tube station, I thought with a flash of resentment. She was safely aboveground in a taxi.

"They didn't have it, either," she said, "but the clerk suggested I try a shop next door to the Portmeirion store which was clear out in Kensington. It took the rest of the day. How was the conference? Was Arthur there?"

You know he was, I thought. She had foreseen his having gotten old, she'd tried to warn me that first morning in the hotel, and I hadn't believed her.

"How was he?" Cath asked.

You already know, I thought bitterly. Your antennae pick up vibrations from everybody. Except your husband.

And even if I tried to tell her, she'd be too wrapped up in her precious china pattern to even hear me.

"He's fine," I said. "We had lunch and then spent the whole afternoon together. He hadn't changed a bit."

"Is he going to the play with us?"

"No," I said and was saved by the Hugheses coming in right then, Mrs. Hughes, looking frail and elderly, and her strapping sons Milford Junior and Paul and their wives.

Introductions all around, and it developed that the blonde with Milford Junior wasn't his wife, it was his fianceé. "Barbara and I just couldn't talk to each other anymore," he confided to me over cocktails. "All she was interested in was buying things, clothes, jewelry, furniture."

China, I thought, looking across the room at Cath.

At dinner I was seated between Paul and Milford Junior, who spent the meal discussing the Decline and Fall of the British Empire.

"And now Scotland wants to separate," Milford said. "Who's next? Sussex? The City of London?"

"At least perhaps then we'd see decent governmental services. The current state of the streets and the transportation system—"

"I was in the Tube today," I said, seizing the opening. "Do either of you know if Charing Cross has ever been the site of a train accident?"

"I shouldn't wonder," Milford said. "The entire system's a disgrace. Dirty, dangerous—the last time I rode the Tube, a thief tried to pick my pocket on the escalator."

"I never go down in the Tube anymore," Mrs. Hughes put in from the end of the table where she and Cath were deep in a discussion of china shops in Chelsea. "I haven't since Milford died."

"There are beggars everywhere," Paul said. "Sleeping on the platforms, sprawled in the passages. It's nearly as bad as it was during the Blitz."

The Blitz. Air raids and incendiaries and fires. Smoke and sulfur and death.

"The Blitz?" I said.

"During Hitler's bombing of London in World War II, masses of people sheltered in the Tube," Milford said. "Along the tracks, on the platforms, even on the escalators."

"Not that it was any safer than staying aboveground," Paul said.

"The shelters were hit?" I said eagerly.

Paul nodded. "Paddington. And Marble Arch. Forty people were killed in Marble Arch."

Marble Arch. Blast and blood and terror.

"What about Charing Cross?" I asked.

"I've no idea," Milford said, losing interest. "They should pass legislation keeping beggars out of the Underground. And requiring cabbies to speak understandable English."

The Blitz. Of course. That would explain the smell of gunpowder or whatever it was. And the blast. A high-explosive bomb.

But the Blitz had been over fifty years ago. Could the air from a bomb blast have stayed down in the Tube all those years without dissipating?

There was one way to find out. The next morning I took the Tube to Tottenham Court Road, where there was a whole street of bookstores, and asked for a book about the history of the Underground in the Blitz.

"The Underground?" the girl at Foyle's, the third place I'd tried, said vaguely. "The Tube Museum might have something."

"Where's that?" I asked.

She didn't know, and neither did the ticket vendor back at the tube station, but I remembered seeing a poster for it on the platform at Oxford Circus during my travels yesterday. I consulted my tube map, took the train to Victoria, and changed for Oxford Circus, where I checked five platforms before I found it.

Covent Garden. The London Transport Museum. I checked the map again, took the Central Line across to Holborn, transferred to the Piccadilly Line, and went to Covent Garden.

And apparently it had been hit, too, because a gust of face-singeing heat struck me before I was a third of the way down the tunnel. There was no smell of explosives, though, or of sulfur or dust. Just ash and fire and hopeless desperation that it was all, all burning down.

The scent of it was still with me as I hurried upstairs and out into the market, through the rows of carts selling T-shirts and postcards and toy double-decker buses, to the Transport Museum.

It was full of T-shirts and postcards, too, all sporting the Underground symbol or replicas of the tube map. "I need a book on the Tube during the Blitz," I asked a boy across a counter stacked with "Mind the Gap" place mats and playing cards.

"The Blitz?" he said vaguely.

"World War II," I said, which didn't elicit any recognition, either.

He waved a hand loosely to the left. "The books are over there."

They weren't. They were on the far wall, past a rack of posters of tube ads from the twenties and thirties, and most of what books they had were about trains, but I finally found two histories of the Tube and a paperback called *London in Wartime*. I bought them all and a notebook with a tube map on the cover.

The Transport Museum had a snack bar. I sat down at one of the plastic tables and began taking notes. Nearly all the tube stations had been used as shelters, and a lot of them had been hit—Euston Station, Aldwych, Monument. "In the aftermath of the bombing, the acrid smell of brick dust and cordite was everywhere," the paperback said. Cordite. That was what I had smelled.

Marble Arch had taken a direct hit, the bomb bursting like a grenade in one of the passages, ripping tiles off the walls as it exploded, sending them slicing through the people sheltered there. Which explained the smell of blood. And the lack of heat. It had been pure blast.

I looked up Holborn. There were several references to its having been used as a shelter, but nothing in any of the books that said it had taken a hit.

Charing Cross had, twice. It had been hit by a high-explosive bomb, and then by a V-2 rocket. The bomb had broken water mains and loosed an avalanche of dirt down onto the room containing the escalators. That was the damp earthiness I'd smelled—mud from the roof collapsing.

Nearly a dozen stations had been hit the night of May 10, 1941: Cannon Street, Paddington, Blackfriars, Liverpool Street—

Covent Garden wasn't on the list. I looked it up in the paperback. The station hadn't been hit, but incendiaries had fallen all around Covent Garden, and the whole area had been on fire. Which meant that Holborn wouldn't have to have taken a direct hit, either. There could have been a bombing nearby, with lots of deaths, that was responsible for Holborn's charnel house smell. And the fact that there had been fires all around Covent Garden fit with the fact that there hadn't been sulfur, or concussion.

It all fit—the smell of mud and cordite in Charing Cross, of smoke in Cannon Street, of blast and blood in Marble Arch. The winds I was feeling were the winds of the Blitz, trapped there by London's inversion layer, caught belowground with no way out, nowhere to go, held and recirculated and intensified through the years in the mazelike tunnels and passages and pockets of the Tube. It all fit.

And there was a way to test it. I copied a list of all the stations I hadn't been to that had been hit—Blackfriars, Monument, Paddington, Liverpool Street. Praed Street, Bounds Green, Trafalgar Square, and Balham had taken direct hits. If my theory was correct, the winds should definitely be there.

I started looking for them, using the tube map on the cover of my notebook. Bounds Green was far north on the Piccadilly Line, nearly to the legendary Cockfosters, and Balham was nearly as far south on the Northern Line. I couldn't find either Praed Street or Trafalgar Square. I wondered if those stations had been closed or given other names. The Blitz had, after all, been fifty years ago.

Monument was the closest. I could get there by way of the Central Line and then follow the Circle Line around to Liverpool Street and from there go on up to Bounds Green. Monument had been down near the docks—it should smell like smoke, too, and the river water they'd sprayed on the fire, and burning cotton and rubber and spices. A warehouse full of pepper had burned. That odor would be unmistakable.

But I didn't smell it. I wandered up and down the passages of the Central and Northern and District Lines, stood on each of the platforms, waited in the corners near the stairways for over an hour, and nothing.

It doesn't happen all the time, I thought, taking the Circle Line to Liverpool Street. There's some other factor—the time of day or the temperature or the weather. Maybe the winds only blew when London was experiencing an inversion layer. I should have checked the weather this morning, I thought.

Whatever the factor was, there was nothing at Liverpool Street, either, but at Euston the wind hit me full force the minute I stepped off the train—a violent blast of soot and dread and charred wood. Even though I knew what it was now, I had to lean against the cold tiled wall a moment till my heart stopped pounding and the dry taste of fear in my mouth subsided.

I waited for the next train and the next, but the wind didn't repeat itself, and I went down to the Victoria Line, thought a minute, and went back up to the surface to ask the ticket seller if the tracks at Bounds Green were aboveground.

"I believe they are, sir," he said in a thick Scottish brogue.

"What about Balham?"

He looked alarmed. "Balham's the other way. It's not on the same line, either."

"I know," I said. "Are they? Aboveground?"

He shook his head. "I'm afraid I don't know, sir. Sorry. If you're going to Balham, you go down to the Northern Line and take the train to Tooting Bec and Morden. Not the one to Elephant and Castle."

I nodded. Balham was even farther out in the suburbs than Bounds Green. The tracks were almost certain to be aboveground, but it was still worth a try.

Balham had taken the worst hit of any of the stations. The bomb had fallen just short of the station, but in the worst possible place. It had plunged the station into darkness, smashed the water and sewer pipes and the gas mains. Filthy water had rushed into the station in torrents, flooding the pitch-black passages, pouring down the stairs and into the tunnels. Three hundred people had drowned. And how could that not still be there, even if Balham was aboveground? And if it was there, the smell of sewage and gas and darkness would be unmistakable.

I didn't follow the ticket vendor's directions. I detoured to Black-friars, since it was nearly on the way, and stood around its yellow-tiled platforms for half an hour with no result before going on to Balham.

The train was nearly deserted for most of the long trip. From London Bridge out there were only two people in my car, a middle-aged woman reading a book and, at the far end, a young girl, crying.

She had spiked hair and a pierced eyebrow, and she cried helplessly, obliviously, making no attempt to wipe her mascaraed cheeks, or even turn her head toward the window.

I wondered if I should go ask her what was wrong or if the woman with the book would think I was hitting on her. I wasn't even sure she would be aware of me if I did go over—there was a complete absorption to her sorrow that reminded me of Cath, intent on finding her china. I wondered if that was what had broken this girl's heart, that they had discontinued her pattern? Or had her friends betrayed her, had affairs, gotten old?

"Borough," the automated voice said, and she seemed to come to herself with a jerk, swiped at her cheeks, grabbed up her knapsack, and got off.

The middle-aged woman stayed on all the way to Balham, never once looking up from her book. When the train pulled in, I went over and stood next to her at the door so I could see what classic of literature she found so fascinating. It was *Gone with the Wind*.

But the winds aren't gone, I thought, leaning against the wall of Balham's platform, listening for the occasional sound of an incoming train, futilely waiting for a blast of sewage and methane and darkness. The winds of the Blitz are still here, endlessly blowing through the tunnels and passages of the Tube like ghosts, wandering reminders of fire and flood and destruction.

If that was what they were. Because there was no smell of filthy water at Balham, or any indication that any had ever been there. The air in the passages was dry and dusty. There wasn't even a hint of mildew.

And even if there had been, it still wouldn't explain Holborn. I waited through three more trains on each side and then caught a train for Elephant and Castle and the Imperial War Museum.

"Experience the London Blitz," the poster had said, but the exhibit didn't have anything about which tube stations had been hit. Its gift shop yielded three more books, though. I scoured them from cover to cover, but there was no mention at all of Holborn or of any bombings near there.

And if the winds were leftover breezes from the Blitz, why hadn't I felt them the first time we were here? We had been in the Tube all the time, going to the conference, going to plays, going off on the Old

Man's wild hares, and there hadn't been even a breath of smoke, of sulfur.

What was different that time? The weather? It had rained nearly nonstop that first time. Could that have affected the inversion layer? Or was it something that had happened since then? Some change in the routing of the trains or the connections between stations?

I walked back to Elephant and Castle in a light rain. A man in a clerical collar and two boys with white surplices over their arms were coming out of the station. There must be a church nearby, I thought, and realized that could be the solution for Holborn.

The crypts of churches had been used as shelters during the Blitz. Maybe they had also been used as temporary morgues.

I looked up "morgue" and then, when that didn't work, "body disposal."

I was right. They had used churches, warehouses, even swimming pools after some of the worst air raids to store bodies.

I doubted if there were any swimming pools near Holborn, but there might be a church.

There was only one way to find out—go back to Holborn and look. I looked at my tube map. Good. I could catch a train straight to Holborn from here. I went down to the Bakerloo Line and got on a northbound train. It was nearly as empty as the one I'd come out on, but when the doors opened at Waterloo, a huge crowd of people surged onto the train.

It can't be rush hour yet, I thought, and glanced at my watch. Six-fifteen. Good God. I was supposed to meet Cath at the theater at seven. And I was how many stops from the theater?

I pulled out my tube map and clung to the overhead pole, trying to count. Embankment and then Charing Cross and Piccadilly Circus. Five minutes each, and another five to get out of the station in this crush. I'd make it. Barely.

"Service on the Bakerloo Line has been disrupted from Embankment north," the automated voice said as we pulled in. "Please seek alternate routes."

Not now! I thought, grabbing for my map. Alternate routes.

I could take the Northern Line to Leicester Square and then change for Piccadilly Circus. No, it would be faster to get off at Leicester Square and run the extra blocks.

I raced off the train the minute the doors opened and down the corridor to the Northern Line. Five to seven, and I was still two stops away from Leicester Square, and four blocks from the theater. A train was coming in. I could hear its rumble down the corridor. I darted around people, shouting, "Sorry, sorry, sorry," and burst onto the packed northbound platform.

The train must have been on the southbound tracks. NEXT TRAIN 4 MIN., the overhead sign said.

Great, I thought, hearing it start up, pushing the air in front of it, creating a vacuum in its wake. Embankment had been hit. And that was all I needed right now, a blast from the Blitz.

I'd no sooner said it than it hit, whipping my hair and my coat lapels back, rattling the unglued edges of a poster for *Showboat*. There was no blast, no heat, even though Embankment was right on the river, where the fires had been the worst. It was cold, cold, but there was no smell of formaldehyde with it, no stench of decay. Only the icy chill and a smothering smell of dryness and of dust.

It should have been better than the other ones, but it wasn't. It was worse. I had to lean against the back wall of the platform for support, my eyes closed, before I could get on the train.

What *are* they? I thought, even though this proved they were the residue of the Blitz. Because Embankment had been hit.

And people must have died, I thought. Because it was death I'd smelled. Death and terror and despair.

I stumbled onto the train. It was jammed tight, and the closeness, the knowledge that any wind, any air, couldn't reach me through this mass of people, revived me, calmed me, and by the time I pulled in to

Leicester Square, I had recovered and was thinking only of how late I was.

Seven-ten. I could still make it, but just barely. At least Cath had the tickets, and with luck Elliott and Sara would get there in the meantime and they'd all be busy saying hello.

Maybe the Old Man changed his mind, I thought, and decided to come. Maybe yesterday he'd been under the weather, and tonight he'd be his old self.

The train pulled in. I raced down the passage, up the escalator, and out onto Shaftesbury. It was raining, but I didn't have time to worry about it.

"Tom! Tom!" a breathless voice shouted behind me.

I turned. Sara was frantically waving at me from half a block away.

"Didn't you hear me?" she said breathlessly, catching up to me. "I've been calling you ever since the Tube."

She'd obviously been running. Her hair was mussed, and one end of her scarf dangled nearly to the ground.

"I know we're late," she said, pulling at my arm, "but I *must* catch my breath. You're not one of those dreadful men who've taken up marathon running in old age, are you?"

"No," I said, moving over in front of a shop and out of the path of traffic.

"Elliott's always talking about getting a Stairmaster." She pulled her dangling scarf off and wrapped it carelessly around her neck. "I have *no* desire to get in shape."

Cath was wrong. That was all there was to it. Her radar had failed her and she was misinterpreting the whole situation.

I must have been staring. Sara put a defensive hand up to her hair. "I know I look a mess," she said, putting up her umbrella. "Oh, well. How late are we?"

"We'll make it," I said, taking her arm, and setting off toward the Lyric. "Where's Elliott?"

"He's meeting us at the theater. Did Cath get her china?"

"I don't know. I haven't seen her since this morning," I said.

"Oh, look, there she is," Sara said, and began waving.

Cath was standing in front of the Lyric, next to the water-spotted sign that said TONIGHT'S PERFORMANCE SOLD OUT, looking numb and cold.

"Why didn't you wait inside out of the rain?" I said, leading them both into the lobby.

"We ran into each other coming out of the Tube," Sara said, pulling off her scarf. "Or, rather, I saw Tom. I had to *scream* to get his attention. Isn't Elliott here yet?"

"No," Cath said.

"He and Mr. Evers came back after lunch. The day was *not* a success, so don't bring up the subject. Mrs. Evers insisted on buying everything in the entire gift shop, and then we couldn't find a taxi. Apparently there are no taxis down in Kew. I had to take the Tube, and it was *blocks* to the station." She put her hand up to her hair. "I got blown to pieces."

"Did you change trains at Embankment?" I asked, trying to remember which line went out to Kew Gardens. Maybe she'd felt the wind, too. "Were you on the Bakerloo Line platform?"

"I don't remember," Sara said impatiently. "Is that the line for Kew? You're the tube expert."

"Do you want me to check your coats?" I said hastily.

Sara handed me hers, jamming her long scarf into one sleeve, but Cath shook her head. "I'm cold."

"You should have waited in the lobby," I said.

"Should I?" she said, and I looked at her, surprised. Was she mad I was late? Why? We still had fifteen minutes, and Elliott wasn't even here yet.

"What's the matter?" I started to say, but Sara was asking, "Did you get your china?"

"No," Cath said, still with that edge of anger in her voice. "Nobody has it."

"Did you try Selfridge's?" Sara asked, and I went off to check Sara's coat. When I came back, Elliott was there.

"Sorry I'm late," he said. He turned to me. "What happened to you this—?"

"We were all late," I said, "except Cath, who, luckily, was the one with the tickets. You *do* have the tickets?"

Cath nodded and pulled them out of her evening bag. She handed them to me, and we went in. "Right-hand aisle and down to your right," the usher said. "Row three."

"No stairs to climb?" Elliott said. "No ladders?"

"No rock axes and pitons," I said. "No binoculars."

"You're kidding," Elliott said. "I won't know how to act."

I stopped to buy programs from the usher. By the time we got to Row 3, Cath and Sara were already in their seats. "Good God," Elliott said as we sidled past the people on the aisle. "I'll bet you can actually *see* from here."

"Do you want to sit next to Sara?" I said.

"Good God, no," Elliott joked. "I want to be able to ogle the chorus girls without her smacking me with her program."

"I don't think it's that kind of play," I said.

"Cath, what's this play about?" Elliott said.

She leaned across Sara. "Hayley Mills is in it," she told him.

"Hayley Mills," he said reminiscently, leaning back, his hands behind his head. "I thought she was truly sexy when I was ten years old. Especially that dance number in *Bye Bye Birdie*."

"You're thinking of Ann-Margret, you fool," Sara said, reaching across me to smack him with her program. "Hayley Mills was in that one where she's the little girl who always saw the positive side of things— what was it called?"

I looked across at Cath, surprised she hadn't chimed in with the answer—she was the Hayley Mills fan. She was sitting with her coat pulled around her shoulders. Her face looked pinched with cold.

"*You* know Hayley Mills," Sara said to Elliott. "We watched her in *The Flame Trees of Thika.*"

Elliott nodded. "I always admired her chest. Or am I thinking of Annette?"

"I don't think this is that kind of play," Sara said.

It wasn't that kind of play. Everyone wore high-necked costumes, including Hayley Mills, who swept in swathed in a bulky coat. "I'm *so* sorry I'm late, dear," she said, taking off her coat to reveal a turtleneck sweater and going over to stand in front of a stage fire. "It's so cold out. And the air's so strange."

Whoever was playing her husband said, "'Into my heart an air that kills from yon far country blows,'" and Elliott leaned over and whispered, "Oh, God, a *literary* play."

I'd missed the rest of the husband's line, but he must have asked Hayley why she was late, because she said, "My assistant cut her hand, and I had to take her to hospital. It took forever for her to get stitched up."

A hospital. I hadn't considered that. Their morgues would have been full during the Blitz. Was there a hospital close to Holborn? I would have to ask Elliott at intermission.

A sudden rattle of applause brought me out of my reverie.

The stage was dark. I'd missed Scene One. When the lights went back up, I tried to focus on the play, so I could discuss it at least halfway intelligibly at the intermission.

"The wind is rising," Hayley Mills said, looking out an imaginary window.

"Storm brewing," a man, not her husband, said.

"That's what I fear," she said, rubbing her hands along her arms to warm them. "Oh, Derek, what if he finds out about us?"

I glanced sideways across Sara at Cath, but couldn't see her face in the darkened theater. She obviously hadn't known what this play was about, or she'd never have chosen it.

But Hayley wasn't acting anything like Sara. She chain-smoked, she paced, she hung up the phone hastily when her husband came into the room and was so obviously guilty no one, least of all her husband, could have failed to miss it.

Elliott certainly didn't. "The husband's got to be a complete moron," he said as soon as the curtain went down for the intermission. "Even the *dog* could deduce that she's having an affair. Why is it characters in plays never act any way remotely resembling real life?"

"Maybe because people in real life don't look like Hayley Mills," Cath said. "She *does* look wonderful, doesn't she, Sara? She hasn't aged a day."

"You're joking, right?" Elliott said. "All right, I know people kid themselves about their spouses having affairs, but—"

"I *have* to go to the bathroom," Cath said. "I suppose there'll be a horrible line. Come with me, Sara, and I'll tell you the saga of my china." They edged past us.

"Get us a glass of white wine," Sara called back from the aisle, and Elliott and I shouldered our way to the bar, which took ten minutes, and another five to get served. Sara and Cath still weren't back.

"So where were you all day?" Elliott asked me, sipping Sara's wine. "I looked for you at lunch."

"I was researching something," I said. "Holborn tube station is in Bloomsbury, isn't it?"

"I think so," he said. "I rarely take the Tube."

"Are there any hospitals near the tube station?"

"Hospitals?" he said bewilderedly. "I don't know. I don't think so."

"Or churches?"

"I don't know. What's this all about?"

"Have you ever heard of a thing called an inversion layer?" I said. "It's when air is trapped—"

"They simply must do something about the women's bathroom situation," Sara said, grabbing her wine and taking a sip. "I thought we were going to be in there the entire third act."

"Sounds like an excellent idea," Elliott said. "I don't mean to sound like the Old Man, but if this is any indication, plays truly have gone to hell! I mean, we're expected to believe that Hayley Mills's husband is so blind that he can't see his wife's in love with—the other one—what's his name—?"

"*Pollyanna*," Cath said. "I've been trying to remember it all through the first two acts. The name of the little girl who always saw the positive side of things."

"Sara," I said, "are there any hospitals near Holborn?"

"The Great Ormond Street Hospital for Sick Children. That's the one James Barrie left all the money to," she said. "Why?"

The Great Ormond Street Hospital. That had to be it. They had used it as a temporary morgue, and the air—

"It's so *obvious*," Elliott said, still on the subject of infidelity. "The excuses Hayley Mills's character makes for where she's been—"

"She looks wonderful, doesn't she?" Cath said. "How old do you suppose she is? She looks so young!"

The end-of-intermission bell chimed.

"Let's go," Cath said, setting her wine down. "I don't want to have to crawl over all those people again."

Sara swallowed her wine at one gulp, and we went back down the aisle. We were too late. The people on the end had to stand up and let us past.

"But don't you agree," Elliott said, sitting down, "that any normal person—"

"Shh," Cath said, leaning all the way across Sara and me to shut him up. "The lights are going down."

They did, and I felt an odd sense of relief, as if we'd just avoided something terrible. The curtain began to go up.

"I still say," Elliott said in a stage whisper, "that nobody could have that many clues thrown at him and not realize his wife's having an affair."

"Why not?" Sara said, "You didn't," and Hayley Mills came on-stage.

Beside me, in the dark, Elliott was applauding like everyone else, and I thought, It's as if nothing happened. Elliott will think he didn't really hear it, like the wind in the Tube, over so fast you wonder if it was really real, and he'll decide it wasn't, he'll lean across me and say, "What do you mean? You're not having an affair, are you?" and Sara will whisper, "Of course not, you idiot. I just meant you never notice anything," and it won't all have blown up, it won't all—

"Who is it?" Elliott said.

His voice echoed in the space between two of Hayley Mills and her husband's lines, and a man in front of us turned around and glared.

"Who is it?" Elliott said again, louder. "Who are you having an affair with?"

Cath said, in a strangled voice, "Don't—"

"No, you're right," Elliott said, standing up. "What the hell difference does it make?" and pushed his way out over the people on the aisle.

Sara sat an endless minute, and then she plunged past us, too, tripping over my foot and nearly falling as she did.

I looked over at Cath, wondering if I should go after Sara. I had the ticket for her coat and scarf in my pocket. Cath was staring stiffly up at the stage, her coat clutched tightly around her.

"This can't go on," Hayley Mills said, looking now fully as old as she was, but still going gamely on with her lines, "I want a divorce," and Cath stood up and pushed past me, me following clumsily after her, muttering, "Sorry, sorry," over and over to the people on the aisle.

"It's *over*," Hayley said from the stage. "Can't you *see* that?"

I didn't catch up to Cath till she was halfway through the lobby.

"Wait," I said, reaching for her arm. "Cath."

Her face was white and set. She pushed unseeingly through the glass doors and out onto the pavement, and then stood there, looking bewildered.

"I'll get a taxi," I said, thinking, At least we won't have to compete with the end-of-the-play crowd.

Wrong. People were streaming out of the Apollo, and farther down the street, *Miss Saigon*, and God knew what else. There were swarms of people on the curb and at the corner, shouting and whistling for taxis.

"Wait here," I said, pushing Cath back under the Lyric's marquee, and plunged out into the melee, my arm thrust out. A taxi pulled toward the curb, but it was only avoiding a clot of people, newspapers over their heads, ducking across the street.

The driver put his arm out and gestured toward the "in use" light on top of the taxi.

I stepped off the curb, scanning the mess for a taxi that didn't have its light on, jerking back again as a motorbike splashed by.

Cath tugged on the back of my jacket. "It's no use," she said. "*Phantom* just let out. We'll never get a taxi."

"I'll go to one of the hotels," I said, gesturing up the street, "and have the doorman get one. You stay here."

"No, it's all right," she said. "We can take the Tube. Piccadilly Circus is close, isn't it?"

"Right down there," I said, pointing.

She nodded and put her purse uselessly over her head against the rain, and we darted out onto the sidewalk, through the crowd, and down the steps into Piccadilly Circus.

"At least it's dry in here," I said, fishing for change for a ticket for her.

She nodded again, shaking the skirt of her coat out.

There was a huge crush at the machines and an even bigger one at the turnstiles. I handed her her ticket, and she put it gingerly in the slot and yanked her hand back before the machine could suck it away.

None of the down escalators was working. People clomped awkwardly down the steps. Two punkers with shaved heads and bad skin shoved their way past, muttering obscenities.

At the bottom there was a nasty-looking puddle under the tube map. "We need the Piccadilly Line," I said, taking her arm and leading her down the tunnel and out onto the jammed platform.

The LED sign overhead said NEXT TRAIN 2 MIN. A train rumbled through on the other side and people poured onto the platform behind us, pushing us forward. Cath stiffened, staring down at the MIND THE GAP sign, and I thought, All we need now is a rat. Or a knifing.

A train pulled in and we pushed onto it, crammed together like sardines. "It'll thin out in a couple of stops," I said, and she nodded. She looked dazed, shell-shocked.

Like Elliott, staring blindly at the stage, saying in a flat voice, "Who are you having an affair with?" and stumbling blindly over people's feet, people's knees, trying to get out of the row, looking like he'd been hit by a blast of sulfurous, deadly wind. Everything fine one minute, sipping wine and discussing Hayley Mills, and the next, a bomb ripping the world apart and everything in ruins.

"Green Park," the loudspeaker said, and the door opened and more people pushed on. "You better watch out!" a woman with matted hair said, shaking a finger in Cath's face. Her fingertip was stained blue-black. "You better! I mean it!"

"That's it," I said, pushing Cath behind me. "We're getting off at the next stop." I put my hand on her back and began propelling her through the mass of people toward the door.

"Hyde Park Corner," the loudspeaker said.

We got off, the door whooshed shut, and the train began to pull out.

"We'll go up top and get a taxi," I said tightly. "You were right. The Tube's gone to hell."

It's all gone to hell, I thought bitterly, starting down the empty tunnel, Cath behind me. Sara and Elliott and London and Hayley Mills. All of it. The Old Man and Regent Street and us.

The wind caught me full in the face. Not from the train we had just gotten off of—from ahead of us somewhere, farther down the tunnel. And worse, worse, worse than before. I staggered back against the wall, doubling up like I'd been punched in the stomach. Disaster and death and devastation.

I straightened up, clutching my stomach, unable to catch my breath, and looked across the tunnel. Cath was standing with her back against the opposite wall, her hands flattened against the tiles, her face pinched and pale.

"You felt it," I said, and felt a vast relief.

"Yes."

Of course she felt it. This was Cath, who sensed things nobody else noticed, who had known Sara was having an affair, that the Old Man had turned into an old man. I should have gone and gotten her the first time it happened, dragged her down here, made her stand in the tunnels with me.

"Nobody else felt them," I said. "I thought I was crazy."

"No," she said, and there was something in her voice, in the way she stood huddled against the green-tiled wall, that told me what should have been obvious all along.

"You felt them the first time we were here," I said, amazed. "That's why you hate the Tube. Because of the winds."

She nodded.

"That's why you wanted to take a taxi to Harrods," I said. "Why didn't you say something that first time?"

"We didn't have enough money for taxis," she said, "and you didn't seem to be aware of them."

I wasn't aware of anything, I thought, not Cath's obvious reluctance to go down into the tube stations, nor her flinching back from the incoming trains. She was watching for the next wind, I thought, remembering her peering nervously into the tunnel. She was waiting for it to hit.

"You should have told me," I said. "If you'd told me, I could have helped you figure out what they were so they wouldn't frighten you anymore."

She looked up. "What they were?" she repeated blankly.

"Yes. I've figured out what's causing them. It's because of the inversion layer. The air gets trapped down here, and there's no way out. Like gas pockets in a mine. So it just stays here, year after year," I said, unbelievably glad I could talk to her, tell her.

"People used these tube stations as shelters during the Blitz," I said eagerly. "Balham was hit, and so was Charing Cross. That's why you can smell smoke and cordite. Because of the high-explosive bombs. And people were killed by flying tiles at Marble Arch. That's what we're feeling—the winds from those events. They're winds from the past. I don't know what this one was caused by. A tunnel collapse, maybe, or a V-2—" I stopped.

She was looking the way she had sitting on the narrow bed in our hotel room, right before she told me Sara was having an affair.

I stared at her.

"You know what's causing the winds," I said finally. Of course she knew. This was Cath, who knew everything. Cath, who had had twenty years to think about this.

I said, "What's causing them, Cath?"

"Don't—" she said, and looked down the passageway, as if hoping somebody would come, a sudden rush of people, hurrying for the trains, pushing between us, cutting her off before she could answer, but the tunnel remained empty, still, no air moving at all.

"Cath," I said.

She took a deep breath, and then said, "They're what's coming."

"What's *coming*?" I repeated stupidly.

"What's waiting for us," she said, and then, bitterly, "Divorce and death and decay. The ends of things."

"They can't be," I said. "Marble Arch took a direct hit. And Charing Cross—"

But this was Cath, who was always right. And what if the scent wasn't of smoke but of fear, not of ashes but of despair?

What if the formaldehyde wasn't the charnel house odor of a temporary morgue but of a permanent one, Death itself, the marble arch that waited for us all? No wonder it had reminded Cath of a cemetery.

What if the direct hits, shrapnel flying everywhere, slashing through youth and marriage and happiness, weren't V-2s, but death and devastation and decline?

The winds all, all smelled of death, and the Blitz hardly had a monopoly on that. Look at Hari Srinivasau. And the pub with the great fish and chips.

"But all of the stations where there are winds were hit," I said. "And in Charing Cross there was a smell of water and dirt. It has to be the Blitz."

Cath shook her head. "I've felt them on BART, too."

"But that's in San Francisco. It might be the earthquake. Or the fire."

"And on the Metro in D.C. And once, at home, in the middle of Main Street," she said, staring at the floor. "I think you're right about the inversion layer. It must concentrate them down here, make them stronger and more—"

She paused, and I thought she was going to say "lethal."

"More noticeable," she said.

But I hadn't noticed. Nobody had noticed except Cath, who noticed everything.

And the old, I thought, remembering the white-haired woman in South Kensington Station, her coat collar clutched closed with a blue-veined hand, the stooped old black man on the platform in Holborn. The old feel them all the time. They walked bent nearly double against a wind which blew all the time.

Or stayed out of the Tube. I thought of the Old Man saying, "I loathe the Tube." The Old Man, who had run us merrily all over London on the Tube after adventure, on at Baker Street and off at Tower Hill, up escalators, down stairs, shouting stories over his shoulder the whole time. "Horrible place," he had said, shuddering, yesterday. "Filthy, smelly, drafty." Drafty.

He felt the winds, and so did Mrs. Hughes. "I never go down in the Tube anymore," she had said at dinner. Not "I never take the Tube." I never *go down* in the Tube. And it wasn't just the stairs or the long distances she had to walk. It was the winds, reeking of separation and loss and sorrow.

And Cath had to be right. They had to be the winds of mortality. What else would blow so steadily, so inexorably, on the old and no one else?

But then why had I noticed them? Maybe the conference was an inversion layer of another kind, bringing me face-to-face with old friends and old places. With cancer and the Gap and the Old Man, railing about newfangled plays and spicy food. Bringing me face-to-face early with death and old age and change.

And a feeling of time running out, that made you go shoving down escalators and racing through corridors, frantic to catch the train before it pulled out. A feeling of panic, that it might be the last one. "The doors are closing."

I thought of Sara, running up out of Leicester Square Station, her hair windblown, her cheeks unnaturally red, of her pushing past my knees in the theater, desperate, pursued.

"Sara felt them," I said.

"Did she?" Cath said, her voice flat.

I looked at her, standing there against the far wall, braced for the next wind, waiting for it to hit.

It was funny. This very passage, this very station had been used as a shelter during the Blitz. But there weren't any shelters that could protect you from this kind of raid.

And no matter what train you caught, no matter which line you took, they all went to the same station. Marble Arch. End of the line.

"So what do we do?" I said.

She didn't answer. She stood there looking at the floor between us as if it had "Mind the Gap" written on it. Mind the Gap.

"I don't know," she said finally.

And what had I thought she would say? That it wouldn't be so bad as long as we had each other? That love conquers all?

That was the whole point, wasn't it, that it didn't? That it was no match for divorce and destruction and death? Look at Milford Hughes Senior. Look at Daniel Drecker's daughter.

"They didn't have my china at any of the shops in Chelsea," she said bleakly. "It never occurred to me it might be discontinued. All those years, I—it never occurred to me it wouldn't still be there." Her voice broke. "It was such a pretty pattern."

And the Old Man was so funny and so full of life, the pub was always jam-packed, Sara and Elliott had a great marriage.

But even that couldn't save them. Divorce and destruction and decay.

And what could anybody do about any of it? Button up your overcoat? Stay aboveground?

But that was the problem, staying aboveground. And somehow getting through the days, knowing the doors were closing and it was all going to go smash. Knowing that everything you ever loved or liked or even thought was pretty was all going to be torn down, burned up, blown away. "Gone with the wind," I said, thinking of the woman on the train.

"What?" Cath said, still in that numb, hopeless voice.

"The novel," I said ruefully. "*Gone with the Wind*. There was a woman on the train to Balham today reading it. When I was tracking down the winds, trying to find out which stations had them, if they were stations that had been hit during the Blitz."

"You went to Balham?" she demanded. "Today?"

"And Blackfriars. And Embankment. And Elephant and Castle. I went to the Transport Museum to find which stations had been hit, and then to Monument and Balham, trying to see if they had winds." I shook my head. "I spent the whole day, trying to figure out the pattern of the— What is it?"

Cath had put her hand up to her mouth as if she were in pain.

"What is it?"

She said, "Sara canceled again today. After you left. I thought maybe we could have lunch." She looked across at me. "Nobody knew where you were."

"I didn't want anybody to know I was running around London chasing winds nobody else could feel," I said.

"Elliott told me you'd disappeared the day before, too," she said, and there was still something I wasn't getting here. "He said he and Arthur wanted you to have lunch with them, but you left."

"I went back to Holborn, to try to see what was causing the winds. And then to Marble Arch."

"Sara told me she and Elliott had to go take Evers and his wife sightseeing, that they wanted to see Kew Gardens."

"Elliott? I thought you said he was at the conference?"

"He was. He said Sara had a doctor's appointment she'd forgotten about," she said. "Nobody knew where you were. And then at the theater, you and Sara—"

Had shown up together, late, out of breath, Sara's cheeks flaming. And the day before, I had lied about lunch, about the afternoon session. To Cath, who could sense when people were lying, who could sense when something was wrong.

"You thought *I* was the one who was having an affair with Sara," I said.

She nodded numbly.

"You thought I was having an affair with *Sara?*" I said. "How could you think that? I *love* you."

"And Sara loved Elliott. People cheat on their spouses, they leave each other. Things . . ."

". . . fall apart," I murmured.

And the air down here registered it all, trapped it belowground, distilled it into an essence of death and destruction and decay.

Cath was wrong. It was the Blitz after all. And the girl crying on the train to Balham, and the arguing American couple.

Estrangement and disaster and despair. I wondered if it would record this, too, Cath's fear and our unhappiness, and send it blowing through the tunnels and tracks and passages of the Tube to hit some poor unsuspecting tourist in the face next week. Or fifty years from now.

I looked at Cath, still standing against the opposite wall, impossibly far away.

"I'm not having an affair with Sara," I said, and Cath leaned weakly against the tiles and started to cry.

"I love you," I said and crossed the passage in one stride and put my arms around her, and for a moment everything was all right. We were together, and safe. Love conquers all.

But only till the next wind—the results of the X-ray, the call in the middle of the night, the surgeon looking down at his hands, not wanting to tell you the bad news. And we were still down in the tube tunnels, still in its direct path.

"Come on," I said, and took her arm. I couldn't protect her from the winds, but I could get her out of the Tube. I could keep her out of the inversion layer. For a few years. Or months. Or minutes.

"Where are we going?" she asked as I propelled her along the passage.

"Up," I said. "Out."

"We're miles from our hotel," she said.

"We'll get a taxi," I said. I led her up the stairs, around a curve, listening as we went for the sound of a train rumbling in, for a tinny voice announcing, "Mind the Gap."

"We'll take taxis exclusively from now on," I said.

Down another passage, down another set of stairs, trying not to hurry, as if hurrying might bring another one on. Through the arch to the escalators. Almost there. Another minute, and I'd have her on the escalator and headed up out of the inversion layer. Out of the wind. Safe for the moment.

A clot of people emerged abruptly from the Circle Line tunnel opposite and jammed up in front of the escalator, chattering in French. Teenagers on holiday, lugging enormous backpacks and a duffel too wide for the escalator steps, stopping, maddeningly, to consult their tube maps at the foot of the escalator.

"Excuse me," I said, *"Pardonnez-moi,"* and they looked up, and, instead of moving aside, tried to get on the escalator, jamming the too-wide duffel between the rubber handholds, mashing it down onto the full width of the escalator steps so no one could get past.

Behind us, in the Piccadilly Line tunnel, I could hear the faint sound of a train approaching. The French kids finally, finally, got the bag onto the escalator, and I pushed Cath onto the bottom step, and stepped onto the one below her.

Come on. Up, up. Past posters for *Remains of the Day* and *Forever, Patsy Cline* and *Death of a Salesman.* Below us, the rumble of the train grew louder, closer.

"What do you say we forget going back to our hotel? We're not far from Marble Arch," I said to cover the sound. "What say we call the Royal Hernia and see if they've got an extra bed?"

Come on, come on. Up. *King Lear. The Mousetrap.*

"What if it's not still there?" Cath said, looking down at the depths below us. We'd come almost three floors. The sound of the train was only a murmur, drowned out by the giggling students and the dull roar of the station hall above us.

"It's still there," I said positively.

Come on, up, up.

"It'll be just like it was," I said. "Steep stairs and the smells of mildew and rotting cabbage. Nice wholesome smells."

"Oh, no," Cath said. She pointed across at the down escalators, suddenly jammed with people in evening dress, shaking the rain from their fur coats and theater programs. *"Cats* just got out. We'll never find a taxi."

"We'll walk," I said.

"It's raining," Cath said.

Better the rain than the wind, I thought. Come on. Up.

We were nearly to the top. The students were already heaving their backpacks onto their shoulders. We would walk to a phone booth and call a taxi. And what then? Keep our heads down. Stay out of drafts. Turn into the Old Man.

It won't work, I thought bleakly. The winds are everywhere. But I had to try to protect Cath from them, having failed to protect her for the last twenty years, I had to try now to keep her out of their deadly path.

Three steps from the top. The French students were yanking on the wedged duffel, shouting, *"Allons! Allons! Vite!"*

I turned to look back, straining to hear the sound of the train over their voices. And saw the wind catch the gray hair of the old woman just stepping onto the top step of the down escalator. She hunched down, ducking her head as it blew down on her from above. From above! It flipped the hair back from the oblivious young faces of the French students above us, lifted their collars, their shirttails.

"Cath!" I shouted and reached for her with one hand, digging the fingers of my other one into the rubber railing as if I could stop the escalator, keep it from carrying us inexorably forward, forward into its path.

My grabbing for her had knocked her off balance. She half-fell off her step and into me. I turned her toward me, pulled her against my chest, wrapped my arms around her, but it was too late.

"I love you," Cath said, as if it was her last chance.

"Don't—" I said, but it was already upon us, and there was no protecting her, no stopping it. It hit us full blast, forcing Cath's hair across her cheeks, blowing us nearly back off the step, hitting me full in the face with its smell. I caught my breath in surprise.

The old lady was still standing poised at the top of the escalator, her head back, her eyes closed. People jammed up behind her, saying irritatedly, "Sorry!" and "May I get past, please!" She didn't hear them. Head tilted back, she sniffed deeply at the air.

"Oh," Cath said, and tilted her head back, too.

I breathed it in deeply. A scent of lilacs and rain and expectation. Of years of tourists reading *England on $40 a Day* and newlyweds holding hands on the platform. Of Elliott and Sara and Cath and me, tumbling laughingly after the Old Man, off the train and through the beckoning passages to the District Line and the Tower of London. The scent of spring and the All Clear and things to come.

Caught in the winding tunnels along with the despair and the terror and the grief. Caught in the maze of passages and stairs and platforms, trapped and magnified and held in the inversion layer.

We were at the top. "May I get past, please?" the man behind us said.

"We'll find your china, Cath," I said. "There's a secondhand market at Portobello Road that has everything under the sun."

"Does the Tube go there?" she said.

"I *beg* your pardon," the man said. "*Sorry.*"

"Ladbroke Grove Station. The Hammersmith and City Line," I said, and bent to kiss her.

"You're blocking the way," the man said. "People are trying to get through."

"We're improving the atmosphere," I said and kissed her again.

We stood there a moment, breathing it in—leaves and lilacs and love.

Then we got on the down escalator, holding hands, and went down to the eastbound platform and took the Tube to Marble Arch.

Afterword for "The Winds of Marble Arch"

My favorite place in London is of course St. Paul's, but my second favorite is not a place, exactly. It's the whole vast network of the London Underground. It has these wonderful wooden-slatted escalators that go all the way down to the center of the earth, and ceramic-tiled platforms, and on every available post and pillar and wall is posted the tube map, the best map ever drawn.

And just as the Tube isn't exactly a place, the tube map's not exactly a map, either. It's more like a circuit diagram (or a scar on Professor Dumbledore's knee), and it was designed, believe it or not, by an Underground employee, Harry Beck, in his spare time. It's a work of genius. It's ridiculously easy to read and understand, and it's beautiful in its own right, with all those lovely blue and purple and green lines. It should be hanging in the Tate Gallery, and the Underground should be on the National Trust for Places of Historic Interest. I mean, Charing Cross Station stands on the site of the blacking factory where Charles Dickens worked as a kid. Petula Clark got her start singing in the Tube during the Blitz. Actors like Laurence Olivier and Alec Guinness and Dame Edith Evans gave impromptu performances in Leicester Square Station as the bombs fell, and hundreds of the British Museum's treasures were stored in the blocked-off tunnels of Chancery Lane. Two men were assigned to guard them, and they lived, cooked, and slept there surrounded by wooden crates full of Pharaohs, Caesars, and Grecian urns.

I discovered the delights of the Underground on my very first trip to London and have adored it ever since, so much so that I was delighted that my novel *Blackout / All Clear* and "The Winds of Marble Arch" made it necessary for me to spend hours in the Tube taking notes, and I'm ridiculously happy whenever I see it in a movie or on an episode of *Dr. Who* or the new *Sherlock*. The TV series *Primeval* used the old deserted tunnels under the Aldwych, complete with bunks from the Blitz days, in one of its episodes (it was infested with giant bugs from the Carboniferous Era), and the Underground is in lots of great movies, from *Hanover Street* to *Love Actually* to *Billy Elliott*.

My favorite, though, has to be *Sliding Doors*, in which catching a train—or missing it—takes on cosmic significance.

Just as it should. This is, after all, the Underground.

ALL SEATED ON THE GROUND

I'd always said that if and when the aliens actually landed, it would be a letdown. I mean, after *War of the Worlds, Close Encounters,* and *E.T.,* there was no way they could live up to the image in the public's mind, good or bad.

I'd also said that they would look nothing like the aliens of the movies, and that they would *not* have come to A) kill us, B) take over our planet and enslave us, C) save us from ourselves à la *The Day the Earth Stood Still,* or D) have sex with Earthwomen. I mean, I realize it's hard to find someone nice, but would aliens really come thousands of light-years just to get a date? Plus, it seemed just as likely they'd be attracted to warthogs. Or yucca. Or air-conditioning units.

I've also always thought A) and B) were highly unlikely, since imperialist invader types would probably be too busy invading their next-door neighbors and being invaded by other invader types to have time to go after an out-of-the-way place like Earth, although you never know. I mean, look at Iraq. And as to C), I'm wary of people *or* aliens who say they've come to save you, as witness Reverend Thresher. And it seemed to me that aliens who were capable of building the spaceships necessary to cross all those light-years would necessarily have complex civilizations and therefore more complicated motives for coming than merely incinerating Washington or phoning home.

What had *never* occurred to me was that the aliens would arrive and we still wouldn't know what those motives were after almost nine months of talking to them.

Now, I'm not talking about an arrival where the UFO swoops down in the Southwest in the middle of nowhere, mutilates a few cows, makes a crop circle or two, abducts an *extremely* unreliable and unintelligent-sounding person, probes them in embarrassing places, and takes off again. I'd never believed the aliens would do that, either, and they didn't, although they did land in the Southwest, sort of.

They landed their spaceship in Denver, in the middle of the DU campus, and marched—well, actually marched is the wrong word; the Altairi's method of locomotion is somewhere between a glide and a waddle—straight up to the front door of University Hall in classic "Take me to your leader" fashion.

And that was it. They (there were six of them) didn't say, "Take us to your leader!" or "One small step for aliens, one giant leap for alien-kind" or even "Earthmen, hand over your females." Or your planet. They just stood there.

And stood there. Police cars surrounded them, lights flashing. TV news crews and reporters pointed cameras at them. F-16s roared overhead, snapping pictures of their spaceship and trying to determine whether A) it had a force field or B) weaponry or C) they could blow it up (they couldn't). Half the city fled to the mountains in terror, creating an enormous traffic jam on I-70, and the other half drove by the campus to see what was going on, creating an enormous traffic jam on Evans.

The aliens, who by now had been dubbed the Altairi because an astronomy professor at DU had announced they were from the star Altair in the constellation Aquila (they weren't), didn't react to any of this, which apparently convinced the president of DU they weren't going to blow up the place à la *Independence Day*. He came out and welcomed them to Earth and to DU.

They continued to stand there. The mayor came and welcomed them to Earth and to Denver. The governor came and welcomed them to Earth and to Colorado, assured everyone it was perfectly safe to visit the state, and implied the Altairi were just the latest in a long line of tourists who had come from all over to see the magnificent Rockies, though that seemed unlikely since they were facing the other way, and they didn't turn around, even when the governor walked past them to point at Pikes Peak. They just stood there, facing University Hall.

They continued to stand there for the next three weeks, through an endless series of welcoming speeches by scientists, State Department officials, foreign dignitaries, and church and business leaders, and an assortment of weather, including a late April snowstorm that broke branches and power lines. If it hadn't been for the expressions on their faces, everybody would have assumed the Altairi were plants.

But no plant ever glared like that. It was a look of utter, withering disapproval. The first time I saw it in person, I thought, Oh, my God, it's Aunt Judith.

She was actually my father's aunt, and she used to come over once a month or so, dressed in a suit, a hat, and white gloves, and sit on the edge of a chair and glare at us, a glare which drove my mother into paroxysms of cleaning and baking whenever she found out Aunt Judith was coming. Not that Aunt Judith criticized Mom's housekeeping or her cooking. She didn't. She didn't even make a face when she sipped the coffee Mom served her or draw a white-gloved finger along the mantelpiece, looking for dust. She didn't have to. Sitting there in stony silence while my mother desperately tried to make conversation, her entire manner indicated disapproval. It was perfectly clear from that glare of hers that she considered us untidy, ill-mannered, ignorant, and utterly beneath contempt.

Since she never said what it was that displeased her (except for the occasional "Properly brought-up children do not speak unless spoken to"), my mother frantically polished silverware, baked petits fours, wrestled my sister Tracy and me into starched pinafores and patent-leather shoes and ordered us to thank Aunt Judith nicely for our birthday presents—a card with a dollar bill in it—and scrubbed and dusted the entire house to within an inch of its life. She even redecorated the entire living room, but nothing did any good. Aunt Judith still radiated disdain.

It would wilt even the strongest person. My mother frequently had to lie down with a cold cloth on her forehead after a visit from Aunt Judith, and the Altairi had the same effect on the dignitaries and scientists and politicians who came to see them. After the first time, the governor refused to meet with them again, and the president, whose polls were already in the low twenties and who couldn't afford any more pictures of irate citizens, refused to meet with them at all.

Instead he appointed a bipartisan commission, consisting of representatives from the Pentagon, the State Department, Homeland Security, the House, the Senate, and FEMA, to study them and find a way to communicate with them, and then, after that was a bust, a second commission consisting of experts in astronomy, anthropology, exobiology, and communications, and then a third, consisting of whoever they were able to recruit and who had anything resembling a theory about the Altairi or how to communicate with them, which is where I come in. I'd written a series of newspaper columns on aliens both before and after the Altairi arrived. (I'd also written columns on tourists, driving with cell phones, the traffic on I-70, the difficulty of finding any nice men to date, and Aunt Judith.)

I was recruited in late November to replace one of the language experts, who quit "to spend more time with his wife and family." I was picked by the chair of the commission, Dr. Morthman (who clearly didn't realize that my columns were humorous), but it didn't matter, since he had no intention of listening to me, or to anyone else on the commission, which at that point consisted of three linguists, two anthropologists, a cosmologist, a meteorologist, a botanist (in case they were plants after all), experts in primate, avian, and insect behavior (in case they were one of the above), an Egyptologist (in case they turned out to have built the Pyramids), an animal psychic, an Air Force colonel, a JAG lawyer, an expert in foreign customs, an expert in nonverbal communications, a weapons expert, Dr. Morthman (who, as far as I could see, wasn't an expert in anything), and, because of our proximity to Colorado Springs, the head of the One True Way Maxichurch, Reverend Thresher, who was convinced the Altairi were a herald of the End Times. "There is a reason God had them land here," he said. I wanted to ask him why, if that was the case, they hadn't landed in Colorado Springs instead, but he wasn't a good listener, either.

The only progress these people and their predecessors had made by the time I joined the commission was to get the Altairi to follow them various places, like in out of the weather and into the various labs that had been set up in University Hall for studying them, although when I saw the videotapes, it wasn't at all clear they were responding to anything the commission said or did. It looked to me like following Dr. Morthman and the others was their own idea, particularly since at nine o'clock every night they turned and glided/waddled back outside and disappeared into their ship.

The first time they did that, everyone panicked, thinking they were leaving. "Aliens Depart. Are They Fed Up?" the evening news logo read, a conclusion which I felt was due to their effect on people rather than any solid evidence. I mean, they could have gone home to watch Jon Stewart on *The Daily Show,* but even after they re-emerged the next morning, the theory persisted that there was some sort of deadline, that if we didn't succeed in communicating with them within a fixed amount of time, the planet would be reduced to ash. Aunt Judith had always made me feel exactly the same way, that if I didn't measure up, I was toast.

But I never did measure up, and nothing in particular happened, except she stopped sending me birthday cards with a dollar in them, and I figured if the Altairi hadn't obliterated us after a few conversations with Reverend Thresher (he was constantly reading them passages from Scripture and trying to convert them), they weren't going to.

But it didn't look like they were going to tell us what they were doing here, either. The commission had tried speaking to them in nearly every language, including Farsi, Navajo code-talk, and Cockney slang. They had played them music, drummed, written out greetings, given them several PowerPoint presentations, text-messaged them, and shown them the Rosetta Stone. They'd also tried Ameslan and panto-mime, though it was obvious the Altairi could hear. Whenever some-one spoke to them or offered them a gift (or prayed over them), their expression of disapproval deepened to one of utter contempt. Just like Aunt Judith.

By the time I joined the commission, it had reached the same state of desperation my mother had when she redecorated the living room and had decided to try to impress the Altairi by taking them to see the sights of Denver and Colorado, in the hope they'd react favorably.

"It won't work," I said. "My mother put up new drapes *and* wallpa-per, and it didn't have any effect at all," but Dr. Morthman didn't listen.

We took them to the Denver Museum of Art and Rocky Mountain National Park and the Garden of the Gods and a Broncos game. They just stood there, sending out waves of disapproval.

Dr. Morthman was undeterred. "Tomorrow we'll take them to the Denver Zoo."

"Is that a good idea?" I asked. "I mean, I'd hate to give them ideas," but Dr. Morthman didn't listen.

Luckily, the Altairi didn't react to anything at the zoo, or to the Christmas lights at Civic Center, or to the *Nutcracker* ballet. And then we went to the mall.

By that point, the commission had dwindled down to seventeen people (two of the linguists and the animal psychic had quit), but it was still a large enough group of observers that the Altairi ran the risk of being trampled in the crowd. Most of the members, however, had stopped going on the field trips, saying they were "pursuing alternate lines of research" that didn't require direct observation, which meant they couldn't stand to be glared at the whole way there and back in the van.

So the day we went to the mall, there were only Dr. Morthman, the aroma expert Dr. Wakamura, Reverend Thresher, and me. We didn't even have any press with us. When the Altairi'd first arrived, they were all over the TV networks and CNN, but after a few weeks of the aliens doing nothing, the networks had shifted to showing more exciting scenes from *Alien, Invasion of the Body Snatchers,* and *Men in Black II,* and then completely lost interest and gone back to Paris Hilton and stranded whales. The only photographer with us was Leo, the teenager Dr. Morthman had hired to videotape our outings, and as soon as we got inside the mall, he said, "Do you think it'd be okay if I ducked out to buy my girlfriend's Christmas present before we start filming? I mean, face it, they're just going to stand there."

He was right. The Altairi glide-waddled the length of several stores and then stopped, glaring impartially at The Sharper Image and Gap window displays and the crowds who stopped to gawk at the six of them and who then, intimidated by their expressions, averted their eyes and hurried on.

The mall was jammed with couples loaded down with shopping bags, parents pushing strollers, children, and a mob of middle-school girls in green choir robes apparently waiting to sing. The malls invited school and church choirs to come and perform this time of year in the food court. The girls were giggling and chattering; a toddler was shriek-ing, "I don't *want* to!"; Julie Andrews was singing "Joy to the World" on the piped-in Muzak; and Reverend Thresher was pointing at the panty-, bra-, and wing-clad mannequins in the window of Victoria's Secret and saying, "Look at that! Sinful!"

"This way," Dr. Morthman, ahead of the Altairi, said, waving his arm like the leader of a wagon train, "I want them to see Santa Claus," and I stepped to the side to get around a trio of teenage boys walking side by side who'd cut me off from the Altairi.

There was a sudden gasp, and the mall went quiet except for the Muzak. "What—?" Dr. Morthman said sharply, and I pushed past the teenage boys to see what had happened.

The Altairi were sitting calmly in the middle of the space between the stores, glaring. A circle of fascinated shoppers had formed a circle around them, and a man in a suit who looked like the manager of the mall was hurrying up, demanding, "What's going on here?"

"This is wonderful," Dr. Morthman said. "I knew they'd respond if we just took them enough places." He turned to me. "You were behind them, Miss Yates. What made them sit down?"

"I don't know," I said. "I couldn't see them from where I was. Did—?"

"Go find Leo," he ordered. "He'll have it on tape."

I wasn't so sure of that, but I went to look for him. He was just coming out of Victoria's Secret, carrying a small bright pink bag. "Meg, what happened?" he asked.

"The Altairi sat down," I said.

"Why?"

"That's what we're trying to find out. I take it you weren't filming them?"

"No, I told you, I had to buy my girlfriend— Jeez, Dr. Morthman will kill me." He jammed the pink bag into his jeans pocket. "I didn't think—"

"Well, start filming now," I said, "and I'll go see if I can find somebody who caught it on their cellphone camera." With all these people taking their kids to see Santa, there was bound to be someone with a camera. I started working my way around the circle of staring spectators, keeping away from Dr. Morthman, who was telling the mall manager he needed to cordon off this end of the mall and everyone in it.

"Everyone in it?" the manager gulped.

"Yes, it's essential. The Altairi are obviously responding to something they saw or heard—"

"Or smelled," Dr. Wakamura put in.

"And until we know what it was, we can't allow anyone to leave," Dr. Morthman said. "It's the key to our being able to communicate with them."

"But it's only two weeks till Christmas," the mall manager said. "I can't just shut off—"

"You obviously don't realize that the fate of the planet may be at stake," Dr. Morthman said.

I hoped not, especially since no one seemed to have caught the event on film, though they all had their cell phones out and pointed at the Altairi now, in spite of their glares. I looked across the circle, searching for a likely parent or grandparent who might have—

The choir. One of the girls' parents was bound to have brought a video camera along. I hurried over to the troop of green-robed girls. "Excuse me," I said to them, "I'm with the Altairi—"

Mistake. The girls instantly began bombarding me with questions. "Why are they sitting down?"

"Why don't they talk?"

"Why are they always so mad?"

"Are we going to get to sing? We didn't get to sing yet."

"They said we had to stay here. How long? We're supposed to sing over at Flatirons Mall at six o'clock."

"Are they going to get inside us and pop out of our stomachs?"

"Did any of your parents bring a video camera?" I tried to shout over their questions, and when that failed, "I need to talk to your choir director."

"Mr. Ledbetter?"

"Are you his girlfriend?"

"No," I said, trying to spot someone who looked like a choir director type. "Where is he?"

"Over there," one of them said, pointing at a tall, skinny man in slacks and a blazer. "Are you going out with Mr. Ledbetter?"

"No," I said, trying to work my way over to him.

"Why not? He's really nice."

"Do you have a boyfriend?"

"No," I said as I reached him. "Mr. Ledbetter? I'm Meg Yates. I'm with the commission studying the Altairi—"

"You're just the person I want to talk to, Meg," he said.

"I'm afraid I can't tell you how long it's going to be," I said. "The girls told me you have another singing engagement at six o'clock."

"We do, and I've got a rehearsal tonight, but that isn't what I wanted to talk to you about."

"She doesn't have a boyfriend, Mr. Ledbetter," one of the girls said.

I took advantage of the interruption to say, "I was wondering if anyone with your choir happened to record what just happened on a video camera or a—"

"Probably. Belinda," he said to the one who told him I didn't have a boyfriend, "go get your mother." She took off through the crowd. "Her mom started recording when we left the church. And if she didn't happen to catch it, Kaneesha's mom probably did. Or Chelsea's dad."

"Oh, thank goodness," I said. "Our cameraman didn't get it on film, and we need it to see what triggered their action."

"What made them sit down, you mean?" he said. "You don't need a video. I know what it was. The song."

"What song?" I said. "A choir wasn't singing when we came in, and anyway, the Altairi have already been exposed to music. They didn't react to it at all."

"What kind of music? Those notes from *Close Encounters*?"

"Yes," I said defensively, "and Beethoven and Debussy and Charles Ives. A whole assortment of composers."

"But instrumental music, not vocals, right? I'm talking about a song. One of the Christmas carols on the piped-in Muzak. I saw them sit down. They were definitely—"

"Mr. Ledbetter, you wanted my mom?" Belinda said, dragging over a large woman with a videocam.

"Yes," he said. "Mrs. Carlson, I need to see the video you shot of the choir today. From when we got to the mall."

She obligingly found the place and handed it to him. He fast-forwarded a minute. "Oh, good, you got it," he said, rewound, and held the camera so I could see the little screen. "Watch."

The screen showed the bus with *First Presbyterian Church* on its side, the girls getting off, the girls filing into the mall, the girls gathering in front of Crate and Barrel, giggling and chattering, though the sound was too low to hear what they were saying. "Can you turn the volume up?" Mr. Ledbetter said to Mrs. Carlson, and she pushed a button.

The voices of the girls came on: "Mr. Ledbetter, can we go to the food court afterward for a pretzel?"

"Mr. Ledbetter, I don't want to stand next to Heidi."

"Mr. Ledbetter, I left my lip gloss on the bus."

"Mr. Ledbetter—"

The Altairi aren't going to be on this, I thought. Wait—there, past the green-robed girls, was Dr. Morthman and Leo with his video camera, and then the Altairi. They were just glimpses, though, not a clear view. "I'm afraid—" I said.

"Shh," Mr. Ledbetter said, pushing down on the volume button again. "Listen."

He had cranked the volume all the way up. I could hear Reverend Thresher saying, "Look at that! It's absolutely disgusting!"

"Can you hear the Muzak on the tape, Meg?" Mr. Ledbetter asked.

"Sort of," I said. "What is that?"

" 'Joy to the World,' " he said, holding it so I could see. Mrs. Carlson must have moved to get a better shot of the Altairi, because there was no one blocking the view of them as they followed Dr. Morthman. I tried to see if they were glaring at anything in particular—the strollers or the Christmas decorations or the Victoria's Secret mannequins or the sign for the restrooms—but if they were, I couldn't tell.

"This way," Dr. Morthman said on the tape, "I want them to see Santa Claus."

"Okay, it's right about here," Mr. Ledbetter said. "Listen."

"'While shepherds watched . . .'" the Muzak choir sang tinnily.

I could hear Reverend Thresher saying, "Blasphemous!" and one of the girls asking, "Mr. Ledbetter, after we sing can we go to McDonald's?" and the Altairi abruptly collapsed onto the floor with a floomphing motion, like a crinolined Scarlett O'Hara sitting down suddenly. "Did you hear what they were singing?" Mr. Ledbetter said.

"No—"

"'All seated on the ground.' Here," he said, rewinding. "Listen."

He played it again. I watched the Altairi, focusing on picking out the sound of the Muzak through the rest of the noise. "'While shepherds watched their flocks by night,'" the choir sang, "'all seated on the ground.'"

He was right. The Altairi sat down the instant the word "seated" ended. I looked at him.

"See?" he said happily. "The song said to sit down and they sat. I happened to notice it because I was singing along with the Muzak. It's a bad habit of mine. The girls tease me about it."

But why would the Altairi respond to the words in a Christmas carol when they hadn't responded to anything else we'd said to them over the last nine months? "Can I borrow this videotape?" I asked. "I need to show it to the rest of the commission."

"Sure," he said, and asked Mrs. Carlson.

"I don't know," she said reluctantly. "I have tapes of every single one of Belinda's performances."

"She'll make a copy and get the original back to you," Mr. Ledbetter told her. "Isn't that right, Meg?"

"Yes," I said.

"Great," he said. "You can send the tape to me, and I'll see to it Belinda gets it. Will that work?" he asked Mrs. Carlson.

She nodded, popped the tape out, and handed it to me. "Thank you," I said and hurried back over to Dr. Morthman, who was still arguing with the mall manager.

"You can't just close the entire mall," the manager was saying. "This is the biggest profit period of the year—"

"Dr. Morthman," I said, "I have a tape here of the Altairi sitting down. It was taken by— "

"Not now," he said. "I need you to go tell Leo to film everything the Altairi might have seen."

"But he's taping the Altairi," I said. "What if they do something else?" but he wasn't listening.

"Tell him we need a video record of everything they might have responded to, the stores, the shoppers, the Christmas decorations, everything. And then call the police department and tell them to cordon off the parking lot. Tell them no one's to leave."

"Cordon off—!" the mall manager said. "You can't hold all these people here!"

"All these people need to be moved out of this end of the mall and into an area where they can be questioned," Dr. Morthman said.

"Questioned?" the mall manager, almost apoplectic, said.

"Yes, one of them may have seen what triggered their action—"

"Someone did," I said. "I was just talking to—"

He wasn't listening. "We'll need names, contact information, and depositions from all of them," he said to the mall manager. "And they'll need to be tested for infectious diseases. The Altairi may be sitting down because they don't feel well."

"Dr. Morthman, they aren't sick," I said. "They—"

"Not *now*," he said. "Did you tell Leo?"

I gave up. "I'll do it now," I said and went over to where Leo was filming the Altairi and told him what Dr. Morthman wanted him to do.

"What if the Altairi do something?" he said, looking at them sitting there glaring. He sighed. "I suppose he's right. They don't look like they're going to move anytime soon." He swung his camera around and started filming the Victoria's Secret window. "How long do you think we'll be stuck here?"

I told him what Dr. Morthman had said.

"Jeez, he's going to question all these people?" he said, moving to the Williams-Sonoma window. "I had somewhere to go tonight."

All these people have somewhere to go tonight, I thought, looking at the crowd—mothers with babies in strollers, little kids, elderly couples, teenagers. Including fifty middle-school girls who were supposed to be at another performance an hour from now. And it wasn't the choir director's fault Dr. Morthman wouldn't listen.

"We'll need a room large enough to hold everyone," Dr. Morthman was saying, "and adjoining rooms for interrogating them," and the mall manager was shouting, "This is a *mall*, not Guantanamo!"

I backed carefully away from Dr. Morthman and the mall manager and then worked my way through the crowd to where the choir director was standing, surrounded by his students. "But, Mr. Ledbetter," one of them was saying, "we'd come right back, and the pretzel place is right over there."

"Mr. Ledbetter, could I speak to you for a moment?" I said.

"Sure. Shoo," he said to the girls.

"But, Mr. Ledbetter—"

He ignored them. "What did the commission think of the Christmas carol theory?" he asked me.

"I haven't had a chance to ask them. Listen, in another five minutes they're going to lock down this entire mall."

"But I—"

"I know, you've got another performance and if you're going to leave, do it right now. I'd go that way," I said, pointing to the east door.

"*Thank* you," he said earnestly, "but won't you get into trouble—?"

"If I need your choir's depositions, I'll call you," I said. "What's your number?"

"Belinda, give me a pen and something to write on," he said. She handed him a pen and began rummaging in her backpack.

"Never mind," he said, "there isn't time." He grabbed my hand and wrote the number on my palm.

"You said we aren't allowed to write on ourselves," Belinda said.

"You're not," he said. "I really appreciate this, Meg."

"Go," I said, looking anxiously over at Dr. Morthman. If they didn't go in the next thirty seconds, they'd never make it, and there was no way he could round up fifty middle-school girls in that short a time. Or even make himself heard . . .

"Ladies," he said, and raised his hands as if he were going to direct a choir. "Line up." And to my astonishment, they instantly obeyed him, forming themselves silently into a line and walking quickly toward the east door with no giggling, no "Mr. Ledbetter—?" My opinion of him went up sharply.

I pushed quickly back through the crowd to where Dr. Morthman and the mall manager were still arguing. Leo had moved farther down the mall to film the Verizon Wireless store and away from the east door. Good. I rejoined Dr. Morthman, moving to his right side so if he turned to look at me, he couldn't see the door.

"But what about *bathrooms*?" the manager was yelling. "The mall doesn't have nearly enough bathrooms for all these people."

The choir was nearly out the door. I watched till the last one disappeared, followed by Mr. Ledbetter.

"We'll get in portable toilets. Miss Yates, arrange for Porta-Potties to be brought in," Dr. Morthman said, turning to me, and it was obvious he had no idea I'd ever been gone. "And get Homeland Security on the phone."

"Homeland Security!" the manager wailed. "Do you know what it'll do to business when the media gets hold—" He stopped and looked over at the crowd around the Altairi.

There was a collective gasp from them and then a hush. Someone must have turned the Muzak off at some point because there was no sound at all in the mall. "What—? Let me through," Dr. Morthman said, breaking the silence. He pushed his way through the circle of shoppers to see what was happening.

I followed in his wake. The Altairi were slowly standing up, a motion somewhat like a string being pulled taut.

"Thank goodness," the mall manager said, sounding infinitely relieved. "Now that that's over, I assume I can reopen the mall."

Dr. Morthman shook his head. "This may be the prelude to another action, or the response to a second stimulus. Leo, I want to see the video of what was happening right before they began to stand up."

"I didn't get it," Leo said.

"Didn't *get* it?"

"You told me to tape the stuff in the mall," he said, but Dr. Morthman wasn't listening. He was watching the Altairi, who had turned around and were slowly glide-waddling back toward the east door.

"Go after them," he ordered Leo. "Don't let them out of your sight, and get it on tape this time." He turned to me. "You stay here and see if the mall has surveillance tapes. And get all these people's names and contact information in case we need to question them."

"Before you go, you need to know—"

"Not *now*. The Altairi are leaving. And there's no telling where they'll go next," he said, and took off after them. "See if anyone caught the incident on a video camera."

As it turned out, the Altairi went only as far as the van we'd brought them to the mall in, where they waited, glaring, to be transported back to DU. When I got back, they were in the main lab with Dr. Wakamura. I'd been at the mall nearly four hours, taking down names and phone numbers from Christmas shoppers who said things like, "I've been here six hours with two toddlers. Six hours!" and "I'll have you know I missed my grandson's Christmas concert." I was glad I'd helped

Mr. Ledbetter and his seventh-grade girls sneak out. They'd never have made it to the other mall in time.

When I was finished taking names and abuse, I went to ask the mall manager about surveillance tapes, expecting more abuse, but he was so glad to have his mall open again, he turned them over immediately. "Do these tapes have audio?" I asked him, and when he said no, "You wouldn't also have a tape of the Christmas music you play, would you?"

I was almost certain he wouldn't—Muzak is usually piped in—but to my surprise he said yes and handed over a CD. I stuck it and the tapes in my bag, drove back to DU, and went to the main lab to find Dr. Morthman. I found Dr. Wakamura instead, squirting assorted food court smells—corn dog, popcorn, sushi—at the Altairi to see if any of them made them sit down. "I'm convinced they were responding to one of the mall's aromas," he said.

"Actually, I think they may have—"

"It's just a question of finding the right one," he said, squirting pizza at them. They glared.

"Where's Dr. Morthman?"

"Next door," he said, squirting essence of funnel cake. "He's meeting with the rest of the commission."

I winced and went next door. "We need to look at the floor coverings in the mall," Dr. Short was saying. "The Altairi may well have been responding to the difference between wood and stone."

"And we need to take air samples," Dr. Jarvis said. "They may have been responding to something poisonous to them in our atmosphere."

"Something poisonous?" Reverend Thresher said. "Something blasphemous, you mean! Angels in filthy underwear! The Altairi obviously refused to go any farther into that den of iniquity, and they sat down in protest. Even aliens know sin when they see it."

"I don't agree, Dr. Jarvis," Dr. Short said, ignoring Reverend Thresher. "Why would the air in the mall have a different composition from the air in a museum or a sports arena? We're looking for variables here. What about sounds? Could they be a factor?"

"Yes," I said. "The Altairi were—"

"Did you get the surveillance tapes, Miss Yates?" Dr. Morthman cut in. "Go through and cue them up to the point just before the Altairi sat down. I want to see what they were looking at."

"It wasn't what they were looking at," I said. "It was—"

"And call the mall and get samples of their floor coverings," he said. "You were saying, Dr. Short?"

I left the surveillance tapes and the lists of shoppers on Dr. Morthman's desk, and then went to the audio lab, found a CD player, and listened to the songs: "Here Comes Santa Claus," "White Christmas," "Joy to the World"—

Here it was. "'While shepherds watched their flocks by night, all seated on the ground, the angel of the Lord came down, and glory shone around.'" Could the Altairi have thought the song was talking about the descent of their spaceship? Or were they responding to something else entirely, and the timing was simply coincidental?

There was only one way to find out. I went back to the main lab, where Dr. Wakamura was sticking lighted candles under the Altairi's noses. "Good grief, what is that?" I asked, wrinkling my nose.

"Bayberry magnolia," he said.

"It's awful."

"You should smell sandalwood violet," he said. "They were right next to Candle in the Wind when they sat down. They may have been responding to a scent from the store."

"Any response?" I said, thinking their expressions, for once, looked entirely appropriate.

"No, not even to spruce watermelon, which smelled *very* alien. Did Dr. Morthman find any clues on the security tapes?" he asked hopefully.

"He hasn't looked at them yet," I said. "When you're done here, I'll be glad to escort the Altairi back to their ship."

"Would you?" he said gratefully. "I'd really appreciate it. They look exactly like my mother-in-law. Can you take them now?"

"Yes," I said, and went over to the Altairi and motioned them to follow me, hoping they wouldn't veer off and go back to their ship since it was nearly nine o'clock. They didn't. They followed me down the hall and into the audio lab. "I just want to try something," I said and played them "While Shepherds Watched."

"'While shepherds watched their flocks,'" the choir sang. I watched the Altairi's unchanging faces. Mr. Ledbetter was wrong, I thought. They must have been responding to something else. They're not even listening. "'. . . by night, all seated . . .'"

The Altairi sat down.

I've got to call Mr. Ledbetter, I thought. I switched off the CD and punched in the number he'd written on my hand. "Hi, this is Calvin Ledbetter," his recorded voice said. "Sorry I can't come to the phone right now," and I remembered too late that he'd said he had a rehearsal. "If you're calling about a rehearsal, the schedule is as follows: Thursday, Mile-High Women's Chorus, eight P.M., Montview Methodist, Friday, chancel choir, eleven A.M., Trinity Episcopal, Denver Symphony, three P.M.—" It was obvious he wasn't home. And that he was far too busy to worry about the Altairi.

I hung up and looked over at them. They were still sitting down, and it occurred to me that playing them the song might have been a bad idea, since I had no idea what had made them stand back up. It hadn't been the Muzak because it had been turned off, and if the stimulus had been something in the mall, we could be here all night. After a few minutes, though, they stood up, doing that odd pulled-string thing, and glared at me. "'While shepherds watched their flocks by night,'" I said to them, "'all seated on the ground.'"

They continued to stand.

"*Seated* on the ground," I repeated. "*Seated*. Sit!"

No response at all.

I played the song again. They sat down right on cue. Which still didn't prove they were doing what the words told them to do. They could be responding to the mere sound of singing. The mall had been noisy when they first walked in. "While Shepherds Watched" might have been the first song they'd been able to hear, and they'd sit down whenever they heard singing. I waited till they stood up again and then played the two preceding tracks. They didn't respond to Bing Crosby singing "White Christmas" or to Julie Andrews singing "Joy to the World." (Or to the breaks between songs.) There wasn't even any indication they were aware anyone was singing.

"'While shepherds watched their flocks by-y night . . .'" the choir began. I tried to stay still and keep my face impassive, in case they were responding to nonverbal cues I was giving them. "'. . . ah-all seated—'"

They sat down at exactly the same place, so it was definitely those particular words. Or the voices singing them. Or the particular configuration of notes. Or the rhythm. Or the frequencies of the notes.

Whatever it was, I couldn't figure it out tonight. It was nearly ten o'clock. I needed to get the Altairi back to their spaceship. I waited for them to stand up and then led them, glaring, out to their ship, and went back to my apartment.

The message light on my answering machine was flashing. It was probably Dr. Morthman, wanting me to go back to the mall and take air samples. I hit play. "Hi, this is Mr. Ledbetter," the choir director's voice said. "From the mall, remember? I need to talk to you about something." He gave me his cellphone number and repeated his home phone, "In case it washed off. I should be home by eleven. Till then, whatever you do, *don't* let your alien guys listen to any more Christmas carols."

There was no answer at either of the numbers. He turns his cell phone off during rehearsals, I thought. I looked at my watch. It was ten-fifteen. I grabbed the yellow pages, looked up the address of Montview Methodist, and took off for the church, detouring past the Altairi's ship to make sure it was still there and hadn't begun sprouting guns from its ports or flashing ominous lights. It hadn't. It was its usual Sphinx-like self, which reassured me. A little.

It took me twenty minutes to reach the church. I hope rehearsal isn't over and I've missed him, I thought, but there were lots of cars in the parking lot, and light still shone though the stained-glass windows. The front doors, however, were locked.

I went around to the side door. It was unlocked, and I could hear singing from somewhere inside. I followed the sound down a darkened hall.

The song abruptly stopped, in the middle of a word. I waited a minute, listening, and when it didn't start up again, began trying doors. The first three were locked, but the fourth opened onto the sanctuary. The women's choir was up at the very front, facing Mr. Ledbetter, whose back was to me. "Top of page ten," he was saying.

Thank goodness he's still here, I thought, slipping in the back.

"From 'O hear the angel voices,'" he said, nodded to the organist, and raised his baton.

"Wait, where do we take a breath?" one of the women asked. "After 'voices'?"

"No, after 'divine,'" he said, consulting the music in front of him on the music stand, "and then at the bottom of page thirteen."

"Another woman said, "Can you play the alto line for us? From 'Fall on your knees'?"

This was obviously going to take a while, and I couldn't afford to wait. I started up the aisle toward them, and the entire choir looked up from their music and glared at me.

Mr. Ledbetter turned around, and his face lit up. He turned to the women again, said, "I'll be right back," and sprinted down the aisle to me. "Meg," he said, reaching me. "Hi. What—?"

"I'm sorry to interrupt, but I got your message, and—"

"You're not interrupting. Really. We were almost done anyway."

"What did you mean, don't play them any more Christmas carols?

I didn't get your message till after I'd played them some of the other songs from the mall—"

"And what happened?"

"Nothing, but on your message you said—"

"Which songs?"

"'Joy to the World' and—"

"All four verses?"

"No, only two. That's all that were on the CD. The first one and the one about 'wonders of his love.'"

"One and four," he said, staring past me, his lips moving rapidly as if he were running through the lyrics. "Those should be okay—"

"What do you mean? Why did you leave that message?"

"Because if the Altairi were responding literally to the words in 'While Shepherds Watched,' Christmas carols are full of dangerous—"

"Dangerous—?"

"Yes. Look at 'We Three Kings of Orient Are.' You didn't play them that, did you?"

"No, just 'Joy to the World' and 'White Christmas.'"

"Mr. Ledbetter," one of the women called from the front of the church. "How long are you going to be?"

"I'll be right there," he said. He turned back to me. "How much of 'While Shepherds Watched' did you play them?"

"Just the part up to 'all seated on the ground.'"

"Not the other verses?"

"No. What—?"

"Mr. Ledbetter," the same woman said impatiently, "some of us have to leave."

"I'll be right there," he called to her, and to me, "Give me five minutes," and sprinted back up the aisle.

I sat down in a back pew, picked up a hymnal, and tried to find "We Three Kings." That was easier said than done. The hymns were numbered, but they didn't seem to be in any particular order. I turned to the back, looking for an index.

"But we still haven't gone over 'Saviour of the Heathen, Come,'" a young, pretty redhead said.

"We'll go over it Saturday night," Mr. Ledbetter said.

The index didn't tell me where "We Three Kings" was, either. It had rows of numbers—5.6.6.5. and 8.8.7.D.—with a column of strange words below them—Laban, Hursley, Olive's Brow, Arizona—like some sort of code. Could the Altairi be responding to some sort of cipher embedded in the carol like in *The Da Vinci Code*? I hoped not.

"When are we supposed to be there?" the women were asking.

"Seven," Mr. Ledbetter said.

"But that won't give us enough time to run over 'Saviour of the Heathen, Come,' will it?"

"And what about 'Santa Claus Is Coming to Town'?" the redhead asked. "We don't have the second soprano part at all."

I abandoned the index and began looking through the hymns. If I couldn't figure out a simple hymnal, how could I hope to figure out a completely alien race's communications? *If* they were trying to communicate. They might have been sitting down to listen to the music, like you'd stop to look at a flower. Or maybe their feet just hurt.

"What kind of shoes are we supposed to wear?" the choir was asking.

"Comfortable," Mr. Ledbetter said. "You're going to be on your feet a long time."

I continued to search through the hymnal. Here was "What Child Is This?" I had to be on the right track. "Bring a Torch, Jeannette, Isabella." It had to be here somewhere. "On Christmas Night, All People Sing—"

They were finally gathering up their things and leaving. "See you Saturday," he said, herding them out the door, all except for the pretty redhead, who buttonholed him at the door to say, "I was wondering if you could stay and go over the second soprano part with me again. It'll only take a few minutes."

"I can't tonight," he said. She turned and glared at me, and I knew *exactly* what that glare meant.

"Remind me and we'll run through it Saturday night," he said, shut the door on her, and sat down next to me. "Sorry, big performance Saturday. Now, about the aliens. Where were we?"

"'We Three Kings.' You said the words were dangerous."

"Oh, right." He took the hymnal from me, flipped expertly to the right page, pointed. "Verse four. 'Sorrowing, sighing, bleeding, dying'—I assume you don't want the Altairi locking themselves in a stone-cold tomb."

"No," I said fervently. "You said 'Joy to the World' was bad, too. What does it have in it?"

"'Sorrow, sins, thorns infesting the ground.'"

"You think they're doing whatever the hymns tell them? That they're treating them like orders to be followed?"

"I don't know, but if they are, there are all kinds of things in Christmas carols you don't want them doing: running around on rooftops, bringing torches, killing babies—"

"Killing *babies*?" I said. "What carol is that in?"

"'The Coventry Carol,'" he said flipping to another page. "The verse about Herod. See?" He pointed to the words. "'Charged he hath this day . . . all children young to slay.'"

"Oh, my gosh, that carol was one of the ones from the mall. It was on the CD," I said. "I'm so glad I came to see you."

"So am I," he said, and grinned at me.

"You asked me how much of 'While Shepherds Watched' I'd played them," I said. "Is there child-slaying in that, too?"

"No, but verse two has got 'fear' and 'mighty dread' in it, and 'seized their troubled minds.'"

"I definitely don't want the Altairi to do that," I said, "but now I don't know *what* to do. We've been trying to establish communications with the Altairi for nine months, and that song was the first thing they've ever responded to. If I can't play them Christmas carols—"

"I didn't say that. We just need to make sure the ones you play them don't have any murder and mayhem in them. You said you had a CD of the music they were playing in the mall?"

"Yes. That's what I played them."

"Mr. Ledbetter?" a voice said tentatively, and a balding man in a clerical collar leaned in the door. "How much longer will you be? I need to lock up."

"Oh, sorry, Reverend McIntyre," he said and stood up. "We'll get out of your way." He ran up the aisle, grabbed his music, and came back. "You'll be at the aches, right?" he said to Reverend McIntyre.

The *aches*? You must have misunderstood what he said, I thought.

"I'm not sure," Reverend McIntyre said. "My handle's pretty rusty."

Handle? What *were* they talking about?

"Especially 'The Hallelujah Chorus.' It's been years since I last sang it."

Oh, Handel, not handle.

"I'm rehearsing it with Trinity Episcopal's choir at eleven tomorrow if you want to come and run through it with us."

"I just may do that."

"Great," Mr. Ledbetter said. "Good night." He led me out of the sanctuary. "Where's your car parked?"

"Out in front."

"Good. Mine, too." He opened the side door. "You can follow me to my apartment."

I had a sudden blinding vision of Aunt Judith glaring disapprovingly at me and saying, "A nice young lady *never* goes to a gentleman's apartment alone."

"You did say you brought the music from the mall with you, didn't you?" he asked.

Which is what you get for jumping to conclusions, I thought, following him to his apartment and wondering if he was going out with the redheaded second soprano.

"On the way over I was thinking about all this," he said when we got to his apartment building, "and I think the first thing we need to do is figure out exactly which element or elements of 'all seated on the ground' they're responding to, the notes—I know you said they'd been exposed to music before, but it could be this particular configuration of notes—or words."

I told him about reciting the lyrics to them.

"Okay, then, the next thing we do is see if it's the accompaniment," he said, unlocking the door. "Or the tempo. Or the key."

"The key?" I said, looking down at the keys in his hand.

"Yeah, have you ever seen *Jumpin' Jack Flash*?"

"No."

"Great movie. Whoopi Goldberg. In it, the key to the spy's code is the key. Literally. B flat. 'While Shepherds Watched' is in the key of C, but 'Joy to the World' is in D. That may be why they didn't respond to it. Or they may only respond to the sound of certain instruments. What Beethoven did they listen to?"

"The Ninth Symphony."

He frowned. "Then that's unlikely, but there might be a guitar or a marimba or something in the 'While Shepherds Watched' accompaniment. We'll see. Come on in," he said, opening the door and immediately vanishing into the bedroom. "There's soda in the fridge," he called back out to me. "Go ahead and sit down."

That was easier said than done. The couch, chair, and coffee table were all covered with CDs, music, and clothes. "Sorry," he said, coming back in with a laptop. He set it down on top of a stack of books and moved a pile of laundry from the chair so I could sit down. "December's a bad month. And this year, in addition to my usual five thousand concerts and church services and cantata performances, I'm directing aches."

Then I hadn't misheard him before. "Aches?" I said.

"Yeah. A-C-H-E-S. The All-City Holiday Ecumenical Sing. ACHES. Or, as my seventh-grade girls call it, Aches and Pains. It's a giant concert—well, not actually a concert because everybody sings, even the audience. But all the city singing groups and church choirs participate." He moved a stack of LPs off the couch and onto the floor and sat down across from me. "Denver has it every year. At the convention center. Have you ever been to a Sing?" he said, and when I shook my head, "It's pretty impressive. Last year three thousand people and forty-four choirs participated."

"And you're directing?"

"Yeah. Actually, it's a much easier job than directing my church choirs. Or my seventh-grade girls' glee. And it's kind of fun. It used to be the All-City *Messiah*, you know, a whole bunch of people getting together to sing Handel's *Messiah*, but then they had a request from the Unitarians to include some Solstice songs, and it kind of snowballed from there. Now we do Hanukkah songs and 'Have Yourself a Merry Little Christmas' and 'The Seven Nights of Kwanzaa,' along with Christmas carols and selections from the *Messiah*. Which, by the way, we can't let the Altairi listen to, either."

"Is there children-slaying in that, too?"

"Head-breaking. 'Thou shalt break them with a rod of iron' and 'dash them in pieces.' There's also wounding, bruising, cutting, deriding, and laughing to scorn."

"Actually, the Altairi already know all about scorn," I said.

"But hopefully not about shaking nations. And covering the earth with darkness," he said. "Okay"—he opened his laptop—"the first thing I'm going to do is scan in the song. Then I'll remove the accompaniment so we can play them just the vocals."

"What can I do?"

"You," he said, disappearing into the other room again and returning with a foot-high stack of sheet music and music books, which he dumped in my lap, "can make a list of all the songs we don't want the Altairi to hear."

I nodded and started through *The Holly Jolly Book of Christmas Songs*. It was amazing how many carols, which I'd always thought were about peace and goodwill, had really violent lyrics. "The Coventry Carol" wasn't the only one with child-slaying in it. "Christmas Day Is Come" did, too, along with references to sin, strife, and militants. "O Come, O Come, Emmanuel" had strife, too, and envy and quarrels. "The Holly and the Ivy" had thorns, blood, and bears, and "Good King

Wenceslas" talked about cruelty, bringing people flesh, freezing their blood, and heart failure.

"I had no idea Christmas carols were so grim," I said.

"You should hear Easter," Mr. Ledbetter said. "While you're looking, see if you can find any songs with the word 'seated' in it so we can see if it's that particular word they're responding to."

I nodded and went back to reading lyrics. In "Let All Mortal Flesh Keep Silence" everyone was standing, not seated, plus it had "fear," "trembling," and a line about giving oneself for heavenly food. "The First Noel" had "blood," and the shepherds were lying, not sitting.

What Christmas song has "seated" in it? I thought, trying to remember. Wasn't there something in "Jingle Bells" about Miss Somebody or Other being seated by someone's side?

There was, and in "Wassail, Wassail," there was a line about "a-sitting" by the fire, but not the word "seated."

I kept looking. The nonreligious Christmas songs were almost as bad as the carols. Even a children's song like "I'm Getting' Nuttin' for Christmas" gaily discussed smashing bats over people's heads, and there seemed to be an entire genre of "Grandma Got Run Over by a Reindeer"–type songs: "Grandma's Killer Fruitcake," "I Came Upon a Roadkill Deer," and "Grandpa's Gonna Sue the Pants Off Santa."

And even when the lyrics weren't violent, they had phrases in them like "rule o'er all the earth" and "over us all to reign," which the Altairi might take as an invitation to global conquest.

There have to be some carols that are harmless, I thought, and looked up "Away in a Manger" in the index (which *The Holly Jolly Book*, unlike the hymnal, did have): ". . . lay down his sweet head . . . the stars in the sky . . ." No mayhem here, I thought. I can definitely add this to the list. "Love . . . blessings . . ."

"And take us to heaven to live with thee there." A harmless enough line, but it might mean something entirely different to the Altairi. I didn't want to find myself on a spaceship heading back to Aquila or wherever it was they came from.

We worked till almost three in the morning, by which time we had separate recordings of the vocals, accompaniment, and notes (played by Mr. Ledbetter on the piano, guitar, and flute and recorded by me) of "all seated on the ground," a list, albeit rather short, of songs the Altairi could safely hear, and another, even shorter list of ones with "seated," "sit," or "sitting" in them.

"Thank you so much, Mr. Ledbetter," I said, putting on my coat.

"Calvin," he said.

"Calvin. Anyway, thank you. I really appreciate this. I'll let you know the results of my playing the songs for them."

"Are you kidding, Meg?" he said. "I want to be there when you do this."

"But I thought— Don't you have to rehearse with the choirs for your ACHES thing?" I said, remembering the heavy schedule he'd left on his answering machine.

"Yes, and I have to rehearse with the symphony, and with the chancel choir and the kindergarten choir and the handbell choir for the Christmas Eve service—"

"Oh, and I've kept you up so late," I said. "I'm really sorry."

"Choir directors never sleep in December," he said cheerfully, "and what I was going to say was that I'm free in between rehearsals and till eleven tomorrow morning. How early can you get the Altairi?"

"They usually come out of their ship around seven, but some of the other commission members may want to work with them."

"And face those bright shiny faces before they've had their coffee? My bet is you'll have the Altairi all to yourself."

He was probably right. I remembered Dr. Jarvis saying he had to work himself up to seeing the Altairi over the course of the day: "They look just like my fifth-grade teacher."

"Are you sure *you* want to face them first thing in the morning?" I asked him. "The Altairi's glares—"

"Are nothing compared to the glare of a first soprano who didn't get the solo she wanted. Don't worry, I can handle the Altairi," he said. "I can't wait to find out what it is they're responding to."

What we found out was nothing.

Calvin had been right. There was no one else waiting outside University Hall when the Altairi appeared. I hustled them into the audio lab, locked the door, and called Calvin, and he came right over, bearing Starbucks coffee and an armload of CDs.

"Yikes!" he said when he saw the Altairi standing over by the speakers. "I was wrong about the first soprano. This is more a seventh-grader's 'No, you can't text-message during the choir concert—or wear face glitter' glare."

I shook my head. "It's an Aunt Judith glare."

"I'm very glad we decided not to play them the part about dashing people's heads into pieces," he said. "Are you sure they didn't come to Earth to kill everybody?"

"No," I said. "That's why we have to establish communications with them."

"Right," he said, and proceeded to play the accompaniment we'd recorded the night before. Nothing, and nothing when he played the notes with piano, guitar, and flute, but when he played the vocal part by itself, the Altairi promptly sat down.

"Definitely the words," he said, and when we played them "Jingle Bells," they sat down again at "seated by my side," which seemed to confirm it. But when he played them the first part of "Sit Down, You're Rocking the Boat" from *Guys and Dolls* and "Sittin' on the Dock of the Bay," they didn't sit down for either one.

"Which means it's the word 'seated,' " I said.

"Or they only respond to Christmas songs," he said. "Do you have some other carol we can play them?"

"Not with 'seated,' " I said. " 'All I Want for Christmas Is My Two Front Teeth' has 'sitting' in it."

We played it for them. No response, but when he played "We Need a Little Christmas," from the musical *Mame*, the Altairi sat down the moment the recording reached the word "sitting."

Calvin cut off the rest of the phrase, since we didn't want the Altairi sitting on our shoulders, and looked at me. "So why did they respond to this 'sitting' and not the one in 'All I Want for Christmas Is My Two Front Teeth'?" he mused.

I was tempted to say, "Because 'All I Want for Christmas' is an absolutely terrible song," but I didn't. "The voices?" I suggested.

"Maybe," he said and shuffled through the CDs till he found a recording of the same song by the Statler Brothers. The Altairi sat down at exactly the same place.

So not the voices. And not just Christmas. When Calvin played them the opening song from *1776*, they sat down again as the Continental Congress sang orders to John Adams to sit down. And it wasn't the verb "to sit." When we played them "The Hanukkah Song," they spun solemnly in place.

"Okay, so we've established it's ecumenical," Calvin said.

"Thank goodness," I said, thinking of Reverend Thresher and what he'd say if he found out they'd responded to a Christmas carol, but when we played them a Solstice song with the phrase "the earth turns round again," they just stood there and glared.

"Words beginning with *s*?" I said.

"Maybe." He played them, in rapid succession, "The Snow Lay on the Ground," "Santa Claus Is Coming to Town," and "Suzy Snowflake." Nothing.

At ten forty-five Calvin left to go to his choir rehearsal. "It's at Trinity Episcopal, if you want to meet me there at noon," he said, "and we can go over to my apartment from there. I want to run an analysis on the frequency patterns of the phrases they responded to."

"Okay," I said, and delivered the Altairi to Dr. Wakamura, who wanted to squirt them with perfumes from the Crabtree and Evelyn store. I left them glaring at him and went up to Dr. Morthman's office.

He wasn't there. "He went to the mall to collect paint samples," Dr. Jarvis said.

I called him on his cell phone. "Dr. Morthman, I've run some tests," I said, "and the Altairi are—"

"Not now. I'm waiting for an important call from ACS," he said, and hung up.

I went back to the audio lab and listened to the Cambridge Boys' Choir, Barbra Streisand, and Barenaked Ladies Christmas albums, trying to find songs with variations of "sit" and "spin" in them and no bloodshed. I also looked up instances of "turn." They hadn't responded to "turns" in the Solstice song, but I wasn't sure that proved anything. They hadn't responded to "sitting" in "All I Want for Christmas," either.

At noon I went to meet Calvin at Trinity Episcopal. They weren't done rehearsing yet, and it didn't sound like they would be for some time. Calvin kept starting and stopping the choir and saying, "Basses, you're coming in two beats early, and altos, on 'singing,' that's an A flat. Let's take it again, from the top of page eight."

They went over the section four more times, with no discernible improvement, before Calvin said, "Okay, that's it. I'll see you all Saturday night."

"We are *never* going to get that entrance right," several of the choir members muttered as they gathered up their music, and the balding minister from last night, Reverend McIntyre, looked totally discouraged.

"Maybe I shouldn't sing after all," he told Calvin.

"Yes, you should," Calvin said, and put his hand on Reverend McIntyre's shoulder. "Don't worry. It'll all come together. You'll see."

"Do you really believe that?" I asked Calvin after Reverend McIntyre had gone out.

He laughed. "I know it's hard to believe listening to them now. I never think they're going to be able to do it, but somehow, no matter how awful they sound in rehearsal, they always manage to pull it off. It's enough to restore your faith in humanity." He frowned. "I thought you were going to come over, and we were going to look at frequency patterns."

"We are," I said. "Why?"

He pointed behind me. The Altairi were standing there with Reverend McIntyre. "I found them outside," he said, smiling. "I was afraid they might be lost."

"Oh, dear, they must have followed me. I'm so sorry," I said, though Reverend McIntyre didn't seem particularly intimidated by them. I said as much.

"I'm not," he said. "They don't look nearly as annoyed as my congregation does when they don't approve of my sermon."

"I'd better take them back," I said to Calvin.

"No, as long as they're here, we might as well take them over to my apartment and try some more songs on them. We need more data."

I somehow squeezed all six of them into my car and took them over to Calvin's apartment, and he analyzed frequency patterns while I played some more songs for them. It definitely wasn't the quality of the songs or the singers they were responding to. They wouldn't sit down for Willie Nelson's "Pretty Paper" and then did for a hideous falsetto children's recording of "Little Miss Muffet" from the 1940s.

It wasn't the words' meaning, either. When I played them *Adeste Fideles* in Latin, they sat down when the choir sang, "*tibi sit gloria.*"

"Which proves they're taking what they hear literally," Calvin said when I took him into the kitchen out of earshot of the Altairi to tell me.

"Yes, which means we've got to make sure they don't hear any words that have double meanings," I said. "We can't even play them 'Deck the Halls,' for fear they might deck someone."

"And we definitely can't play them 'laid in a manger,'" he said, grinning.

"It's not funny," I said. "At this rate, we aren't going to be able to play them *anything.*"

"There must be some songs—"

"*What* songs?" I said in frustration. "'I've Got My Love to Keep Me

Warm' talks about hearts that are on fire, 'Christmastide' might bring on a tsunami, and 'be born in us today' sounds like a scene out of *Alien*."

"I know," he said. "Don't worry, we'll find something. Here, I'll help you." He cleared off the kitchen table, brought in the stacks of sheet music, albums, and CDs, and sat me down across from him. "I'll find songs and you check the lyrics."

We started through them. "No . . . no . . . what about 'I Heard the Bells on Christmas Day'?"

"No," I said, looking up the lyrics. "It's got 'hate,' 'wrong,' 'dead,' and 'despair.'"

"Cheery," he said. There was a pause while we looked through more music. "John Lennon's 'Happy Xmas'?"

I shook my head. "'War.' Also 'fights' and 'fear.'"

Another pause, and then he said, "All I want for Christmas is you."

I looked up at him, startled. "What did you say?"

"'All I Want for Christmas is You,'" he repeated. "Song title. Mariah Carey."

"Oh." I looked up the lyrics. "I think it might be okay. I don't see any murder or mayhem." But he was shaking his head.

"On second thought, I don't think we'd better. Love can be even more dangerous than war."

I looked into the living room where the Altairi stood glaring through the door at me. "I seriously doubt they're here to steal Earthwomen."

"Yeah, but we wouldn't want to give anybody any ideas."

"No," I said. "We definitely wouldn't want to do that."

We went back to searching for songs. "How about 'I'll Be Home for Christmas'?" he said, holding up a Patti Page album.

"I'll Be Home" passed muster, but the Altairi didn't respond to it, or to Ed Ames singing "Ballad of the Christmas Donkey" or Miss Piggy singing "Santa Baby."

There didn't seem to be any rhyme or reason to their responses. The keys weren't the same, or the notes, or the accompaniment. They responded to the Andrews Sisters but not to Randy Travis, and it wasn't the voices, either, because they responded to Julie Andrews's "Awake, Awake Ye Drowsy Souls." We played them her "Silver Bells." They didn't laugh (which didn't really surprise me) or bustle, but when the song got to the part about the traffic lights blinking red and green, all six of them blinked their eyes. We played them her "Rise Up, Shepherd, and Follow." They just sat there.

"Try the 'Christmas Waltz,'" I said, looking at the album cover.

He shook his head. "It's got love in it, too. You *did* say you didn't have a boyfriend, didn't you?"

"That's right," I said, "and I have no intention of dating the Altairi."

"Good," he said. "Can you think of any other songs with 'blink' in them?"

By the time he left to rehearse with the symphony, we didn't know any more than when we'd started. I took the Altairi back to Dr. Wakamura, who didn't seem all that happy to see them, tried to find a song with "blink" in it, to no avail, had dinner, and went back over to Calvin's apartment.

He was already there, working. I started through the sheet music. "What about 'Good Christian Men, Rejoice'?" I said. "It's got 'bow' in it," and the phone rang.

Calvin answered it. "What is it, Belinda?" he said, listened a moment, and then said, "Meg, turn on the TV," and handed me the remote.

I switched on the television. Marvin the Martian was telling Bugs Bunny he planned to incinerate the earth. "CNN," Calvin said. "It's on forty."

I punched in the channel and then was sorry. Reverend Thresher was standing in the audio lab in front of a mob of reporters, saying, "—happy to announce that we have found the answer to the Altairi's actions in the mall yesterday. Christmas carols were playing over the sound system in the mall—"

"Oh, no," I said.

"I thought the surveillance tapes didn't have any sound," Calvin said.

"They don't. Someone else in the mall must have had a videocam."

"—and when the Altairi heard those holy songs," Reverend Thresher was saying, "they were overcome by the truth of their message, by the power of God's blessed word—"

"Oh, no," Calvin said.

"—and they sank to the ground in repentance for their sins."

"They did not," I said. "They sat down."

"For the past nine months, scientists have been seeking to discover the reason why the Altairi came to our planet. They should have turned to our Blessed Savior instead, for it is in Him that all answers lie. Why have the Altairi come here? To be saved! They've come to be born again, as we shall demonstrate." He held up a CD of Christmas carols.

"Oh, *no!*" we both said. I grabbed for my cell phone.

"Like the wise men of old," Reverend Thresher was saying, "they have come seeking Christ, which proves that Christianity is the only true religion."

Dr. Morthman took forever to answer his phone. When he did, I said, "Dr. Morthman, you mustn't let the Altairi listen to any Christmas carols—"

"I can't talk now," he said. "We're in the middle of a press conference," and hung up.

"Dr. Morthman—" I hit redial.

"There's no time for that." Calvin, who'd snatched up his keys and my coat, said, "Come on, we'll take my car," and as we racketed downstairs, "There were a lot of reporters there, and he just said something that will make every Jew, Muslim, Buddhist, Wiccan, and non-evangelical Christian on the planet go ballistic. If we're lucky, he'll still be answering questions when we get there."

"And if we're not?"

"The Altairi will be out seizing troubled minds, and we'll have a holy war on our hands."

We almost made it. There were, as Calvin had predicted, a *lot* of questions, particularly after Reverend Thresher stated that the Altairi agreed with him on abortion, gay marriage, and the necessity of electing Republicans to all political offices in the next election.

But the clamoring reporters clogging the steps, the door, and the hall made it nearly impossible to get through, and by the time we reached the audio lab, Reverend Thresher was pointing proudly to the Altairi kneeling on the other side of the one-way mirror and telling the reporters, "As you can see, their hearing the Christmas message has made them kneel in reverence—"

"Oh, no, they must be listening to 'O Holy Night,'" I said, "or 'As with Gladness Men of Old.'"

"What did you play them?" Calvin demanded. He pointed at the kneeling Altairi.

"The One True Way Maxichurch Christmas CD," Reverend Thresher said proudly, holding up the case, which the reporters obligingly snapped, filmed, and downloaded to their iPods. "*Christmas Carols for True Christians.*"

"No, no, what *song?*"

"Do the individual carols hold a special significance for them?" the reporters were shouting, and "What carol were they listening to in the mall?" and "Have they been baptized, Reverend Thresher?" while I tried to tell Dr. Morthman, "You've got to turn the music off."

"Off?" Dr. Morthman said incredulously, yelling to be heard over the reporters. "Just when we're finally making progress communicating with the Altairi?"

"You *have* to tell us which songs you've played!" Calvin shouted.

"Who are *you?*" Reverend Thresher demanded.

"He's with me," I said, and to Dr. Morthman, "You have to turn it off right now. Some of the carols are dangerous."

"*Dangerous?*" he bellowed, and the reporters' attention swiveled to us.

"What do you mean, dangerous?" they asked.

"I mean dangerous," Calvin said. "The Altairi aren't repenting of anything. They're—"

"How dare you accuse the Altairi of not being born again?" Reverend Thresher said. "I saw them respond to the hymnwriter's inspiring words with my own eyes, saw them fall on their knees—"

"They responded to 'Silver Bells,' too," I said, "and to 'The Hanukkah Song.'"

"'The Hanukkah Song?'" the reporters said, and began pelting us with questions again. "Does that mean they're Jewish?" "Orthodox or Reformed?" "What's their response to Hindu chants?" "What about the Mormon Tabernacle Choir? Do they respond to that?"

"This doesn't have anything to do with religion," Calvin said. "The Altairi are responding to the literal meaning of certain words in the songs. Some of the words they're listening to right now could be dangerous for them to—"

"Blasphemy!" Reverend Thresher bellowed. "How could the blessed Christmas message be dangerous?"

"'Christmas Day Is Come' tells them to slay young children," I said, "and the lyrics of other carols have blood and war and stars raining fire. That's why you've got to turn off the music right now."

"Too late," Calvin said and pointed through the one-way mirror.

The Altairi weren't there. "Where are they?" the reporters began shouting. "Where did they go?" and Reverend Thresher and Dr. Morthman both turned to me and demanded to know what I'd done with them.

"Leave her alone. She doesn't know where they are any more than you do," Calvin said in his choir director voice.

The effect on the room was the same as it had been on his seventh-graders. Dr. Morthman let go of me, and the reporters shut up. "Now, what song were you playing?" Calvin said to Reverend Thresher.

"'God Rest Ye Merry, Gentlemen,'" Reverend Thresher said, "but it's one of the oldest and most beloved Christmas carols. It's ridiculous to think hearing it could endanger anyone—"

"Is 'God Rest Ye' why they left?" the reporters were shouting, and "What are the words? Is there any war in it? Or children-slaying?"

"'God rest ye merry, gentlemen,'" I muttered under my breath, trying to remember the lyrics, "'let nothing you dismay . . .'"

"Where did they go?" the reporters clamored.

"'. . . oh, tidings of comfort and joy,'" I murmured. I glanced over at Calvin. He was doing the same thing I was. "'. . . to save us all . . . when we are gone . . .'"

"Where do you think they've gone?" a reporter called out.

Calvin looked at me. "Astray," he said grimly.

The Altairi weren't in the other labs, in any of the other buildings on campus, or in their ship. Or at least no one had seen the ramp to it come down and them go inside. No one had seen them crossing the campus, either, or on the surrounding streets.

"I hold you entirely responsible for this, Miss Yates," Dr. Morthman said. "Send out an APB," he told the police. "And put out an Amber Alert."

"That's for when a child's been kidnapped," I said. "The Altairi haven't—"

"We don't know that," he snapped. He turned back to the police officer. "And call the FBI."

The police officer turned to Calvin. "Dr. Morthman said you said the aliens were responding to the words, 'gone astray.' Were there any other words in the song that are dangerous?"

"Sa—" I began.

"No," Calvin said and, while Dr. Morthman was telling the officer to call Homeland Security and tell them to declare a Code Red, hustled me down the sidewalk and behind the Altairi's ship.

"Why did you tell them that?" I demanded. "What about 'scorn'? What about 'Satan's power'?"

"Shh," he whispered. "He's already calling Homeland Security. We don't want him to call out the Air Force. And the nukes," he said. "And there's no time to explain things to them. We've got to find the Altairi."

"Do you have any idea where they could have gone?"

"No. At least their ship's still here," he said, looking over at it.

I wasn't sure that meant anything, considering the Altairi had been able to get out of a lab with a locked door. I said as much, and Calvin agreed. "'Gone astray' may not even be what they were responding to. They may be off looking for a manger or shepherds. And there are different versions. *Christmas Carols for True Christians* may have used an older one."

"In which case we need to go back to the lab and find out exactly what it was they heard," I said, my heart sinking. Dr. Morthman was likely to have me arrested.

Apparently Calvin had reached the same conclusion, because he said, "We can't go back in there. It's too risky, and we've got to find the Altairi before Reverend Thresher does. There's no telling what he'll play them next."

"But how—?"

"If they did go astray, then they may still be in the area. You go get your car and check the streets north of the campus, and I'll do south. Do you have your cell phone?"

"Yes, but I don't have a car. Mine's at your apartment. We came over in yours, remember?"

"What about the van you use to take the Altairi places in?"

"But won't that be awfully noticeable?"

"They're looking for six aliens on foot, not in a van," he said, "and besides, if you find them, you'll need something to put them in."

"You're right," I said and took off for the faculty parking lot, hoping Dr. Morthman hadn't had the same idea.

He hadn't. The parking lot was deserted. I slid the van's back door open, half-hoping this was the Altairi's idea of astray, but they weren't inside, or on any of the streets for an area two miles north of DU. I drove up University Boulevard and then slowly up and down the side streets, terrified I'd find them squished on the pavement.

It was already dark. I called Calvin. "No sign of them," I told him. "Maybe they went back to the mall. I'm going to go over there and—"

"No, don't do that," he said. "Dr. Morthman and the FBI are there. I'm watching it on CNN. They're searching Victoria's Secret. Besides, the Altairi aren't there."

"How do you know?"

"Because they're here at my apartment."

"They are?" I said, weak with relief. "Where did you find them?"

He didn't answer me. "Don't take any major streets on your way over here," he said. "And park in the alley."

"Why? What have they done?" I asked, but he'd already hung up.

The Altairi were standing in the middle of Calvin's living room when I got there. "I came back here to check on alternate lyrics for 'God Rest Ye' and found them waiting for me," Calvin explained. "Did you park in the alley?"

"Yes, at the other end of the block. What have they done?" I repeated, almost afraid to ask.

"Nothing. At least nothing that's been on CNN," he said, gesturing at the TV, which was showing the police searching the candle store. He had the sound turned down, but across the bottom of the screen was the logo "Aliens AWOL."

"Then why all the secrecy?"

"Because we can't afford to let them find the Altairi till we've figured out why they're doing what they're doing. Next time it might not be as harmless as going astray. And we can't go to your apartment. They know where you live. We're going to have to hole up here. Did you tell anybody you were working with me?"

I tried to think. I'd attempted to tell Dr. Morthman about Calvin when I got back from the mall, but I hadn't gotten far enough to tell him Calvin's name, and when Reverend Thresher had demanded, "Who are you?" all I'd said was, "He's with me."

"I didn't tell anybody your name," I said.

"Good," he said. "And I'm pretty sure nobody saw the Altairi coming here."

"But how can you be sure? Your neighbors—"

"Because the Altairi were waiting for me inside," he said. "Right where they are now. So either they can pick locks, walk through walls, or teleport. My money's on teleportation. And it's obvious the commission doesn't have any idea where they are," he said, pointing at the TV, where a mugshot-like photo of the Altairi was displayed, with "Have you seen these aliens?" and a phone number to call across their midsections. "And luckily, I went to the grocery store and stocked up the other day so I wouldn't have to go shopping in between all my concerts."

"Your concerts! And the All-City Sing! I forgot all about them," I said, stricken with guilt. "Weren't you supposed to have a rehearsal tonight?"

"I canceled it," he said, "and I can cancel the one tomorrow morning if I have to. The Sing's not till tomorrow night. We've got plenty of time to figure this out."

If they don't find us first, I thought, looking at the TV, where they were searching the food court. Eventually, when they couldn't find the Altairi anywhere, they'd realize I was missing, too, and start looking for us. And the reporters today, unlike Leo, had all been videotaping. If they put Calvin's picture on TV with a number to call, one of his church choir members or his seventh-graders would be certain to call in and identify him.

Which meant we'd better work fast. I picked up the list of songs and actions we'd compiled. "Where do you want to start?" I asked Calvin, who was starting through a stack of LPs.

"Not with 'Frosty the Snowman,'" he said. "I don't think I can stand any chasing here and there."

"How about, 'I Wonder as I Wander'?"

"Very funny," he said. "Since we know they respond to 'kneeling,' why don't we start with that?"

"Okay." We played them "fall on your knees" and "come adore on bended knee" and "whose forms are bending low," some of which they responded to and some of which they didn't, for no reason we could see.

"'The First Noel' has 'full reverently upon their knee' in it," I said, and Calvin started toward the bedroom to look for it.

He stopped as he passed in front of the TV. "I think you'd better come look at this," he said, and turned it up.

"The Altairi were not at the mall, as we had hoped," Dr. Morthman was saying, "and it has just come to our attention that a member of our commission is also missing, Margaret Yates." Video of the scene at the lab came on behind Dr. Morthman and the reporter, with me shouting for him to shut the music off. Any second a picture of Calvin would appear, demanding to know which carol they were playing.

I grabbed up my phone and called Dr. Morthman, hoping against hope they couldn't trace cellphone calls and that he'd answer even though he was on TV.

He did, and the camera blessedly zoomed in on him so only a tiny piece of the video remained visible. "Where are you calling from?" he demanded. "Did you find the Altairi?"

"No," I said, "but I think I have an idea where they might be."

"Where?" Dr. Morthman said.

"I don't think they've gone astray. I think they may be responding to one of the other words in the song. 'Rest' or possibly—"

"I knew it," Reverend Thresher said, shoving in front of Dr. Morthman. "They were responding to the words 'Remember Christ our Savior was born on Christmas Day.' They've gone to church. They're at the One True Way right this minute."

It wasn't what I had in mind, but at least a photo of the One True Way Maxichurch was better than one of Calvin. "That should give us at least two hours. His church is way down in Colorado Springs," I said, turning the TV back down, and went back to playing songs to the Altairi and logging their responses and non-responses, but half an hour later, when Calvin went into the bedroom to try to find a Louis Armstrong CD, he stopped in front of the TV again and frowned.

"What happened?" I said, dumping the pile of sheet music on my lap on the couch beside me and sidling past the Altairi to get to him. "Didn't they take the bait?"

"Oh, they took it, all right," he said and turned up the TV.

"We believe the Altairi are in Bethlehem," Dr. Morthman was saying. He was standing in front of a departures board at DIA.

"*Bethlehem?*" I said.

"It's mentioned in the lyrics twice," Calvin said. "At least if they're off in Israel it gives us more time."

"It also gives us an international incident," I said. "In the Middle East, no less. I've got to call Dr. Morthman." But he must have turned his cell phone off, and I couldn't get through to the lab.

"You could call Reverend Thresher," Calvin said, pointing to the TV screen.

Reverend Thresher was surrounded by reporters as he got into his Lexus. "I'm on my way to the Altairi right now, and tonight we will hold a Praise Worship Service, and you'll be able to hear their Christian witness and the Christmas carols that first brought them to the Lord—"

Calvin switched the TV off. "It's a sixteen-hour flight to Bethlehem," he said encouragingly. "It surely won't take us that long to figure this out."

The phone rang. Calvin shot me a glance and then picked it up. "Hello, Mr. Steinberg," he said. "Didn't you get my message? I canceled tonight's rehearsal." He listened awhile. "If you're worried about your entrance on page twelve, we'll run over it before the Sing." He listened some more. "It'll all come together. It always does."

I hoped that would be true of our solving the puzzle of the Altairi. If it wasn't, we'd be charged with kidnapping. Or starting a religious war. But both were better than letting Reverend Thresher play them "slowly dying" and "thorns infest the ground." Which meant we'd better figure out what the Altairi were responding to, and fast. We played them Dolly Parton and Manhattan Transfer and the Barbershop Choir of Toledo and Dean Martin.

Which was a bad idea. I'd had almost no sleep the last two days, and I found myself nodding off after the first few bars. I sat up straight and tried to concentrate on the Altairi, but it was no use. The next thing I knew, my head was on Calvin's shoulder, and he was saying, "Meg? Meg? Do the Altairi sleep?"

"Sleep?" I said, sitting up and rubbing my eyes. "I'm sorry, I must have dozed off. What time is it?"

"A little after four."

"In the *morning*?"

"Yes. Do the Altairi sleep?"

"Yes, at least we think so. Their brain patterns alter, and they don't respond to stimuli, but then again, they *never* respond."

"Are there visible signs that they're asleep? Do they close their eyes or lie down?"

"No, they sort of droop over, like flowers that haven't been watered. And their glares diminish a little. Why?"

"I have something I want to try. Go back to sleep."

"No, that's okay," I said, suppressing a yawn. "If anybody needs to sleep, it's you. I've kept you up the last two nights, and you've got to direct your Sing thing tonight. I'll take over and you go—"

He shook his head. "I'm fine. I told you, I never get any sleep this time of year."

"So what's this idea you want to try?"

"I want to play them the first verse of 'Silent Night.'"

"'Sleep in heavenly peace,'" I said.

"Right, and no other action verbs *and* I've got at least fifty versions of it. Johnny Cash, Kate Smith, Britney Spears—"

"Do we have time to play them fifty different versions?" I asked, looking over at the TV. A split screen showed a map of Israel and the outside of the One True Way Maxichurch. When I turned the volume up, a reporter's voice said, "Inside, thousands of members are awaiting the appearance of the Altairi, whom Reverend Thresher expects at any minute. A twenty-four-hour High-Powered Prayer Vigil—"

I turned it back down. "I guess we do. You were saying?"

"'Silent Night' is a song everybody—Gene Autry, Madonna, Burl Ives—has recorded. Different voices, different accompaniments, different keys. We can see which versions they respond to—"

"And which ones they don't," I said, "and that may give us a clue to what they're responding to."

"Exactly," he said, opening a CD case. He stuck it in the player and hit Track 4. "Here goes."

The voice of Elvis Presley singing "'Silent night, holy night'" filled the room. Calvin came back over to the couch and sat down next to me. When Elvis got to "'tender and mild,'" we both leaned forward expectantly, watching the Altairi. "'Sleep in heavenly peace,'" Elvis crooned, but the Altairi were still stiffly upright. They remained that way through the repeated "'sleep in heavenly peace.'" And through Alvin the Chipmunk's solo of it. And Celine Dion's.

"Their glares don't appear to be diminishing," Calvin said. "If anything, they seem to be getting worse."

They were. "You'd better play them Judy Garland," I said.

He did, and Dolly Parton and Harry Belafonte. "What if they don't respond to any of them?" I asked.

"Then we try something else. I've also got twenty-six versions of 'Grandma Got Run Over by a Reindeer.'" He grinned at me. "I'm kidding. I do, however, have nine different versions of 'Baby, It's Cold Outside.'"

"For use on redheaded second sopranos?"

"No," he said. "Shh, I love this version. Nat King Cole."

I shh-ed and listened, wondering how the Altairi could resist falling asleep. Nat King Cole's voice was even more relaxing than Dean Martin's. I leaned back against the couch. "'All is calm . . .'"

I must have fallen asleep again, because the next thing I knew, the music had stopped and it was daylight outside. I looked at my watch. It said two P.M. The Altairi were standing in the exact same spot they'd been in before, glaring, and Calvin was sitting hunched forward on a kitchen chair, his chin in his hand, watching them and looking worried.

"Did something happen?" I glanced over at the TV. Reverend Thresher was talking. The logo read "Thresher Launches Galaxywide Christian Crusade." At least it didn't say "Air Strikes in Middle East."

Calvin was slowly shaking his head.

"Wasn't there any response to 'Silent Night'?" I asked.

"No, there was," he said. "You responded to the version by Nat King Cole."

"I know," I said. "I'm sorry. I meant the Altairi. They didn't respond to any of the 'Silent Nights'?"

"No, they responded," he said, "but just to one version."

"But that's good, isn't it?" I asked. "Now we can analyze what it was that was different about it that they were responding to. Which version was it?"

Instead of answering, he walked over to the CD player and hit play. A loud chorus of nasal female voices began belting out, "Silent night, holy night," shouting to be heard over a cacophony of clinks and clacks. "What *is* that?" I asked.

"The Broadway chorus of the musical *42nd Street* singing and tap-dancing to 'Silent Night.' They recorded it for a special Broadway Christmas charity project."

I looked over at the Altairi, thinking maybe Calvin was wrong and they hadn't really fallen asleep, but in spite of the din, they had sagged limply over, their heads nearly touching the ground, looking almost peaceful. Their glares had faded from full-bore Aunt Judith to only mildly disapproving.

I listened to the *42nd Street* chorines tapping and belting out "Silent Night" at the top of their lungs some more. "It is kind of appealing," I said, "especially the part where they shout out 'Mother and child!'"

"I know," he said. "I'd like it played at our wedding. And obviously the Altairi share our good taste. But aside from that, I'm not sure *what* it tells us."

"That the Altairi like show tunes?" I suggested.

"God forbid. Think what Reverend Thresher would do with that," he said. "Besides, they didn't respond to 'Sit Down, You're Rocking the Boat.'"

"No, but they did to that song from *Mame*."

"And to the one from *1776* but not to *The Music Man* or *Rent*," he said frustratedly. "Which puts us right back where we started. I have no clue what they're responding to!"

"I know," I said. "I'm so sorry. I should never have gotten you involved in this. You have your ACHES thing to direct."

"It doesn't start till seven," he said, rummaging through a stack of LPs, "which means we've got another four hours to work. If we could just find another 'Silent Night' they'll respond to, we might be able to figure out what in God's name they're doing. What the hell happened to that *Star Wars Christmas* album?"

"Stop," I said. "This is ridiculous." I took the albums out of his hands. "You're exhausted, and you've got a big job to do. You can't direct all those people on no sleep. This can wait."

"But—"

"People think better after a nap," I said firmly. "You'll wake up, and the solution will be perfectly obvious."

"And if it isn't?"

"Then you'll go direct your choirs, and—"

"Choirs," he said thoughtfully.

"Or All-City Sing or Aches and Pains or whatever you call it, and

I'll stay here and play the Altairi some more 'Silent Nights' till you get back and—"

"'Sit Down, John' was sung by the chorus," he said, looking past me at the drooping Altairi. "And so was 'While Shepherds Watched.' And the *42nd Street* 'Silent Night' was the only one that wasn't a solo." He grabbed my shoulders. "They're all choruses. That's why they didn't respond to Julie Andrews singing 'Rise Up, Shepherd, and Follow,' or to Stubby Kaye singing 'Sit Down, You're Rocking the Boat.' They only respond to groups of voices."

I shook my head. "You forgot 'Awake, Awake, Ye Drowsy Souls.'"

"Oh," he said, his face falling, "you're right. Wait!" He lunged for the Julie Andrews CD and stuck it in the recorder. "I think Julie Andrews sings the verse and then a chorus comes in. Listen."

He was right. The chorus had sung "Awake, awake."

"Who sang the 'Joy to the World' you played them on the CD from the mall?" Calvin asked.

"Just Julie Andrews," I said. "And Brenda Lee sang 'Rockin' Around the Christmas Tree.'"

"And Johnny Mathis sang 'Angels from the Realms of Glory,'" he said happily. "But the Hanukkah song, which they *did* respond to, was sung by the . . ." he read it off the CD case, "the Shalom Singers. That's got to be it." He began looking through the LPs again.

"What are you looking for?" I asked.

"The Mormon Tabernacle Choir," he said. "They've *got* to have recorded 'Silent Night.' We'll play it for the Altairi, and if they fall asleep, we'll know we're on the right track."

"But they're already asleep," I pointed out, gesturing to where they stood looking like a week-old flower arrangement. "How—?"

He was already digging again. He brought up a Cambridge Boys' Choir album, pulled the LP out, and read the label, muttering, "I know it's on here . . . Here it is." He put it on, and a chorus of sweet boys' voices sang, "'Christians awake, salute the happy morn.'"

The Altairi straightened immediately and glared at us. "You were right," I said softly, but he wasn't listening. He had the LP off the turntable and was reading the label again, muttering, "Come on, you have to have done 'Silent Night.' Everyone does 'Silent Night.'" He flipped the LP over, said, "I *knew* it," popped it back on the turntable, and dropped the needle expertly. "'. . . and mild,'" the boys' angelic voices sang, "'sleep . . .'"

The Altairi drooped over before the word was even out. "That's definitely it!" I said. "That's the common denominator."

He shook his head. "We need more data. It could just be a coincidence. We need to find a choral version of 'Rise Up, Shepherd, and Follow.' And 'Sit Down, You're Rocking the Boat.' Where did you put *Guys and Dolls?*"

"But that was a solo."

"The first part, the part *we* played them was a solo. Later on all the gamblers come in. We should have played them the whole song."

"We couldn't, remember?" I said, handing it to him. "Remember the parts about dragging you under and drowning, not to mention gambling and drinking?"

"Oh, right," he said. He put headphones on, listened, and then unplugged them. "'Sit down . . .'" a chorus of men's voices sang lustily, and the Altairi sat down.

We played choir versions of "All I Want for Christmas Is My Two Front Teeth" and "Rise Up, Shepherds, and Follow." The Altairi sat down and stood up. "You're right," he said after the Altairi knelt to the Platters singing "The First Noel." "It's the common denominator, all right. But why?"

"I don't know," I admitted. "Maybe they can't understand things said to them by fewer voices than a choir. That would explain why there are six of them. Maybe each one only hears certain frequencies, which singly are meaningless, but with six of them—"

He shook his head. "You're forgetting the Andrews Sisters. And Barenaked Ladies. And even if it is the choir aspect they're responding to, it still doesn't tell us what they're doing here."

"But now we know how to get them to tell us," I said, grabbing up *The Holly Jolly Book of Christmas Songs*. "Can you find a choir version of '*Adeste Fideles*' in English?"

"I think so," he said. "Why?"

"Because it's got 'we greet thee' in it," I said, running my fingers down the lyrics of "Good Christian Men, Rejoice."

"And there's 'Watchmen, Tell Us of the Night,'" he said. "And 'great glad tidings tell.' They're bound to respond to one of them."

But they didn't. Peter, Paul, and Mary ordered the Altairi to go tell (we blanked out the "on the mountain" part), but either the Altairi didn't like folk music, or the Andrews Sisters had been a fluke.

Or we had jumped to conclusions. When we tried the same song again, this time by the Boston Commons Choir, there was still no response. And none to choral versions of "Deck the Halls" ("while I tell"), "Jolly Old St. Nicholas" ("don't you tell a single soul" minus "don't" and "a single soul"). Or to "The Friendly Beasts," even though all six verses had "tell" in them.

Calvin thought the tense might be the problem and played parts of "Little St. Nick" ("tale" and "told") and "The Carol of the Bells" ("telling"), but to no avail. "Maybe the word's the problem," I said. "Maybe they just don't know the word 'tell.'" But they didn't respond to "say" or "saying" or "said," to "messages" or to "proclaim."

"We must have been wrong about the choir thing," Calvin said, but that wasn't it, either. While he was in the bedroom putting his tux on for the Sing, I played them snatches of "The First Noel" and "Up on the Rooftop" from the Barenaked Ladies CD, and they knelt and jumped right on cue.

"Maybe they think Earth's a gym and this is an exercise class," Calvin said, coming in as they were leaping to the St. Paul's Cathedral Choir singing "The Twelve Days of Christmas." "I don't suppose the word 'calling' had any effect on them."

"No," I said, tying his bow tie, "and 'I'm bringing you this simple phrase' didn't, either. Has it occurred to you that the music might not be having any effect at all, and they just happen to be sitting and leaping and kneeling at the same time as the words are being sung?"

"No," he said. "There's a connection. If there wasn't, they wouldn't look so irritated that we haven't been able to figure it out yet."

He was right. Their glares had, if anything, intensified, and their very posture radiated disapproval.

"We need more data, that's all," he said, going to get his black shoes. "As soon as I get back, we'll—" He stopped.

"What is it?"

"You'd better look at this," he said, pointing at the TV. The screen was showing a photo of the ship. All the lights were on, and exhaust was coming out of assorted side vents. Calvin grabbed the remote and turned it up.

"It is now believed that the Altairi have returned to their ship and are preparing to depart," the newscaster said. I glanced over at the Altairi. They were still standing there. "Analysis of the ignition cycle indicates that takeoff will be in less than six hours."

"What do we do now?" I asked Calvin.

"We figure this out. You heard them. We've got six hours till blast-off."

"But the Sing—"

He handed me my coat. "We know it's got *something* to do with choirs, and I've got every kind you could want. We'll take the Altairi to the convention center and hope we think of something on the way."

We didn't think of anything on the way. "Maybe I should take them back to their ship," I said, pulling into the parking lot. "What if I cause them to get left behind?"

"They are *not* E.T.," he said.

I parked at the service entrance, got out, and started to slide the back door of the van open. "No, leave them there," Calvin said. "We've got to find a place to put them before we take them in. Lock the car."

I did, even though I doubted if it would do any good, and followed Calvin through a side door marked "Choirs Only" and through a maze of corridors lined with rooms marked "St. Peter's Boys Choir," "Red Hat Glee Club," "Denver Gay Men's Chorus," "Sweet Adelines Show Chorus," "Mile High Jazz Singers." There was a hubbub in the front of the building, and when we crossed the main corridor, we could see people in gold and green and black robes milling around talking.

Calvin opened several doors one after the other, ducked inside the rooms, shutting the door after him, and then re-emerged, shaking his head. "We can't let the Altairi hear the *Messiah*, and you can still hear the noise from the auditorium," he said. "We need someplace sound-proof."

"Or farther away," I said, leading the way down the corridor and turning down a side hall. And running smack into his seventh-graders coming out of one of the meeting rooms. Mrs. Carlson was videotaping them, and another mother was attempting to line them up to go in, but as soon as they saw Calvin, they clustered around him saying, "Mr. Ledbetter, where have you been? We thought you weren't coming," and "Mr. Ledbetter, Mrs. Carlson says we have to turn our cell phones off, but can't we just have them on vibrate?" and "Mr. Ledbetter, Shelby and I were supposed to go in together, but she says she wants to be partners with Danika."

Calvin ignored them. "Kaneesha, could you hear any of the groups rehearsing when you were in getting dressed?"

"Why?" Belinda asked. "Did we miss the call to go in?"

"Could you, Kaneesha?" he persisted.

"A little bit," she said.

"That won't work, then," he said to me. "I'll go check the room at the end. Wait here." He sprinted along the hall.

"You were at the mall that day," Belinda said accusingly to me. "Are you and Mr. Ledbetter going out?"

We may all be going out together—with a bang—if we don't figure out what the Altairi are doing, I thought. "No," I said.

"Are you hooking up?" Chelsea asked.

"Chelsea!" Mrs. Carlson said, horrified.

"Well, are you?"

"Aren't you supposed to be lining up?" I asked.

Calvin came back at a dead run. "It should work," he said to me. "It seems fairly soundproof."

"Why does it have to be soundproof?" Chelsea asked.

"I bet it's so nobody can hear them making out," Belinda said, and Chelsea began making smooching noises.

"Time to go in, ladies," he said in his choir director's voice, "line up," and he really was amazing. They immediately formed pairs and began making a line.

"Wait till everybody's gone into the auditorium," he said, pulling me aside, "and then go get them and bring them in. I'll do a few minutes' intro of the orchestra and the organizing committee so the Altairi won't hear any songs while you're getting them to the room. There's a table you can use to barricade the door so nobody can get in."

"And what if the Altairi try to leave?" I asked. "A barricade won't stop them, you know."

"Call me on my cell phone, and I'll tell the audience there's a fire drill or something. Okay? I'll make this as short as I can." He grinned. "No 'Twelve Days of Christmas.' Don't worry, Meg. We'll figure this out."

"I *told* you she was his girlfriend."

"*Is* she, Mr. Ledbetter?"

"Let's go, ladies," he said and led them down the hall and into the auditorium. Just as the auditorium doors shut on the last stragglers, my cell phone rang. It was Dr. Morthman, calling to say, "You can stop looking. The Altairi are in their ship."

"How do you know? Have you seen them?" I asked, thinking, I knew I shouldn't have left them in the car.

"No, but the ship's begun the ignition process, and it's going faster than NASA previously estimated. They're now saying it's no more than four hours to takeoff. Where are you?"

"On my way back," I said, trying not to sound like I was running out to the parking lot and unlocking the van, which, thank goodness, was at least still there and intact.

"Well, hurry it up," Dr. Morthman snapped. "The press is here. You're going to have to explain to them exactly how you let the Altairi get away." I pulled open the van's door.

The Altairi weren't inside.

Oh, no. "I blame this entire debacle on you," Dr. Morthman said. "If there are international repercussions—"

"I'll be there as soon as I can," I said, hung up, and turned to run around to the driver's side.

And collided with the Altairi, who had apparently been standing behind me the entire time. "Don't scare me like that," I said. "Now come on," and led them rapidly into the convention center, past the shut doors of the auditorium, where I could hear talking but not singing, thank goodness, and along the long hall to the room Calvin had indicated.

It was empty except for the table Calvin had mentioned. I herded the Altairi inside and then tipped the table on its side, pushed it in front of the door, wedging it under the doorknob, and leaned my ear against it to see if I could hear any sound from the auditorium, but Calvin had been right. I couldn't hear anything, and they should have started by now.

And now what? With takeoff only four hours away, I needed to take advantage of every second, but there was nothing in the room I could use—no piano or CD player or LPs. We should have used his seventh-graders' dressing room, I thought. They'd at least have had iPods or something.

But even if I played the Altairi hundreds of Christmas carols being sung by a choir, and they responded to them all—bowing, decking halls, dashing through snow in one-horse open sleighs, following yonder stars—I'd still be no closer to figuring out why they were here or why they'd decided to leave. Or why they'd taken the very loud tap-dancing chorus of *42nd Street* singing "Sleep in heavenly peace" as a direct order. If they even knew what the word "sleep"—or "seated" or "spin" or "blink"—meant.

Calvin had surmised they could only hear words sung to them with more than one voice, but that couldn't be it. Someone hearing a word for the first time would have no idea what it meant, and they'd never heard "'all seated on the ground'" till that day in the mall. They had to have heard the word before to have known what it meant, and they'd only have heard it spoken. Which meant they could hear spoken words as well as sung ones.

They could have read the words, I thought, remembering the Rosetta Stone and the dictionaries Dr. Short had given them. But even if they'd somehow taught themselves to read English, they wouldn't know how it was pronounced. They wouldn't have recognized it when they heard it spoken. The only way they could do that was by hearing the spoken word. Which meant they'd been listening to and understanding every word we'd said for the past nine months. Including Calvin's and my conversations about them slaying babies and destroying the planet. No wonder they were leaving.

But if they understood us, then that meant one of two things—they were either unwilling to talk to us or were incapable of speaking. Had their sitting down and their other responses been an attempt at sign language?

No, that couldn't be it, either. They could have responded just as easily to a spoken "sit" and done it months earlier. And if they were trying to communicate, wouldn't they have given Calvin and me some hint we were on the right—or the wrong—track instead of just standing there with that we-are-not-amused glare? And I didn't believe for a moment those expressions were an accident of nature. I knew disapproval when I saw it. I'd watched Aunt Judith too many years not to—

Aunt Judith. I took my cell phone out of my pocket and called my sister Tracy. "Tell me everything you can remember about Aunt Judith," I said when she answered.

"Has something happened to her?" she said, sounding alarmed. "When I talked to her last week she—"

"Last week?" I said. "You mean Aunt Judith's still *alive?*"

"Well, she was last week when we had lunch."

"*Lunch?* With Aunt Judith? Are we talking about the same person? Dad's Aunt Judith? The Gorgon?"

"Yes, only she's not a Gorgon. She's actually very nice when you get to know her."

"Aunt Judith," I said, "the one who always glared disapprovingly at everybody?"

"Yes, only she hasn't glared at me in years. As I say, when you get to know her—"

"And exactly how did you do that?"

"I thanked her for my birthday present."

"And—?" I said. "That can't have been all. Mom always made both of us thank her nicely for our presents."

"I know, but they weren't proper thank-yous. 'A prompt handwritten note expressing gratitude is the only proper form of thanks,'" Tracy said, obviously quoting. "I was in high school, and we had to write a thank-you letter to someone for class. She'd just sent me my birthday card with the dollar in it, so I wrote her, and the next day she called and gave me this long lecture about the importance of good manners and how shocking it was that no one followed the most basic rules of etiquette anymore and how she was delighted to see that at least one young person knew how to behave, and then she asked me if I'd like to go see *Les Miz* with her, and I bought a copy of Emily Post, and we've gotten along great ever since. She sent Evan and me a sterling silver fish slice when we got married."

"For which you sent her a handwritten thank-you note," I said absently. Aunt Judith had been glaring because we were boorish and unmannered. Was that why the Altairi looked so disapproving, because they were waiting for the equivalent of a handwritten thank-you note from us?

If that was the case, we were doomed. Rules of etiquette are notoriously illogical and culture-specific, and there was no intergalactic Emily Post for me to consult. And I had, oh, God, less than two hours till liftoff.

"Tell me exactly what she said that day she called you," I said, unwilling to give up the idea that she was somehow the key.

"It was eight years ago—"

"I know. Try to remember."

"Okay . . . there was a lot of stuff about gloves and how I shouldn't wear white shoes after Labor Day and how I shouldn't cross my legs. 'Well-bred young ladies sit with their ankles crossed.'"

Had the Altairi's sitting down in the mall been an etiquette lesson in the proper way to sit? It seemed unlikely, but so did Aunt Judith's refusal to speak to people because of the color of their shoes on certain calendar dates.

". . . and she said if I got married, I needed to send out engraved invitations," Tracy said. "Which I did. I think that's why she gave us the fish slice."

"I don't care about the fish slice. What did she say about your thank-you note?"

"She said, 'Well, it's about time, Tracy. I'd nearly given up hope of anyone in your family showing any signs of civilized behavior.'"

Civilized behavior. That was it. The Altairi, like Aunt Judith sitting in our living room glaring, had been waiting for a sign that we were civilized. And singing—correction, *group* singing—was that sign. But was it an arbitrary rule of etiquette, like white shoes and engraved invitations, or was it a symbol of something else? I thought of Calvin telling his chattering seventh-graders to line up, and the milling, giggling, chaotic muddle of girls coming together in an organized, beautifully behaved, *civilized* line.

Coming together. That was the civilized behavior the Altairi had been waiting for a sign of. And they'd seen precious little of it in the nine months they'd been here: the disorganized commission with members quitting and those who were left not listening to anyone; that awful rehearsal where the basses couldn't get the entrance right to save them; the harried shoppers in the mall, dragging their screaming children after them. The piped-in choir singing "While Shepherds Watched" might have been the first indication they'd seen—correction, *heard*—that we were capable of getting along with each other at all.

No wonder they'd sat down right there in the middle of the mall. They must have thought, like Aunt Judith, "Well, it's about time!" But then why hadn't they done the equivalent of calling us and asking us to go see *Les Miz*?

Maybe they hadn't been sure that what they'd seen—correction, heard—was what they thought it was. They'd never *seen* people sing, except for Calvin and those pathetic basses. They'd seen no signs we were capable of singing beautifully in harmony.

But "While Shepherds Watched" had convinced them it might be possible, which was why they'd followed us around and why they'd sat and slept and gone astray whenever they heard more than one voice, hoping we'd get the hint, waiting for further proof.

In which case we should be in the auditorium, listening to the Sing instead of in this soundproof room. Especially since the fact that their ship was getting ready to take off indicated they'd given up and decided they were mistaken after all. "Come on," I said to the Altairi and stood up. "I need to show you something." I shoved the table away from the door, and opened it.

On Calvin. "Oh, good, you're here," I said. "I— Why aren't you in directing?"

"I announced an intermission so I could tell you something. I think I've got it, the thing the Altairi have been responding to," he said, grabbing me by the arms, "the reason they reacted to Christmas songs. I thought of it while I was directing 'Chestnuts Roasting on an Open Fire.' What do nearly all Christmas songs have in them?"

"I don't know," I said. "Chestnuts? Santa Claus? Bells?"

"Close," he said. "Choirs."

Choirs? "We already knew they responded to songs sung by choirs," I said, confused.

"Not just to songs sung by choirs. Songs *about* choirs. Christmas carols being sung by the choir, angel choirs, children's choirs, wassailers, carolers, strike the harp and join the *chorus*," he said. "The angels in 'Angels We Have Heard on High' are sweetly singing o'er the plains. In 'It Came Upon the Midnight Clear,' all the world gives back the song they sing. They're all about singing," he said excitedly. "'That glorious song of old,' 'whom angels greet with anthems sweet.' Look," he flipped through the pages of his music, pointing out phrases, "'oh, hear the angel voices,' 'as men of old have sung,' 'whom shepherds guard and angels sing,' 'let men their songs employ.' There are references to singing in songs by Randy Travis, the Peanuts kids, Paul McCartney, *How the Grinch Stole Christmas*. It wasn't just that 'While Shepherds Watched' was sung by a choir. It was that it was a song *about* choirs singing. And not just singing, but what they're singing." He thrust the song in front of me, pointing to the last verse. "'Goodwill, henceforth from heaven to men.' That's what they've been trying to communicate to us."

I shook my head. "It's what they've been waiting for us to communicate to them. Just like Aunt Judith."

"Aunt Judith?"

"I'll explain later. Right now we've got to prove we're civilized before the Altairi leave."

"And how do we do that?"

"We sing to them, or rather, the All-City Holiday Ecumenical Sing does."

"What do we sing?"

I wasn't sure it mattered. I was pretty certain what they were looking for was proof we could cooperate and work together in harmony, and in that case, "Mele Kalikimaka" would work as well as "The Peace Carol." But it wouldn't hurt to make things as clear to them as we could. And it would be nice if it was also something that Reverend Thresher couldn't use as ammunition for his Galaxywide Christian Crusade.

"We need to sing something that will convince the Altairi we're a civilized species," I said, "something that conveys goodwill and peace. Especially peace. And not religion, if that's possible."

"How much time have we got to write it?" Calvin asked. "And we'll have to get copies made—"

My cell phone rang. The screen showed it was Dr. Morthman. "Hang on," I said, hitting talk. "I should be able to tell you in a second. Hello?"

"Where *are* you?" Dr. Morthman shouted. "The ship's beginning its final ignition cycle."

I whirled around to make sure the Altairi were still there. They were, thank goodness, and still glaring. "How long does the final cycle take?" I asked.

"They don't know," Dr. Morthman said, "ten minutes at the outside. If you don't get here immediately—"

I hung up.

"Well?" Calvin said. "How much time have we got?"

"None," I said.

"Then we'll have to use something we've already got," he said and began riffling through his sheaf of music, "and something people know the harmony to. Civilized . . . civilized . . . I think . . ." He found what he was looking for and scanned it. ". . . Yeah, if I change a couple of words, this should do the trick. Do you think the Altairi understand Latin?"

"I wouldn't put it past them."

"Then we'll just do the first two lines. Wait five minutes—"

"Five minutes—?"

"So I can brief everybody on the changes, and then bring the Altairi in."

"Okay," I said, and he took off at a run for the auditorium.

There was an expectant buzz in the audience when we came through the double doors, and the ranks of choirs arrayed around the stage, a sea of maroon and gold and green and purple robes, began whispering to each other behind their music.

Calvin had apparently just finished his briefing. Some of the choirs and the audience were busily scribbling notes on their music, and passing pencils, and asking each other questions. The orchestra, on one side of the stage, was warming up in a jumbled cacophony of screeches and hoots and blats.

On the other side, the sopranos of the Mile-High Women's Chorus were apparently filling the altos in on my interrupting rehearsal the other night, because they all turned to glare at me. "I think it's ridiculous that we can't sing the words we know," an elderly woman wearing gloves and a hat with a veil said to her companion.

Her companion nodded. "If you ask me, they're carrying this entire ecumenical thing too far. I mean, humans are one thing, but *aliens!*"

There's no way this is going to work, I thought, looking over at Calvin's seventh-graders, who were leaning over the backs of each other's chairs, giggling and chewing gum. Belinda was text-messaging someone on her cell phone, and Kaneesha was listening to her iPod. Chelsea had her hand up and was calling, "Mr. Ledbetter! Mr. Ledbetter, Shelby took my music."

Over in the orchestra, the percussionist was practicing crashing his cymbals. It's hopeless, I thought, looking over at the glaring Altairi. There's no way we can convince them we're sentient, let alone civilized.

My cell phone rang. And that's it, the straw that's going to break the camel's back, I thought, fumbling for it. Now everyone, even the musician with the cymbals, was glaring at me. "How rude!" the elderly woman in the white gloves said.

"The ship's started its countdown!" Dr. Morthman bellowed in my ear.

I hit "end" and turned the phone off. "Hurry," I mouthed to Calvin, and he nodded and stepped up on the dais.

He tapped the music stand with his baton, and the entire auditorium fell silent. *"Adeste Fideles,"* he said, and everyone opened their music.

"Adeste Fideles?" What's he doing? I thought. "O come, all ye faithful" isn't what we need. I ran mentally through the lyrics: "Come ye to Bethlehem . . . come let us adore him . . ." No, no, not religious!

But it was too late. Calvin had already spread his hands out, palms up, and lifted them, and everyone was getting to their feet. He nodded to the orchestra, and they began playing the introduction to *"Adeste Fideles."*

I turned to look at the Altairi. They were glaring even more condemningly than usual. I moved between them and the doors.

The symphony was reaching the end of the introduction. Calvin glanced at me. I smiled, I hoped encouragingly, and held up crossed fingers. He nodded and then raised his baton again and brought it down.

"Have you ever been to a Sing?" Calvin had said. "It's pretty impressive." There had to be nearly four thousand people in that auditorium, all of them singing in perfect harmony, and if they'd been singing "The Chipmunks Song," it would still have been awe-inspiring. But the words they were singing couldn't have been more perfect if Calvin and I had written them to order. " 'Sing, earthly choirs,' " they trilled, " 'sing in exultation. Sing to the citizens of heaven above,' " and the Altairi glide-waddled up the aisle to the stage and sat down at Calvin's feet.

I ducked outside to the hall and called Dr. Morthman. "What's happening with the ship?" I asked him.

"Where *are* you?" he demanded. "I thought you said you were on your way over here."

"There's a lot of traffic," I said. "What's the ship doing?"

"It's aborted its ignition sequence and shut down its lights," he said.

Good, I thought. That means what we're doing is working.

"It's just sitting there on the ground."

"How appropriate," I murmured.

"What do you mean by that?" he said accusingly. "Spectrum analysis shows the Altairi aren't in their ship. You've got them, don't you? Where are you and what have you done to them? If—"

I hung up, switched off my phone, and went back inside. They'd finished *"Adeste Fideles"* and were singing "Hark, the Herald Angels Sing." The Altairi were still sitting at Calvin's feet. "'. . . Reconciled,'" the assemblage sang, "'Joyful, all ye nations rise,'" and the Altairi rose.

And rose, till they were a good two feet above the aisle. There was a collective gasp, and everyone stopped singing and stared at them floating there.

No, don't stop, I thought, and hurried forward, but Calvin had it under control. He turned a glare worthy of Aunt Judith on his seventh-grade girls, and they swallowed hard and started singing again, and after a moment everyone else recovered themselves and joined in to finish the verse.

When the song ended, Calvin turned and mouthed at me, "What do I do next?"

"Keep singing," I mouthed back.

"Singing what?"

I shrugged him an "I don't know," and mouthed, "What about this?" and pointed at the fourth song on the program.

He grinned, turned back to his choirs, and announced, "We will now sing, 'There's a Song in the Air.'"

There was a rustle of pages, and they began singing. I eyed the Altairi warily, looking for a lessening in elevation, but they continued to hover, and when the choir reached, "'and the beautiful sing,'" it seemed to me their glares became slightly less fierce.

"'And that song from afar has swept over the earth,'" the assemblage sang, and the auditorium doors burst open and Dr. Morthman, Reverend Thresher, and dozens of FBI agents and police and reporters and cameramen came rushing in. "Stay where you are," one of the FBI agents shouted.

"Blasphemous!" Reverend Thresher roared. "Look at this! Witches, homosexuals, liberals—!"

"Arrest that young woman," Dr. Morthman said, pointing at me, "and the young man directing—" He stopped and gaped at the Altairi hovering above the stage. Flashes began to go off, reporters started talking into microphones, and Reverend Thresher positioned himself squarely in front of one of the cameras and clasped his hands. "Oh, Lord," he shouted, "drive Satan's demons out of the Altairi!"

"No!" I shouted to Calvin's seventh-graders, "don't stop singing," but they already had. I looked desperately at Calvin. "Keep directing!" I said, but the police were already moving forward to handcuff him, stepping cautiously around the Altairi, who were drifting earthward like slowly leaking balloons.

"And teach these sinners here the error of their ways," Dr. Thresher was intoning.

"You can't do this, Dr. Morthman," I said desperately. "The Altairi—"

He grabbed my arm and dragged me to one of the police officers. "I want both of them charged with kidnapping," he said, "and I want her charged with conspiracy. She's responsible for this entire—" He stopped and stared past me.

I turned around. The Altairi were standing directly behind me, glaring. The police officer, who'd been about to clamp a pair of handcuffs on me, let go of my wrist and backed away, and so did the reporters and the FBI.

"Your excellencies," Dr. Morthman said, taking several steps back, "I want you to know the commission had nothing to do with this. We knew nothing about it. It's entirely this young woman's fault. She . . ."

"We acknowledge your greetings," the Altairus in the center said, bowing to me, "and greet you in return."

A murmur of surprise rumbled through the auditorium, and Dr. Morthman stammered, "Y-you speak English?"

"Of course," I said and bowed to the Altairi. "It's nice to finally be able to communicate with you."

"We welcome you into the company of citizens of the heavens," the one on the end said, "and reciprocate your offers of goodwill, peace on earth, and chestnuts."

"We assure you that we come bearing gifts as well," the Altairus on the other end said.

"It's a miracle!" Reverend Thresher shouted. "The Lord has healed them! He has unlocked their lips!" He dropped to his knees and began to pray. "Oh, Lord, we know it is our prayers which have brought this miracle about—"

Dr. Morthman bounded forward. "Your excellencies, allow me to be the first to welcome you to our humble planet," he said, extending his hand. "On behalf of the government of the—"

The Altairi ignored him. "We had begun to think we had erred in our assessment of your world," the one who'd spoken before said to me, and the one next to her? him? said, "We doubted your species was fully sentient."

"I know," I said. "I doubt it myself sometimes."

"We also doubted you understood the concept of accord," the one on the other end said, and turned and glared pointedly at Calvin's wrists.

"I think you'd better un-handcuff Mr. Ledbetter," I said to Dr. Morthman.

"Of course, of course," he said, motioning to the police officer. "Explain to them it was all a little misunderstanding," he whispered to me, and the Altairi turned to glare at him and then at the police officer.

When Calvin was out of the handcuffs, the one on the end said, "As the men of old, we are with gladness to be proved wrong."

So are we, I thought. "We're delighted to welcome you to our planet," I said.

"Now if you'll accompany me back to DU," Dr. Morthman cut in, "we'll arrange for you to go to Washington to meet with the president and—"

The Altairi began to glare again. Oh, no, I thought, and looked frantically at Calvin. "We have not yet finished greeting the delegation,

Dr. Morthman," Calvin said. He turned to the Altairi. "We would like to sing you the rest of our greeting songs."

"We wish to hear them," the Altairus in the center said, and the six of them immediately turned, walked back up the aisle, and sat down.

"I think it would be a good idea if you sat down, too," I said to Dr. Morthman and the FBI agents.

"Can some of you share your music with them?" Calvin said to the people in the last row. "And help them find the right place?"

"I have no intention of singing with witches and homo—" Reverend Thresher began indignantly, and the Altairi all turned to glare at him. He sat down, and an elderly man in a yarmulke handed him his music.

"What do we do about the words to the 'Hallelujah Chorus'?" Calvin whispered to me, and the Altairi stood up and walked back down the aisle to us.

"There is no need to alter your joyful songs. We wish to hear them with the native words," the one in the center said.

"We have a great interest in your planet's myths and superstitions," the one on the end said, "the child in the manger, the lighting of the Kwanzaa menorah, the bringing of toys and teeth to children. We are eager to learn more."

"We have many questions," the next one in line said. "If the child was born in a desert land, then how can King Herod have taken the children on a sleigh ride?"

"Sleigh ride?" Dr. Morthman said, and Calvin looked inquiringly at me.

"'All children young to sleigh,'" I whispered.

"Also, if holly is jolly, then why does it bark?" the one on the other end said. "And, Mr. Ledbetter, *is* Ms. Yates your girlfriend?"

"There will be time for questions, negotiations, and gifts when the greetings have been completed," the second Altairus on the left, the one who hadn't said anything up till then, said, and I realized he must be the leader. Or the choir director, I thought. When he spoke, the

Altairi instantly formed themselves into pairs, walked back up the aisle, and sat down.

I picked up Calvin's baton and handed it to him. "What do you think we should sing first?" he asked me.

"All I want for Christmas is you," I said.

"Really? I was thinking maybe we should start with 'Angels We Have Heard on High,' or—"

"That wasn't a song title," I said.

"Oh," he said and turned to the Altairi. "The answer to your question is yes."

"These are tidings of great joy," the one in the center said.

"There shall be many mistletoeings," the one on the end added.

The second Altairus on the left glared at them. "I think we'd better sing," I said, and squeezed into the first row, between Reverend McIntyre and an African American woman in a turban and dashiki.

Calvin stepped onto the podium. "The Hallelujah Chorus," Calvin said, and there was a shuffling of pages as people found their music. The woman next to me held out her music to me so we could share and whispered, "It's considered proper etiquette to stand for this. In honor of King George the Third. He's supposed to have stood up the first time he heard it."

"Actually," Reverend McIntyre whispered to me, "he may merely have been startled out of a sound sleep, but rising out of respect and admiration is still an appropriate response."

I nodded. Calvin raised his baton, and the entire auditorium, except for the Altairi, rose as one and began to sing. And if I'd thought "Adeste Fideles" sounded wonderful, "The Hallelujah Chorus" was absolutely breathtaking, and suddenly all those lyrics about glorious songs of old and anthems sweet and repeating the sounding joy made sense. "And the whole world give back the song," I thought, "which now the angels sing."

And apparently the Altairi were as overwhelmed by the music as I was. After the fifth "Hal-leh-eh-lu-jah!" they rose into the air like they'd done before. And rose. And rose, till they floated giddily just below the high domed ceiling.

I knew just how they felt.

It was definitely a communications breakthrough. The Altairi haven't stopped talking since the All-City Sing, though we're not actually much farther along than we were before. They're much better at asking questions than answering them. They did finally tell us where they came from—the star Alsafi in the constellation Draco. But since the meaning of Altair is "the flying one" (and Alsafi means "cooking tripod"), everyone still calls them the Altairi.

They also told us why they'd turned up at Calvin's apartment and kept following me ("We glimpsed interesting possibilities of accord between you and Mr. Ledbetter") and explained, more or less, how their spaceship works, which the Air Force has found extremely interesting. But we still don't know why they came here. Or what they want. The only thing they've told us specifically was that they wanted to have Dr. Morthman and Reverend Thresher removed from the commission and to have Dr. Wakamura put in charge. It turns out they like being squirted, at least as much as they like anything we do. They still glare.

So does Aunt Judith. She called me the day after the All-City Sing to tell me she'd seen me on CNN and thought I'd done a nice job saving the planet, but what on earth was I wearing? Didn't I know one was supposed to dress up for a concert? I told her everything that had happened was all thanks to her, and she glared at me (I could feel it, even over the phone) and hung up.

But she must not be too mad. When she heard I was engaged, she called my sister Tracy and told her she expected to be invited to the wedding shower. My mother is cleaning like mad.

I wonder if the Altairi will give us a fish slice. Or a birthday card with a dollar in it. Or faster-than-light travel.

Afterword for "All Seated on the Ground"

When I wrote this story, I relied heavily on my thirty-odd years of experience singing in church choirs, during which I sang every Christmas carol ever written and learned way more than I ever wanted to know about them. And about everything else.

As I have often said, everything you need to know about the world can be learned by singing in a church choir. Comedy, drama, intrigue, romance, revenge, pride, lust, envy, greed, vainglory . . . You name it, church choirs have it all. Plus, you find out a bunch of other useful stuff to get you through life. Like:

1. If the person singing next to you is flat, it's fairly easy to stay on pitch. If they're sharp, you're doomed.

2. The third verse of any hymn (or the fifth if it has six verses) is where they stick the really terrible lyrics, which is why so many ministers opt for "verses 1, 2, and 4." Verse 3 is where you'll find gems like "sorrowing, sighing, bleeding, dying" and "O mysterious condescending! O abandonment sublime!"

3. On the other hand, at least hymns with bad lyrics are *interesting,* unlike most of modern praise music, which is boring beyond belief. I'll take "Nor thorns infest the ground" over "Oh, God, you're so awesome" any day.

4. Divinely inspired is not the same as good. Many beloved hymns and Christmas carols are actually hideous, which you would know if you had to sing them every year.

I particularly loathe "O Little Town of Bethlehem." During one of those Christmas Eve services where they tell the carol's history and then the choir sings it (the carol, not the history), the minister described in detail the circumstances under which "O Little Town" had been written.

The author, the minister said, an Episcopal priest named Phillips Brooks, had visited the Holy Land, ridden to Bethlehem on horseback, and, once there, sat through a five-hour church service, and had been so inspired by the whole experience that he'd immediately sat down (really? I find the entire story somewhat questionable) and written the carol.

After which account, my daughter (also in the choir and sitting next to me) leaned over and whispered to me, "Oh, well, I guess it's the thought that counts, Mom," followed by sputters of suppressed laughter and our not being allowed to sit together anymore.

THE LAST OF THE WINNEBAGOS

On the way out to Tempe I saw a dead jackal in the road. I was in the far left lane of Van Buren, ten lanes away from it, and its long legs were facing away from me, the squarish muzzle flat against the pavement so it looked narrower than it really was, and for a minute I thought it was a dog.

I had not seen an animal in the road like that for fifteen years. They can't get onto the dividers, of course, and most of the multiways are fenced. And people are more careful of their animals.

The jackal was probably somebody's pet. This part of Phoenix was mostly residential, and after all this time people still think they can turn the nasty, carrion-loving creatures into pets. Which was no reason to have hit it and, worse, left it there. It's a felony to strike an animal and another one to not report it, but whoever had hit it was long gone.

I pulled the Hitori over onto the center shoulder and sat there awhile, staring at the empty multiway. I wondered who had hit it and whether they had stopped to see if it was dead.

Katie had stopped. She had hit the brakes so hard she sent her car into a skid that brought it up against the ditch, and jumped out of the jeep. I was still running toward him, floundering in the snow. We made it to him almost at the same time. I knelt beside him, the camera dangling from my neck, its broken case hanging half-open.

"I hit him," Katie had said. "I hit him with the jeep."

I looked in the rearview mirror. I couldn't even see over the pile of camera equipment in the backseat with the eisenstadt balanced on top. I got out. I had come nearly a mile, and looking back, I couldn't see the jackal, though I knew now that that was what it was.

"McCombe! David! Are you there yet?" Ramirez's voice said from inside the car.

I leaned in. "No," I shouted in the general direction of the phone's receiver. "I'm still on the multiway."

"Mother of God, what's taking you so long? The governor's conference is at twelve, and I want you to go out to Scottsdale and do a layout on the closing of Taliesin West. The appointment's for ten. Listen, McCombe, I got the poop on the Amblers for you. They bill themselves as 'One-Hundred Percent Authentic,' but they're not. Their RV isn't really a Winnebago, it's an Open Road.

"It *is* the last RV on the road, though, according to Highway Patrol. A man named Eldridge was touring with one, also *not* a Winnebago, a Shasta, until March, but he lost his license in Oklahoma for using a tanker lane, so this is it. Recreation vehicles are banned in all but four states. Texas has legislation in committee, and Utah has a full-divided bill coming up next month. Arizona will be next, so take lots of pictures, Danny Boy. This may be your last chance. And get some of the zoo."

"What about the Amblers?" I said.

"Their name *is* Ambler, believe it or not. I ran a lifeline on them. He was a welder. She was a bank teller. No kids. They've been doing this since eighty-nine when he retired. Nineteen years. David, are you using the eisenstadt?"

We had been through this the last three times I'd been on a shoot. "I'm not *there* yet," I said.

"Well, I want you to use it at the governor's conference. Set it on his desk if you can."

I intended to set it on a desk, all right. One of the desks at the back, and let it get some nice shots of the rear ends of reporters as they reached wildly for a little clear airspace to shoot their pictures in, some of them holding their vidcams in their upstretched arms and aiming them in what they hope is the right direction because they can't see the governor at all, or let it get a nice shot of one of the reporter's arms as he knocked it facedown on the desk.

"This one's a new model. It's got a trigger. It's set for faces, full-lengths, and vehicles."

So great. I come home with a hundred-frame cartridge full of passersby and tricycles. How the hell did it know when to click the shutter or which one was the governor in a press conference of eight hundred people, full-length *or* face? It was supposed to have all kinds of fancy light-metrics and computer-composition features, but all it could really do was mindlessly snap whatever passed in front of its idiot lens, just like the highway speed cameras.

It had probably been designed by the same government types who'd put the highway cameras along the road instead of overhead so that all it takes is a little speed to reduce the new side license plates to a blur, and people go faster than ever. A great camera, the eisenstadt. I could hardly wait to use it.

"Sun-co's very interested in the eisenstadt," Ramirez said. She didn't say good-bye. She never does. She just stops talking and then starts up again later. I looked back in the direction of the jackal.

The multiway was completely deserted. New cars and singles don't use the undivided multiways much, even during rush hours. Too many of the little cars have been squashed by tankers. Usually there are at least a few obsoletes and renegade semis taking advantage of the Patrol's being on the divideds, but there wasn't anybody at all.

I got back in the car and backed up even with the jackal. I turned off the ignition but didn't get out. I could see the trickle of blood from its mouth from here. A tanker went roaring past out of nowhere, trying to beat the cameras, straddling the three middle lanes and crushing the jackal's rear half to a bloody mush. It was a good thing I hadn't been trying to cross the road. He never would have even seen me.

I started the car and drove to the nearest off-ramp to find a phone. There was one at an old 7-Eleven on McDowell.

"I'm calling to report a dead animal on the road," I told the woman who answered the Society's phone.

"Name and number?"

"It's a jackal," I said. "It's between Thirtieth and Thirty-second on Van Buren. It's in the far right lane."

"Did you render emergency assistance?"

"There was no assistance to be rendered. It was dead."

"Did you move the animal to the side of the road?"

"No."

"Why not?" she said, her tone suddenly sharper, more alert.

Because I thought it was a dog. "I didn't have a shovel," I said, and hung up.

I got out to Tempe by eight-thirty, in spite of the fact that every tanker in the state suddenly decided to take Van Buren. I got pushed out onto the shoulder and drove on that most of the way.

The Winnebago was set up in the fairgrounds between Phoenix and Tempe, next to the old zoo. The flyer had said they would be open from nine to nine, and I had wanted to get most of my pictures before they opened, but it was already a quarter to nine, and even if there were no cars in the dusty parking lot, I was probably too late.

It's a tough job being a photographer. The minute most people see a camera, their real faces close like a shutter in too much light, and all that's left is their camera face, their public face. It's a smiling face, except for Saudi terrorists and senators, but, smiling or not, it shows no real emotion. Actors, politicians, people who have their picture taken all the time are the worst. The longer the person's been in the public eye, the easier it is for me to get great vidcam footage and the harder it is to get anything approaching a real photograph, and the Amblers had been at this for nearly twenty years. By a quarter to nine they would already have their camera faces on.

I parked down at the foot of the hill next to the clump of ocotillos and yucca where the zoo sign had been, pulled my Nikon longshot out of the mess in the backseat, and took some shots of the sign they'd set up by the multiway: See a Genuine Winnebago. One-Hundred Percent Authentic.

The Genuine Winnebago was parked longways against the stone banks of cactus and palms at the front of the zoo. Ramirez had said it wasn't a real Winnebago, but it had the identifying W with its extending stripes running the length of the RV, and it seemed to me to be the right shape, though I hadn't seen one in at least ten years.

I was probably the wrong person for this story. I had never had any great love for RVs, and my first thought when Ramirez called with the assignment was that there are some things that should be extinct, like mosquitoes and lane dividers, and RVs are right at the top of the list. They had been everywhere in the mountains when I'd lived in Colorado, crawling along in the left-hand lane, taking up two lanes even in the days when a lane was fifteen feet wide, with a train of cursing cars behind them.

I'd been behind one on Independence Pass that had stopped cold while a ten-year-old got out to take pictures of the scenery with an Instamatic, and one of them had tried to take the curve in front of my house and ended up in my ditch, looking like a beached whale. But that was always a bad curve.

An old man in an ironed short-sleeved shirt came out the side door and around to the front end and began washing the Winnebago with a sponge and a bucket. I wondered where he had gotten the water. According to Ramirez's advance work, which she'd sent me over the modem about the Winnebago, it had maybe a fifty-gallon water tank, tops, which is barely enough for drinking water, a shower, and maybe washing a dish or two, and there certainly weren't any hookups here at the zoo, but he was swilling water onto the front bumper and even over the tires as if he had more than enough.

I took a few shots of the RV standing in the huge expanse of parking lot and then hit the longshot to full for a picture of the old man working on the bumper. He had large reddish-brown freckles on his arms and the top of his bald head, and he scrubbed away at the bumper with a vengeance.

After a minute he stopped and stepped back, and then called to his wife. He looked worried, or maybe just crabby. I was too far away to tell if he had snapped out her name impatiently or simply called her to come and look, and I couldn't see his face. She opened the metal side door, with its narrow louvered window, and stepped down onto the metal step.

The old man asked her something, and she, still standing on the step, looked out toward the multiway and shook her head, and then came around to the front, wiping her hands on a dish towel, and they both stood there looking at his handiwork.

They were One-Hundred Percent Authentic, even if the Winnebago wasn't, down to her flowered blouse and polyester slacks, probably also One-Hundred Percent, and the cross-stitched rooster on the dish towel. She had on brown leather slip-ons like I remembered my grandmother wearing, and I was willing to bet she had set her thinning white hair on bobby pins.

Their bio said they were in their eighties, but I would have put them in their nineties, although I wondered if they were too perfect and therefore fake, like the Winnebago. But she went on wiping her hands on the dish towel the way my grandmother had when she was upset, even though I couldn't see if her face was showing any emotion, and that action at least looked authentic.

She apparently told him the bumper looked fine because he dropped the dripping sponge into the bucket and went around behind the Winnebago. She went back inside, shutting the metal door behind her even though it had to be already at least a hundred and ten out, and they hadn't even bothered to park under what scanty shade the palms provided.

I put the longshot back in the car.

The old man came around the front with a big plywood sign. He propped it against the vehicle's side. "The Last of the Winnebagos," the sign read in somebody's idea of what Indian writing should look like. "See a vanishing breed. Admission—Adults—$8.00, Children under twelve—$5.00 Open 9 A.M. to Sunset."

He strung up a row of red and yellow flags, and then picked up the bucket and started toward the door, but halfway there he stopped and took a few steps down the parking lot to where I thought he probably had a good view of the road, and then went back, walking like an old man, and took another swipe at the bumper with the sponge.

"Are you done with the RV yet, McCombe?" Ramirez said on the car phone.

I slung the camera into the back. "I just got here. Every tanker in Arizona was on Van Buren this morning. Why the hell don't you have me do a piece on abuses of the multiway system by water haulers?"

"Because I want you to get to Tempe alive. The governor's press conference has been moved to one, so you're okay. Have you used the eisenstadt yet?"

"I told you, I just got here. I haven't even turned the damned thing on."

"You don't turn it on. It self-activates when you set it bottom down on a level surface."

Great. It had probably already shot its hundred-frame cartridge on the way here.

"Well, if you don't use it on the Winnebago, make sure you use it at the governor's conference," she said. "By the way, have you thought any more about moving to investigative?"

That was why Sun-co was really so interested in the eisenstadt. It had been easier to send a photographer who could write stories than it had been to send a photographer and a reporter, especially in the little one-seater Hitoris they were ordering now, which was how I'd gotten to be a photojournalist.

And since that had worked out so well, why send either? Send an eisenstadt and a DAT deck and you won't need a Hitori and way-mile credits to get them there. You can send them through the mail. They can sit unopened on the old governor's desk, and after a while somebody in a one-seater who wouldn't have to be either a photographer *or* a reporter can sneak in to retrieve them and a dozen others.

"No," I said, glancing back up the hill. The old man gave one last swipe to the front bumper and then walked over to one of the zoo's old stone-edged planters and dumped the water bucket on a tangle of prickly pear, which would probably think it was a spring shower and bloom before I made it up the hill. "Look," I said, "if I'm going to get any pictures before the touristas arrive, I'd better go."

"I wish you'd think about it. And use the eisenstadt this time. You'll like it once you try it. Even *you'll* forget it's a camera."

"I'll bet," I said. I looked back down the multiway. Nobody at all was coming now. Maybe that was what all the Amblers' anxiety was about—I should have asked Ramirez what their average daily attendance was and what sort of people used up credits to come this far out and see an old beat-up RV. The curve into Tempe alone was three point two miles. Maybe nobody came at all. If that was the case, I might have a chance of getting some decent pictures. I got in the Hitori and drove up the steep drive.

"Howdy," the old man said, all smiles, holding out his reddish-brown freckled hand to shake mine. "Name's Jake Ambler. And this here's Winnie," he said, patting the metal side of the RV, "last of the Winnebagos. Is there just the one of you?"

"David McCombe," I said, holding out my press pass. "I'm a photographer. Sun-co. Phoenix *Sun*, Tempe-Mesa *Tribune*, Glendale *Star*, and affiliated stations. I was wondering if I could take some pictures of your vehicle?" I touched my pocket and turned the taper on.

"You bet. We've always cooperated with the media, Mrs. Ambler and me. I was just cleaning old Winnie up," he said. "She got pretty dusty on the way down from Globe." He didn't make any attempt to tell his wife I was there, even though she could hardly avoid hearing us, and she didn't open the metal door again. "We been on the road now with Winnie for almost twenty years. Bought her in 1989 in Forest City, Iowa, where they were made. The wife didn't want to buy her, didn't know if she'd like traveling, but now she's the one wouldn't part with it."

He was well into his spiel now, an open, friendly, I-have-nothing-to-hide expression on his face that hid everything. There was no point in taking any stills, so I got out the vidcam and shot the TV footage while he led me around the RV.

"This up here," he said, standing with one foot on the flimsy metal ladder and patting the metal bar around the top, "is the luggage rack, and this is the holding tank. It'll hold thirty gallons and has an automatic electric pump that hooks up to any waste hookup. Empties in five minutes, and you don't even get your hands dirty." He held up his fat pink hands, palms forward, as if to show me. "Water tank," he said, slapping a silver metal tank next to it. "Holds forty gallons, which is plenty for just the two of us. Interior space is a hundred fifty cubic feet with six feet four of headroom. That's plenty even for a tall guy like yourself."

He gave me the whole tour. His manner was easy, just short of slap-on-the-back hearty, but he looked relieved when an ancient VW bug came chugging catty-cornered up through the parking lot. He must have thought they wouldn't have any customers, either.

A family piled out, Japanese tourists, a woman with short black hair, a man in shorts, two kids. One of the kids had a ferret on a leash.

"I'll just look around while you tend to the paying customers," I told him.

I locked the vidcam in the car, took the longshot, and went up toward the zoo. I took a wide-angle of the zoo sign for Ramirez. I could see it now. She'd run a caption like, "The old zoo stands empty today. No sound of lion's roar, of elephant's trumpeting, of children's laughter, can be heard here. The old Phoenix Zoo, last of its kind, while just outside its gates stands yet another last of its kind. Story on page 10." Maybe it *would* be a good idea to let the eisenstadts and the computers take over.

I went inside. I hadn't been out here in years. In the late eighties there had been a big flap over zoo policy. I had taken the pictures, but I hadn't covered the story since there were still such things as reporters back then. I had photographed the cages in question, and the new zoo director who had caused all the flap by stopping the zoo's renovation project cold and giving the money to a wildlife protection group.

"I refuse to spend money on cages when in a few years we'll have nothing to put in them. The timber wolf, the California condor, the grizzly bear, are in imminent danger of becoming extinct, and it's our responsibility to save them, not make a comfortable prison for the last survivors."

The Society had called him an alarmist, which just goes to show you how much things can change.

Well, he was an alarmist, wasn't he? The grizzly bear isn't extinct in the wild—it's Colorado's biggest tourist draw, and there are so many whooping cranes Texas is talking about limited hunting.

In all the uproar, the zoo had ceased to exist, and the animals all went to an even more comfortable prison in Sun City—sixteen acres of savannah land for the zebras and lions, and snow manufactured daily for the polar bears.

They hadn't really been cages, in spite of what the zoo director said. The old capybara enclosure, which was the first thing inside the gate, was a nice little meadow with a low stone wall around it. A family of prairie dogs had taken up residence in the middle of it.

I went back to the gate and looked down at the Winnebago. The family circled the Winnebago, the man bending down to look underneath the body. One of the kids was hanging off the ladder at the back of the RV. The ferret was nosing around the front wheel Jake Ambler had so carefully scrubbed down, looking like it was about ready to lift its leg, if ferrets do that.

The kid yanked on its leash and then picked it up in his arms. The mother said something to him. Her nose was sunburned.

Katie's nose had been sunburned. She had had that white cream on it that skiers used to use. She had been wearing a parka and jeans and bulky pink and white moon boots that she couldn't run in, but she still made it to Aberfan before I did. I pushed past her and knelt over him.

"I hit him," she said bewilderedly. "I hit a dog."

"Get back in the jeep, damn it!" I shouted at her.

I stripped off my sweater and tried to wrap him in it. "We've got to get him to the vet."

"Is he dead?" Katie said, her face as pale as the cream on her nose.

"No!" I had shouted. "No, he isn't dead!"

The mother turned and looked up toward the zoo, her hand shading her face. She caught sight of the camera, dropped her hand, and smiled, a toothy, impossible smile. People in the public eye are the worst, but even people having a snapshot taken close down somehow, and it isn't just the phony smile. It's as if that old superstition is true and cameras do really steal the soul.

I pretended to take her picture and then lowered the camera. The zoo director had put up a row of tombstone-shaped signs in front of the gate, one for each endangered species. They were covered with plastic, which hadn't helped much.

I wiped the streaky dust off the one in front of me. "*Canis latrans,*" it said, with two green stars after it. "Coyote. North American wild dog. Due to large-scale poisoning by ranchers, who saw it as a threat to cattle and sheep, the coyote is nearly extinct in the wild." Underneath there was a photograph of a ragged coyote sitting on its haunches and an explanation of the stars. Blue—endangered species. Yellow—endangered habitat. Red—extinct in the wild.

After Misha died, I had come out here to photograph the dingo and the coyotes and the wolves, but they were already in the process of moving the zoo, so I couldn't get any pictures, and it probably wouldn't have done any good. The coyote in the picture had faded to a greenish yellow and its yellow eyes were almost white, but it stared out of the picture looking as hearty and unconcerned as Jake Ambler, wearing its camera face.

The mother had gone back to the bug and was herding the kids inside. Mr. Ambler walked the father back to the car, shaking his shining bald head, and the man talked some more, leaning on the open door, and then got in and drove off. I walked back down.

If he was bothered by the fact that they had only stayed ten minutes and that, as far as I had been able to see, no money had changed hands, it didn't show in his face. He led me around to the side of the RV and pointed to a chipped and faded collection of decals along the painted bar of the W. "These here are the states we've been in." He pointed to the one nearest the front. "Every state in the Union, plus Canada and Mexico. Last state we were in was Nevada."

Up this close it was easy to see where he had painted out the name of the original RV and covered it with the bar of red. The paint had the dull look of inauthenticity. He had covered up the words "Open Road" with a burnt-wood plaque that read, "The Amblin' Amblers."

He pointed at a bumper sticker next to the door that said "I got lucky in Vegas at Caesar's Palace" and had a picture of a naked showgirl. "We couldn't find a decal for Nevada. I don't think they make them anymore. And you know something else you can't find? Steering wheel covers. You know the kind. That keep the wheel from burning your hands when it gets hot?"

"Do you do all the driving?" I asked.

He hesitated before answering, and I wondered if one of them didn't have a license. I'd have to look it up in the lifeline.

"Mrs. Ambler spells me sometimes, but I do most of it. Mrs. Ambler reads the map. Damn maps nowadays are so hard to read. Half the time you can't tell what kind of road it is. They don't make them like they used to."

We talked for a while more about all the things you couldn't find a decent one of anymore and the sad state things had gotten in generally, and then I announced I wanted to talk to Mrs. Ambler, got the vidcam and the eisenstadt out of the car, and went inside the Winnebago.

She still had the dish towel in her hand, even though there couldn't possibly be space for that many dishes in the tiny RV. The inside was even smaller than I had thought it would be, low enough that I had to duck and so narrow I had to hold the Nikon close to my body to keep from hitting the lens on the passenger seat. It felt like an oven inside, and it was only nine o'clock in the morning.

I set the eisenstadt down on the kitchen counter, making sure its concealed lens was facing out. If it would work anywhere, it would be here. There was basically nowhere for Mrs. Ambler to go that she could get out of range. There was nowhere I could go, either, and sorry, Ramirez, there are just some things a live photographer can do better than a preprogrammed one, like stay out of the picture.

"This is the galley," Mrs. Ambler said, folding her dish towel and hanging it from a plastic ring on the cupboard below the sink with the cross-stitch design showing.

It wasn't a rooster after all. It was a poodle wearing a sunbonnet and carrying a basket. "Shop on Wednesday," the motto underneath said.

"As you can see, we have a double sink with a hand-pump faucet. The refrigerator is LP-electric and holds four cubic feet. Back here is the dinette area. The table folds up into the rear wall, and we have our bed. And this is our bathroom."

She was as bad as her husband. "How long have you had the Winnebago?" I said to stop the spiel. Sometimes, if you can get people talking about something besides what they intended to talk about, you can disarm them into something like a natural expression.

"Nineteen years," she said, lifting up the lid of the chemical toilet. "We bought it in 1989. I didn't want to buy it—I didn't like the idea of selling our house and going gallivanting off like a couple of hippies, but Jake went ahead and bought it, and now I wouldn't trade it for anything. The shower operates on a forty-gallon pressurized water system."

She stood back so I could get a picture of the shower stall, so narrow you wouldn't have to worry about dropping the soap. I dutifully took some vidcam footage.

"You live here full-time, then?" I said, trying not to let my voice convey how impossible that prospect sounded. Ramirez had said they were from Minnesota. I had assumed they had a house there and only went on the road for part of the year.

"Jake says the great outdoors is our home," she said. I gave up trying to get a picture of her and snapped a few high-quality detail stills for the papers: the "Pilot" sign taped on the dashboard in front of the driver's seat, the crocheted granny-square afghan on the uncomfortable-looking couch, a row of salt and pepper shakers in the back windows—Indian children, black Scottie dogs, ears of corn.

"Sometimes we live on the open prairies and sometimes on the seashore," she said.

She went over to the sink and hand-pumped a scant two cups of water into a little pan and set it on the two-burner stove. She took down two turquoise Melmac cups and matching saucers and a jar of freeze-dried coffee and spooned a little into the cups.

"Last year we were in the Colorado Rockies. We can have a house on a lake or in the desert, and when we get tired of it, we just move on. Oh, my, the things we've seen."

I didn't believe her. Colorado had been one of the first states to ban recreation vehicles, even before the gas crunch and the multiways. It had banned them on the passes first and then shut them out of the national forests, and by the time I left they weren't even allowed on the interstates.

Ramirez had said RVs were banned outright in forty-six states. New Mexico was one, Utah had heavy restricks, and daytime travel was forbidden in all the western states. Whatever they'd seen, and it sure as

hell wasn't Colorado, they had seen it in the dark or on some unpa-
trolled multiway, going like sixty to outrun the cameras. Not exactly the
footloose and fancy-free life they tried to paint.

The water boiled. Mrs. Ambler poured it into the cups, spilling a
little on the turquoise saucers. She blotted it up with the dish towel.
"We came down here because of the snow. They get winter so early in
Colorado."

"I know," I said.

It had snowed two feet, and it was only the middle of September.
Nobody even had their snow tires on. The aspens hadn't even turned
yet, and some of the branches had broken under the weight of the snow.
Katie's nose had still been sunburned from the summer.

"Where did you come from just now?" I asked Mrs. Ambler.

"Globe," she said, and opened the door to yell to her husband.
"Jake! Coffee!" She carried the cups to the table-that-converts-into-a-
bed. "It has leaves that you can put in it so it seats six," she said.

I sat down at the table so she was on the side where the eisenstadt
could catch her. The sun was coming in through the cranked-open
back windows, already hot. Mrs. Ambler got onto her knees on the plaid
cushions and let down a woven cloth shade, carefully, so it wouldn't
knock the salt and pepper shakers off.

There were some snapshots stuck up between the ceramic ears of
corn. I picked one up. It was a square Polaroid from the days when you
had to peel off the print and glue it to a stiff card. The two of them,
looking exactly the way they did now, with that friendly, impenetrable
camera smile, were standing in front of a blur of orange rock—the
Grand Canyon? Zion? Monument Valley? Polaroid had always chosen
color over definition. Mrs. Ambler was holding a little yellow blur in her
arms that could have been a cat but wasn't.

It was a dog.

"That's Jake and me at Devil's Tower," she said, taking the picture
away from me. "And Taco. You can't tell from this picture, but she was
the cutest little thing. A chihuahua."

She handed it back to me and rummaged behind the salt and pepper shakers. "Sweetest little dog you ever saw. This will give you a better idea."

The picture she handed me was considerably better, a matte print done with a decent camera. Mrs. Ambler was holding the chihuahua in this one, too, standing in front of the Winnebago.

"She used to sit on the arm of Jake's chair while he drove and when we came to a red light she'd look at it, and when it turned green she'd bark to tell him to go. She was the smartest little thing."

I looked at the dog's flaring, pointed ears, its bulging eyes and rat's snout.

The dogs never come through. I took dozens of pictures, there at the end, and they might as well have been calendar shots. Nothing of the real dog at all. I decided it was the lack of muscles in their faces—they could not smile, in spite of what their owners claimed.

It is the muscles in the face that make people leap across the years in pictures. The expressions on dogs' faces were what breeding had fastened on them—the gloomy bloodhound, the alert collie, the rakish mutt—and anything else was wishful thinking on the part of the doting master, who would also swear that a color-blind chihuahua with a brain pan the size of a Mexican jumping bean could tell when the light changed.

My theory of the facial muscles doesn't really hold water, of course. Cats can't smile, either, and they come through. Smugness, slyness, disdain—all of those expressions come through beautifully, and they don't have any muscles in their faces, either, so maybe it's love that you can't capture in a picture because love was the only expression dogs were capable of.

I was still looking at the picture. "She is a cute little thing," I said and handed it back to her. "She wasn't very big, was she?"

"I could carry Taco in my jacket pocket. We didn't name her Taco. We got her from a man in California that named her that," she said, as if she could see herself that the dog didn't come through in the picture.

As if, had she named the dog herself, it would have been different. Then the name would have been a more real name, and Taco would have, by default, become more real as well. As if a name could convey what the picture didn't—all the things the little dog did and was and meant to her.

Names don't do it, either, of course. I had named Aberfan myself. The vet's assistant, when he heard it, typed it in as Abraham.

"Age?" he had said calmly, even though he had no business typing all this into a computer, he should have been in the operating room with the vet.

"You've got that in there, damn it!" I shouted.

He looked calmly puzzled. "I don't show any Abraham . . ."

"Aberfan, damn it. Aberfan!"

"Here it is," the assistant said imperturbably.

Katie, standing across the desk from me, glanced up from looking at the screen. "He had the newparvo and lived through it?" she said, and her face was wide open.

"He had the newparvo and lived through it," I said, "until you came along."

"I had an Australian shepherd," I told Mrs. Ambler.

Jake came into the Winnebago, carrying the plastic bucket. "Well, it's about time," Mrs. Ambler said. "Your coffee's getting cold."

"I was just going to finish washing off Winnie," he said. He wedged the bucket into the tiny sink and began pumping vigorously with the heel of his hand. "She got mighty dusty coming down through all that sand."

"I was telling Mr. McCombe here about Taco," she said, getting up and taking him the cup and saucer. "Here, drink your coffee before it gets cold."

"I'll be in in a minute," he said. He stopped pumping and tugged the bucket out of the sink.

"Mr. McCombe had a dog," she said, still holding the cup out to him. "He had an Australian shepherd. I was telling him about Taco."

"He's not interested in that," Jake said. They exchanged one of those warning looks that married couples are so good at. "Tell him about the Winnebago. That's what he's here for."

Jake went back outside. I screwed the longshot's lens cap on and put the vidcam back in its case. She took the little pan off the miniature stove and poured the coffee back into it. "I think I've got all the pictures I need," I said to her back.

She didn't turn around. "He never liked Taco. He wouldn't even let her sleep on the bed with us. Said it made his legs cramp. A little dog like that that didn't weigh anything."

I took the longshot's lens cap back off.

"You know what we were doing the day she died?" she said bitterly. "We were out shopping. I didn't want to leave her alone, but Jake said she'd be fine. It was ninety degrees that day, and he just kept on going from store to store, and when we got back she was dead."

She set the pan on the stove and turned on the burner. "The vet said it was the newparvo, but it wasn't. She died from the heat, poor little thing."

I set the Nikon down gently on the formica table and estimated the settings.

"When did Taco die?" I asked her, to make her turn around.

"Ninety," she said. She turned back to me, and I let my hand come down on the button in an almost soundless click, but her public face was still in place, apologetic now, smiling, a little sheepish. "My, that was a long time ago."

I stood up and collected my cameras. "I think I've got all the pictures I need," I said again. "If I don't, I'll come back out."

"Don't forget your briefcase," she said, handing me the eisenstadt. "Did your dog die of the newparvo, too?"

"He died fifteen years ago," I said. "In ninety-three."

She nodded understandingly. "The third wave," she said.

I went outside. Jake was standing behind the Winnebago, under the back window, holding the bucket. He shifted it to his left hand and held out his right hand to me. "You get all the pictures you needed?" he asked.

"Yeah," I said. "I think your wife showed me about everything." I shook his hand.

"You come on back out if you need any more pictures," he said, and sounded, if possible, even more jovial, openhanded, friendly than he had before. "Mrs. Ambler and me, we always cooperate with the media."

"Your wife was telling me about your chihuahua," I said, more to see the effect on him than anything else.

"Yeah, the wife still misses that little dog after all these years," he said, and he looked the way she had, mildly apologetic, still smiling. "It died of the newparvo. I told her she ought to get it vaccinated, but she kept putting it off."

He shook his head. "Of course, it wasn't really her fault. You know whose fault the newparvo really was, don't you?"

Yeah, I knew. It was the Communists' fault, and it didn't matter that all their dogs had died, too, because he would say their chemical warfare had gotten out of hand or that everybody knows Commies hate dogs. Or maybe he'd say it was the fault of the Japanese, though I doubted that. He was, after all, in a tourist business. Or the Democrats or the atheists or all of them put together, and even that was One-Hundred Percent Authentic—portrait of the kind of man who drives a Winnebago—but I didn't want to hear it. I walked over to the Hitori and slung the eisenstadt in the back.

"You know who really killed your dog, don't you?" he called after me.

"Yes," I said, and got in the car.

I went home, fighting my way through a fleet of red-painted water tankers who weren't even bothering to try to outrun the cameras and thinking about Taco. My grandmother had had a chihuahua. Perdita. Meanest dog that ever lived. Used to lurk behind the door waiting to take Labrador-sized chunks out of my leg. And my grandmother's. It developed some lingering chihuahuan ailment that made it incontinent and even more ill-tempered, if that was possible.

Toward the end, it wouldn't even let my grandmother near it, but she refused to have it put to sleep and was unfailingly kind to it, even though I never saw any indication that the dog felt anything but unrelieved spite toward her. If the newparvo hadn't come along, it probably would still have been around making her life miserable.

I wondered what Taco, the wonder dog, able to distinguish red and green at a single intersection, had really been like, and if it had died of heat prostration. And what it had been like for the Amblers, living all that time in a hundred and fifty cubic feet together and blaming each other for their own guilt.

I called Ramirez as soon as I got home, breaking in without announcing myself, the way she always did. "I need a lifeline," I said.

"I'm glad you called," she said. "You got a call from the Society. And how's this as a slant for your story? 'The Winnebago and the Winnebagos.' They're an Indian tribe. In Minnesota, I think—why the hell aren't you at the governor's conference?"

"I came home," I said. "What did the Society want?"

"They didn't say. They asked for your schedule. I told them you were with the governor in Tempe. Is this about a story?"

"Yeah."

"Well, you run a proposal past me before you write it. The last thing the paper needs is to get in trouble with the Society."

"The lifeline's for Katherine Powell." I spelled it.

She spelled it back to me. "Is she connected with the Society story?"

"No."

"Then what is she connected with? I've got to put something on the request-for-info."

"Put down background."

"For the Winnebago story?"

"Yes," I said. "For the Winnebago story. How long will it take?"

"That depends. When do you plan to tell me why you ditched the governor's conference? *And* Taliesin West. Jesus Maria, I'll have to call the *Republic* and see if they'll trade footage. I'm sure they'll be thrilled to have shots of an extinct RV. That is, assuming you got any shots. You did make it out to the zoo, didn't you?"

"Yes. I got vidcam footage, stills, the works. I even used the eisenstadt."

"Mind sending your pictures in while I look up your old flame, or is that too much to ask? I don't know how long this will take. It took me two days to get clearance on the Amblers. Do you want the whole thing—pictures, documentation?"

"No. Just a résumé. And a phone number."

She cut out, still not saying good-bye. If phones still had receivers, Ramirez would be a great one for hanging up on people. I highwired the vidcam footage and the eisenstadts in to the paper and then fed the eisenstadt cartridge into the developer. I was more than a little curious about what kind of pictures it would take, in spite of the fact that it was trying to do me out of a job. At least it used high-res film and not some damn two-hundred-thousand-pixel TV substitute. I didn't believe it could compose, and I doubted if the eisenstadt would be able to do foreground-background, either, but it might, under certain circumstances, get a picture I couldn't.

The doorbell rang. I answered the door. A lanky young man in a Hawaiian shirt and baggies was standing on the front step, and there was another man in a Society uniform out in the driveway.

"Mr. McCombe?" he said, extending a hand. "Jim Hunter. Humane Society."

I don't know what I'd expected—that they wouldn't bother to trace the call? That they'd let somebody get away with leaving a dead animal on the road?

"I just wanted to stop by and thank you on behalf of the Society for phoning in that report on the jackal. Can I come in?"

He smiled, an open, friendly, smug smile, as if he expected me to be stupid enough to say "I don't know what you're talking about" and slam the screen door on his hand.

"Just doing my duty," I said, smiling back at him.

"Well, we really appreciate responsible citizens like you. It makes our job a whole lot easier." He pulled a folded readout from his shirt pocket. "I just need to double-check a couple of things. You're a reporter for Sun-co, is that right?"

"Photojournalist," I said.

"And the Hitori you were driving belongs to the paper?"

I nodded.

"It has a phone. Why didn't you use it to make the call?"

The uniform was bending over the Hitori.

"I didn't realize it had a phone. The paper just bought the Hitoris. This is only the second time I've had one out."

Since they knew the paper had had phones put in, they also knew what I'd just told them. I wondered where they'd gotten the info. Public phones were supposed to be tap-free, and if they'd read the license number off one of the cameras, they wouldn't know who'd had the car unless they'd talked to Ramirez, and if they'd talked to her, she wouldn't have been talking blithely about the last thing she needed being trouble with the Society.

"You didn't know the car had a phone," he said, "so you drove to—"

He consulted the readout, somehow giving the impression he was taking notes. I'd have bet there was a taper in the pocket of that shirt. "—the 7-Eleven at McDowell and Fortieth Street, and made the call from there. Why didn't you give the Society rep your name and address?"

"I was in a hurry," I said. "I had two assignments to cover before noon, the second out in Scottsdale."

"Which is why you didn't render assistance to the animal, either. Because you were in a hurry."

You bastard, I thought.

"No," I said. "I didn't render assistance because there wasn't any assistance to be rendered. The—it was dead."

"And how did you know that, Mr. McCombe?"

"There was blood coming out of its mouth," I said.

I had thought that that was a good sign, that he wasn't bleeding anywhere else. The blood had come out of Aberfan's mouth when he tried to lift his head, just a little trickle, sinking into the hard-packed snow. It had stopped before we even got him into the car. "It's all right, boy," I told him. "We'll be there in a minute."

Katie started the car, killed it, started it again, backed it up to where she could turn around.

Aberfan lay limply across my lap, his tail against the gearshift. "Just lie still, boy," I said. I patted his neck. It was wet, and I raised my hand and looked at my palm, afraid it was blood. It was only water from the melted snow. I dried his neck and the top of his head with the sleeve of my sweater.

"How far is it?" Katie said. She was clutching the steering wheel with both hands and sitting stiffly forward in the seat. The windshield wipers flipped back and forth, trying to keep up with the snow.

"About five miles," I said, and she stepped on the gas pedal and then let up on it again as we began to skid. "On the right side of the highway."

Aberfan raised his head off my lap and looked at me. His gums were gray, and he was panting, but I couldn't see any more blood. He tried to lick my hand. "You'll make it, Aberfan," I said. "You made it before, remember?"

"But you didn't get out of the car and go check, to make sure it was dead?" Hunter said.

"No."

"And you don't have any idea who hit the jackal?" he said, and made it sound like the accusation it was.

"No."

He glanced back at the uniform, who had moved around the car to the other side. "Whew," Hunter said, shaking his Hawaiian collar, "it's like an oven out here. Mind if I come in?" which meant the uniform needed more privacy. Well, then, by all means, give him more privacy. The sooner he sprayed print-fix on the bumper and tires and peeled off the incriminating traces of jackal blood that weren't there and stuck them in the evidence bags he was carrying in the pockets of that uniform, the sooner they'd leave.

I opened the screen door wider.

"Oh, this is great," Hunter said, still trying to generate a breeze with his collar. "These old adobe houses stay so cool." He glanced around the room at the developer and the enlarger, the couch, the dry-mounted photographs on the wall. "You don't have any idea who might have hit the jackal?"

"I figure it was a tanker," I said. "What else would be on Van Buren that time of morning?"

I was almost sure it had been a car or a small truck. A tanker would have left the jackal a spot on the pavement. But a tanker would get a license suspension and two weeks of having to run water into Santa Fe instead of Phoenix, and probably not that. Rumor at the paper had it the Society was in the Water Board's pocket. If it was a car, on the other hand, the Society would take away the car and stick its driver with a prison sentence.

"They're all trying to beat the cameras," I said. "The tanker probably didn't even know it'd hit it."

"What?" he said.

"I said, it had to be a tanker. There isn't anything else on Van Buren during rush hour."

I expected him to say, "Except for you," but he didn't. He wasn't even listening. "Is this your dog?" he said.

He was looking at the photograph of Perdita. "No," I said. "That was my grandmother's dog."

"What is it?"

A nasty little beast. And when it died of the newparvo, my grandmother had cried like a baby. "A chihuahua."

He looked around at the other walls. "Did you take all these pictures of dogs?" His whole manner had changed, taking on a politeness that made me realize just how insolent he had intended to be before. The one on the road wasn't the only jackal around.

"Some of them," I said. He was looking at the photograph next to it. "I didn't take that one."

"I know what this one is," he said, pointing at it. "It's a boxer, right?"

"An English bulldog," I said.

"Oh, right. Weren't those the ones that were exterminated? For being vicious?"

"No," I said.

He moved on to the picture over the developer, like a tourist in a museum. "I bet you didn't take this one, either," he said, pointing at the high shoes, the old-fashioned hat on the stout old woman holding the dogs in her arms.

"That's a photograph of Beatrix Potter, the English children's author," I said. "She wrote *Peter Rabbit*."

He wasn't interested. "What kind of dogs are those?"

"Pekingese."

"It's a great picture of them."

It is, in fact, a terrible picture of them. One of them has wrenched its face away from the camera, and the other sits grimly in its owner's hand, waiting for its chance. Obviously neither of them liked having its picture taken, though you can't tell that from their expressions. They reveal nothing in their little flat-nosed faces, in their black little eyes.

Beatrix Potter, on the other hand, comes through beautifully, in spite of the attempt to smile for the camera and the fact that she must have had to hold on to the Pekes for dear life, or maybe because of that. The fierce, humorous love she felt for her fierce, humorous little dogs is all there in her face. She must never, in spite of *Peter Rabbit* and its attendant fame, have developed a public face. Everything she felt was right there, unprotected, unshuttered. Like Katie.

"Are any of these your dog?" Hunter asked. He was standing looking at the picture of Misha that hung above the couch.

"No," I said.

"How come you don't have any pictures of your dog?" he asked, and I wondered how he knew I had had a dog and what else he knew.

"He didn't like having his picture taken."

He folded up the readout, stuck it in his pocket, and turned around to look at the photo of Perdita again. "He looks like he was a real nice little dog," he said.

The uniform was waiting on the front step, obviously finished with whatever he had done to the car. "We'll let you know if we find out who's responsible," Hunter said, and they left. On the way out to the street the uniform tried to tell him what he'd found, but Hunter cut him off. The suspect has a house full of photographs of dogs, therefore he didn't run over a poor facsimile of one on Van Buren this morning. Case closed.

I went back over to the developer and fed the eisenstadt film in. "Positives, one two three order, five seconds," I said, and watched as the pictures came up on the developer's screen.

Ramirez had said the eisenstadt automatically turned on whenever it was set upright on a level surface. She was right. It had taken a half-dozen shots on the way out to Tempe. Two shots of the Hitori it must have taken when I set it down to load the car, open door of same with prickly pear in the foreground, a blurred shot of palm trees and buildings with a minuscule, sharp-focused glimpse of the traffic on the expressway. Vehicles and people. There was a great shot of the red tanker that had clipped the jackal and ten or so of the yucca I had parked next to at the foot of the hill.

It had gotten two nice shots of my forearm as I set it down on the kitchen counter of the Winnebago and some beautifully composed Still Lifes of Melmac with Spoons. Vehicles and people. The rest of the pictures were dead losses: my back, the open bathroom door, Jake's back, and Mrs. Ambler's public face.

Except the last one. She had been standing right in front of the eisenstadt, looking almost directly into the lens. "When I think of that poor thing, all alone," she had said, and by the time she turned around she had her public face back on, but for a minute there, looking at what she thought was a briefcase and remembering, there she was, the person I had tried all morning to get a picture of.

I took it into the living room and sat down and looked at it awhile.

"So you knew this Katherine Powell in Colorado," Ramirez said, breaking in without preamble, and the highwire slid silently forward and began to print out the lifeline. "I always suspected you of having some deep dark secret in your past. Is she the reason you moved to Phoenix?"

I was watching the highwire advance the paper. Katherine Powell. 4628 Dutchman Drive, Apache Junction. Forty miles away.

"Holy Mother, you were really cradle-robbing. According to my calculations, she was seventeen when you lived there."

Sixteen.

"Are you the owner of the dog?" the vet had asked her, his face slackening into pity when he saw how young she was.

"No," she said. "I'm the one who hit him."

"My God," he said. "How old are you?"

"Sixteen," she said, and her face was wide open. "I just got my license."

Ramirez said, "Aren't you even going to tell me what she has to do with this Winnebago thing?"

"I moved down here to get away from the snow," I said, and cut out without saying good-bye.

The lifeline was still rolling silently forward. Hacker at Hewlett-Packard. Fired in ninety-nine, probably during the unionization. Divorced. Two kids. She had moved to Arizona five years after I did. Management programmer for Toshiba. Arizona driver's license.

I went back to the developer and looked at the picture of Mrs. Ambler. I had said dogs never came through. That wasn't true. Taco wasn't in the blurry Polaroids Mrs. Ambler had been so anxious to show me, in the stories she had been so anxious to tell. But she was in this picture, reflected in the pain and love and loss on Mrs. Ambler's face. I could see her plain as day, perched on the arm of the driver's seat, barking impatiently when the light turned green.

I put a new cartridge in the eisenstadt and went out to see Katie.

I had to take Van Buren—it was almost four o'clock, and the rush hour would have started on the divideds—but the jackal was gone anyway. The Society is efficient. Like Hitler and his Nazis.

"How come you don't have any pictures of your dog?" Hunter had asked.

The question could have been based on the assumption that anyone who would fill his living room with photographs of dogs must have had one of his own, but it wasn't. He had known about Aberfan, which meant he'd had access to my lifeline, which meant all kinds of things. My lifeline was privacy-coded, so I had to be notified before anybody could get access, except, it appeared, the Society.

A reporter I knew at the paper, Dolores Chiwere, had tried to do a story a while back claiming that the Society had an illegal link to the lifeline banks, but she hadn't been able to come up with enough evidence to convince her editor. I wondered if this counted.

The lifeline would have told them about Aberfan but not about how he died. Killing a dog wasn't a crime in those days, and I hadn't pressed charges against Katie for reckless driving or even called the police.

"I think you should," the vet's assistant had said. "There are less than a hundred dogs left. People can't just go around killing them."

"My God, man, it was snowing and slick," the vet had said angrily, "and she's just a kid."

"She's old enough to have a license," I said, looking at Katie. She was fumbling in her purse for her driver's license. "She's old enough to have been on the roads."

Katie found her license and gave it to me. It was so new it was still shiny. Katherine Powell. She had turned sixteen two weeks ago.

"This won't bring him back," the vet had said, and taken the license out of my hand and given it back to her. "You go on home now."

"I need her name for the records," the vet's assistant had said.

She had stepped forward. "Katie Powell," she had said.

"We'll do the paperwork later," the vet had said firmly.

They never did do the paperwork, though. The next week the third wave hit, and I suppose there hadn't seemed any point.

I slowed down at the zoo entrance and looked up into the parking lot. The Amblers were doing a booming business. There were at least five cars and twice as many kids clustered around the Winnebago.

"Where the hell are you?" Ramirez said. "And where the hell are your pictures? I talked the *Republic* into a trade, but they insisted on scoop rights. I need your stills now!"

"I'll send them in as soon as I get home," I said. "I'm on a story."

"The hell you are! You're on your way out to see your old girlfriend. Well, not on the paper's credits, you're not."

"Did you get the stuff on the Winnebago Indians?" I asked her.

"Yes. They were in Wisconsin, but they're not anymore. In the mid-seventies there were sixteen hundred of them on the reservation and about forty-five hundred altogether, but by 1990, the number was down to five hundred, and now they don't think there are any left, and nobody knows what happened to them."

I'll tell you what happened to them, I thought. Almost all of them were killed in the first wave, and people blamed the government and the Japanese and the ozone layer, and after the second wave hit, the Society passed all kinds of laws to protect the survivors, but it was too late, they were already below the minimum survival population limit, and then the third wave polished off the rest of them, and the last of the Winnebagos sat in a cage somewhere, and if I had been there I would probably have taken his picture.

"I called the Bureau of Indian Affairs," Ramirez said, "and they're supposed to call me back, and you don't give a damn about the Winnebagos. You just wanted to get me off the subject. What's this story you're on?"

I looked around the dashboard for an exclusion button.

"What the hell is going on, David? First you ditch two big stories, now you can't even get your pictures in. Jesus, if something's wrong, you can tell me. I want to help. It has something to do with Colorado, doesn't it?"

I found the button and cut her off.

Van Buren got crowded as the afternoon rush spilled over off the dividers. Out past the curve, where Van Buren turns into Apache Boulevard, they were putting in new lanes. The cement forms were already up on the eastbound side, and they were building the wooden forms up in two of the six lanes on my side.

The Amblers must have just beaten the workmen, though at the rate the men were working right now, leaning on their shovels in the hot afternoon sun and smoking stew, it had probably taken them six weeks to do this stretch.

Mesa was still open multiway, but as soon as I was through downtown, the construction started again, and this stretch was nearly done—forms up on both sides and most of the cement poured.

The Amblers couldn't have come in from Globe on this road. The lanes were barely wide enough for the Hitori, and the tanker lanes were gated. Superstition is full-divided, and the old highway down from Roosevelt is, too, which meant they hadn't come in from Globe at all. I wondered how they had come in—probably in some tanker lane on a multiway.

"Oh, my, the things we've seen," Mrs. Ambler had said. I wondered how much they'd been able to see skittering across the dark desert like a couple of kangaroo mice, trying to beat the cameras.

The road workers didn't have the new exit signs up yet, and I missed the exit for Apache Junction and had to go halfway to Superior, trapped in my narrow, cement-sided lane, till I hit a change-lanes and could get turned around.

Katie's address was in Superstition Estates, a development pushed up as close to the base of Superstition Mountain as it could get. I thought about what I would say to Katie when I got there. I had said maybe ten sentences altogether to her, most of them shouted directions, in the two hours we had been together. In the jeep on the way to the vet's I had talked to Aberfan, and after we got there, sitting in the waiting room, we hadn't talked at all.

It occurred to me that I might not recognize her. I didn't really remember what she looked like—only the sunburned nose and that terrible openness, and now, fifteen years later, it seemed unlikely that she would have either of them. The Arizona sun would have taken care of the first, and she had gotten married and divorced, been fired, had who knows what else happened to her in fifteen years to close her face. In which case, there had been no point in my driving all the way out here.

But Mrs. Ambler had had an almost impenetrable public face, and you could still catch her off guard. If you got her talking about the dogs. If she didn't know she was being photographed.

Katie's house was an old-style passive solar, with flat black panels on the roof. It looked presentable, but not compulsively neat. There wasn't any grass—tankers won't waste their credits coming this far out, and Apache Junction isn't big enough to match the bribes and incentives of Phoenix or Tempe—but the front yard was laid out with alternating patches of black lava chips and prickly pear. The side yard had a parched-looking palo verde tree, and there was a cat tied to it. A little girl was playing under it with toy cars.

I took the eisenstadt out of the back and went up to the front door and rang the bell. At the last moment, when it was too late to change my mind, walk away, because she was already opening the screen door, it occurred to me that she might not recognize me, that I might have to tell her who I was.

Her nose wasn't sunburned, and she had put on the weight a

sixteen-year-old puts on to get to be thirty, but otherwise she looked the same as she had that day in front of my house. And her face hadn't completely closed. I could tell, looking at her, that she recognized me and that she had known I was coming. She must have put a notify on her lifeline to have them warn her if I asked her whereabouts. I thought about what that meant.

She opened the screen door a little, the way I had to the Humane Society. "What do you want?" she said.

I had never seen her angry, not even when I turned on her at the vet's. "I wanted to see you," I said.

I had thought I might tell her I had run across her name while I was working on a story and wondered if it was the same person or that I was doing a piece on the last of the passive solars. "I saw a dead jackal on the road this morning," I said.

"And you thought I killed it?" she said. She tried to shut the screen door.

I put out my hand without thinking, to stop her. "No," I said.

I took my hand off the door. "No, of course I don't think that. Can I come in? I just want to talk to you."

The little girl had come over, clutching her toy cars to her pink T-shirt, and was standing off to the side, watching curiously.

"Come on inside, Jana," Katie said, and opened the screen door a fraction wider. The little girl scooted through. "Go on in the kitchen," she said. "I'll fix you some Kool-Aid." She looked up at me. "I used to have nightmares about your coming. I'd dream that I'd go to the door and there you'd be."

"It's really hot out here," I said and knew I sounded like Hunter. "Can I come in?"

She opened the screen door all the way. "I've got to make my daughter something to drink," she said, and led the way into the kitchen, the little girl dancing in front of her.

"What kind of Kool-Aid do you want?" Katie asked her, and she shouted, "Red!"

The kitchen counter faced the stove, refrigerator, and water cooler across a narrow aisle that opened out into an alcove with a table and chairs. I put the eisenstadt down on the table and then sat down myself so she wouldn't suggest moving into another room.

Katie reached a plastic pitcher down from one of the shelves and stuck it under the water tank to fill it. Jana dumped her cars on the counter, clambered up beside them, and began opening the cupboard doors.

"How old's your little girl?" I asked.

Katie got a wooden spoon out of the drawer next to the stove and brought it and the pitcher over to the table. "She's four," she said. "Did you find the Kool-Aid?" she asked the little girl.

"Yes," the little girl said, but it wasn't Kool-Aid. It was a pinkish cube she peeled a plastic wrapping off of. It fizzed and turned a thin-nish red when she dropped it in the pitcher. Kool-Aid must have be-come extinct, too, along with Winnebagos and passive solar. Or else changed beyond recognition. Like the Humane Society.

Katie poured the red stuff into a glass with a cartoon whale on it.

"Is she your only one?" I asked.

"No, I have a little boy," she said, but warily, as if she wasn't sure she wanted to tell me, even though if I'd requested the lifeline I already had access to all this information. Jana asked if she could have a cookie and then took it and her Kool-Aid back down the hall and outside. I could hear the screen door slam.

Katie put the pitcher in the refrigerator and leaned against the kitchen counter, her arms folded across her chest. "What do you want?"

She was just out of range of the eisenstadt, her face in the shadow of the narrow aisle.

"There was a dead jackal on the road this morning," I said. I kept my voice low so she would lean forward into the light to try and hear me. "It'd been hit by a car, and it was lying funny, at an angle. It looked like a dog. I wanted to talk to somebody who remembered Aberfan, somebody who knew him."

"I didn't know him," she said. "I only killed him, remember? That's why you did this, isn't it, because I killed Aberfan?"

She didn't look at the eisenstadt, hadn't even glanced at it when I set it on the table, but I wondered suddenly if she knew what I was up to. She was still carefully out of range.

And what if I said to her, "That's right. That's why I did this, because you killed him, and I didn't have any pictures of him. You owe me. If I can't have a picture of Aberfan, you at least owe me a picture of you remembering him."

Only she didn't remember him, didn't know anything about him except what she had seen on the way to the vet's, Aberfan lying on my lap and looking up at me, already dying. I had had no business coming here, dredging all this up again. No business.

"At first I thought you were going to have me arrested," Katie said, "and then after all the dogs died, I thought you were going to kill me."

The screen door banged. "Forgot my cars," the little girl said and scooped them into the tail of her T-shirt. Katie tousled her hair as she went past, and then folded her arms again.

" 'It wasn't my fault,' I was going to tell you when you came to kill me," she said. " 'It was snowy. He ran right in front of me. I didn't even see him.' I looked up everything I could find about newparvo. Preparing for the defense. How it mutated from parvovirus and from cat distemper before that and then kept on mutating, so they couldn't come up with a vaccine. How even before the third wave they were below the minimum survival population. How it was the fault of the people who owned the last survivors because they wouldn't risk their dogs to breed them. How the scientists didn't come up with a vaccine until only the jackals were left.

" 'You're wrong,' I was going to tell you. 'It was the puppy mill owners' fault that all the dogs died. If they hadn't kept their dogs in such unsanitary conditions, it never would have gotten out of control in the first place.' I had my defense all ready. But you'd moved away."

Jana banged in again, carrying the empty whale glass. She had a red smear across the whole lower half of her face. "I need some more," she said, making "some more" into one word. She held the glass in both hands while Katie opened the refrigerator and poured her another glassful.

"Wait a minute, honey," she said, "you've got Kool-Aid all over you," and bent to wipe Jana's face with a paper towel.

Katie hadn't said a word in her defense while we waited at the vet's, not "It was snowy," or "He ran right out in front of me," or "I didn't even see him." She had sat silently beside me, twisting her mittens in her lap, until the vet came out and told me Aberfan was dead, and then she had said, "I didn't know there were any left in Colorado. I thought they were all dead."

And I had turned to her, to a sixteen-year-old not even old enough to know how to shut her face, and said, "Now they all are. Thanks to you."

"That kind of talk isn't necessary," the vet had said warningly.

I had wrenched away from the hand he tried to put on my shoulder. "How does it feel to have killed one of the last dogs in the world?" I shouted at her. "How does it feel to be responsible for the extinction of an entire species?"

The screen door banged again. Katie was looking at me, still holding the reddened paper towel.

"You moved away," she said, "and I thought maybe that meant you'd forgiven me, but it didn't, did it?" She came over to the table and wiped at the red circle the glass had left. "Why did you do it? To punish me? Or did you think that's what I'd been doing the last fifteen years, roaring around the roads murdering animals?"

"What?" I said.

"The Society's already been here."

"The Society?" I said, not understanding.

"Yes," she said, still looking at the red-stained towel. "They said you had reported a dead animal on Van Buren. They wanted to know where I was this morning between eight and nine A.M."

I nearly ran down a road worker on the way back into Phoenix. He leaped for the still-wet cement barrier, dropping the shovel he'd been leaning on all day, and I ran right over it.

The Society had already been there. They had left my house and gone straight to hers. Only that wasn't possible, because I hadn't even called Katie then. I hadn't even seen the picture of Mrs. Ambler yet. Which meant they had gone to see Ramirez after they left me, and the last thing Ramirez and the paper needed was trouble with the Society.

"I thought it was suspicious when he didn't go to the governor's conference," she had told them, "and just now he called and asked for a lifeline on this person here. Katherine Powell. 4628 Dutchman Drive. He knew her in Colorado."

"Ramirez!" I shouted at the car phone. "I want to talk to you!" There wasn't any answer.

I swore at her for a good ten miles before I remembered I had the exclusion button on. I punched it off. "Ramirez, where the hell are you?"

"I could ask you the same question," she said. She sounded even angrier than Katie, but not as angry as I was. "You cut me off, you won't tell me what's going on."

"So you decided you had it figured out for yourself, and you told your little theory to the Society."

"What?" she said, and I recognized that tone, too. I had heard it in my own voice when Katie told me the Society had been there.

Ramirez hadn't told anybody anything, she didn't even know what I was talking about, but I was going too fast to stop. "You told the Society I'd asked for Katie's lifeline, didn't you?" I shouted.

"No," she said. "I didn't. "Don't you think it's time you told me what's going on?"

"Did the Society come see you this afternoon?"

"No. I told you. They called this morning and wanted to talk to you. I told them you were at the governor's conference."

"And they didn't call back later?"

"No. Are you in trouble?"

I hit the exclusion button. "Yes," I said. "Yes, I'm in trouble."

Ramirez hadn't told them. Maybe somebody else at the paper had, but I didn't think so. There had, after all, been Dolores Chiwere's story about them having illegal access to the lifelines. "How come you don't have any pictures of your dog?" Hunter had asked me, which meant they'd read my lifeline, too. So they knew we had both lived in Colorado, in the same town, when Aberfan died.

"What did you tell them?" I had demanded of Katie. She had been standing there in the kitchen still messing with the Kool-Aid-stained towel, and I had wanted to yank it out of her hands and make her look at me. "What did you tell the Society?"

She looked up at me. "I told them I was on Indian School Road, picking up the month's programming assignments from my company. Unfortunately, I could just as easily have driven in on Van Buren."

"About Aberfan!" I shouted. "What did you tell them about Aberfan?"

She looked steadily at me. "I didn't tell them anything. I assumed you'd already told them."

I had taken hold of her shoulders. "If they come back, don't tell them anything. Not even if they arrest you. I'll take care of this. I'll . . ."

But I hadn't told her what I'd do because I didn't know. I had run out of her house, colliding with Jana in the hall on her way in for another refill, and roared off for home, even though I didn't have any idea what I would do when I got there.

Call the Society and tell them to leave Katie alone, that she had nothing to do with this? That would be even more suspicious than everything else I'd done so far, and you couldn't get much more suspicious than that.

I had seen a dead jackal on the road (or so I said), and instead of reporting it immediately on the phone right there in my car, I'd driven to a convenience store two miles away. I'd called the Society, but I'd refused to give them my name and number. And then I'd canceled two shoots without telling my boss and asked for the lifeline of one Katherine Powell, whom I had known fifteen years ago and who could have been on Van Buren at the time of the accident.

The connection was obvious, and how long would it take them to make the connection that fifteen years ago was when Aberfan had died?

Apache was beginning to fill up with rush hour overflow and a whole fleet of tankers. The overflow obviously spent all their time driving dividers—nobody bothered to signal that they were changing lanes. Nobody even gave an indication that they knew what a lane was. Going around the curve from Tempe and onto Van Buren they were all over the road. I moved over into the tanker lane.

My lifeline didn't have the vet's name on it. They were just getting started in those days, and there was a lot of nervousness about invasion of privacy. Nothing went online without the person's permission, especially not medical and bank records, and the lifelines were little more than puff bios: family, occupation, hobbies, pets. The only things on the lifeline besides Aberfan's name was the date of his death and my address at the time, but that was probably enough. There were only two vets in town.

The vet hadn't written Katie's name down on Aberfan's record. He had handed her driver's license back to her without even looking at it, but Katie had told her name to the vet's assistant. He might have written it down. There was no way I could find out. I couldn't ask for the vet's lifeline because the Society had access to the lifelines. They'd get to him before I could. I could maybe have the paper get the vet's records for me, but I'd have to tell Ramirez what was going on, and the phone was probably tapped, too. And if I showed up at the paper, Ramirez would confiscate the car. I couldn't go there.

Wherever the hell I was going, I was driving too fast to get there. When the tanker ahead of me slowed down to ninety, I practically climbed up his back bumper. I had gone past the place where the jackal had been hit without ever seeing it.

Even without the traffic, there probably hadn't been anything to see. What the Society hadn't taken care of, the overflow probably had, and anyway, there hadn't been any evidence to begin with. If there had been, if the cameras had seen the car that hit it, they wouldn't have come after me. And Katie.

The Society couldn't charge her with Aberfan's death—killing an animal hadn't been a crime back then—but if they found out about Aberfan, they would charge her with the jackal's death, and it wouldn't matter if a hundred witnesses, a hundred highway cameras had seen her on Indian School Road. It wouldn't matter if the print-fix on her car was clean. She had killed one of the last dogs, hadn't she? They would crucify her.

I should never have left Katie. "Don't tell them anything," I had told her, but she had never been afraid of admitting guilt. When the receptionist had asked her what had happened, she had said, "I hit him," just like that, no attempt to make excuses, to run off, to lay the blame on someone else.

I had run off to try to stop the Society from finding out that Katie had hit Aberfan, and meanwhile the Society was probably back at Katie's, asking her how she'd happened to know me in Colorado, asking her how Aberfan died.

I was wrong about the Society. They weren't at Katie's house. They were at mine, standing on the porch, waiting for me to let them in.

"You're a hard man to track down," Hunter said.

The uniform grinned. "Where you been?"

"Sorry," I said, fishing my keys out of my pocket. "I thought you were all done with me. I've already told you everything I know about the incident."

Hunter stepped back just far enough for me to get the screen door open and the key in the lock. "Officer Segura and I just need to ask you a couple more questions."

"Where'd you go this afternoon?" Segura asked.

"I went to see an old friend of mine."

"Who?"

"Come on, come on," Hunter said. "Let the guy get in his own front door before you start badgering him with a lot of questions."

I opened the door. "Did the cameras get a picture of the tanker that hit the jackal?" I asked.

"Tanker?" Segura said.

"I told you," I said, "I figure it had to be a tanker. The jackal was lying in the tanker lane."

I led the way into the living room, depositing my keys on the computer and switching the phone to exclusion while I talked. The last thing I needed was Ramirez bursting in with "What's going on? Are you in trouble?"

"It was probably a renegade that hit it, which would explain why he didn't stop." I gestured at them to sit down.

Hunter did. Segura started for the couch and then stopped, staring at the photos on the wall above it. "Jesus, will you look at all the dogs!" he said. "Did you take all these pictures?"

"I took some of them. That one in the middle is Misha."

"The last dog, right?"

"Yes," I said.

"No kidding. The very last one."

No kidding. She was being kept in isolation at the Society's research facility in St. Louis when I saw her. I had talked them into letting me shoot her, but it had to be from outside the quarantine area. The picture had an unfocused look that came from shooting it through a wire-mesh-reinforced window in the door, but I wouldn't have done any better if they'd let me inside. Misha was past having any expression to photograph. She hadn't eaten in a week at that point. She lay with her head on her paws, staring at the door, the whole time I was there.

"You wouldn't consider selling this picture to the Society, would you?"

"No, I wouldn't."

He nodded understandingly. "I guess people were pretty upset when she died."

Pretty upset. They had turned on anyone who had anything to do with it—the puppy mill owners, the scientists who hadn't come up with a vaccine, Misha's vet—and a lot of others who hadn't. And they had handed over their civil rights to a bunch of jackals who were able to grab them because everybody felt so guilty. Pretty upset.

"What's this one?" Segura asked. He had already moved on to the picture next to it.

"It's General Patton's bull terrier Willie."

They had fed and cleaned up after Misha with those robot arms they used to use in the nuclear plants. Her owner, a tired-looking woman, had been allowed to watch her through the wire mesh window, but she'd had to stay off to the side because Misha flung herself barking against the door whenever she saw her.

"You should make them let you in," I had told her. "It's cruel to keep her locked up like that. You should make them let you take her back home."

"And let her get the newparvo?" she said.

There was nobody left for Misha to get the newparvo from, but I didn't say that. I set the light readings in the camera, trying not to lean into Misha's line of vision.

"You know what killed them, don't you?" she said. "The ozone layer. All those holes. The radiation got in and caused it."

It was the Communists, it was the Mexicans, it was the government. And the only people who acknowledged their guilt weren't guilty at all.

"This one here looks kind of like a jackal," Segura said. He was looking at a picture I had taken of a German shepherd after Aberfan died. "Dogs were a lot like jackals, weren't they?"

"No," I said, and sat down on the shelf in front of the developer's screen, across from Hunter. "I already told you everything I know about the jackal. I saw it lying in the road, and I called you."

"You said when you saw the jackal it was in the far right lane," Hunter said.

"That's right."

"And you were in the far left lane?"

"I was in the far left lane."

They were going to take me over my story, point by point, and when I couldn't remember what I'd said before, they were going to say, "Are you sure that's what you saw, Mr. McCombe? Are you sure you didn't see the jackal get hit? Katherine Powell hit it, didn't she?"

"You told us this morning you stopped, but the jackal was already dead. Is that right?" Hunter asked.

"No," I said.

Segura looked up. Hunter touched his hand casually to his pocket and then brought it back to his knee, turning on the taper.

"I didn't stop for about a mile. Then I backed up and looked at it, but it was dead. There was blood coming out of its mouth."

Hunter didn't say anything. He kept his hands on his knees and waited—an old journalist's trick, if you wait long enough, they'll say something they didn't intend to, just to fill the silence.

"The jackal's body was at a peculiar angle," I said, right on cue. "The way it was lying, it didn't look like a jackal. I thought it was a dog."

I waited till the silence got uncomfortable again. "It brought back a lot of terrible memories," I said. "I wasn't even thinking. I just wanted to get away from it. After a few minutes I realized I should have called the Society, and I stopped at the 7-Eleven."

I waited again, till Segura began to shoot uncomfortable glances at Hunter, and then started in again. "I thought I'd be okay, that I could go ahead and work, but after I got to my first shoot, I knew I wasn't going to make it, so I came home." Candor. Openness. If the Amblers can do it, so can you. "I guess I was still in shock or something. I didn't even call my boss and have her get somebody to cover the governor's conference. All I could think about was—"

I stopped and rubbed my hand across my face. "I needed to talk to somebody. I had the paper look up an old friend of mine, Katherine Powell."

I stopped, I hoped this time for good. I had admitted lying to them and confessed to two crimes: leaving the scene of the accident and using press access to get a lifeline for personal use, and maybe that would be enough to satisfy them. I didn't want to say anything about going out to see Katie. They would know she would have told me about their visit and decide this confession was an attempt to get her off, and maybe they'd been watching the house and knew it anyway, and this was all wasted effort.

The silence dragged on. Hunter's hands tapped his knees twice and then subsided. The story didn't explain why I'd picked Katie, who I hadn't seen in fifteen years, who I knew in Colorado, to go see, but maybe, maybe they wouldn't make the connection.

"This Katherine Powell," Hunter said, "you knew her in Colorado, is that right?"

"We lived in the same little town."

We waited.

"Isn't that when your dog died?" Segura said suddenly. Hunter shot him a glance of pure rage, and I thought, It isn't a taper he's got in that shirt pocket. It's the vet's records, and Katie's name is on them.

"Yes," I said. "He died in September of ninety-three."

Segura opened his mouth.

"In the third wave?" Hunter asked before he could say anything.

"No," I said. "He was hit by a car."

They both looked genuinely shocked. The Amblers could have taken lessons from them. "Who hit it?" Segura asked, and Hunter leaned forward, his hand moving reflexively toward his pocket.

"I don't know," I said. "It was a hit and run. Whoever it was just left him lying there in the road. That's why when I saw the jackal, it . . . That was how I met Katherine Powell. She stopped and helped me. She helped me get him into her car, and we took him to the vet's, but it was too late."

Hunter's public face was pretty indestructible, but Segura's wasn't. He looked surprised and enlightened and disappointed all at once.

"That's why I wanted to see her," I added unnecessarily.

"Your dog was hit on what day?" Hunter asked.

"September thirtieth."

"What was the vet's name?"

He hadn't changed his way of asking the questions, but he no longer cared what the answers were. He had thought he'd found a connection, a cover-up, but here we were, a couple of dog lovers, a couple of good Samaritans, and his theory had collapsed. He was done with the interview, he was just finishing up, and all I had to do was be careful not to relax too soon.

I frowned. "I don't remember his name. Cooper, I think."

"What kind of car did you say hit your dog?"

"I don't know," I said, thinking, not a jeep. Make it something besides a jeep. "I didn't see him get hit. The vet said it was something big, a pickup maybe. Or a Winnebago."

And I knew who had hit the jackal. It had all been right there in front of me—the old man using up their forty-gallon water supply to wash the bumper, the lies about their coming in from Globe—only I had been too intent on keeping them from finding out about Katie, on getting the picture of Aberfan, to see it. It was like the damned parvovirus. When you had it licked in one place, it broke out somewhere else.

"Were there any identifying tire tracks?" Hunter said.

"What?" I said. "No. It was snowing that day."

It had to show in my face, and he hadn't missed anything yet. I passed my hand over my eyes. "I'm sorry. These questions are bringing it all back."

"Sorry," Hunter said.

"Can't we get this stuff from the police report?" Segura asked.

"There wasn't a police report," I said. "It wasn't a crime to kill a dog when Aberfan died."

It was the right thing to say. The look of shock on their faces was the real thing this time, and they looked at each other in disbelief instead of at me. They asked a few more questions and then stood up to leave. I walked them to the door.

"Thank you for your cooperation, Mr. McCombe," Hunter said. "We appreciate what a difficult experience this has been for you."

I shut the screen door between us. The Amblers would have been going too fast, trying to beat the cameras because they weren't even supposed to be on Van Buren. It was almost rush hour, and they were in the tanker lane, and they hadn't even seen the jackal till they hit it, and then it was too late. They had to know the penalty for hitting an animal was jail and confiscation of the vehicle, and there wasn't anybody else on the road.

"Oh, one more question," Hunter said from halfway down the walk. "You said you went to your first assignment this morning. What was it?"

Candid. Open. "It was out at the old zoo. A sideshow kind of thing."

I watched them all the way out to their car and down the street. Then I latched the screen, pulled the inside door shut, and locked it, too. It had been right there in front of me—the ferret sniffing the wheel, the bumper, Jake anxiously watching the road.

I had thought he was looking for customers, but he wasn't. He was expecting to see the Society drive up. "He's not interested in that," he had said when Mrs. Ambler said she had been telling me about Taco.

He had listened to our whole conversation, standing under the back window with his guilty bucket, ready to come back in and cut her off if she said too much, and I hadn't tumbled to any of it. I had been so intent on Aberfan I hadn't even seen it when I looked right through the lens at it.

And what kind of an excuse was that? Katie hadn't even tried to use it, and she was learning to drive.

I went and got the Nikon and pulled the film out of it. It was too late to do anything about the eisenstadt pictures or the vidcam footage, but

I didn't think there was anything in them. Jake had already washed the bumper by the time I'd taken those pictures.

I fed the longshot film into the developer. "Positives, one two three order, fifteen seconds," I said, and waited for the image to come on the screen.

I wondered who had been driving. Jake, probably. "He never liked Taco," she had said, and there was no mistaking the bitterness in her voice. "I didn't want to buy the Winnebago."

They would both lose their licenses, no matter who was driving, and the Society would confiscate the Winnebago. They would probably not send two octogenarian specimens of Americana like the Amblers to prison. They wouldn't have to. The trial would take six months, and Texas already had legislation in committee.

The first picture came up. A light-setting shot of an ocotillo.

Even if they got off, even if they didn't end up taking away the Winnebago for unauthorized use of a tanker lane or failure to purchase a sales tax permit, the Amblers had six months left at the outside. Utah was all ready to pass a full-divided bill, and Arizona would be next. In spite of the road crews' stew-slowed pace, Phoenix would be all-divided by the time the investigation was over, and they'd be completely boxed in. Permanent residents of the zoo. Like the coyote.

A shot of the zoo sign, half-hidden in the cactus. A close-up of the Amblers' flag-trailing sign. The Winnebago in the parking lot.

"Hold," I said. "Crop." I indicated the areas with my finger. "Enlarge to full screen."

The longshot takes great pictures, sharp contrast, excellent detail. The developer only had a five-hundred-thousand-pixel screen, but the dark smear on the bumper was easy to see, and the developed picture would be much clearer. You'd be able to see every splatter, every grayish-yellow hair. The Society's computers would probably be able to type the blood from it.

"Continue," I said, and the next picture came on the screen. Artsy shot of the Winnebago and the zoo entrance. Jake washing the bumper.

Red-handed.

Maybe Hunter had bought my story, but he didn't have any other suspects, and how long would it be before he decided to ask Katie a few more questions? If he thought it was the Amblers, he'd leave her alone.

The Japanese family clustered around the waste-disposal tank. Close-up of the decals on the side. Interiors—Mrs. Ambler in the galley, the upright-coffin shower stall, Mrs. Ambler making coffee.

No wonder she had looked that way in the eisenstadt shot, her face full of memory and grief and loss. Maybe in the instant before they hit it, it had looked like a dog to her, too.

All I had to do was tell Hunter about the Amblers, and Katie was off the hook. It should be easy. I had done it before.

"Stop," I said to a shot of the salt and pepper collection. The black and white Scottie dogs had painted red-plaid bows and red tongues.

"Expose," I said. "One through twenty-four."

The screen went to question marks and started beeping. I should have known better. The developer could handle a lot of orders, but asking it to expose perfectly good film went against its whole memory, and I didn't have time to give it the step-by-steps that would convince it I meant what I said.

"Eject," I said. The Scotties blinked out. The developer spat out the film, rerolled into its protective case.

The doorbell rang. I switched on the overhead and pulled the film out to full length and held it directly under the light.

I had told Hunter an RV hit Aberfan, and he had said on the way out, almost an afterthought, "That first shoot you went to, what was it?"

And after he left, what had he done, gone out to check on the side-show kind of thing, gotten Mrs. Ambler to spill her guts? There hadn't been time to do that and get back. He must have called Ramirez. I was glad I had locked the door.

I turned off the overhead. I rerolled the film, fed it back into the developer, and gave it a direction it could handle. "Permanganate bath, full strength, one through twenty-four. Remove one hundred percent emulsion. No notify."

The screen went dark. It would take the developer at least fifteen minutes to run the film through the bleach bath, and the Society's computers could probably enhance a picture out of two crystals of silver and thin air, but at least the detail wouldn't be there. I unlocked the door.

It was Katie.

She held up the eisenstadt. "You forgot your briefcase," she said.

I stared blankly at it. I hadn't even realized I didn't have it. I must have left it on the kitchen table when I went tearing out, running down little girls and stewed road workers in my rush to keep Katie from getting involved. And here she was, and Hunter would be back any minute, saying, "That shoot you went on this morning, did you take any pictures?"

"It isn't a briefcase," I said.

"I wanted to tell you," she said, and stopped. "I shouldn't have accused you of telling the Society I'd killed the jackal. I don't know why you came to see me today, but I know you're not capable of—"

"You have no idea what I'm capable of," I said. I opened the door enough to reach for the eisenstadt. "Thanks for bringing it back. I'll get the paper to reimburse your way-mile credits."

Go home. Go home. If you're here when the Society comes back, they'll ask you how you met me, and I just destroyed the evidence that could shift the blame to the Amblers.

I took hold of the eisenstadt's handle and started to shut the door.

She put her hand on the door. The screen door and the fading light made her look unfocused, like Misha. "Are you in trouble?"

"No," I said. "Look, I'm very busy."

"Why did you come to see me?" she asked. "Did you kill the jackal?"

"No," I said, but I opened the door and let her in.

I went over to the developer and asked for a visual status. It was only on the sixth frame. "I'm destroying evidence," I said to Katie. "I took a picture this morning of the vehicle that hit it, only I didn't know it was the guilty party until half an hour ago."

I motioned for her to sit down on the couch. "They're in their eighties. They were driving on a road they weren't supposed to be on, in an obsolete recreation vehicle, worrying about the cameras and the tankers. There's no way they could have seen it in time to stop. The Society won't see it that way, though. They're determined to blame somebody, anybody, even though it won't bring them back."

She set her canvas carryit and the eisenstadt down on the table next to the couch.

"The Society was here when I got home," I said. "They'd figured out we were both in Colorado when Aberfan died. I told them it was a hit and run, and you'd stopped to help me. They had the vet's records, and your name was on them."

I couldn't read her face. "If they come back," I said, "you tell them that you gave me a ride to the vet's."

I went back to the developer. The longshot film was done. "Eject," I said, and the developer spit it into my hand. I fed it into the recycler.

"McCombe! Where the hell are you?" Ramirez's voice exploded into the room, and I jumped and started for the door, but she wasn't there.

The phone was flashing. "McCombe! This is important!"

Ramirez was on the phone and using some override I didn't even know existed. I went over and pushed it back to access. The flashing lights went off. "I'm here," I said.

"You won't believe what just happened!" She sounded outraged. "A couple of terrorist types from the Society just stormed in here and confiscated the stuff you sent me!"

All I'd sent her was the vidcam footage and the shots from the eisenstadt, and there shouldn't have been anything on those. Jake had already washed the bumper. "What stuff?" I said.

"The prints from the eisenstadt!" she said, still shouting. "Which I didn't have a chance to look at when they came in because I was too busy trying to work a trade on your governor's conference, not to mention trying to track you down! I had hardcopies made and sent the originals straight down to composing with your vidcam footage. I finally got to them half an hour ago, and while I'm sorting through them, this Society creep just grabs them away from me. No warrant, no 'would you mind?,' nothing. Right out of my hand. Like a bunch of—"

"Jackals," I said. "You're sure it wasn't the vidcam footage?" There wasn't anything in the eisenstadt shots except Mrs. Ambler and Taco, and even Hunter couldn't have put that together, could he?

"Of course I'm sure," Ramirez said, her voice bouncing off the walls. "It was one of the prints from the eisenstadt. I never even saw the vidcam stuff. I sent it straight to composing. I told you."

I went over to the developer and fed the cartridge in. The first dozen shots were nothing, stuff the eisenstadt had taken from the back-seat of the car. "Start with frame ten," I said. "Positives. One two three order. Five seconds."

"What did you say?" Ramirez demanded.

"I said, did they say what they were looking for?"

"Are you kidding? I wasn't even there as far as they were concerned. They split up the pile and started through them on *my* desk."

The yucca at the foot of the hill. More yucca. My forearm as I set the eisenstadt down on the counter. My back.

"Whatever it was they were looking for, they found it," Ramirez said.

I glanced at Katie. She met my gaze steadily, unafraid. She had never been afraid, not even when I told her she had killed all the dogs, not even when I'd shown up on her doorstep after fifteen years.

"The one in the uniform showed it to the other one," Ramirez was saying, "and said, 'You were wrong about the woman doing it. Look at this.'"

"Did you get a look at the picture?"

Still life of cups and spoons. Mrs. Ambler's arm. Mrs. Ambler's back.

"I tried. It was a truck of some kind."

"A truck? Are you sure? Not a Winnebago?"

"A truck. What the hell is going on over there?"

I didn't answer. Jake's back. Open shower door. Still life with Sanka. Mrs. Ambler remembering Taco.

"What woman are they talking about?" Ramirez said. "The one you wanted the lifeline on?"

"No," I said. The picture of Mrs. Ambler was the last one on the sheet. The developer went back to the beginning. Bottom half of the Hitori. Open car door. Prickly pear. "Did they say anything else?"

"The one in uniform pointed to something on the hardcopy and said, 'See, there's his number on the side. Can you make it out?'"

Blurred palm trees and the expressway. The tanker hitting the jackal.

"Stop," I said.

The image froze.

"What?" Ramirez said.

It was a great action shot, the back wheels passing right over the mess that had been the jackal's hind legs. The jackal was already dead, of course, but you couldn't see that or the already drying blood coming out of its mouth because of the angle. You couldn't see the truck's license number, either, because of the speed the tanker was going, but the number was there, waiting for the Society's computers. It looked like the tanker had just hit it.

"What did they do with the picture?" I asked.

"They took it into the chief's office. I tried to call up the originals from composing, but the chief had already sent for them *and* your vidcam footage. Then I tried to get you, but I couldn't get past your damned exclusion."

"Are they still in there with the chief?"

"They just left. They're on their way over to your house. The chief told me to tell you he wants 'full cooperation,' which means hand over the negatives and any other film you took this morning. He told *me* to keep my hands off. No story. Case closed."

"How long ago did they leave?"

"Five minutes. You've got plenty of time to make me a print. Don't highwire it. I'll come pick it up."

"What happened to 'The last thing I need is trouble with the Society'?"

"It'll take them at least twenty minutes to get to your place. Hide it somewhere the Society won't find it."

"I can't," I said, and listened to her furious silence. "My developer's broken. It just ate my longshot film," I said, and hit the exclusion button again.

"You want to see who hit the jackal?" I said to Katie, and motioned her over to the developer. "One of Phoenix's finest."

She came and stood in front of the screen, looking at the picture. If the Society's computers were really good, they could probably prove the jackal was already dead, but the Society wouldn't keep the film long enough for that. Hunter and Segura had probably already destroyed the highwire copies.

Maybe I should offer to run the cartridge sheet through the permanganate bath for them when they got here, just to save time.

I looked at Katie. "It looks guilty as hell, doesn't it?" I said. "Only it isn't."

She didn't say anything, didn't move.

"It would have killed the jackal if it had hit it. It was going at least ninety. But the jackal was already dead."

She looked across at me.

"The Society would have sent the Amblers to jail. It would have confiscated the house they've lived in for nearly twenty years for an accident that was nobody's fault. They didn't even see it coming. It just ran right out in front of them."

Katie put her hand up to the screen and touched the jackal's image.

"They've suffered enough," I said, looking at her.

It was getting dark. I hadn't turned on any lights, and the red image of the tanker made her nose look sunburned.

"All these years she's blamed her husband for her dog's death, and he didn't do it," I said. "A Winnebago's a hundred square feet on the inside. That's about as big as this developer, and they've lived inside it for fifteen years, while the lanes got narrower and the highways shut down, hardly enough room to breathe, let alone live, and her blaming him for something he didn't do."

In the ruddy light from the screen she looked sixteen.

"They won't do anything to the driver, not with the tankers hauling thousands of gallons of water into Phoenix every day. Even the Society won't run the risk of a boycott. They'll destroy the negatives and call the case closed. And the Society won't go after the Amblers," I said. "Or you."

I turned back to the developer. "Go," I said, and the image changed. Yucca. Yucca. My forearm. My back. Cups and spoons.

"Besides," I said. "I'm an old hand at shifting the blame." Mrs. Ambler's arm. Mrs. Ambler's back. Open shower door. "Did I ever tell you about Aberfan?"

Katie was still watching the screen, her face pale now from the light blue One-Hundred Percent formica shower stall.

"The Society already thinks the tanker did it. The only one I've got to convince is my editor." I reached across to the phone and took the exclusion off. "Ramirez," I said, "wanta go after the Society?"

Jake's back. Cups, spoons, and Sanka.

"I did," Ramirez said in a voice that could have frozen the Salt River, "but your developer was broken, and you couldn't get me a picture."

Mrs. Ambler and Taco.

I hit the exclusion button again and left my hand on it. "Stop," I said. "Print." The screen went dark, and the print slid out into the tray.

"Reduce frame. Permanganate bath by one percent. Follow on screen." I took my hand off. "What's Dolores Chiwere doing these days, Ramirez?"

"She's working investigative. Why?"

I didn't answer. The picture of Mrs. Ambler faded a little, a little more.

"The Society *does* have a link to the lifelines!" Ramirez said, not quite as fast as Hunter, but almost. "That's why you requested your old girlfriend's line, isn't it? You're running a sting."

I had been wondering how to get Ramirez off Katie's trail, and she had done it herself, jumping to conclusions just like the Society. With a little effort, I could convince Katie, too: Do you know why I really came to see you today? To catch the Society. I had to pick somebody the Society couldn't possibly know about from my lifeline, somebody I didn't have any known connection with.

Katie watched the screen, looking like she already half-believed it. The picture of Mrs. Ambler faded some more. Any known connection.

"Stop," I said.

"What about the truck?" Ramirez demanded. "What does it have to do with this sting of yours?"

"Nothing," I said. "And neither does the Water Board, which is an even bigger bully than the Society. So do what the chief says. Full co-operation. Case closed. We'll get them on lifeline tapping."

She digested that, or maybe she'd already hung up and was calling Dolores Chiwere. I looked at the image of Mrs. Ambler on the screen. It had faded enough to look slightly overexposed but not enough to look tampered with. And Taco was gone.

I looked at Katie. "The Society will be here in another fifteen minutes," I said, "which gives me just enough time to tell you about Aberfan." I gestured at the couch. "Sit down."

She came and sat down. "He was a great dog," I said. "He loved the snow. He'd dig through it and toss it up with his muzzle and snap at the snowflakes, trying to catch them."

Ramirez had obviously hung up, but she would call back if she couldn't track down Chiwere. I put the exclusion back on and went over to the developer. The image of Mrs. Ambler was still on the screen. The bath hadn't affected the detail that much. You could still see the wrinkles, the thin white hair, but the guilt, or blame, the look of loss and love, was gone. She looked serene, almost happy.

"There are hardly any good pictures of dogs," I said. "They lack the necessary muscles to take good pictures, and Aberfan would lunge at you as soon as he saw the camera."

I turned the developer off. Without the light from the screen, it was almost dark in the room. I turned on the overhead.

"There were less than a hundred dogs left in the United States, and he'd already had the newparvo once and nearly died. The only pictures I had of him had been taken when he was asleep. I wanted a picture of Aberfan playing in the snow."

I leaned against the narrow shelf in front of the developer's screen. Katie looked the way she had at the vet's, sitting there with her hands clenched, waiting for me to tell her something terrible.

"I wanted a picture of him playing in the snow, but he always lunged at the camera," I said, "so I let him out in the front yard, and then I sneaked out the side door and went across the road to some pine trees where he wouldn't be able to see me. But he did."

"And he ran across the road," Katie said. "And I hit him."

She was looking down at her hands. I waited for her to look up, dreading what I would see in her face. Or not see.

"It took me a long time to find out where you'd gone," she said to her hands. "I was afraid you'd refuse me access to your lifeline. I finally saw one of your pictures in a newspaper, and I moved to Phoenix, but after I got here I was afraid to call you for fear you'd hang up on me."

She twisted her hands the way she had twisted her mittens at the vet's. "My husband said I was obsessed with it, that I should have gotten over it by now, everybody else had. That they were only dogs anyway." She looked up, and I braced my hands against the developer. "He said forgiveness wasn't something somebody else could give you, but I didn't want you to forgive me exactly. I just wanted to tell you I was sorry."

There hadn't been any reproach, any accusation in her face when I told her she was responsible for the extinction of a species that day at the vet's, and there wasn't now. Maybe she doesn't have the facial muscles for it, I thought bitterly.

"Do you know why I came to see you today?" I said angrily. "My camera broke when I tried to catch Aberfan. I didn't get any pictures."

I grabbed the picture of Mrs. Ambler out of the developer's tray and flung it at her. "Her dog died of newparvo. They left it in the Winnebago, and when they came back, it was dead."

"Poor thing," she said, but she wasn't looking at the picture. She was looking at me.

"Mrs. Ambler didn't know she was having her picture taken. I thought if I got you talking about Aberfan, I could get a picture like that of you."

And surely now I would see it, the look I had really wanted when I set the eisenstadt down on Katie's kitchen table, the look I still wanted, even though the eisenstadt was facing the wrong way, the look of betrayal the dogs had never given us. Not even Misha. Not even Aberfan. How does it feel to be responsible for the extinction of an entire species?

I pointed at the eisenstadt. "It's not a briefcase. It's a camera. I was going to take your picture without your even knowing it."

She had never known Aberfan. She had never known Mrs. Ambler, either, but in that instant before she started to cry she looked like both of them. She put her hand up to her mouth. "Oh," she said, and the love, the loss was there in her voice, too. "If you'd had it then, it wouldn't have happened."

I looked at the eisenstadt. If I had had it then, I could have set it on the porch and Aberfan would never have even noticed it. He would have burrowed through the snow and tossed it up with his nose, and I could have thrown snow up in big glittering sprays that he would have leaped at, and it never would have happened.

Katie Powell would have driven past, and I would have stopped to wave at her, and she, sixteen years old and just learning to drive, would maybe even have risked taking a mittened hand off the steering wheel to wave back, and Aberfan would have wagged his tail into a blizzard and then barked at the snow he'd churned up.

He wouldn't have caught the third wave. He would have lived to be an old dog, fourteen or fifteen, too old to play in the snow anymore, and even if he had been the last dog in the world I would not have let them lock him up in a cage, I would not have let them take him away. If I had had the eisenstadt.

No wonder I hated it.

It had been at least fifteen minutes since Ramirez called. The Society would be here any minute. "You shouldn't be here when the Society comes," I said, and Katie nodded and smudged the tears off her cheeks and stood up, reaching for her carryit.

"Do you ever take pictures?" she said, shouldering the carryit. "I mean, besides for the papers?"

"I don't know if I'll be taking pictures for them much longer. Photo-journalists are becoming an extinct breed."

"Maybe you could come take some pictures of Jana and Kevin. Kids grow up so fast, they're gone before you know it."

"I'd like that," I said. I opened the screen door for her and looked both ways down the street at the darkness. "All clear," I said, and she went out. I shut the screen door between us.

She turned and looked at me one last time with her dear, open face that even I hadn't been able to close. "I miss them," she said.

I put my hand up to the screen. "I miss them, too."

I watched her to make sure she turned the corner and then went back in the living room and took down the picture of Misha. I propped it against the developer so Segura would be able to see it from the door.

In a month or so, when the Amblers were safely in Texas and the

Society had forgotten about Katie, I'd call Segura and tell him I might be willing to sell it to the Society, and then in a day or so I'd tell him I'd changed my mind. When he came out to try to talk me into it, I'd tell him about Perdita and Beatrix Potter, and he would tell me about the Society.

Chiwere and Ramirez would have to take the credit for the story—I didn't want Hunter putting anything else together—and it would take more than one story to break them, but it was a start.

Katie had left the print of Mrs. Ambler on the couch. I picked it up and looked at it a minute and then fed it into the developer. "Recycle," I said.

I picked up the eisenstadt from the table by the couch and took the film cartridge out. I started to pull the film out to expose it, and then shoved it into the developer instead and turned it on. "Positives, one two three order, five seconds."

I had apparently set the camera on its activator again—there were ten shots or so of the backseat of the Hitori. Vehicles and people. The pictures of Katie were all in shadow. There was a Still Life of Kool-Aid Pitcher with Whale Glass and another one of Jana's toy cars, and some near-black frames that meant Katie had laid the eisenstadt facedown when she brought it to me.

"Two seconds," I said, and waited for the developer to flash the last shots so I could make sure there wasn't anything else on the cartridge and then expose it before the Society got here. All but the last frame was of the darkness that was all the eisenstadt could see lying on its face.

The last one was of me.

The trick in getting good pictures is to make people forget they're being photographed. Distract them. Get them talking about something they care about.

"Stop," I said, and the image froze.

Aberfan was a great dog. He loved to play in the snow, and after I had murdered him, he lifted his head off my lap and tried to lick my hand.

The Society would be here any minute to take the longshot film and destroy it, and this one would have to go, too, along with the rest of the cartridge. I couldn't risk Hunter's being reminded of Katie. Or Segura taking a notion to do a print-fix and peel on Jana's toy cars.

It was too bad. The eisenstadt takes great pictures. "Even you'll forget it's a camera," Ramirez had said in her spiel, and that was certainly true. I was looking straight into the lens.

And it was all there, Misha and Taco and Perdita and the look he gave me on the way to the vet's while I stroked his poor head and told him it would be all right, that look of love and pity I had been trying to capture all these years. The picture of Aberfan.

The Society would be here any minute. "Eject," I said, and cracked the cartridge open, and exposed it to the light.

Afterword for "The Last of the Winnebagos"

The End of the World is back in fashion these days, what with the whole Mayan calendar thing, nuclear terrorists in the news, and the ever more dire threat of global warming, but what people forget is that it's *always* ending.

Extinction happens on a daily basis: pay phones, soda fountains, carbon paper, LPs, metal merry-go-rounds, Woolworth's, clothespins, VCRs, swimming caps, dial telephones, ocean liners, linen handkerchiefs, Beeman's chewing gum. And we never really appreciate any of it till it's too late, till it's already gone.

I particularly miss cherry phosphates, drive-in movies, and those great swings with linked-metal chains and wooden seats. And I know, I know, they were dangerous, but you could swing so high on them, all the way out over the landscape and up into the sky. And on the way home from the drive-in, you could lean your head out of the car (which had no air-conditioning) and look up at the moonlit summer clouds and the dark, star-filled sky.

I miss roller coasters—the old-fashioned kind with white-painted wooden frameworks and rackety cars. And passenger trains with Pullman berths and dining cars with white tablecloths, and Green River soda pop, and canvas sneakers.

And soon, I fear, I will also miss books.

Even the stories in this collection are testimony to how quickly things vanish, and not just "The Last of the Winnebagos." Many were written before the advent of cell phones and the Internet; Egypt and Iraq have changed a lot, film is nearly extinct, and in a few more years the sheet music in "All Seated on the Ground" and the paperbacks and travel guides in "Death on the Nile" will seem oddly quaint. "Why didn't they just have a Kindle?" readers will ask.

Science fiction seems especially vulnerable to questions like that, since we're supposed to be predicting the future and all, and it's tempting to update the stories when they're reprinted, especially after you've just watched a movie in which the actors are all talking on shoebox-sized cell phones. Or are standing in front of the World Trade Center. It's tempting to change the dates (especially if they've already passed) and the technology.

But once you change one thing, you have to change another, and another, and eventually the entire plot. And besides, it's a little too much like the Egyptian pharaohs chiseling out all mention of the previous Ramses, erasing the past.

So let them stand, reminders of the past we had and the future we thought was coming, and of how ephemeral it all is. And remember what Albert Camus had to say on the subject: "Do not wait upon the Day of Judgment. It happens every day."

Connie Willis is known not only for her amazing fiction—some of which is on dazzling display in this volume, and much of which is still out there for you to discover, if you have not done so already—but also for her signature speeches at various events and conventions. These speeches are moving and funny and so very quintessentially Connie that you can't help falling in love with her not only as a writer, but as an incredible human being.

So, as a special added bonus, we are publishing three of her speeches here, for your reading pleasure. Two have been delivered before—one at the 2006 Worldcon, where Connie was Guest of Honor, and one at the 2012 Nebula Awards, where Connie received the Damon Knight Memorial Grand Master Award. The third was never delivered.

I know the reading experience can't quite replicate Connie's expert delivery (although the format of the speeches will give you some insight into how they are meant to be read), but I still found myself smiling and with tears in my eyes at the end of each one.

Enjoy! And thank you, Connie, for everything you do.

—*Anne Lesley Groell*
Executive Editor
(and LSE: Long-Suffering Editor)

---

* See Grand Master Acceptance Speech, though I think MDE—Much Delighted Editor—is by far the better designation.

2006 WORLDCON
GUEST OF HONOR SPEECH

(Given August 17, 2006)

A MIRACLE OF RARE DEVICE:
ON BOOKS, SF, AND MY LIFE AMONG THEM

The thing that's so great about being a guest of honor at Worldcon
is that it gives me the chance
to thank all the people who helped me become a writer:

like my junior high school teacher Mrs. Werner
who read Rumer Godden's *An Episode of Sparrows*
out loud to us
and first introduced me to the Blitz

and my high school English teacher
Mrs. Juanita Jones,
who encouraged me in my writing
even though I showed no signs of talent whatsoever,
and I forced her to read my story about how I'd met George
Maharis of the TV series *Route 66*,
a story which includes deathless lines like,
"His face lit up like a birthday cake."
And in which the heroine,
while driving in downtown Manhattan, manages to run into a
tree—
obviously the tree from *A Tree Grows in Brooklyn*.

It also gives me a chance to thank all those people who've helped
me keep writing all these years:
   —my long-suffering secretary Laura Lewis

   —and my even more long-suffering family

   —my miracle-working agents: Patrick Delahunt, Ralph Vicinanza, and Vince Gerardis

   —my extremely patient editors Anne Groell
and Sheila Williams
and Gardner Dozois

   —my EXTREMELY patient readers

   —and my friends,
my fellow soldiers in the trenches,
who've kept me from getting discouraged
and more than once talked me out of quitting altogether.

All my best moments in science fiction I owe to you guys—

—staying up all night after that first Nebula Awards banquet
with John Kessel and Jim Kelly,
eating chocolate chip cookies and red pistachio nuts
and getting red-stained hands that didn't fade for weeks
—sitting in workshops with Ed Bryant
and Cynthia Felice
and Mike Toman
and George R.R. Martin

—driving to Portales to see Jack Williamson
with Charlie Brown
and Scott Edelman
and Walter Jon Williams

—gossiping with Nancy Kress
and Ellen Datlow
and Eileen Gunn

—laughing at something
Michael Cassutt
or Eileen Gunn
or Howard Waldrop said.

—laughing at something Gardner Dozois said so hard I snorted
a piece of lettuce up my nose, nearly killing myself.

You guys are the wittiest, smartest, nicest people in the world,
and I would not have lasted five minutes in science fiction without
you.

But most important,
I need to thank
   Robert Heinlein
   and Louisa May Alcott
   and Kit Reed
   and Damon Runyon
   and Sigrid Undset
   and Theodore Sturgeon
   and Agatha Christie
   and Jerome K. Jerome
   and Daphne du Maurier
   and Philip K. Dick
   and Rumer Godden
   and L. M. Montgomery
   and Ray Bradbury
   and Shirley Jackson
   and Bob Shaw
   and James Herriot
   and Mildred Clingerman
   and P. G. Wodehouse
   and Dorothy L. Sayers
   and Daniel Keyes
   and J. R. R. Tolkien
   and Judith Merril
   and Charles Williams
   and William Shakespeare.

Which brings me to the subject of this speech.

You're supposed to talk about something significant in a guest-of-
honor speech—
   global warming
   or the coming Singularity

or space travel
or tougher sentences for parole violators.
Or world peace.

But I want to talk about something completely personal.

I want to talk about books and what they have meant to me.
Which is everything in the world.

I owe books my vocation, my life, even my family.

I'm not kidding.
You probably don't know this, but I only got married because of a book.
And, no, I'm not talking about love poems.
And, NO, not *Lolita*.
I got married because of *Lord of the Rings*.

To quote Kip Russell in *Have Space Suit, Will Travel*, "How it happened was this way."

I was flying out to Connecticut
for the express purpose of breaking up with my boyfriend
and I bought this set of three paperbacks to read on the plane
and by the time I got to New Haven
I was so worried about Frodo and Sam
that I said to my boyfriend, "It's awful. They're trying to sneak into Mordor and the Ringwraiths are after them and I don't trust Gollum and . . ."

and I completely forgot to break up with him.

And, as of yesterday, we've been married thirty-nine years.

I owe my daughter's name to a book, too. We named her after the
good daughter in *King Lear*
and she has lived up to her name in absolutely every way.

And I owe all the books I've written to books.

They taught me how to write.
   Agatha Christie taught me plotting
   Mary Stewart suspense
   Heinlein dialogue
   P. G. Wodehouse comedy
   Shakespeare irony
   and Philip K. Dick how to pull the rug out from under the
   reader.

Books also gave me all sorts of good advice on how to cope with
everything,
from following the rules—

"There are three rules for writing a novel," W. Somerset Maugham
said. *"Unfortunately, no one knows what they are."*

to the stupid questions people ask writers—

Heavens! [Harriet Vane thought.] *Here was that awful woman,
Muriel Campshott, coming up to claim acquaintance. Campshott
had always simpered. She still simpered . . . She was going to say,
"How do you think of all your plots?" She did say it. Curse the
woman.*

to coping with the pressure to write what your publisher—or your
readers—want—

"The only thing you can do," Dorothy Sayers said, *"is write what you want to write and hope for the best."*

to feeling like you've made a hideous mistake in your choice of career—

"It took me fifteen years to discover I had no talent for writing," Robert Benchley told me, *"but I couldn't give it up because by that time I was famous."*

They even showed me what to write and how to write it.

When I went to England for the first time,
I remembered that book about the Blitz Mrs. Werner had read out loud when I was in the eighth grade,
and it made me go to St. Paul's,
where I found the fire watch and Oxford's time-traveling historians
and my life's work.

Above all, they taught me what it meant to be a writer.

"Storytellers make us remember what mankind would have been like had not fear, and the failing will, and the laws of nature tripped up its heels," William Butler Yeats said.

And books—

Wait, I'm getting ahead of myself.
Let me begin at the beginning.

I loved books from the moment I saw them, from before I could even read.

And as soon as I did learn,
I read everything I could get my grubby little hands on.

You couldn't get a library card till you were eight years old when I
was a kid
(These were dark, benighted times)
and you were only allowed to check out three at a time
(Really dark and benighted times).

So the day I got my library card,
I checked out three of L. Frank Baum's Oz books.

Rita Mae Brown says, "When I got my library card, that's when my
life began."

Mine, too.

I read all three Oz books that night
and took them back the next day
and checked out three more.

And then I checked out all the other Oz books
and all the Maida's Little Shop books
and all the Elsie Dinsmore books—
possibly the worst books ever written—
and all the Betsy, Tacy, and Tib books
and the Blue, Green, Yellow, Red, and Violet fairy books.

No one else in my family liked to read,
and they were always telling me to "get my nose out of that book
and go outside to play,"
an order which had no apparent effect on me
because I went right ahead and read

all the Anne of Green Gables books
and all the Nancy Drew books
and all the Mushroom Planet books
and *Alice in Wonderland*
and *A Little Princess*
and *Cress Delahanty*
and *The Water Babies.*

When I was in sixth grade,
I read *Little Women*
and decided I wanted to be a writer like Jo March.

When I was in seventh grade,
I read *A Tree Grows in Brooklyn*
and decided to read my way straight through the library
from A to Z
like Francie does in that book.

When I was in eighth grade,
my teacher Mrs. Werner read us
An Episode of Sparrows by Rumer Godden, a book about an orphan who plants a garden in the bombed-out rubble of a church,
and I fell in love with the Blitz.

And then, when I was thirteen,
I read *Have Space Suit, Will Travel,*
and it was all over.

How it happened was this way.

I was thirteen
and shelving books in the junior high library,

and I picked up a yellow book—I can still see it—
with a guy in a space suit on the cover.

The title was *Have Space Suit, Will Travel*,
and I opened it and read:

"You see, I had this space suit.
How it happened was this way:
'Dad,' I said, 'I want to go to the Moon.'
'Certainly,' he answered and looked back at his book. It was Jerome
K. Jerome's Three Men in a Boat, *which he must know by heart.*
I said, 'Dad, please! I'm serious!'"

There's a scene at the end of *Star Wars*.
The Death Star has cleared the planet
and Luke Skywalker is going in for one last run.
Princess Leia is back at command headquarters,
listening intently to the battle.
All the other fighter pilots are dead or out of action
and Darth Vader has Luke clearly in his sights.
And all of a sudden,
Han Solo comes zooming in from left field
to blast Darth Vader
and says,
"Yahoo! You're all clear, kid. Now let's blow this thing."

Now, when he does this,
Princess Leia doesn't look up from the battle map
or even change her expression,
but my daughter, who was eight years old at the time,
leaned over to me and said, "Oh, she's hooked, Mother."

And when I opened that yellow book
and read those first lines of *Have Space Suit, Will Travel,*
I was hooked.

I raced through *Have Space Suit* and then—
after a brief detour to read *Three Men in a Boat*—
I read *Citizen of the Galaxy*
and *Time for the Stars*
and *The Star Beast*
and *Double Star*
and *Tunnel in the Sky*
and *The Door into Summer*
and everything else Heinlein had ever written.

And then Asimov
    and Clarke
    and *The Martian Chronicles*
    and *A Canticle for Leibowitz*

and then, oh my God,
I discovered the Year's Best short story collections
and the world exploded into dazzling possibilities.

Here, side by side, were the most astonishing short stories
and novelettes
and novellas
and poems

"Vintage Season"
and "Lot"
and "The Man Who Lost the Sea"
and "I Have No Mouth and I Must Scream"

and "Flowers for Algernon"
and "Houston, Houston, Do You Read?"

stories by Kit Reed
and William Tenn
and James Blish
and Fredric Brown
and Zenna Henderson
and Philip K. Dick,
all in one book

nightmarish futures
and high-tech futures
marvelous Shangri-Las
and strange distant planets

aliens
and time travel
and robots
and unicorns
and monsters

tragedies
and adventures
and fantasies
and romances
and comedies
and horrors

"Surface Tension"
"Evening Primrose"
"Day Million"

"Continued on Next Rock"
"When We Went to See the End of the World"
"I Hope I Shall Arrive Soon"
and "One Ordinary Day, with Peanuts,"

stories that in only a few pages,
a few thousand words,
could turn reality upside down and inside out
and make you look at the world,
at the universe,
a whole new way,
could make you laugh,
make you think,
break your heart.

I was beyond hooked.
I was stunned.
I was speechless with wonder,

like Kip and Peewee looking at their own Milky Way from the
Magellanic Clouds,

like the two hobos in Ray Bradbury's "A Miracle of Rare Device,"
gazing at the beautiful city in the air.

And I knew I wanted to spend the rest of my life reading.

And writing.

I stopped reading my way through the library from A to Z
and started reading all the books I could find
with the little atom and rocketship symbol on their spines.

I had only gotten as far as the *D*s on my plan to read my way
through the alphabet when I stopped,
but, as it turned out,
it was a good thing I'd gotten that far.

Because when I was twelve,
my mother died suddenly and shatteringly,
and my world fell apart,
and I had nobody to turn to but books.

They saved my life.

I know what you're thinking,
that books provided an escape for me.

And it's certainly true books can offer refuge from worries and despair—

As Leigh Hunt says, *"I entrench myself in books equally against sorrow and the weather."*

I remember particularly
a night in the hospital at my five-year-old daughter's bedside
waiting for tests to show if she had appendicitis
or something worse,
clinging to James Herriot's *All Creatures Great and Small*
like it was a life raft.

During the Blitz,
in the makeshift libraries set up in the tube shelters,
the most popular books were Agatha Christie's mysteries,
in which the murderer's always caught and punished,

justice always triumphs,
and the world makes sense.

And when I'm anxious about things, I reread Agatha Christie, too.

And Mary Stewart.
And Lenora Mattingly Weber's Beany Malone books.

Books can help you get through
    long nights and long trips
    the wait for the phone call
    and the judge's verdict
    and the doctor's diagnosis

    can switch off your squirrel-caging mind,
    can make you forget your own troubles in the troubles of
    Kip and Peewee
    and Frodo
    and Viola
    and Harry
    and Charlie
    and Huck.

But it wasn't escape I needed when my mother died.
It was the truth.
And I couldn't get anyone to tell it to me.

Instead, they said things like:

"There's a reason this happened,"
and "You'll get over this,"
and "God never sends us more than we can bear."

Lies, all lies.

I remember an aunt saying sagely, "The good die young"—
not exactly a motivation to behave yourself—

and more than one person telling me, "It's all part of God's plan."
I remember thinking, even at age twelve,
What kind of moron is God?
I could come up with a better plan than this.

And the worst lie of all, "It's for the best."

Everybody lied—relatives, clergymen, friends.

So it was a good thing I'd reached the Ds because I had
    Margery Allingham
    and James Agee's A *Death in the Family*
    and Peter Beagle's A *Fine and Private Place*
    and Peter De Vries's *The Blood of the Lamb* to tell me the truth.

"*Time heals nothing*," Peter De Vries said.

And Margery Allingham said, "*Mourning is not forgetting. It is an
undoing. Every minute tie has to be untied, and something permanent and valuable recovered and assimilated from the knot.*"

And when I discovered science fiction a year later,
Robert Sheckley said,
"*Never try to explain to yourselves why some things happen and
why other things don't happen. Don't ask and don't imagine that an
explanation exists. Get it?*"

And Bob Shaw's "The Light of Other Days"
and John Crowley's "Snow"
and Tom Godwin

taught me everything there is to know about death
and memory
and the cold equations.

But there were also hopeful messages in those books.

"There is a land of the living and a land of the dead," Thornton
Wilder said, *"and the bridge is love, the only survival, the only
meaning."*

And Dorothy, in *The Patchwork Girl of Oz*, said, "Never give
up. . . . No one ever knows what's going to happen next."

"If you look for truth," C. S. Lewis wrote, *"you may find comfort in
the end: if you look for comfort, you will not get either comfort or
truth, only soft soap and wishful thinking to begin with, and in the
end, despair."*

I found what I was looking for,
what I needed,
what I wanted,
what I loved
in books

when I couldn't find it anywhere else.

Francie and the public library and books saved my life.

And taught me the most important lesson books have to teach.

"You think your pain and your heartbreak are unprecedented in the history of the world," James Baldwin says, *"but then you read. It was[books that] taught me that the things that tormented me most were the very things that connected me with all the people who were alive, or who ever had been alive."*

And the narrator in the movie *Matilda* says it even better: *"Matilda read all kinds of books and was nurtured by the voices of all those authors who had sent their books out into the world like ships onto the sea. These books gave Matilda a hopeful and comforting message: 'You are not alone.'"*

I told you about falling in love with books
that day I got my library card,
that day I opened *Have Space Suit* and read that first page,
that day I discovered the Year's Best collections,

but it wasn't just that I fell in love with books,
with science fiction.

It wasn't just that they were there when I needed them.
It was that when I found them,
I also found,

like one of Zenna Henderson's People,
or the Ugly Duckling
or Anne of Green Gables
or Harry Potter,

my true family,
my "kindred spirits," as Anne calls them,
my own kind.

And, finding them,
for the first time I knew,

like Ozma released from the witch's spell,
like Deckard in *Do Androids Dream of Electric Sheep?*
like Bethie and Jemmy and Valancy,

who I really was.

I had escaped,
but it was not from the real world.
It was from exile.

I had come home.

Just like in a story.

And I lived happily ever after.

Books are an amazing thing.
Anyone who thinks of them as an escape from reality
or as something you should get your nose out of and go outside
and play

as merely a distraction
or an amusement
or a waste of time

is dead wrong.

Books are the most important
the most powerful

the most beautiful thing
humans have ever created.

When Kip and Peewee find themselves on trial for earth
and trying to defend it against the charge
that it's a danger which should be destroyed, Kip says,
"Have you heard our poetry?"

And what better defense of us could you come up with?

Books can reach out across space
and time
and language
and culture
and customs,
gender
and age
and even death
and speak to someone they never met,
to someone who wasn't even born when they were written

and give them help
and advice
and companionship
and consolation.

In the words of Clarence Day, Jr.,
"The world of books is the most remarkable creation of man.
Nothing else that he builds ever lasts.
Monuments fall;
nations perish;
civilizations grow old and die out;

and, after an era of darkness,
new races build others.

But in the world of books
are volumes that have seen this happen again and again
and yet live on,
still young,
still as fresh as the day they were written
still telling men's hearts of the hearts of men centuries dead."

They are a miracle of rare device.

I never met Louisa May Alcott
or Robert Heinlein
or Rumer Godden or L. Frank Baum or Philip K. Dick
or Thornton Wilder or Dean Matthews of St. Paul's,
but they reached out to me
across time,
across space,
and spoke to me
encouraged me
inspired me
taught me everything I know.

Saved my life.

And filled it with wonder.

And I just wanted to say thank you.

Being the sort of obsessive neurotic I am, I wasn't sure exactly what would be required of me when I was given the Grand Master Nebula Award, so I wrote a couple of speeches, "just in cases," as Aurelia says in Love Actually.

I only ended up having to give one speech, but here, for your delectation, is the other.

GRAND MASTER BACKUP SPEECH
(never delivered)

People keep asking me how I feel now that I'm a Grand Master, and there are a lot of answers to that.

I feel incredibly honored
and humbled
and awestruck to find myself in such exalted company
as Robert Heinlein
and Joe Haldeman
and Bob Silverberg

and my dear friend Jack Williamson.
(My first thought when I found out about the Grand Master Award was, "He would be so proud of me.")

I feel all of those things,
plus dismayed to find myself old enough to be made

a Grand Master
and delighted to have been named
and worried that I'll wake up any moment now
and find that it was all a dream.

In short, I feel like Frodo
and Kip Russell
and Alice.

But mostly,
I feel like Beatrix Potter.

In the middle of World War II,
a reporter interviewed Beatrix Potter.
She was a very old lady by that time—
she would have been eighty-four, I think—
and she was living on a farm in the Lake District,
raising sheep for the army to turn into wool for uniforms,
and dealing with rationing
and food shortages
and fuel shortages.

At that particular moment,
she was dealing with a German plane
that had crashed in one of her fields,
as well as the aches and pains of being eighty-four.

And with the war.
Because Hitler had conquered Europe
and was sinking dozens of convoys
and bombing cities all over England,
and it looked like he might invade any minute.

And if he did, everybody knew what would happen—
   conquest and executions and concentration camps.

But when the interviewer asked Beatrix Potter
what her greatest wish was,
she said,
"To live till the end of the war.
I can't *wait* to see how it all turns out!"

That's exactly how I feel.

It's how I've always felt.

It's why I started reading in the first place:

to find out what happened to Cinderella
and to Peter Pan,
to find out whether the twelve dancing princesses got caught
and whether Peter Rabbit made it out from under
Mr. McGregor's flowerpot
and whether the prince was able to break the spell.

And it's still the reason I read,
and I think the reason everybody reads.

Forget subtext
and symbolism
and lofty, existential themes.

We want to know—
what happens to Elizabeth Bennet and Mr. Darcy
and Frodo and Sam

and Scout
and the Yearling.

Does Lear get there in time to save Cordelia?
Does Eliza Doolittle come back to Henry Higgins?
Does Orpheus make it all the way back to the surface
without turning around to make sure Eurydice is following him?

We've *got* to know.

A friend of mine said that when she went to see
the Leonardo DiCaprio–Claire Danes version
of *Romeo and Juliet,*
she saw two young girls come out of the theater crying.
"I didn't know they *died!*" one of them sobbed to the other.

I know. I laughed, too.

But what if you didn't know how *Romeo and Juliet* ended?
What if you were seeing it for the first time?

How fast did you race through the pages
the first time you read *Lord of the Rings?*
or "The Cold Equations"?
or *The Hunger Games?*

Or *Rebecca?*
Or *Les Misérables?*

How late did you stay up to finish the book?

When *The Old Curiosity Shop* was coming out
in serial installments,

people in America thronged the docks
and called up to ships arriving from England,
"Did Little Nell die?"

I recently got addicted to *Primeval,*
a British TV series about dinosaur hunters in modern-day London
and I watched Season One in one fell swoop
and then called my daughter at five in the morning—
and she lives in California, so it was four there—
but she didn't answer the phone drowsily,
or in a panic because the only reason you get a call at five in the
morning is because something terrible has happened.

Instead, she said calmly, "Hello, Mother. I assume you've just
watched Episode Six."

I had indeed.

And then I neglected everything else in my life
to watch Season Two.
And Three.

Both seasons were out on DVD,
but then I had to watch Season Four
as the episodes came out—a week apart—
and then wait six months for Season Five to start—
and it nearly killed me.

Trust me.
If there'd been a ship I could have shouted up to, to ask,
"Do Connor and Abby make it back okay?"
I'd have been down at the docks in a flash—
and I live a thousand miles from the nearest coast.

Why is that such a powerful desire, to know what happened?
And what is it we really want to know?
Is it what's going to happen to Frodo and Sam?
Or what's going to happen to us?

Characters in stories grow up
and go off on quests
and fall in love
and find out terrible things about their parents
and even worse things about themselves
and explore strange planets
and travel through time
and lose battles
and win wars
and give way to despair
and solve mysteries
and figure out what matters
and find love
and save the kingdom

and in the process they tell us about ourselves.
They show us what matters
and what doesn't.
They teach us how to be human.
And tell us how our own stories might turn out.

But Beatrix Potter already knew how her life had turned out.
She already knew
that you can't ever tell what's going to happen next.

She wrote a story for her niece
and became a world-famous author.

She fell in love with her publisher
and got secretly engaged to him against her parents' wishes,
and he *died*.

And then,
when all hope seemed lost,
she fell in love again
and found all the things she'd ever dreamed of.

She already knew what had happened in her life.
So what did she mean when she said she wanted to see
how it all turned out?

Was it who won the war?
Or something bigger?

Did she mean did they win the war? Or something else?

In *Blackout* and *All Clear*,
the elderly Shakespearean actor Sir Godfrey
asks the time-traveler Polly, "Did we win the war?"

and when she says yes,
meaning far more than just the war they're in at that moment,
he asks,
"Was it a comedy or a tragedy?"

I think that's what we really want to know when we read.

And we don't mean just our own stories,
we mean the whole shebang—
the world

and the war we're always in
and the whole arc of history—past and future.

Is it a comedy?
Or a tragedy?
Or, horrible thought, a TV show that gets canceled
before it has a chance to wrap things up properly?

Literature is the only thing that can tell us.
History could, maybe,
but we're not around long enough to find out what it has to say.

Will Ferrell's character
in *Stranger Than Fiction*
carries around a notebook and tries to keep track of the clues
to what sort of story he's in,
but that doesn't work, either.

So literature's our only hope.

And no single book
knows the whole answer

No single fictional detective
—not even Miss Marple,
not even Sherlock Holmes—
can solve this mystery.

But each character
each book
each author,
from Graham Greene
to Homer

to P. G. Wodehouse
to Philip K. Dick
to Beatrix Potter
holds a clue.

And every book we read,
every movie
and TV show we watch,

Dr. Who
and *Moby Dick*
and Nancy Drew
and "The Light of Other Days"
and *Lolita*
and "One Ordinary Day with Peanuts"
and *Oedipus Rex*
and *Bridget Jones's Diary*
and "The Ugly Duckling"
and *Barefoot in the Park*
and *Gaudy Night*
and "Nightfall"
and *Our Town*
and "The Veldt"
and *Le Morte d'Arthur*
and *Miracle on 34th Street*
and even *Twilight*
has a piece of the answer.

It's like a giant jigsaw puzzle.

When my husband's teaching how science figures things out,
he does a science experiment
in which he cuts up a mystery novel

and then passes out random single pages of it to his students,
and they try to figure out what's going on,
to solve the mystery.

That's what we do, too.

We'll never have all the pieces.
But with the help of books
and movies
and even TV shows about dinosaur hunters,
we can get a glimpse of the answer.

That's why I read
and why I write,
adding my own fragment to the tangle of clues,
and will go on doing both till I can't anymore.
To find out what happens
To find out what kind of story we're in.

When Sir Godfrey asks Polly, "Is it a tragedy or a comedy?"
she answers with certainty, "A comedy."

I think so, too.

Mostly because of clues I've found
in *Have Space Suit, Will Travel*
and *Three Men in a Boat*
and *The Tempest*.

I wanted desperately to find out what happened to Kip and Peewee,
but I also wanted them to be okay,
to get home safely.

I think that's a good sign,
that we not only want happy endings for ourselves,
but for the people we love,
both real and fictional:
for Connor and Abby on *Primeval*
and Elinor Dashwood and Edward Ferrars,
and Kate and Petruchio,
and Lord Peter Wimsey and Harriet Vane.

And I think another good sign is that
J and George and Harris,
the three men in a boat
(to say nothing of the dog Montmorency),
make us laugh out loud a hundred years after they made
their trip up the Thames.

But I think the best clue of all is that
Shakespeare, whom nobody would accuse of being unrealistic
about the human race—
or of always looking "on the bright side of life"—
was a huge fan of happy endings.

He put them in all of his comedies
and even some of his tragedies.

Cordelia's hanged and Lear dies,
but not before they're reunited,
not before all their sins against each other are forgiven
and they have a chance to "sing like birds in a cage" together.

And even more significant
is the fact that he went *back* to comedy
after he'd written the tragedies.

His last word on the subject isn't *Macbeth*,
but *The Tempest*.

The Tempest is a play that's famous for its elegiac speech:
"*Our revels now are ended . . .*
And, like the baseless fabric of this vision,
The cloud-capp'd towers, the gorgeous palaces,
The solemn temples, the great globe itself,
Yea, all which it inherit, shall dissolve,
And, like this insubstantial pageant faded,
Leave not a rack behind."

But the play doesn't end with that.
It ends with a reconciliation
And a blessing
And a wedding.
I think it's definitely a comedy.

I'm not absolutely certain, of course.
But I have hopes.
And, just like Beatrix Potter,
I can't wait to find out.

GRAND MASTER ACCEPTANCE SPEECH

*(Given by Connie Willis at the Nebula Awards Banquet
in Washington, D.C., on Saturday, May 19, 2012)*

As Barbra Streisand said when she won the Oscar, "Hello, Gorgeous!"

Those of you who know me
know that I faithfully watch the Oscars,

mostly for the clothes—
like that awful pink thing Gwyneth Paltrow wore a couple of years ago
and that thing with the giant red bow that Emma Stone wore this year,

but I also watch for the acceptance speeches

Like when Jack Palance dropped to the floor and started doing
push-ups.

Or when Sally Field kept hugging her Oscar to her and saying,
"You like me, you really like me!"

No, we didn't.

Or when James Cameron shouted, "I'm king of the world!"

And Richard Attenborough compared himself to Gandhi and
Martin Luther King, Jr.

All this research came in handy the last couple of weeks.

No, not to show me how to give a *bad* speech.
To show me how to do a good one.

Meryl Streep did it.
She gave a great one this year
when she won Best Actress for *Iron Lady*.

Emma Thompson did it.
John Wayne did it.
The guy from Flight of the Conchords did it, for heaven's sake.
How hard can it be?

But it must be fairly hard
because there have been *lots* of bad speeches.

Now, when I say bad speeches,
I'm not talking about people being rambling and incoherent.
That's to be expected.

They're excited.
And I don't mind if they get all choked up.
Crying is fine.

And so is putting on their reading glasses,
pulling out a list,
and thanking everybody they've ever known,
including the third-grade teacher
who cast them as the pumpkin in their school production
of *Cinderella*.

I totally get that,
especially the part about the third-grade teacher,
although in my case
it was my sixth-grade teacher, who introduced me to *Little
Women*,
and my eighth-grade teacher, who introduced me to the Blitz,
and my high school English teacher,
who took me to meet Lenora Mattingly Weber.

I wouldn't be here without them.

And I wouldn't be here without my BFFs—truly my Best Friends
Forever
    Jim Kelly
    and Sheila Williams
    and Cynthia Felice
    and Michael Cassutt
    and Melinda Snodgrass
    and John Kessel
    and Nancy Kress

and without my BHE—Best Husband Ever, Courtney
and my DTD—Dearer than Daughter, Cordelia.

Without my WWCIA—Writer's Workshop Comrades in Arms
  Ed Bryant
  and John Stith
  and Mike Toman
  and Walter Jon Williams

and my LSEs—Long-Suffering Editors
  Anne Groell
  and Gardner Dozois
  and Ellen Datlow
  and Liza Trombi
  and Shawna McCarthy

and my FWAGMs—Friends Who Are Grand Masters (is that
cool, or what?)
  Robert Silverberg
  and Joe Haldeman
  and Fred Pohl

and all the wonderful people who've befriended me over the years
from Chris Lotts
to *Dr.* Neil Gaiman
and Rose Beetum
and Lee Whiteside
and Craig Chrissinger
and Patrice Caldwell and Betty Williamson

and SFWA

and all the great science-fiction people I've known,
some of whom are here
and some of whom—

Charlie Brown
and Ralph Vicinanza
and Isaac Asimov
and Jack Williamson—
aren't.

As Meryl Streep said in her acceptance speech,
"The thing that counts the most is the friendship
and the love we've shared.
I look out here and see my life before my eyes."

And I do:
    —driving all night to the Chicago Worldcon with Cee
    —eating chocolate donuts with George R.R. Martin
    —and getting thrown out of the Tupperware Museum with
    Sheila Williams and Jim Kelly
    —and driving Charlie Brown to Jack Williamson's in Portales
    —and getting thrown out of the Grand Ole Opry with Sheila
    Williams and Jim Kelly
    —and sparring, onstage and off, with Mike Resnick and Bob
    Silverberg
    —and laughing so hard at dinner with Gardner Dozois and Ei-
    leen Gunn that I snorted a piece of lettuce up my nose
    —and staying up all night eating red pistachios and talking
    about the Nebulas with Jim Kelly and John Kessel
    —and having wonderful conversations about
    Star Wars
    and Shakespeare
    and sangria
    and the Algonquin Round Table
    and *Primeval*
    and the Marx Brothers

and how e-books are going to kill us
and what happens after we die

and meeting, oh, so many people,
making, oh, so many friends.

Now this is the place where the music starts to come up
and the winner starts talking faster and faster to get everything in
before they drag them off the stage,
and I'm going to do it, too,
because I have to thank the people to whom I owe the most:

—Robert A. Heinlein,
for introducing me to Kip and Peewee
and to *Three Men in a Boat*
and to the whole wonderful world of science fiction

—and Kit Reed and Charles Williams and Ward Moore,
who showed me its amazing possibilities

—Philip K. Dick and Shirley Jackson and Howard Waldrop and
William Tenn,
who taught me how science fiction should be written

—and Bob Shaw and Daniel Keyes and Theodore Sturgeon,
whose stories:
"The Light of Other Days"
and "Flowers for Algernon"
and "The Man Who Lost the Sea"
taught me to love it.

I wouldn't be here without them.
Or without you.

As Meryl Streep put it,
"My friends, thank you, all of you,
for this inexplicably wonderful career."

Or, as Sally Field *should* have said it,
"I love you.
I really, really love you."

Thank you for this inexplicably wonderful award.

ABOUT THE AUTHOR

CONNIE WILLIS has received seven Nebula Awards and eleven Hugo awards for science fiction, and her novel *Passage* was nominated for both. Her other works include *Doomsday Book, Lincoln's Dreams, Bellwether, Impossible Things, Remake, Uncharted Territory, To Say Nothing of the Dog, Fire Watch, Miracle and Other Christmas Stories, Blackout,* and *All Clear.* Connie Willis lives in Colorado with her family.